APOCALYPSE
IN PARADISE

APOCALYPSE IN PARADISE

by
Nancy E. Rose

Gotham Books

30 N Gould St.
Ste. 20820, Sheridan, WY 82801
https://gothambooksinc.com/

Phone: 1 (307) 464-7800

© 2025 *Nancy E. Rose*. All rights reserved.

No part of this book may be reproduced, stored in a retrieval system, or transmitted by any means without the written permission of the author.

Published by Gotham Books (March 6, 2025)

ISBN: 979-8-3485-3891-0 (P)
ISBN: 979-8-3485-3892-7 (E)

Because of the dynamic nature of the Internet, any web addresses or links contained in this book may have changed since publication and may no longer be valid.

The views expressed in this work are solely those of the author and do not necessarily reflect the views of the publisher, and the publisher hereby disclaims any responsibility for them.

TABLE OF CONTENTS

Prologue viii
Chapter 1 1
Chapter 2 5
Chapter 3 9
Chapter 4 14
Chapter 5 18
Chapter 6 22
Chapter 7 27
Chapter 8 32
Chapter 9 37
Chapter 10 41
Chapter 11 46
Chapter 12 50
Chapter 13 54
Chapter 14 59
Chapter 15 66
Chapter 16 71
Chapter 17 76
Chapter 18 80
Chapter 19 87
Chapter 20 92
Chapter 21 96
Chapter 22 101
Chapter 23 106
Chapter 24 111
Chapter 25 118
Chapter 26 123
Chapter 27 127
Chapter 28 130
Chapter 29 136
Chapter 30 139
Chapter 31 142
Chapter 32 145
Chapter 33 149
Chapter 34 152

Chapter 35	156
Chapter 36	164
Chapter 37	168
Chapter 38	174
Chapter 39	180
Chapter 40	188
Chapter 41	195
Chapter 42	202
Chapter 43	206
Chapter 44	211
Chapter 45	215
Chapter 46	220
Chapter 47	225
Chapter 48	230
Chapter 49	234
Chapter 50	239
Chapter 51	242
Chapter 52	248
Chapter 53	252
Chapter 54	255
Chapter 55	260
Chapter 56	267
Chapter 57	271
Chapter 58	276
Chapter 59	280
Chapter 60	284
Chapter 61	289
Chapter 62	292
Chapter 63	294
Chapter 64	298
Chapter 65	301
Chapter 66	304
Chapter 67	308
Chapter 68	312
Chapter 69	316
Chapter 70	318
Chapter 71	321
Chapter 72	324

Chapter 73 327
Chapter 74 331
Chapter 75 335
Chapter 76 339
Chapter 77 343
Chapter 78 352
Chapter 79 355
Chapter 80 357
Chapter 81 361
References 364

Prologue

Kaiko ʻo ke awa, popo ʻI ka nalu, ʻa ʻohe ʻike ʻia ka poʻe nana i heʻe ka nalu.

(The harbor is rough, the surf rolls, and the rider of the surf cannot be seen; A stormy circumstance with uncertain results).

It was inevitable.

Weather events in the south Pacific region are not uncommon. In fact, flash floods are common – too common. Two years ago during torrential rains, a reservoir in the mountains broke and a thirty-foot wave was unleashed on an unsuspecting neighborhood. The inland tidal wave that was generated killed all thirty-seven people who lived in the affected community.

That particular day happened to be the wedding day for an expectant mother and father-to-be. Family and friends from Oahu and Kauai had arrived to share in their momentous day. What was supposed to be a day of celebration became a day of death and destruction.

There are other serious weather-related perils in the tropics. Swimmers caught in riptides drown; torrential rains cause severe, often fatal accidents, and hikers who fall off steep cliffs while attempting to get the perfect photo. There are killer bacteria in the waters of the ocean and in the fresh water rivers and lakes. Killer bacteria like leptospirosis and necrotizing fasciitis, better known as strept-eating flesh bacteria, can be found on occasion in the waters and claim unsuspecting visitors. Necrotizing fasciitis is an especially swift killer. Not a pretty sight. Not a pretty smell.

Of more serious consequences, every fifty years or so, islands in the Pacific Ocean are confronted by a destructive tsunami.

Offshore marine birds were flocking to higher elevations, soaring to the top of Mount Hi'iake, the volcanic mountain. Unbeknownst to the island people, a tsunami was coming. Kimo was initially unaware of the pending giant wave that was headed their way as Honolulu had not sent a warning. Eighteen hours ago, an earthquake of a magnitude of 7.9 Mw, 1700 miles southeast of the Polynesian Islands had gone unnoticed. Locally, the earthquake had generated a 440-foot wave. It annihilated a nearby small island, wiping out the entire population.

How had it gone undetected?

As the sentinel birds approached the island of Nardei and the weather became volatile, the community's leader, Kimo, began to suspect that some sort of major weather event was approaching. He attempted to contact The Pacific Tsunami Warning Centre (PTWC) in Honolulu but communications were down. All he heard was static on the line. What was that about?

Clearly, the prophecies from their passed loved ones were accurate.

There was a strange, electrical charge in the air that was not the residual effects of thunder and lightning. And yet, the air sizzled. A pungent odor that smelled like a dead animal filled the air.

Was it the foul odor of the Night Marchers?

Kimo soon became aware that the events happening on his tropical island were the actions of Kanaloa or the Great Serpent.

He had returned to Nardei.

The static charge and foul odor hung over the island like a New England fog. A neon, lime- green mist began to creep onshore. The air became as heavy as black strap molasses, making it difficult to breathe. The skies darkened and thunder boomed like a cannon. It was starting to rain.

The animals were spooked. Herds of wild pigs and goats were fleeing to the highlands. Clouds of red dirt were kicked up behind them. Smaller animals like dogs, cats, ducks and chickens weren't far behind them. Their cries of terror were deafening. Like the creatures who marched on to Noah's ark, they rushed to safety, climbing up the steep hillside to the wooden cross on the hill. There was an island-wide rule that if a tsunami approached Nardei, they should run to the cross. Maybe, the animals understood this too.

The power of the Polynesian people's *mana* and their knowledge of ancient secrets, allowed them to transmit messages to the animal kingdom. Historically, the Polynesian people had been able to grasp the force of nature and utilize this force or mana to their benefit. However, on mornings like this one, it was often *mutually* beneficial.

Chaos ensued. Cattle and horses were busting out of their pens. Fences were stomped down as they too fled to higher ground. Immediately, the older folks knew what the animal antics meant. It was the first sign. It wasn't as though they had never experienced a tsunami before for they surely had on several occasions. 'Course, the younger ones had never experienced a tsunami. The youngest wailed with fear.

In 1957, an earthquake the magnitude of 9.1 Mw occurred south of the Andreanof Islands, Aleutian Islands in Alaska, causing a 1780-feet tsunami to crash onto the shorelines of most of the islands in the southern Pacific Ocean. The older Nardei residents remember it well. It was a gigantic wave that came upon shore and so, they had fled to the cross. It was all that remained of a small church that had been constructed centuries ago when missionaries first came to the islands. The church had been burned down by the Polynesians in retaliation for the fatal diseases that they had also brought along with their white man's religion. The cross had endured much like the Native Polynesians.

Once again, in 1968, an 8.2 Mw earthquake off the coast of Honshu Island, Japan had generated a 1270-foot high wave that had found its way to Nardei. It was a wave that hit with such a great force that it produced a loud, crashing noise. The sheer force of the giant wave removed all trees and vegetation from elevations as high as 1740 feet above sea level. But each time after the tsunami, a lower sea level left the reefs and lagoons high and dry above a new shoreline, the wind blowing the sand inland.

Like before, they had run to the cross. Nearby, several caves in the mountain-side offered refuge. With foresight, preparations had been made. Supplies could be found inside the protective caves for just such an occasion.

They were prepared.

But were they prepared for the great battle that lay ahead?

Their dead ancestors had warned them and they had heeded the warning.

Non-perishable food, water, lanterns, flashlights, paper goods, sanitary supplies, fishing poles and lures, blankets and pillows, medical supplies and some medicinal concoctions made from indigenous products found in the ocean waters and the vegetation found in the mountains, were housed there. These magical potions were made by Hannah, the Kapuna or High Priestess of the island's people. Unfortunately, these pharmaceuticals would be sorely needed in the days that lay ahead.

Days earlier, they had gathered their belongings, and they had journeyed to the safety of the cross, and the nearby sacred caves.

Regretfully, not all. Not all could leave their home and possessions.

Many brought their Bibles as they held on strong to their faith because they also understood there was nothing similar about this coming tidal wave. It was unlike any of the others. They could smell it in the air. They could hear it in the wind. They could see it in the strange green mist that continued to slowly creep onto the shore.

As the storm approached, Kimo gazed up into the dark and moonless night sky, crossed himself and uttered, "O, all you gods, Come to our aid!"

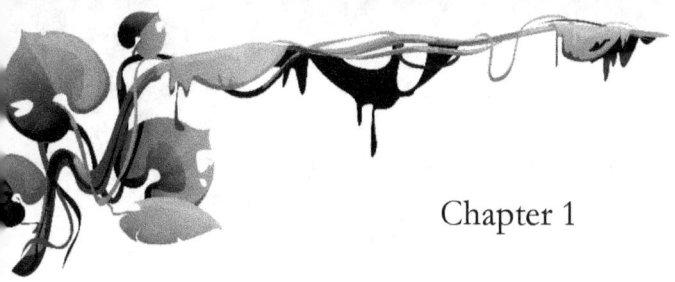

Chapter 1

'A 'ohe pua 'I leo.

(Not a sound gushed forth; not a single word was spoken)

After a brief morning rain, the sun emerged. A vivid rainbow graced the azure-blue sky. The turquoise-blue ocean waters shimmered like a swath of silk and the marine birds broke the glass-like surface foraging for their breakfast of small fish. Kate, now the mother of three children, watched them playing near the shoreline.

Little Hannah (named after her godmother, Kupuna Hannah), only seven and a half years old, was using her bucket and shovel to make a hole to "put the fishies in a pool." Her strawberry-blonde curls framed her cherub face. Pink cheeks and bright blue eyes peered out from under her sun bonnet. She was the image of her mother. Her older brother, Luke, was helping her dig the hole. Hina, her older sister at age 12, was bogie boarding in the small waves. Family bliss prevailed.

Kate and Kimo had wed after the apocalyptic events that had occurred on Nardei just over 5 years ago. At that time, they had "hanai" or adopted Luke and Hina whose parents had perished from the smallpox disease that had plagued their island. Luke, now 16 years old, was the best older brother that a girl could have. Both little Hannah and Hina agreed. Hina just couldn't say so. Now, she remained mute.

She had not spoken since the 10 frightening days of the epic tribulation that had been a time of great trauma for little Hina. While possessed by the devil, Luke had almost sacrificed little Hina to the evil one. Without the Divine intervention from Pastor Kua, Hina would have been murdered by the brother she so cherished. Finally, the loss of her parents had overwhelmed her. A descendent of the Mu or Quiet people, Hina had responded to these traumatic experiences by shutting down, holding on tightly to those horrors that she could not verbally express. Her lips were sealed.

Little Hina had been named after the legendary ocean and moon goddess. She is the oldest goddess known in the Hawai'ian legends. The goddess, Hina, is associated with all things having to do with the ocean, including the moon and weather events. It is said that a full moon is associated with a favorable mood of the moon goddess. However, a blood-red moon is said to be the action of an upset Hina.

Hina can take other forms. She has been known to be an `elepaio bird, coral, a type of banana and a special gourd. It is said that she lives in the peaceful and quiet environment of the moon. A powerful healer, Hina has intervened on behalf of mankind on more than one occasion. Humans had repeatedly needed to be saved from themselves and their own stupidity.

In human form, Hina has been depicted as a beautiful woman with hair like fire and ice-blue eyes. She carries a calabash (coconut gourd) containing the moon and the stars. Hina is depicted as the female generating force in Hawaiian cosmology. Hina was known as the moon goddess and was worshipped as creatrix, mother, protector and sometimes a wrathful destroyer.

"Kate," spoke a familiar voice. She turned and saw Kekela, and as always, with his sidekick, Pua, a small white terrier, faithfully at his side. His white cane tapped the way in front of him. He was legally blind as a result of being sick with the debilitating smallpox virus. Death had been knocking on his door and he had barely survived. He was a testament to the resiliency of the Hawai'ian people.

He was a testament to the power of faith.

"Hi Kekela. Come sit and keep me company for a bit."

Kekela sat down beside Kate as Pua jumped all over her, licking her face.

Squeezing his hand, she asked, "Howzit goin'?"

"I needed a break from the office. Kimo's on the warpath this morning." "Really? What's going on?" asked Kate. Kimo was not easily angered.

"He's trying to reach the Department of Agriculture in Honolulu. There is some kind of blight on the crops. The taro has little green bugs or something on 'em. Some of the plants are dying off. He's afraid that it'll spread quickly if we don't get a grip on it."

"Hum. That's curious." Kate pondered that information. A blight of little green bugs?

Hannah noticed Kekela and came rushing up, "Uncle! Uncle!" She threw her arms around him as Pua barked with excitement, licking Hannah's face. She giggled with glee.

"Uncle, you want to see the pool I made for the fishies?" She forgot that Kekela couldn't see.

Meanwhile, Hina, dressed in a pink suit that showed off her dark, tanned skin and blue-black hair, came out of the water with her board and joined the group. At that awkward age of pre-adolescence, little Hina was not as little anymore as she shot up in height. When she wasn't doing ocean activities, Hina could be found on the basketball court. She was a skilled athlete.

Maybe her other heightened senses played a role in her winning abilities.

She and Kekela had their own way to communicate to each other. A special language between the blind man and the mute girl. Some called it telepathy. Others believed that they were like their *aumakua*, passed ancestral spirits, who made their voices heard through certain vessels.

Hina rushed up to her Uncle too. A new set of dog antics resumed. The laughter and joy that Kate heard was music to her ears. She loved her island home and family. Smiling, she reflected on the young woman who had left California to pursue an adventure. And she'd gotten one.

Fortunately, the following years after the dark days of the tribulation had been peaceful, as she settled into the island way of life and family life. She still worked as a nurse two days a week at the ambulatory health center on Nardei. Kupuna Hannah babysat those days. All three children adored her. Little Hannah was her "baby-angel."

Kate invited Kekela to join the gang for lunch. Amid the pleas of the children, he could hardly decline the invitation. They packed up the kids and beach stuff and headed home. Their Hanalei green and white plantation house was in good condition and both she and Kimo prided themselves on a well-groomed yard. They enjoyed gardening together, but it was mostly Kate who kept it up. The children ran ahead and rushed into the house, sand and all. Kate and Kekela, with Pua in tow, walked up the seven steps to the front porch. Kate took Kekela's arm. As they climbed the stairs, Kate paused.

"What?" asked Kekela.

"Nothing," she responded. "Nothing at all."

He couldn't see what she saw.

In the flower beds beside the steps, the tropical foliage plants' called Coleus, were looking sickly. Their bright-red leaves were turning yellow and dying. Go figure, they'd been fine last evening when she had watered the yard.

Chapter 2

'A 'a I ka hula, waiho ka hilahila I ka hale.
(When one wants to dance the hula, bashfulness should be left at home).

The small plane burst through the clouds and prepared to approach the runway on the northern shore of Nardei. The runway was once part of a military installation that was destroyed during the battle between the villagers and the United States military which took place during the tribulation period.

As the plane made its descent, the tourists on board were treated to majestic views of the dense rain forest on the north side of the island. Hawai'ian rain forests are characterized by heavy rainfall with an annual range of 150 to 300 inches. This particular tropical range forest was one of the most diverse, species-rich areas of vegetation in the world. There were plant species here that were found nowhere else on earth. This enabled the native Kapuna to manufacture unique medicinal products. Much would be lost if this rich assemblage of species wasn't protected. The Hawai'ian people deemed it sacred ground. It was *kapu*, or taboo, to enter this area without the Kupuna's permission.

The afternoons and nights were usually cloudy and rainy, making mornings the best time to fly in and out of the island.

The passengers were tourists who had come to spend a week on this island paradise, touted by tourist agents as being "an experience in ancient Hawaii culture, unlike no other." While on Nardei, the tourists enjoy an authentic island vacation, including a luau with a pig roasted on a spit over an open fire, traditional hulas, fire-eating and fire-dancing men, scuba diving, snorkeling in coral reef bays, and hiking in lush valleys and majestic mountains with panoramic vistas. There is a wildlife bird sanctuary on the island's east side which offers guided tours during their layover. It is the nesting ground for rare tropical birds, like the red-footed booby.

On the south and west side of the island, pristine white sand beaches grace its shores. During the summer months, monk seals find refuge on these shores, enjoying an afternoon siesta. In any season, the weather is generally best off the leeward coast which is influenced by the trade winds. Those easy, breezy, tropical days.

Most of the tropical islands are fringed with coral, but their origin is evident in the numerous craters of extinct volcanoes up and down the Pacific waters, except for the blazing fires spewing from the mountains on the island of Hawaii.

After a smooth landing, the 10 passengers de-planed. Some on them were on wobbly feet and some were pale in the face. It had been a bumpy flight. On high heels too small for her feet, a rather obese, loud woman precariously negotiated the descending staircase, before her husband caught her.

She cried out, "Lordy, Lordy!" She slipped once, banging the back of her lower leg, before her husband caught her like a sack of rutabagas.

"Thank God, we're finally here," exclaimed the middle-aged woman when she touched down on solid ground. She was dressed in a red pant suit that was way too small for her. Obviously, she was in denial about her real size. Lips, fingernails and toenails were all blood-red. Even her hair was flaming red, styled in a severe bob with bangs. Obviously, the lady had a thing for red.

"Earnest, ain't this somethin'!" the fat lady exclaimed as she gazed at the Mountain View. She could see a waterfall cascading down its precipice, like a curtain of shimmering water. A short, thin bald man with large ears (maybe she tugged on them a lot), nodded.

"Honey-bun, get the camera!" The man ignored her.

"I mean it, baby-cakes, fetch the camera," she demanded in her mid-west accent. She was an Idaho country-bumpkin sort. Slowly, the man removed the carry-on bag from his shoulder and searched for the camera. He handed her the camera and she smiled sweetly (which was just for show). Some of the other passengers were chuckling under their breathe. Yiks! It takes all kinds.

"I'll take some photos and you get our luggage." Gladys had trouble taking the shots because her red, acrylic nails were very long. Scary-kind. Then, the expected occurred. A nail snapped and broke off.

"Earnest! Damn it! I broke a nail. It ripped right off. I need to see a manicurist right away," she pouted and sucked on her nail. How old was she, 16 or 46? Her poor husband. He must not believe in divorce. Or, he had the "little man" complex. Or perhaps he had a "mommy" complex.

Earnest returned with their four pieces of red luggage. Gladys complained that he'd gotten one dirty.

"What'd you do? Drag it through the grass?" she snapped.

Poor Earnest.

The other visitors had retrieved their luggage as well. Right on time, the resort bus arrived. They traveled 15 miles down the paved road to the entrance of The Lodge at Mount Hi'iake. On both sides of the long driveway, Norfolk Island pine trees stood tall. These trees grow as high as 200 feet. The lodge was set in an enchanting hillside location. Mountains loomed in the background.

On the wrap-around porch around the large, white plantation house, formerly the home of a wealthy owner of a sugar plantation, several guests were playing cards or reading, sipping ice tea. It was a peaceful sight.

Inside, the resort was filled with antiques and wooden floors covered by large, vivid Chinese, handmade wool rugs. Wood paneled walls and grand chandeliers could be found in the living areas, dining areas, and the noble library. Most rooms had numerous panels of ceiling-to-floor French windows where one could look in awe at the majestic, larger-than-life showcase of nature. It filled one with wonder.

Gladys had been quiet on the ride to the lodge. She closed her eyes and rested her head against the window. It was no doubt, a relief to Earnest.

But Gladys wasn't sleeping. She was thinking about having a drink. She hadn't had one for over 6 months. But, what the hell. They were on vacation. She told herself that she'd only have one. Something exotic with a slice of pineapple and a pretty umbrella in it. After all, one wouldn't hurt. Would it? No. She could just sip it. Nice and easy.

The bus pulled up and, once again, the group emerged to get their luggage. Gladys was now active, pushing Earnest to get a movin'! She wanted to check out the lodge's bar. After they got to the room, she'd get him to lie down and rest a bit. Then, she would sneak out.

After they settled into their room, Earnest readily agreed with the idea of a nap. Later, they could take a walk in the botanical gardens and get an early dinner. Gladys readily agreed.

"I'm gonna' run downstairs to look for a book to read in the library," Gladys claimed. She opened one of her red suitcases and took out a vivid orange skirt and a yellow blouse. Quickly, she changed, checked her make-up, over-sprayed her perfume, and got ready to exit. The desire to have a drink was overwhelming.

"Since when did you give up your magazines and start reading books?" he mumbled.

"I wanna read about the island." With that, she opened the door and left to find the bar.

Earnest drifted off, snoring loudly. And, while he slept, little specks of green bugs, no bigger than fleas, marched out from the opened suitcase and headed under the bed. These hitchhikers were getting off here too.

Chapter 3

'A'ohe wawae o ka I'a; o 'oe ka mea wawae, ki'I mai.
(Fish have no feet; you who have feet must come and get it).

Ray Taba was a master fisherman. After years of hunting and harvesting from the nearby reefs to the open sea, Ray had become very skilled in his vocation.

Fishing is one of the most skilled occupations of the early Polynesians. It required knowledge of the stars, of the winds, of the currents, and of the clouds. The stars at night guided the fisherman to navigate the seas and stay on course. The wind and the ocean water currents affect the run of the fish, and knowledge of the clouds is helpful in forecasting the weather the next day. More importantly, the fisherman had to go through different stages in his preparation, much like a journey carpenter, before he was accepted as a fisherman.

The fisherman was a revered person in ancient Polynesia, and not everyone could become one.

Ray's older brother, Joe, had been the town sheriff but, sadly, he had died during the time of the tribulation and Ray had inherited his boat, the *Noalani,* named after Joe's wife. Joe had taught Ray everything he knows about fishing, from lucky lures to spotting the right birds.

Many years ago, Joe had been incarcerated in Honolulu for the possession and distribution of methamphetamine. They called it ICE. They should have called it, DEATH. If it didn't kill them, ICE changed people dramatically. Ultimately, it caused paranoid schizophrenia. Brain intact, Ray had cleaned up and turned his life around. Now, he was well liked and respected in the community. People trusted him.

Like his older brother, to fish was his passion. So many times, Joe had brought his younger brother out to sea to learn the art of fishing. Ray had caught his first Blue Marlin – almost four hundred pounds – at age 12. Of course, he had needed Joe's help to reel it in. Big time. It was a day he would always remember because it had been the most exciting day of his young life. Joe still held the record, bringing in a 512 pound prize, eight years ago. Ray planned on breaking that record (again, with Joe's help).

Now Ray takes his nephew, 10-year old David, with him fishing just as Joe had taken and mentored him when he was a boy. This summer morning, Ray and David were up before dawn, getting ready for a day on the ocean waters. Always hoping to catch the big-one.

David, who is usually very excited to set out on another fishing adventure, was unusually quiet this morning. His dark eyes were down-cast, his black hair askew.

Ray looked at his nephew and inquired, "Dude, why are you so quiet this mornin'? Not feeling good?"

"Uncle, I feel okay. I'm just tired." David sighed like a little old man. "I had a bad dream last night."

"About the snake?"

"Yeah, it was Kanaloa, the serpent," said David. His eyes were wide. "He was stickin' out his pointed, red tongue, claiming he's coming to eat me! Just like before!" During the early days of the tribulation, David had encountered the devil in the form of *Kanaloa* (meaning the Great Serpent), a black snake with yellow spots and glowing red eyes like a werewolf. He'd tried to warn them that evil was present on their island but he was discounted. After all, back then David was known for his keen imagination. Still was.

"He's not coming back. He was sent back to the fire pit by Pastor. No worries, Dude."

Despite the reassurance, David was frightened. In fact, he was down-right terrified. He could recall the horrific events that took place seven years ago after he'd encountered Kanaloa. And, before he had met up with the evil one, he had first dreamed of him. Ray wasn't aware of that.

Now, he had returned again to David's dreams. That awareness was chilling the boy's bones, making him shudder with fright.

As dawn broke, the Noalani was underway. Ray was at the wheel and David was keeping an eye out for the birds that would lead them to the fishing grounds. David had tucked away his dark thoughts and was focusing on the chase.

Four hours later, they still had not had a bite. Bored with the lack of action, Ray decided to tell David the legend of *Kauhuhu*, the shark-god of Maui, while they ate their peanut butter and jelly sandwiches, pineapple slices, taro chips, and they drank sweetened, freshly squeezed lemonade (Ray has a lemon tree in his backyard). David was at that age where he consumed large amounts of food. He ate 3 sandwiches before he was satisfied. And that's only because that was all they had brought. He was already tall for his age and skinny like a waif.

Hawai'ians use the term, *kaao*, for a fictional story or one in which imagination is an important component of the tale. However, they use the term, *moolelo*, for those stories that are based on actual historical events.

Stories of gods and goddesses are moolelo. These stories are considered sacred and can only be told in the light of day. So this was a good time to tell David the tale of Kauhuhu.

"Kauhuhu was and still is, for that matter, the god in charge of all mariners and fishermen," begins Ray. "He first appeared as the friend of a priest who was seeking revenge for the killing of his two sons. Kamalo was the name of the priest."

"He appeared as a man, not a shark?' asked the curious boy.

"Right. Hawaii's legendary gods and goddesses are all shape-changers," replied his uncle. "His heiau (temple) was in a village which faced the channel between Molokai and Maui."

Awesome fishing in that channel." Ray smiled. He'd fished there on several occasions. "Back to the two sons - they were younger than you. 'Bout 8 years old. Like boys that age, they were full of mischief. Like daring each other to do stupid stuff. You know, boys will be boys, even centuries ago."

"I'm not like that," declared David rather quickly.

"No, no…not you." David had been a dare devil at that age, especially when it came to sports.

"Well, near this heiau, a high chief, an *alii*, named Kupa lived in his own temple. He'd built a home inside the temple for his family. And, inside his home, he had two sacred drums. Very special drums." Ray stopped to turn the boat to the right, he had spotted some ewa birds in the distance.

"Okay, where was I? Oh yeah, the boys and the drums. One day, the chief was out fishin' in the channel, so the boys snuck into his home and began pounding on the drums. When the chief returned and heard about the boy's drum session, he ordered his *mu*, or temple sacrifice seekers, to kill the boys and bring their bodies to the heiau to be placed on the alter."

"*He killed them?*" asked the curious boy. "His mu did."

"Why?" David's eyes were open wide.

"Because to play the sacred drums was *kapu. Forbidden.*" Ray kept an eye on the birds adjusting the steering wheel again. "When the priest Kamalo heard of the murder of his sons, he sought revenge."

"So, what'd he do?"

"He went and found a priest who could direct him to the heiau of the god-shark, Kauhuhu. He lived in a cave off a steep cliff. It was a hard climb. Finally, he found the temple built within a cave. They had security like a guarded fortress for the shark-god. When he got there, he discovered that the great shark-god was not there. He was out fishing in the Molokai channel. His guardians were there, Waka and Mo-o, the great dragons of Polynesian legends. When Kamalo came upon the dragon guardians, he escaped them and hid deep inside the cave. He hid for three long days."

"What did he eat? What did he drink? Oh and how did he pee?" asked David. "Bugs, mice. I don't know. Maybe he drank his urine."

"Gross." David's face looked like he had just sucked on a lemon.

"Anyways, Kauhuhu returned and said he could smell a human man. He found Kamalo and was about to eat him, until Kamalo said to wait and hear the story about his two dead sons. After hearing the tale, the shark-god took pity on him, 'cause he had a heart. He vowed to help seek revenge on the chief, Kupa, and his clan. The shark-god created a mighty storm, with gale force winds and torrential rains that wiped out his entire family and clan. And the chief? He was fed to the dragons."

"What happened to the shark…" David was interrupted by the familiar squeal of the big, gold reel going off, announcing the hook-up of a fish. The louder the noise, the bigger the fish. This reel was screaming.

Back at the resort, Gladys was screaming too.

Chapter 4

'A 'ohe paha he 'uhane.

(Said of one who behaves in a shameful manner).

After leaving Earnest in the room, Gladys made a bee-line to the bar. Similar to the other rooms, the elegant bar had floor-to-ceiling French windows where one could see that the setting sun was painting the evening sky a magenta color. High ceilings and dim lighting rendered a *lokahi* or peaceful milieu. Well-polished wooden, pine floors shone in the candlelight. The magnificent wooden bar was a work of craftsmanship with hand- carved Polynesian images. It looked very old. The bar was fairly quiet tonight but that would soon change.

In her too-tight, orange polyester skirt and bright yellow blouse (also too tight for the well- endowed woman), she was noticed by the other patrons as she sashayed into the bar. She sat at the bar on the high, wooden chair with the red leather seat and back. Gladys's favorite color.

It appeared that she was almost too big for the stool and she might easily tumble. Sure enough, it would became a self-fulfilling prophecy.

Practically drooling, she asked for a mai tai with a "pineapple slice and a pretty little parasol in it." When it arrived, she wet her lips and took a long drink. So much for sipping it. The second went down easily, providing that sweet, warm glow at her core. Gladys was feeling good.

In the background, you could hear music. A disco song from the seventies, *I Will Survive,* began playing. Right away, Gladys perked up. "Turn that up. I love this song!" The bartender rolled his eyes. "Sorry ma'am. We can't turn it up."

"But I wanna dance," she pouted. "There is no dance floor, ma'am."

"Well, piss on that. I'm gonna dance anyways." Gladys slipped off her chair and began shuffling her feet and pumping her arms. She was twirling around on the floor, as though the silver disco ball was turning above her moving body. Small back shoes were kicked off her feet. Some large women can be very agile on their feet, but not Gladys. The other folks in the bar, mostly couples, were unable to hold back their laughter. It was like watching a Carol Burnett skit. It was difficult to look at her and not feel utterly embarrassed for her. Her bright orange skirt was twisted up her butt and her yellow blouse was transparent, wet with her perspiration. It was not a pretty picture.

Finally, out of breath, she returned to her seat at the bar and ordered another mai tai.

After her third drink, she struck up a conversation with a young, African-American soldier who was sitting quietly (or trying to) at the bar, watching the sun set over the ocean as the evening stars emerged.

Gladys tapped the soldier's arm, and struck up a conversation. "So, you was over in the middle-east fighting those bastard Muslims. Did you kill many?" "Excuse me, ma'am?" asked the man.

"Did you kill many of 'em?" Her speech was slurred.

"Quite frankly, it's a time I don't like to think about," replied the young man.

"Ten, twenty, one hundred? How many of those bastards did you put down?" she persisted in asking. "Come on, how many? Don't be shy, young man."

"I prefer not to talk about it, ma'am." He turned away. Enough of this nosy woman!

This angered Gladys. "Don't turn your back on me, boy! I'm talking to you. You hear me?"

Other folks in the bar stopped their conversations and stared at the loud, rude woman. The bartender came to ask her to leave but the soldier decided to leave instead. With the bartender watching, Gladys apologized to the soldier in an effort to get another drink. And, what do you know? It worked.

While consuming her fourth drink, Gladys accidently broke another red nail. This evoked alarm in Gladys and, immediately, she tried to dig her cell phone out of her purse to call the room and tell Earnest to schedule an appointment with the manicurist for her tomorrow. She couldn't find her phone.

"Hey, handsome, can I borrow your phone? It's an emergency." Gladys smiled sweetly, completely unaware that her make-up had run. Black smudges were under both of her eyes. Her ruby-red lipstick was messed up, some of it coating her teeth. Reluctantly, the bartender allowed her to use the phone but there was no answer in the room. Earnest must be sleeping soundly.

After the consumption of her fifth mai tai, she reached too far for a bowl of nuts and tumbled off the chair. She was drunk as a skunk.

Now, she was cut off.

"Ouch! I hurt my back!" she cried out in obvious discomfort. The bartender couldn't help but think, *serves you right*.

While Gladys lay on the wooden floor, the room began spinning. Gladys became pale, her brow sweating. She continued her lament.

"I'm gonna puke!" she yelled. And, she did.

"Geez, somebody help me get her up," said the bartender. A waitress came to assist. They wiped her off as best they could and then hauled her up. They considered calling a tow truck. Finally, she stumbled out of the bar. The waitress got a mop and cleaned up the floor. What an obnoxious woman!

She did not notice a few green, little flea-bugs that were under the woman's stool.

Gladys made it out to a chase lounge in the lobby, where she promptly fell asleep. Bruises were developing on the back of her leg where she had slipped earlier in the day. Her skirt was jacked up, hugging her fat thighs. Vomit was spattered down her blouse. In her hand, was the blue and pink parasol.

As morning approached, Gladys stirred. She resisted waking up because her head pounded. But, her thirst was great. Her mouth tasted nasty. Slowly, Gladys sat up and moaned. She had trouble remembering what had transpired last evening. Her legs and back ached. Had she fallen again?

Barely able to stand, Gladys got up and headed back to the room. She had to pee like a racehorse. She staggered down the hallway to her room, minus her shoes. The door to the room was unlocked. Upon opening the door, she smelled a foul odor.

The stench of urine and feces filled the air.

Gladys approached the bed. Earnest lay with his mouth open, his face a mask of pain. The color of his skin was gray. There was a bluish-tinged to his cold body. His eyes were open and glazed over. Obviously, he had released his bladder and bowels.

Death was always unbecoming.

Gladys screamed. And then, she released her urine too.

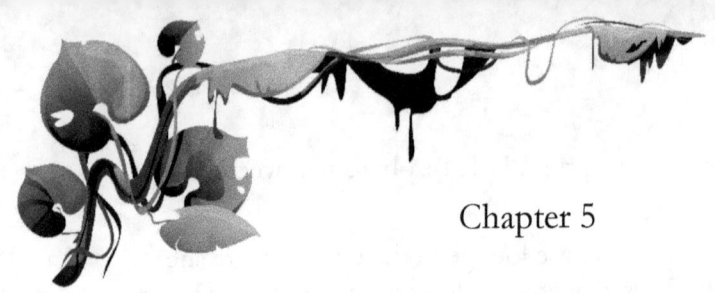

Chapter 5

Ka wela o ka ua.

(Heated rain).

Ten days ago, a Russian ship that was an Oscar-II class, nuclear-powered cruise missile submarine, named *Kursk* after the Russian city, left its home port in the Sea of Okhotsk. The 17-ton ship was four stories high. On board, were two OK-650b nuclear reactors, two steam engines and two 7-bladed propellers. Its impervious hull was made of high-nickel, high-chrome content stainless steel. The ship's flag, *Pyotr Velikiy,* named after Peter the Great, was proudly blowing in the brisk wind. The ship traveled around the island of Kamchatka, and then it headed to the Aleutian Islands. From there, the submarine crossed over the International Date Line. Its destination was the South Pacific Ocean, near the Polynesian islands.

Recently, Russia had resumed nuclear submarine patrols in the South Seas after a hiatus of more than 25 years. Now, President Vladimir Putin was building up the Russian military force, including the Navy, due to increasing tensions between Russia and the United States. President Putin had spared no costs to build a fleet of new submarines that boasted the most recent technological features. He claimed that the vessels possessed cutting-edge technology, including anti-radar software. These new Navy ships made a potent striking force. These submarines can be deployed quickly and covertly anywhere in the world.

And, they did.

Constantly breaking international law, the Russian nuclear subs roamed the waters in places where they had no business being. Alas, spying was a game that all countries engaged in as part of homeland security. However, sometimes Russia really overstepped the boundaries that have been set.

Sometimes, they chose to act boldly and without apology. After all, President Putin's reputation was that of a tough guy. Very much a macho man. Very much a dangerous man.

These vessels traversed the ocean waters silently. Because of their nuclear propulsion, these submarines can remain underwater, unseen under the waves. Quiet, powerful machines, these submarines moved swiftly and stealthy, remaining undetected. Their ability to circumnavigate the world without having to surface (ever) contributed to their skill to sneak around in places where they didn't belong.

America and her territories is enemy number one to the Russian government. Tensions have been building since the end of the cold war.

Today, they were at an all-time high.

The post-Crimean invasion and the takeover of Ukraine by the arrogant President of Russia had escalated the situation. Now, unprovoked war against the Ukraninian people has well demonstrated his utter ruthlessness. Putin wanted to restore the old Soviet Union.

Russian spies were gathering intelligence with surveillance equipment. Part two of the cold war ratcheting up.

As the Russian submarine crossed the expansive pacific waters, one of the Kursk's hydroxide peroxide-fueled Type 65 torpedo's failed. HTP, a form of highly concentrated hydrogen peroxide used as a propellant for the torpedo, seeped through some rust in the torpedo casing.

The sailors had very little warning. In the enclosed submarine, the temperature rose. The men began to get nervous as the temperature continued to rise, getting hotter and hotter.

78 degrees; 83 degrees; 89 degrees; 94 degrees; 100 degrees: *Boom!!*

A Hiroshima-like explosion blasted the ship apart! The explosion produced a blast equal to 550 lb. of TNT and registered 7.8 on the Richter scale!

It was a massive explosion. It produced heated rain.

A second explosion, 135 seconds after the initial event, measured 7.9 Mw. It was catastrophic. All the crew members perished.

The bodies of the sailors were completely obliterated. For a five hundred mile radius, the entire aquatic environment was destroyed. A small island, approximately 250 miles away was no longer there. Nor were its 431 residents.

A huge cloud of toxic gases filled the air and a large deposit of toxic waste was dumped into the ocean.

Unfortunately, the location where the ship exploded was directly over a subduction zone. It is the subduction zone earthquakes, in this case an explosion, of these magnitudes that are most likely to generate a tsunami.

As a matter of history, a huge tidal wave would travel across the vast ocean waters until it hit a mass of land. In this case, that land mass was the island of Nardei.

As the radiation from the two nuclear reactors spread in the ever-moving waters of the Pacific Ocean, the process of *eutrophication* began. This biological process occurs when toxic bacteria proliferate in the absence of healthy plankton and other nutrients. This creates an oxygen-deprived environment that kills marine life. These toxins are spread by ocean currents, contaminating a growing aquatic area.

Plankton raised in radioactive mud carry the radiation with them into the ocean, where it is introduced into the entire food chain.

From plankton- to marine life- to the fisherman's dinner plate.

The process of eutrophication was occurring to the marine world under the South Pacific Ocean, only 1300 miles away from the island of Nardei. Worse yet, as the approaching tsunami gained size and speed, it gathered up with it the radioactive particulars in the polluted water. The massive tidal wave was headed directly towards Nardei, and no one even knew about the calamity that was about to manifest.

Well, almost no one.

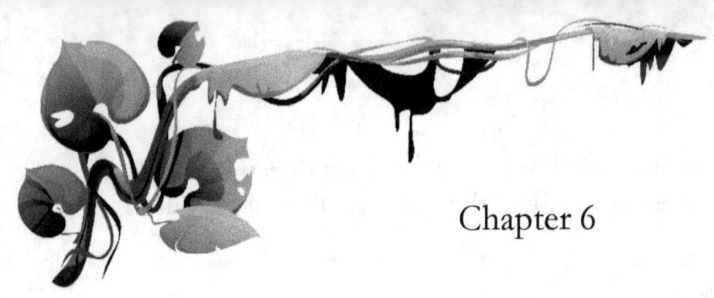

Chapter 6

Ke nae iki nei no.

(Said of one who is dying).

Hearing the screams from Gladys, several resort workers rushed to the room. They found her on the floor, unconscious beside the bed where her dead husband lay. The putrid smell was overwhelming.

"I'll call 911!" cried the housekeeper who was the first to arrive on the scene, right behind her was the daytime resort manager, Mary. She was a quick thinker.

Mary squatted down besides Gladys, noting that she was breathing and that she had a pulse.

Mary knew CPR and had been prepared to administer heart compressions.

"Don't touch anything," said Mary. "Wait until the paramedics and police come."

"I'll go wait outside," said Elena, the housekeeper. The approaching sirens announced the imminent arrival of the emergency vehicles. Besides, Elena couldn't stand the smell.

The paramedics followed Elena down the hallway to the room. As they drew near, the offensive smell hit them. After ensuring that the body on the bed was indeed dead, they focused on Gladys.

"She's breathing on her own but her pulse is rapid and thready, and her blood pressure is low. Is she bleeding anywhere?" asked the tall, Hawai'ian man, who wore his hair tied back in a ponytail. The female paramedic, Malia, had already begun to carefully inspect Gladys's body for any skin lacerations or breaks in skin integrity.

She found none. However, she did notice the bright yellow and green bruises on the back of her legs. The area was swollen as well.

The woman felt so hot that Malia took her temperature per axilla. Gladys had a fever of 102.8 F.

After starting an IV of normal saline and administering oxygen, they wasted no more time and transported Gladys to the emergency room at the local hospital.

Upon her arrival to the hospital, Gladys began to regain consciousness.

She was taken into an examination room. With the assistance of a nurse, the paramedics moved Gladys onto the examination table. By now, Gladys was fully awake.

Taking off her oxygen mask and grabbing her head with both hands, she cried out, "My head! My head is killing me! Do something! Ohhhh!" The nurse, Kakalina (meaning Katherine), told her to relax and that the doctor would be here soon. And right on cue, he entered.

"What have we got here?" inquired Dr. Benjamin Fukina.

"The patient was found unconscious in her room. Her vitals were: respirations 16 and shallow, pulse fast and thready at 127, and blood pressure 106 over 60. There was evidence of recent vomiting and some significant bruising and swelling on the posterior aspect of her right lower leg. I noticed that she also has some bruising and swelling on her right hand, both back and front."

"Help me for God's sake! My head is fuckin' killing me!"
"Anything else?" asked Dr. Fukina.

"Well...yes. Malia said that her husband was found dead in the bed. And she was found on the floor beside him. Then she said that the husband looked really bad, like he'd had some kind of infectious disease. He had some sort of red rash."

"Then why the hell are we not in protective gear? Go do so now, as will I." "Wait! I need something for my headache right now!" exclaimed Gladys.

"We'll be right back," explained Kakalina, and then she quickly left the room, hoping that her lapse in judgment would not come back to bite her. After all, there probably was nothing to worry about – tourists often came with nasty flu bugs from the mainland – and, fortunately, she'd had a flu vaccine recently.

After donning the appropriate protective gear, Kakalina returned to Gladys's examination area. She had already alerted the other staff that this might be an infectious disease case and to prepare an isolation room upstairs in the hospital.

"It's about time you came back! My fuckin' head is killing me. I told you that! Did you bring me something?" Gladys held her face in her hand. She was diaphoretic and, therefore, slick with sweat.

"I can't give you anything until the doctor examines you and says it's okay."

"Fuck that!" Gladys grumbled. She lay back down, moaning and groaning, like a woman in labor.

As the nurse went to put her oxygen mask back on, she noticed a little blood dripping from

Gladys's left nostril. Wiping her nose, she saw that there was a sore inside her left nostril.

Dr. Fukina re-entered the room, with gown, mask, gloves, and booties in place.

The monitors were showing that her vital signs were improving. Dr. Fukina examined the patient from head to toe, noting any abnormalities. He ordered lab work *stat*. Urine and stool cultures and a chest x-ray because she was not perfusing very well, cyanosis apparent in her blue-tinged lips and fingertips, because she was oxygen deprived. Not good.

The pulseoximeter attached to her right fingertip indicated that her oxygen saturation was only at 86%. Already, her oxygen was running at 3.5 liters. Because her neurological exam was unremarkable, he finally ordered Gladys an analgesic. Maybe if she was pain-free, her breathing would improve. He also ordered an anti-pyretic for her fever. She seemed to be burning up.

Her gown was soaked with perspiration.

Kakalina hurried to get the woman her medication because her patient was in apparent discomfort.

"Okay, I have your medication." Kakalina handed Gladys the cup containing her pills. Gladys tried to sit up and take off her oxygen mask but she was too weak. She fell back on the bed.

She looked frightened under the mask, her bright, red hair plastered to her head, greasy from her profuse sweating.

Kakalina assisted her. Gratefully, Gladys took the medication and drifted right off to sleep.

She began to dream of a time from her childhood when she visited a relative's farm in the summertime. They lived on a farm in Montana. In the early morning hours as dawn emerged and brightened the dark sky, Gladys would chase butterflies. They were a light yellow color. In flight, they looked like daises blowing in the summer breeze. She would give chase, trying to catch one. If she did, which had only happened a few times, she would release them back into the sky.

Just as always, Gladys was excited with the pursuit of a beautiful butterfly. And luck was with her! She caught one! She opened her hand to look at it. She shrieked. There was no butterfly there, only little green bugs. They began crawling up her arm, leaving a burning sensation as they moved upward. My God, they itched! And burned like hot fireflies. She began to scratch at the affected area, until she drew blood.

Her arm was on fire now.

In the distance, she heard people shouting, "She's trying to pull her IV out! Get some restraints, look at her right arm, there's a rash ...she's burning up, call the doctor..."

In her dream, Gladys brushed her arm but couldn't get the damn things off. She decided to run down to the river, north on the 100 acre farm. Quickly, she ran, tears streaming down her face because she was both in pain and scared. For goodness sake, she was only 12 years old in her dream. Finally, hot and exhausted, she ran down the river bank and began to walk toward the cool water, glimmering in the summer sun like sparkling diamonds. Of course, that's what Gladys would think. Gladys always had expensive tastes. Flashy gaudy stuff, but nonetheless, expensive. It had been a significant character flaw.

Greed, lust, and gluttony. Serious flaws that offered nothing but misery.

She approached the calm and soothing waters, trying not to scratch her bloodied arm.

A fish jumped out of the calm river onto the river's bank. Oh no, it wasn't a fish. It was a scary-looking black snake, with yellow spots. His red, pointed tongue would whip out of his mouth. One time, he caught a fly. Stricken with terror, Gladys peed herself.

"I am Kanaloa. Do you remember me? We made a deal. Lavish living for your soul. I'm going to collect soon." Twelve year old Gladys fainted.

Shortly thereafter, she was taken up to her room. While being transferred to her bed, Gladys began vomiting.

Her emesis was tinged with fresh blood.

Moments later, she had a seizure. A grand mal seizure that totally taxed her low oxygen reserves. Now, her oxygen saturation had dipped dangerously down to 74%. Her temperature was 103.8F and climbing. It was looking more and more likely that she had contracted some sort of contagious infection.

Gladys was fighting for her life.

She heard, "Code blue, code blue in room 212." Then she heard nothing.

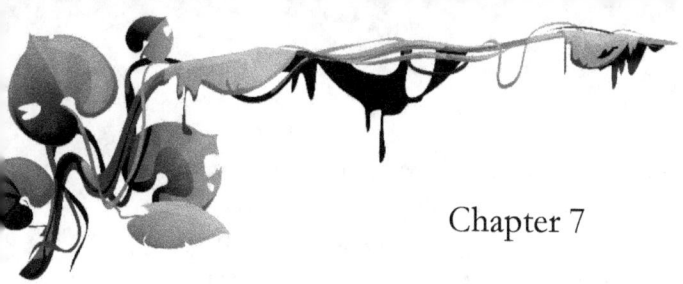

Chapter 7

O ka makua ke ko 'o o ka hale e pa 'a ai.
(The parent is the support that holds the household together).

It was an especially pleasant evening in paradise. The cool, night air was filled with a ginger pungence of scented night-blooming flowers. Kimo's family, which included Kekela, was enjoying their evening meal together. For Kate, it was her favorite time of the day.

It was a typical dinner time for Kimo, Kate and their three children. Like most nights, Uncle Kekela joined them. Pua was at his feet under the table, always hoping for some scraps.

Usually, getting nothing for her trouble. Tonight, they were enjoying freshly-caught ahi. Caught by whom else? Expert fisherman, Ray, of course. Hands down, he was the best fisherman on the island.

"That guy is so lucky. He always catches something. Ray never comes back in with nothin' to show for his time," said Kekela. He was enjoying the grilled fresh catch, along with jasmine rice and fresh green beans. Kate had made a mango and cilantro sauce for the fish. After all, summertime was mango season. Kekela's favorite purple, sweet potato dinner rolls were on the table beside his elbow, well within his reach. He'd already had three and still counting......

"This is so good Kate. You've done it again. No wonder Kimo married you," Kekela teased. "Thing is, he got to you before I could, but here I am at your table anyway." He chuckled. So did the kids.

Kimo smiled and held Kate's hand, "I know I'm a lucky guy. And I guess you are too, bra."

"Oh Dad………enough of the mushy talk." Luke rolled his eyes. He wasn't much for love talk at the age of 15. It embarrassed him because he was secretly in love with a girl in his school named Alemea. Her name means precious and she was just that to him. He planned on marrying her someday. Young love.

"Mama, can I have some more water?" asked little Hannah. Before Kate could respond, Hina reached over and poured her a glass from the pitcher. Mute, but not deaf. Always protective and helpful to the little sister she adored like no other.

Hannah giggled. "He's licking my feet." "That's because he loves you," replied Uncle.

"I love him too. And you too, Uncle." Little Hannah was a sweet and affection child, with a sunny disposition. She could melt the coldest of hearts.

"I love you too, pumpkin," replied Kekela, hiding the tears behind his dark glasses.

Hannah was playing with her rice and ahi, making quite the mess. She was tired out from another day at the beach. Sun and fun makes little girls sleepy.

Suddenly, Kimo's cell phone rang. Kimo asked not to be called during his family's dinner time unless it was an emergency. They all knew that, so the table got quiet as they listened. For their eavesdropping, they got nothing except "a hum, a hum, yeah, okay," then, "I'll be right there." However, from the look on Kimo's face, it wasn't good.

"So what?" asked Kekela.

"There's a couple of dead cattle at the Kane ranch. Says they looked real sick or somethin'." "Maybe I should come with you."

"Nah, no sense both of us missin' Kate's mango pie, bra. Besides, you can keep her company." And with that, he was out the door.

Luke left for a dress rehearsal at the high school. A classic play by Shakespeare – Romeo and Juliet. His leading lady was Alemea. His Juliet. Hina had taken little Hannah upstairs for her

bath. She could hear the little girl singing a Nemo song. Little Mermaid.

Kate and Kekela enjoyed a cup of coffee. Kekela had a second piece of pie. Where did he put it all? He was thin and wiry. No fat on him. Despite his lack of vision, Kekela was still active in the ocean waters, body surfing and riding a long board. He knew the waters and the mountains like the back of his hand. He used his highly developed senses to navigate through different terrains. His sense of smell was very much heightened. He could sniff the wind and glean all kinds of information. His nose was like Rudolph's, an accurate instrument at predicting the weather, especially the approach of storms. How else do you think that Rudolph got to be the leader of the pack?

"I saw Kupuna this afternoon," said Kate. "She had one of her *pokii* dreams." A pokii dream is one that was sent from the spirit world with images and messages that can only be attained in a dream state. "She said she thought the message in it was really a warning."

"A warning about what?" asked Kekela. He was well aware that Kupuna Hannah accurately predicted upcoming events because he had witnessed it on a number of occasions. She'd never been wrong.

"She dreamt about a great tidal wave." Kate went on, "but, that's not the worst of it. She relative who has passed on to the other side. It is believed that after the death of a family member, their spirit could still protect and influence the remaining family, acting through the vessel's body. They can inhabit a variety of vessels, but most often, the favored one was the Pueo or the Hawai'ian barn owl, considerate a sacred bird over the ages. Kai, Kupuna Hannah's late husband, had visited her on several previous occasions, after transmigrating into an owl.

"What did Kai say?"

"The owl in her dream told her to gather the noni plant and fruit to make anti-cancer pharmaceuticals, without delay. And then give them to all of the island's people. Again, without delay. She already has Puna and some of the other men gathering the needed ingredients."

Noni or the morinda plant is a tropical evergreen that grows to approximately 10 feet tall in the Pacific Islands. The noni fruit has been used as a nutritional, wellness product for centuries among the Polynesians. During WW II, soldiers in the South Pacific ate the fruit for added sustenance. Different parts of the noni plant are used as a juice, a tonic, a poultice, and a tea. Most often it is made as a juice, which has an unpleasant taste and odor, so it is mixed with other tropical fruit juices like guava, pineapple or lilikoi to mask the vile taste. Today, it is used to treat or prevent a variety of diseases, including diabetes and cancer.

Researchers at the University of Hawaii have identified a compound in the root and the fruit of the noni plant that inhibits a chemical process that turns normal cells into cancer cells.

"Then, we must do that. Our aumakua is calling." Besides, Kekela had a sense of impending doom and, since he became blind, he was somewhat telepathic. There were bad vibes in the air. That's what he smelled.

After saying their good-byes, Kate cleaned off the table, and began doing the dishes. She noticed green little flecks on two of the kid's plates. Neither Hannah nor Luke liked green beans. Come to think about it, these looked like dead little, green bugs. Yuck! It couldn't be bugs! Well, at least they were dead. So, how dangerous could they be? It wasn't like her kids had never eaten bugs before. Are you kidding? This was the tropics, the land of all bugs, big or small.

Kate headed upstairs to put her two youngest children to bed.

The Hawai'ian Prayer to Lono

Lono the rolling thunder,
The heaven that rumbles,
The disturbed sea,
Lono and Keakea-lani,
Living together, fructifying the earth,
Observing the tapu of women,
Clouds bow down over the sea,
The earthquake sounds Within the earth,
Tumbling down there Below Malama.

Beckwith, Martha (1976). The God Lono, Hawai'ian Mythology, The University of Hawaii Press:Honolulu., Hawaii, p. 32.

Chapter 8

Ke kani nei ka ʻalana.

(The gift is sounded; said of an offering to the gods with a loudly spoken prayer).

The next day, Puna, Luke and some other young men, gathered load after load of noni plants and fruits. Puna, being Kupuna Hannah's son and so much like her, was the group leader. They worked together efficiently, much like a paddling team at a canoe race. It was all about team work. As they collected the requisite ingredients necessary for the anti-cancer medicines, an owl watched over them, supervising their efforts.

Without saying so, they all knew it was Kai. He was ensuring that they were following his instructions. The survival of his people depended on it.

Later that afternoon, Kimo, as mayor, had announced a meeting at the town pavilion for all of Nardei's people. Whenever there was a crisis, they gathered in the town square at the pavilion. Folks thought something was up. By now, through the coconut wireless, they'd heard about the dead cattle at William Kane's farm. Word had it that they were covered in lesions and they had lost all their hair. Pink, naked cattle with blood-red lesions. Their eyes, nose, and ears had bleed out. Word also had it that there was a lot of blood involved everywhere. Major bleeding.

Spooky.

At 5 p.m., the town people began to gather at the pavilion on the front, well-shaded lawn in front of the county building. There were picnic tables scattered around the lawn. At any gathering, Hawai'ians always bring food. This was no different. Soon food began to appear. Fish poki, chicken wings, poi, potato and macaroni salad, seafood salad, and fresh fruit, including lots of pickled mango, taro chips and *haupia* or coconut pudding. Whatever was going on, they'd need to eat. Eat when you can, especially during a period of duress.

There were several chairs on the stage of the pavilion. Pastor Kua walked on stage, leaning on his cane, and sat in one of the chairs. This was something big.

Next, Kupuna Hannah walked slowly on stage and sat down by pastor. This was something *really* big.

Puna crossed the stage, taking a chair beside his mother. Proud mother, proud son.

Kimo walked to the center of the stage, waiting for the crowd to quiet. He had a microphone in his hand, wanting to make sure that everyone could hear him. Some of the crowd quieted quickly, but anticipation was running high. Adults murmured their fears and the children were picking the vibe. They were running around and shouting, so happy to be on the big lawn with a large pavilion and a playground area with slides and swings and a large sandbox.

"My friends and neighbors, my elders and co-workers, once again we must come together for the sake of our island and our people," Kimo began. "Just like seven years ago, there are some dark days ahead. How do I know this? Kupuna Hannah has heard the voices of our aumakua."

There was silence as everyone realized the gravity of the situation. Even the children became silent.

"A tsunami is coming!" shouted an elderly Polynesian man, named Tanti. "I too heard from my dead wife in a dream the other night. On the night of the full moon. She said a giant wave is coming and we must get to high ground!"

"Is that true Kimo?" cried out several individuals. The crowd was stirring, getting worked up like caged cattle.

"Now, quiet down everyone. There are no reports of a significant earthquake anywhere in the world today, or any time in the past week. I've checked with Honolulu, they report there's been no activity. That's the science of it. But, we've got our own ways of knowing." The crowd murmured their agreement. Kimo continued, "There's more than a tsunami coming. The aumakua told Hannah to gather the noni plant and its fruit and make a special juice. He said we must all consume it right away and do so every day. I expect there must be some kind of disease a-foot."

"Is that related to Kane's dead cattle? We heard they was real sick." A woman in the crowd asked the question they were all wondering about. They'd been thinking about the grizzly, gruesome dead bodies of the cattle.

"Maybe, maybe," Kimo told them. "I'm not sure yet."

"What disease? Is anyone actually sick already? What are the symptoms? Is it contagious?" Mrs. Tanaka, the high school principle asked. Her assertive nature rendered her an effective leader in the community.

"We're not sure about any of that right now. Not yet. Nonetheless, we should all start drinking the noni drink Kupuna has made." The town folk all looked at Kupuna Hannah, nodding their approval. "In the cafeteria at the high school, there are enough drinks for all of us to start taking it right away. But, we need more help. Help to gather the plants and fruit. Help to assist Kupuna to make the drink."

"I can help!" shouted one, then another, including Tanti. Soon, plans were being made to utilize every helper wisely. Age had to be considered. Some of the elders weren't always realistic about what their physical limitations were. Tanti thought he could climb up the steep mountains at the age of 72. He was re-assigned to help in the kitchen and given an apron.

Kupuna Hannah rose from her chair and walked over beside Kimo. Her beautiful, long silver hair was piled high on her head and tropical flowers adorned it. With her commanding demeanor, she took the microphone.

"The message was clear, my friends. We must act and act quickly. Everyone's *kokua* (co- operation) is needed. Dark days lay

Mutation in Paradise

ahead, but we, as a people will endure. Just like we have throughout the centuries."

"Amen," said the Pastor out loud. The crowd echoed him.

"Let me be clear: *drink the noni every day and put salt around your home frequently, especially after it rains.*" Kupuna repeated it once again to emphasis what must be done.

"We must call upon the god of the clouds and all storms, Lono, to disperse the tsunami and block it from coming onto our island. Let us please Lono by making the offering of the symbolic food gourd, along with the appropriate prayer."

Throughout the centuries, each householder kept in his place of worship, called the *mua,* a food gourd or *hulilau.* The gourd of Lono was covered with wickerwork and hung by strings to a notched stick. Inside the gourd were kept food, fish, and *awa,* which is a root from a native shrub that has medicinal and narcotic uses. Another small piece of the awa was tied onto the handle outside. Every morning and every evening, the head of the household would take down the gourd and lay it at the house, and face outward to the outdoors, then pray to Lono.

Kupuna was calling upon them again to put into practice this ritual that pleases the god of storms.

Finally, Kupuna said, "Pastor is having a prayer service tonight at 7:00 p.m. Please come and *pule* with us. We need all the prayers that we can get."

After the meeting shut down, folks came to the cafeteria and got their noni drink. Smaller size drinks for children under 12 years old. Lili, named after the last reigning Hawai'ian queen, Queen Liliuokalani, was helping to serve the noni drink. She had grown up with Puna and Napua. She was just a couple of years older than her friends. In fact, Napua was her cousin. She had been heartbroken when Napua had died during the days of the great tribulation.

Lili Lange was born and raised on Nardei, yet she had left her tropical home to attend the John Burn's School of Medicine at the University of Hawaii on Oahu. Lili was as smart as a whip. While attending high school, she had completed on-line courses for her pre-med studies. Lili was a total brainiac, and she was also very beautiful. A hapa child. Part-Hawai'ian, part- Caucasian. She was as exotic as the extinct clouded leopard. An animal of majestic strength, power and beauty.

Now, Puna and Lili were an item. Since she had returned to the island, they had resumed their friendship.

He approached her, smiling. "Hey. How's it going?" He was always taken by her raw beauty.

"People are scared. Everybody is making sure that they get the noni. Not a problem." Lili looked tired. Because of the potential cases of some communicable disease, she'd been at the hospital around the clock. She'd taken Doc's position, including being the medical examiner. Tomorrow, she would be performing the autopsy on Gladys Goldberg. Tonight, she would be doing Earnest's autopsy.

Suddenly, arms were flung around Puna's waist. Hina was embracing her secret crush. She looked up at him and grinned. She ignored Lili.

"Hey, how's my favorite girl?" he asked, smiling back at the mute girl. When would Hina finally break her silence?

Lili was right. The people of Nardei were frightened. They lingered to talk about moving to higher elevations. They would stay in the caves. Fortunately, there were many caves. First daylight, they would begin to bring supplies up to the sanctuary of the caves. They figured time was short.

They would make haste in their preparations. After, they had salted their yards.

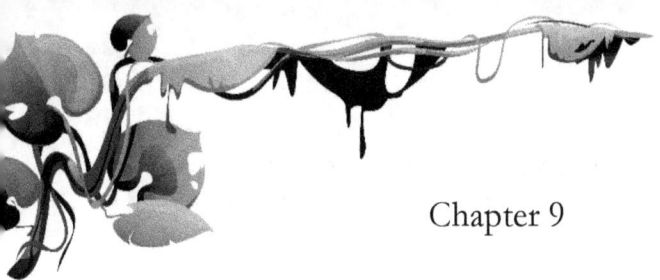

Chapter 9

Ha 'ale 'ale I ka pu 'uwai.
(A heart full to the brim with love).

After finishing up at the cafeteria, Lili and Puna decided to take a walk on the beach under the moonlight. They strolled hand-in-hand along the shoreline, Pua following behind. The almost-full moon shone brightly, illuminating the way. The water sparkled, dancing in the moonbeams. Hundreds of stars twinkled in the dark sky.

Starry, starry night. The kind of night for romancing.

They made a handsome couple. Both with thick, dark hair, both were tall, and both were blessed with attractive looks. He was a warrior and she was a healer.

"What do you really think is going on?' she asked Puna. Her dark eyes shone in the night. He could smell the scent of her passion-fruit, scented shampoo in her hair.

"I think that a tidal wave is really coming. I never doubt the aumakua's warnings. Even Kekela smells it in the air. Something's coming. But, what about the disease? What do you know about that?"

"I'll know more by tomorrow afternoon. Tonight, I'm autopsying one of the dead tourists – the wife. Tomorrow, I'll do the husband." replied Lili. "Quite frankly, I'm afraid of what I'm going to find." She wished that her mentor, Doc, was still alive. He too had perished during the dark days. She recalled, that as a kid, he'd let her play with his stethoscope so she could listen to her heart beating in her chest. As she got older, she became proficient with the tuning fork.

"You'll take precautions, right?" he asked, concern showing on his handsome face. He stopped under the moonlight, seeking out her dark eyes, flecked with gold.

"Of course. You can count on it." She touched his cheek with her cupped hand. He kissed her deeply. Pua began jumping up and down on the couple.

Jealous, little doggie!

"You know, you'll never get past first base with me if that dog is always around!" laughed Lili.

"Oh, so *that's* the problem," Puna teased. Pua starting barking and ran up ahead. What had gotten into her? Soon, she was way ahead of the couple.

"Probably chasing chickens." Puna wanted to talk to Lili about the future. Even though they had only been seeing each other for 9 months, Puna knew that he wanted to make a life with her. Raise a family of their own. He wanted to tell her how he felt but he had a hard time expressing his feelings. After the death of Napua, he was emotionally numb. Lili had changed all that. Maybe, he was afraid that she might leave him too. Her brains and beauty intimidated him. She's a doctor and he was just a high school teacher, after all. Well, he was the athletic director too. What if she rejected him? He didn't think he could handle that. He did not want to grieve the loss of another woman that he loved.

They sat on the beach, ignoring Pua's barking rant.

"Lili, I've been wanting to talk to you about something…" he began. "I know we've only been seeing each other for a short time, but, I already feel really comfortable with you, and…"

Her cell phone rang.

"It's the hospital. I have to take it but hold that thought," she said, smiling. She thought she knew where this conversation was headed. Her smile faded as she listened.

"Okay. I get it. I'll be right there." Lili ended her call. "I gotta run. They're having a number of unexpected admissions."

Mutation in Paradise

"What's going on?"

"I'm not sure." She hurried away. Her long dark hair was swaying across her back. "Call me later, if you can!" shouted Puna. Damn. Foiled again!

He set off to see what was up with Pua, she was acting crazy tonight. Maybe, she was picking up on the fear quietly permeating the town folks. Puna could feel it too. Like his mother, he had also had a dream in which his father had visited him. He told him to make an offering to Lono, the god of weather and the phenomena of storms, even massive storms.

Lono, who can control all weather events: thunder and lightning, earthquakes, dark storms, whirlwinds that sweep the earth, water spouts and gushing mountain streams. The god, Lono, goes back a long way. A poetic Hawai'ian song, "The god Lono", was noted in a diary of a young, British sailor on a large, trading ship that visited the port of Honolulu in 1725.

He would set up a House of Mana at the heiau in the morning. These Hawai'ian gods or akua, the gods of Nature and of Creation, had their public temples or heiaus. As ritual demanded, he would erect a small hut for the purpose of accepting and housing the food offerings to Lono.

This god did not require an animal sacrifice. Lono was also the god of the harvest so he was pleased by offerings of island-grown plants and fruits. Offerings were to be placed on a white, tapa cloth that was blessed by the Kupuna using the proper chant, making sure to use the appropriate rituals in preparation to receive the gifts.

Puna planned to make offerings that included ti leaves, coconuts, bananas, kiwi, red fish and sugar cane. This would generate great mana or power for the god of weather in the days ahead.

Mana was the invisible force that flowed from the most senior spirits to energize everything in the universe, including the wind, the growth of a plant, or a shift in the ocean currents. In humans, mana manifests as exceptional talents.

Following in his mother's footsteps, Puna was a budding Kahuna himself. He knew the required ritual to begin the process of making the offerings to Lono. For the ritual, the attire would consist of only a white, loin cloth and a lei of fragrant, white plumeria flowers, whose fragrance was the utter smell of the tropics. He scattered salt, a natural purifier, around the House of Mana.

Puna was familiar with the Lono's House of Mana chant, *"Lono, god high in the heavens, po'o huna I kea o lewa (with your head hidden in the dark clouds above), please intervene in the fate of the people of Nardei. Lono, god of all weather phenomenon, we seek your help again. As in the past, from the beginning of our ancestors, we turn to you as a tsunami bears down on us.*

Show our island and its people mercy, once again. Oh Lono, father of the harvest, father of fertility, and new beginnings, we humbly submit our gifts."

Tonight, he would enlist the help of his friends to gather the offering items, first thing at dawn. His father had emphasized to do it immediately.

He finally caught up to Pua. She had settled down but she was covered in sticky hitchhikers, from a gnarly plant. She looked like she had just done battle with some foe. What a dog!

Always chasing chickens. Except there were no feathers around.

From the dark, under some bushes, two red eyes glowed from the bushes.

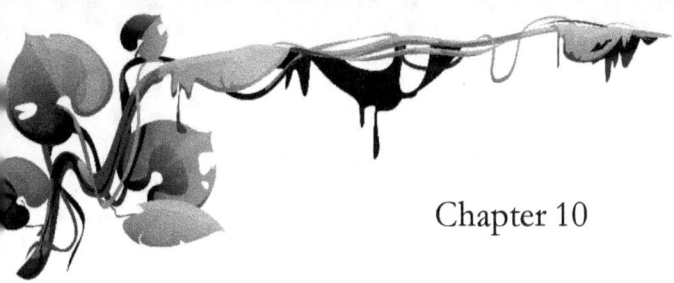

Chapter 10

Hui aku, hui mai, hui kalo me ka nawao.
(Said of a great mix-up; Chaos).

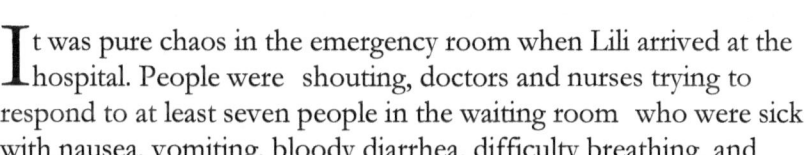

It was pure chaos in the emergency room when Lili arrived at the hospital. People were shouting, doctors and nurses trying to respond to at least seven people in the waiting room who were sick with nausea, vomiting, bloody diarrhea, difficulty breathing, and some had bleeding from their nose, mouth and other orifices. Some had lesions on their skin. Obviously, they had been exposed to the same contagion as Gladys and Earnest.

It was a madhouse, reminiscent of an episode of E.R.

"Lili, over here!" shouted Kakalina. Her gown was bloody, her hair disheveled. She was in protective gear. "We need to intubate this guy!"

Without delay, Lili went to the exam room and donned her own protective gear to avoid getting contaminated from a potentially infectious disease. How contagious was it?

An elderly man, a tourist from Ottawa, Canada, was clearly in respiratory distress. The nurse had opened the sterile intubation tray, getting ready for the doctor to insert it. Mr.

Worthington was barely hanging on. His skin was cyanotic, evidence of poor oxygenation at the cellular level, and his oxygen saturation rate was dangerously low. His blue face and body were covered in the characteristic red lesions, including his bald head. He was perspiring profusely due to a high fever.

Lili snapped on her sterile blue, latex gloves and opened Mr. Worthington's airway in preparation to insert the tube to assist him to breathe. She began inserting the tube when the elderly man began to seize. Blood began to trickle out of his mouth. Bloody, frothy urine ran down his legs. As his arms flailed in the throes of a seizure, he arrested.

Respiratory arrest.

"Code blue, code blue in the E.R., exam room 4." The nurse had called a code while Lili managed the patient, administrating IV Valium to stop the seizure. She needed to intubate this patient right now. Help arrived. Dr. Fukina began ordering medications, as Kakalina took over for Lili and administered the meds into the patient's IV. Lili returned to inserting the airway and this time she got it.

Beeeeep!!

The cardiac monitor started sounding the alarm. Mr. Worthington was going into cardiac arrest. Ventricular arrhythmia, a death sentence. They shocked him several times, but to no avail. The monitor indicated there was no activity.

Asystole. Flat line.

There was the death sentence.

Dr. Fukina called the time of death at 8:52 p.m. There were other sick patients to deal with.

Another patient was wheeled into the exam room, after Mr. Worthington's body was removed to the morgue. This patient was only 5 years old. Jessica was Mr. Worthington's granddaughter. *I'm not going to lose this one*, thought Lili.

It was a long night. By the end of it, there were two more dead patients and six who were admitted to the in-patient floors, including little Jessica. She reminded Lili of little Hannah. Of course, Lili never got to the autopsy of Gladys, and now there were a total of five bodies in the morgue freezers. She'd have to call Honolulu and tell them that they had some type of infectious disease outbreak occurring on their island. Assistance from the Department of

Health would be needed. This was something contagious and lethal and now it was an official epidemic.

They had taken extensive lab work from each patient. Every type of specimen was collected for the purpose of analyzing the offending organism. But, in the meantime, Lili had just received Gladys's lab work, including her CBC. Her blood count revealed that she had been profoundly anemic. Not only was she low in her red blood cells, her WBCs (white blood cells) were extremely low, rendering her totally vulnerable to an infection. Did she have a problem with her bone marrow? But, was it the chicken or the egg? Did an illness strike and she then depleted her WBCs fighting it, or did she have a problem with her immune system as evidenced by the low WBCs, and, therefore, she had acquired an infectious illness?

What a minute! The blood work also indicated that there had been some microscopic organisms in the red blood cells. Well, parasites could also explain a low WBC and anemia. Parasites weren't that uncommon in the tropics, where all living organisms proliferate. Lili needed more data and that would come from the autopsies. What the hell was going on? Lili knew she needed to perform the autopsies on the descendants in the morgue.

She decided to check on Jessica before she went home to sleep. She desperately needed sleep. It was already 3:00 a.m. First thing tomorrow, she would perform the autopsy on Gladys.

When she entered her room, she saw that her mother was sitting at the bedside, holding Jessica's small hand. She was sleeping comfortably, despite being hooked-up to a variety of monitors that were beeping. Heart beat after heart beat. She looked so small in the bed with the oxygen mask covering two-thirds of her face. Her blond hair was wet with the sweat of a fever. Her IV of normal saline was running into her small, left hand.

Jessica had been catheterized to keep track of her urine. Poor urine output was a red flag for profound dehydration. With her high fever, diarrhea and vomiting, this little girl was at high-risk for severe dehydration. In a 5 year old, that could be the kiss of death. The bag containing her urine was a pinkish-red color. Where was she bleeding? From her kidneys? Her bladder?

"Hi, I'm Dr. Lange," said Lili as she approached the bed. The mother looked gaunt and haggard. Was she getting sick too?

"I'm Jessie's mom, Mrs. Alexander," said the mother. "What's wrong with her, doctor?" Her anxiety was apparent, as she wrung her hands, destroying a tissue in the process.

"I'm not sure yet. We're still working on it."

"Is she gonna die like my daddy did?" Her deepest, darkest fear revealed.

"I'm going to do everything in my power to not let that happen," was all the reassurance she could truthfully muster. "Mrs. Alexander, did your father or daughter have any interactions with the Goldberg's?" inquired Lili, determined to get some history.

"That woman! She and her husband were on the same plane that we came on. After that, we steered clear of them – or rather, *her*. She was a little over the top, if you ask me." "What about your room at the resort? Is it near their room?" asked Lili.

"Unfortunately, we have the room next to them. Or rather, we did. I heard they both died. Is that true?" She wanted Lili to say no. Lili just nodded to affirm it. The mother understood that her young daughter was in imminent danger. Death was knocking on her door.

One significant piece of medical information that Lili gleaned was that Jessica had diabetes, type I, insulin-dependent. Her mother showed Lili the insulin she had brought along. This only complicated the case. Management of juvenile diabetes was difficult at best, never mind with a child who was vomiting. Furthermore, it rendered the poor girl at an even greater risk for life- threatening dehydration. Immediately, she was moving Jessica to the ICU to have her monitored constantly. On a dime, the situation could take a turn for the worse.

Lili asked a host of specific questions from the food they ingested to the places they had been, and on and on…

Finally, Lili asked perhaps the most important question: "And you're not sick, Mrs. Alexander, no flu-like symptoms?"

"No, Dr. Lange. I'm fine." She shrugged. It was obviously a mystery to her too.

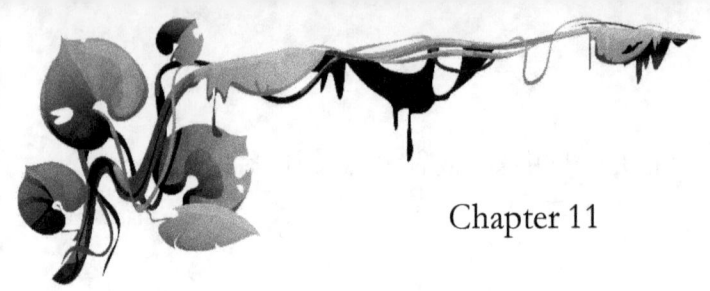

Chapter 11

Ahe no ka manu o Ka'ula, he la 'ino.

(When the birds of Ka'ula appear wild, it denotes a stormy day).

Ancient Hawai'ians possessed expert knowledge of fishing methods. Revealed by recent discoveries of fish hooks of many varieties, it was clear that they had their own lucky lures. The fisherman had to make careful preparations prior to going out fishing. Hooks had to be lashed the day before fishing. There were many *kapus* or rules to be observed by the fisherman and his family.

Old traditions must be respected.

The Hawai'ians use a multitude of names for fish species, clouds, winds, sea states, ocean currents, sea birds, seasonal changes, and other natural phenomena. This reflected their intimacy with the sea. Some fish had several names, distinguishing a different phase of growth. Lawai'a or fishermen have developed an extensive body of knowledge regarding their quarry.

On this sunny morning, Ray and David were headed out to sea in the Noalani. They wanted to see if there were any signs of an approaching storm.

Before the early departure at dawn, Ray had talked to his aumakua, his brother Joe.

Hawaiian families included the spirits of venerated ancestors who had died as part of their *ohana*. They were regarded as important family members to whom acts of respect must be paid often.

For his vessel of worship, Ray used a *kuula*. Every fisherman had his own kuula. It was a pile of stones with great mana, as they came from the ocean depths. He and Joe had retrieved these particular stones on lucky days that they had caught some bounty. Ray had been a child but, even then, he understood they were sacred stones.

More mana, more sacredness.

He had a sense of foreboding, a feeling of impending doom. He had salted around his home and had hung the gourd of Lono on his door, just as the old tradition demanded.

Today, they would venture out as far as possible, perhaps 75 miles, and look for the signs of weather events by observing the currents, feeling and smelling the wind, and examining the clouds.

"Dude, you're mighty quiet this mornin'. Another dream about the snake?" "No, it's not that."

"So, what is it?"

"Uncle? What if we run into the tidal wave?" David's eyes were wide and glassy with fear.

He obviously was feeling the same bad vibe. "I don't want to drown."

"Dude, not to worry. I know the signs that will warn us long before a tsunami could ever hit us," reassured Ray.

"What signs?"

"I'll let you know if I see any. Just watch for any changes in the ocean, skies, clouds, wind and birds." Ray knew that David was a keen observer. David gazed at the ocean waters and the clear, blue skies. It was a glorious day.

Would tomorrow or the next day be the same? Or would they be facing a giant wave coming on shore, destroying Nardei. Was a disaster looming? And, if so, when? After all, there still were no reports from Honolulu about an earthquake or a tidal wave. Nothing.

Only the voices of the aumakua.

As they cruised through the deep, ocean waters, they saw a school of dolphins dashing through the waters, headed farther out to sea. All appeared as it should be. Blue, cloudless skies, a cooling ocean breeze, and turquoise-blue water, glittering with the touch of the sun's rays. Ho, hum…just another perfect day in paradise.

"David, do you smell something funky in the air?" Ray was picking up the scent of something in the breeze. A burnt toast odor. There was static in the air, an electrical charge, yet there was not a dark, cloud in the sky. How could a storm be coming?

"Not really uncle. I only smell the salt in the air."

The farther and deeper they traveled over the ocean waters, the wind began to pick up.

Whatever faint, malodorous scent that had been in the air, it was now dispersed in the slightly, stronger breeze. And still, the skies were clear, the ocean calm, and the wind at a comfortable 18 miles per hour.

So, they traveled a little further.

After one hour, Ray knew that he needed to turn back to ensure they had enough gas to get back.

As he began to make the turn, David shouted, "Look! Look over there!" He pointed to the west. "Not too far. I see something floating in the water. It's fluorescent! Like neon!"

"Okay. I see it." Ray slowed the boat and pulled alongside what appeared to be a dead, 40- pound ahi. He cut the motor. It was bloated with the decomposition of death. He gagged with the smell. But, David was right. There were neon-green flecks of color on the dead fish. In the sunlight, it shone like a fluorescent light. What the hell?

Ray decided to bring the fish back to Nardei and have somebody look at it. He'd never seen

anything like this. A florescent-green fish. It was a mystery to this seasoned fisherman.

"David, hand me the spear." Ray had no intention of touching the dead marlin. What if it had something contagious?

David handed his uncle the sharp spear. Ray gripped it and aimed for the dead fish. It was an easy task. He pulled the fish up and onto the boat. David went to move it.

"No, David! We don't know what killed this fish and that green stuff on it is weird, so stay clear of it," warned Ray. "We best be heading back."

"But, uncle…what do you think was wrong with the fish? What's the green stuff?" David was curious. Well, so was Ray.

Mighty curious.

"To tell you the truth, I have no idea." It was the first time that his uncle didn't know about something related to the ocean and its marine life. That too puzzled the young man.

Ray started the two twin Honda motors and turned the boat, heading back to the safe harbor of home.

He didn't notice that, in his wake, hundreds of other dead, green-speckled fish were floating in the ocean waters. Nor was he aware that in the near distance behind him, a shiny, green mist was shimmering as it rose like steam from the waters. The mist could have been a beautiful, mystic place which housed Peter Pan and his friends, but it wasn't anything like Netherland.

This mist was a deadly shroud and all who encountered it would surely die.

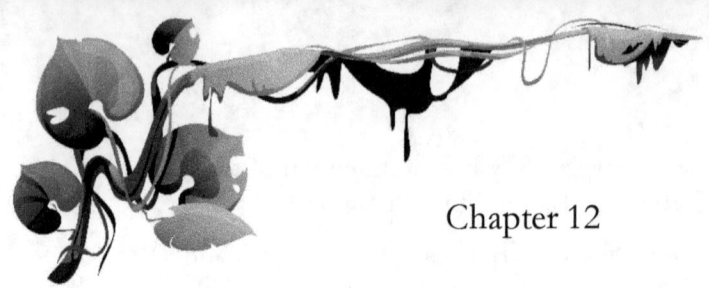

Chapter 12

Hilo mahi ha ʻaheo
(Hilo of the proud farmers).

Kimo's phone at the mayor's office was ringing off the hook. Kekela had been answering a number of calls too. Local taro farmers were reporting that there was some kind of blight on the plants. The taro crops were withering and dying.

The ancient Hawai'ian farmers were of a caliber that was years ahead of other early civilizations. They were able to make the land yield enough to feed over three hundred inhabitants during the days of Captain Cook's visit. A failure to produce crops was an affront to Hawai'ian farmers.

Taro is a major starch in the diet of Hawai'ians. In ancient Hawaii, taro played a much bigger role, beyond being a major dietary staple. Since the earliest agricultural societies, taro was at the heart of the economic, political and spiritual center of the Hawai'ian community. Thus, the taro plant and its history grew into mythological proportions.

Like all things Hawai'ian, great tales regarding the important taro plant were spun. The taro plant was considered an elder sibling to the Hawai'ian race. In the folklore of taro's origin, it is the stillborn, first child of Wakea, the sky father, and his daughter Ho'ohokukalani (daughter to Papa, the earth mother). This child was buried near the house and grew into a taro plant they named Holoanaka, or long stalk trembling. The second son born to Wakea and Ho`ohokukalani took human form and was named Haloa, named after his older brother. Hence, Hawai'ians as a people believed themselves to be closely related to taro.

Taro is made into both local and business products including taro paste or poi. Poi is a slightly fermented paste made from the large, bulbous taro root. Taro cakes, taro batter, taro bread or rolls, taro pancakes, taro chunks in casseroles and *kulolo* (a type of fudge-like candy).

"Calvin, I hear you. Kekela's on the phone to Honolulu right now." Kimo hoped to hell that somebody would finally check out their situation and offer help. "Help me by describing what it looks like." Kimo took out a pen and paper.

"Well, let's see. There's dark spots on the leaves and they got some kind of a lime-green ring around the spots. Some of 'em have these red lesions that puts out a smelly, yellow ooze. It took over the whole crop pretty quick. I'm gonna lose the whole crop."

"I'll get back to you today. Has the sheriff been out yet?" asked Kimo.

"I expect him any minute. Call me soon as you know something." Calvin signed off. Kimo saw that Kekela was off the phone. "What did Honolulu say?"

"To send 'em some information. Take photos." Kekela said that they couldn't send anyone to come right now. "There's some kind of problem with crops with blight. Sorta like us. They said ain't nothin' you can do about a bacterial blight. It gets in the crop's roots, so you gotta burn the fields if you wanna plant new taro."

"Bacterial blight happens in hot temperature zones. Not even fungicides work on bacterial diseases." Kimo knew this would not be good. Bad jujube.

"Well, let's go take a look for ourselves." Kimo grabbed his cell phone and keys. Kekela grabbed his cane. His cane assisted his ability to walk and it also assisted him to see. To ascertain the way forward. He refused to let anyone assist him with his ambulation, being a proud and stubborn blind man. That whole macho guy trip.

As they drove to the north side, they could see the withered, dying crops. Large patches of yellow in the valleys. They rolled their windows up in an attempt to avoid the foul odor in the air. But there was no avoiding it. It smelled like rotten, poopy baby diapers. Multiply by the hundreds, maybe thousands and you've got the idea. Stinky to da max.

"Damn, I'll have to burn my clothes after this. I've never smelt anything like it." Kimo had put a bandana around his nose and mouth. He didn't really want to taste it in his mouth. It would require more than Listerine to take the taste out of his mouth.

"We'll stop at Calvin's place and take some pictures there." They drove down into the terraced valley until they reached Calvin's farm. Now, they'd get to see the plants up close.

As they drove up Calvin's red dirt driveway, Calvin emerged from his house. He looked old and weary. He'd lost some weight too. They got out of the car and walked toward the farmer. Nope, Calvin wasn't looking so good.

"Woowee! That smell is too much! Man, I can hardly handle it," exclaimed Kekela.

"Howdy," greeted Calvin and smiled. There was blood all over his teeth! As a result, his smile was ghoulish. He took out a handkerchief from his overall pocket and wiped his mouth.

"Sorry. Been having a problem with bleeding gums. Gotta get to the dentist before my teeth fall out." That wasn't the only thing falling out. Calvin was losing his hair, heading towards baldness. The curse of hair loss was every man's phobia.

"Bra, you better get those gums checked or you won't be eating any ribs or corn on the cob," said Kekela. He knew Calvin sure enjoyed his food. Not having teeth would reduce his quality of life markedly. No wonder he'd lost some weight.

"Yeah Calvin, you ain't looking so good. Are you sick?" inquired Kimo.

"Maybe not feeling so good these days." That seemed like an understatement. He looked like he had one foot in the grave.

"You best get yourself to the health clinic," warned Kimo. "How's Nadine?"

"She's not feelin' so good herself. We figure we both been suffering from a flu bug even though we had our flu shots. "Course, now we got this situation. Nadine's worried about money."

"Calvin, have you and the wife been drinking your daily noni drink?" asked Kimo. "When we can get into town and pick it up."

"Okay. You go on into the house Calvin and check on the missus. Go take care of Nadine. We'll go take our pictures and be gone. And remember, you both need to see the doc." Kimo was concerned. Usually, when they stopped here, Nadine would come out with some lemonade and snacks. "I'll be checkin' up with you later. Tell Nadine not to worry about money. There'll be disaster relief money."

"You take care now," said Kekela. He had a strong premonition that Calvin and Nadine wouldn't be around much longer. He felt a chill go up his spine. Something deadly was happening. Of that, he was convinced.

"Let's get this done and get outta here. I'll get some quick pictures. Bra, why don't you wait in the car. At least, you can roll up the windows and try to get away from the smell."

Kekela turned and headed back to the car. For some reason, alarms were going off in his head. Kimo headed out to the terraced taro fields.

Once up close, Kimo could see the smelly, yellow ooze was dripping from the dying or dead plants. It was obviously a toxin that was fatal to the plant. He snapped several photos and decided that was it. The smell was giving him a major headache. Time to head out of Dodge.

Snaaaaap! Crackle!

Kimo jumped as the ground next to him sizzled, as though struck by lightning. *Yikes!* There was an electrical charge in the air.

Kimo ran to the car. Damn straight, it was time to head out of Dodge.

Chapter 13

Mai keieki
(Sick Child)

The next morning, Lili went to the school cafeteria to get her daily supply of noni. She returned to the hospital for rounds at 0800.

Jessie had survived the night. At this time, she was stable. Critical, but holding her own.

Her fever was down and that was a very good sign. Even better, her blood sugar was within acceptable parameters following the hook-up of an insulin pump and a glucose and electrolytes rich IV.

But, by no means, was she out of the woods. Jessie's blood work revealed that she was waging a war against some kind of foreign invader. Some type of contagion that was causing her nausea, vomiting, and diarrhea. A formula for disaster in the form of dehydration.

After getting the night report and reviewing the chart, Lili proceeded to the pediatric unit.

She put on her protective gear and entered the room. She saw that Jessie's mother was brushing her daughter's long hair. Curly, beautiful, strawberry-blond hair. The mother's hair was brown. Nothing like her daughter's mane.

"Good morning, Mrs. Alexander," said Lili. "How's she doing?"

"Hi Dr. Lange. She's some better, I think." Jessie's mother looked very tired. The stress she was experiencing was undoubtedly exhausting. The good news was Jessie seemed to be improving a little. Jessie was breathing with ease, although she still needed the assistance of oxygen therapy. Her color had also improved and she was alert. Her blue eyes were no longer glazed over from a high fever. "She's not vomiting as much," reported the mother, announcing a fragile sense of hope.

However, her medical record showed that her emesis was still blood-tinged. As was her urine. Lili was awaiting the results of the urinalysis and the scans of her urinary system.

Lili began to exam her young patient. She took the girl's vital signs. Her blood pressure was low, her pulse a little fast, and respirations were at a rate that indicated she was still experiencing air hunger. Her oxygen saturation was low at 86%. Next, she auscultated heart, lung and bowel sounds. Of concern, her lungs sounded badly congested accounting for her poor gas exchange. Bowel sounds were hyperactive, but that was expected given the nausea and vomiting. The girl had bloody vomit, bloody urine and bloody stools. That accounted for her low blood pressure.

Jessica was a fighter. That's for sure. It was a curiosity that her mother wasn't symptomatic.

There was a knock on the door. Kakalina entered. She smiled at the mother.

"Excuse me, Dr. Lange, but Dr. Tanaka is asking to see you right away. He's in the E.R." "Okay. I'll be right there." It was probably more bad news. She inhaled deeply.

Lili turned to Mrs. Alexander, "She's holding her own. I'll be back to check on her later."

Lili felt Jessie's small hand reaching out to her. The girl wanted to say something. So, Lili removed the oxygen mask to enable Jessie to speak.

"Doctor, please don't let me die like Grandpa," she said in a whispered voice. The mother let out a sob. Those were hard words to hear from a little girl.

"I'm not going to let you die," she promised the little, vulnerable girl. She squeezed her hand. And put her mask back on. Lili knew one thing. She intended to keep that promise.

Lili stripped off her mask, gown, hair cover, and booties, disposing them in the red bin outside the door. Jessie was on isolation and precautions orders. Her hair was disheveled as she put on her lab coat. Her swollen feet ached and her back was in knots.

She pushed on.

Heading down to the emergency room she wondered, *what now?* She needed to get to her autopsies. She'd absolutely insist on it.

As she approached the unit, she heard people screaming, some crying, and some moaning. Loud chaos had ensued. Lili opened the door and entered the unit.

My God! There were whole families in the waiting room. She noticed that these folks were from the North shore. Some individuals ran up to her and pleaded for her to save their loved one. Some were uttering *Kanaloa* (the evil serpent), under their breathe.

Kate went to the exam area to look for Dr. Tanaka. He may be small, but he was like a samurai soldier. A warrior doctor. And, he was sorely needed right now. He was soft-spoken but yet, powerful in his professional demeanor. He was also brilliant.

Already, she could tell these patients were burn victims. Why so many? She saw Kate who was obviously pitching in right now. As a Nurse Practitioner, she was a valuable asset. Besides, she was a really good clinician. She saw Lili and smiled.

Dr. Tanaka saw Lili. "Lili, over here." He waved her over. He was cleaning the burn areas on a teenaged boy. Third-degree burns over 50% of his body. Then the young man would go up to the O.R. to debride the burn areas. It was life-threatening situation for this kid. Suddenly, Kate recognized the boy. It was Peter, the son of Amos. He was the brave, young boy who had saved his little sister during the tribulation days.

"What happened to all these patients?" inquired Kate with a pained expression on her face.

Burns are a challenge to treat.

"I'm not quite sure. They're saying that the air filled with electricity and caused fires in the fields, in their homes, barns, animal pens. Everything was gone. They were claiming that lightning bolts just erupted in the air. No rain, a beautiful sunny day. Go figure." He shrugged his shoulders, perplexed by the information.

"That does sound kind of science fiction." Kate thought that the life they knew just days ago no longer existed.

"I need you to start treating some of these patients. I've called in two extra surgeons." "Shouldn't I get at least one autopsy done?"

"Our priority is to treat the living, the dead can wait." With that, Dr. Tanaka returned to his patient.

Lili knew that she wouldn't be able to see Puna again tonight. He'd been bringing supplies up the mountain to the caves. Preparations, in anticipation of the arrival of a tsunami, were continuing. Something evil was afoot on their beloved island. They would need the wisdom and guidance of the Kupuna Hannah and Pastor Kua.

Lili knew the answer lay in the evidence from the autopsy. But, for now, she would assist the living.

The Prayer of Kane

O Kane-Kanaloa!
O Kane-of-the-great-lightning flashes-in-the-heavens,
O Kane-the-render-of-heaven,
O Kane-of-the-rainbow, O Kane-of-the-rain,
O Kane-the-heavenly-cloud, O Kane-of-the-red-rainbow,
O Kane-of-the-great-wind, O Kane-of-the-little-wind,
O Kane-of-the-peaceful-breeze,
O Kane-dwelling-in-the-mountain,
O Kane-dwelling-by-the-sea,
O Kane-dwelling-by-the-lower-precipice,
O Kane-of-the-coral,
O Kane-traveling-mountain-ward,
O Kane-traveling-seaward, O Kane!
I will live through you, my god.

Adapted from, Hawaiian Mythology (1970) by Martha Beckwith. University of Hawaii Press, Honolulu, Hawaii. (p. 53-54).

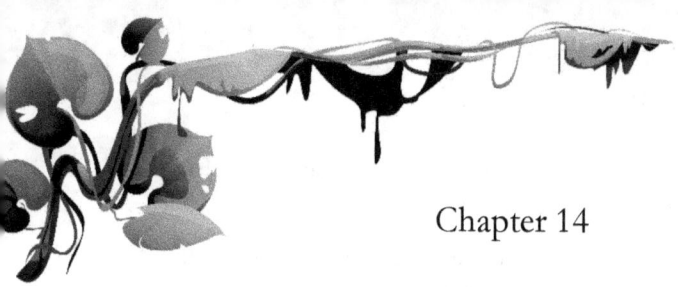

Chapter 14

Mai ka po mai

(From the time of night, darkness, chaos)

Kupuna Hannah was in the fellowship hall at the church talking to Pastor Kua. Her snow- white hair was piled high on her head, making her appear very regal. Her dark-lined skin reflected a life of toil in the tropics. It was a starry, summer evening with trade winds. Cooling, gentle breezes that helped to revive one after an especially hot day. Today, the temperatures had soared to 97 degrees Fahrenheit. Yet, Hannah remained as fresh as a plumeria flower.

The two, old sages were having their evening meal together. The Pastor looked physically drained from the insufferable heat. He looked years older than his chronological age. During the ten days of the great tribulation, Pastor had stood against the evil one. He had sent him and his agents back to the pit of fire. Overnight, Pastor had turned completely gray. Now, he used a cane as his right leg had been damaged during the battle. The thing of it was that Pastor could not remember how his leg had been hurt. He suspected that it might have been a snake bite.

Kupuna was 76 years old. The elder woman was very fatigued from hours spent each day on making all the drinks for the folks in the community. For both of them, there was much to do in the upcoming days. Danger was in the air. The worst was yet to come, like a runaway train; peril was barreling down on the people of Nardei.

They were both picking at their food, too tired and too hot to have an appetite. On the table, there was a pitcher of green ice tea, fish, poi, and seaweed salad. A plate of fruit sat between them.

"So tell me, Mason, do you think it's happening again? Is he back?" asked Hannah. She took a long drink of tea.

Pastor sighed, "Sadly, I do." He had had a prophetic dream in which he had seen the black serpent with yellow spots. Who could forget the red glowing eyes? Kanaloa had issued a challenge: *I will finally win. I will bring down your people and your God will not be able to save you this time.*

Another battle was being waged.

"My dear Hannah, thank you for the respect, but I know very well you already know. True?" asked Pastor. Kupuna was always aware of what was going on. That's why she was the Kupuna, the High Priestess. He picked up a piece of pineapple. The sweet juice ran down his chin.

She let out a deep sigh, "Yes. It's true," affirmed Hannah. "And, I know, as you do too, what we must do. We must gather the people at the heiau tomorrow."

In many important past events, prayers and chants had been offered up to the giver of life. Once again, they would offer up a petition to Kane. The god, Kane, was considered superior to all other gods. In fact, he was considered the Supreme Being. Kane was known to be a god of great mana; great power and great wisdom. One tale talks about the day that Kane took human form. It is said that when Kane walked through a Polynesian village, humans and animals flocked to see him. Even the cockroaches lined up to see Kane.

Without a doubt, Kane was the ultimate god, but lesser gods like Lono and Ku still remained very important to the Hawai'ian people. The god of fertility and harvest blessed the earth with abundance. More importantly, Lono is associated with the phenomena of tropical storms. In prayers to Lono, the signs of the god are named as, lightning, the dark cloud, waterspouts, rain and wind and gushing red mountain streams rushing to the seas.

The god Ku represented both the male or husband and the female or wife. They are considered great ancestral gods of both heaven and earth and have control over the fruitfulness of earth and the generations over the ages. Ku is both the male generating great power and Hina is the female fecundity and the power of growth and production. Hence, Ku and Hina are invoked as inclusive of the entire ancestral line, those from the past and those yet to come.

According to Hawaiian history, from the beginning, Hawai'ians believed in a trinity of gods.

These gods were: *Kane* – the originator; *Ku* – the architect and builder; and *Lono* – the executor and director of the elements.

They called the trinity, *Hikapoloa,* meaning the united will of the gods. This triad of gods: Kane, Ku, and Lono were also referred to as the Sunlight, the Substance, and the Sound. They brought the sunlight into the *Po*, or the darkness and chaos, thus, destroying the Po. Out of that bright illumination, creation was born. After the light was brought in, they next created the heavens, the earth, the sun, the moon, and the stars.

Myths purport that, in the beginning, Kane as a triad existed alone in the intense, dark night until the time when he brought about the first light, then the heavens, then the earth and the ocean, then sun, moon, and stars. Kane existing alone chanted,

"Here am I on the peak of day, on the peak of night.

The spaces of air,

The blue sky I will make, a heaven, A heaven for Ku, for Lono,

A heaven for me, for Kane, Three heavens, a heaven. Behold the heavens!

There is the heaven, The great heaven,

Here am I in heaven, the heaven is mine."

(Beckwith, Martha. 1976. Hawai'ian Mythology. University of Hawaii Press, p.44).

Lastly, Kane, Ku, and Lono, conceived as a single godhead, created the first man. His body was made from red earth mingled with the spittle of Kane, and his head of whitish clay brought by Lono from the four corners of the earth. Interestingly, the meaning of Adam is red and the Hawaiian Adam was formed from *alaea* or red earth. Man was made in the image of the god Kane, who breathed into his nostrils, and gave him life. Afterwards, from one of his ribs which was taken while he slept, a woman was created. The man was called *Kumu-honua*, and the woman *Ke-ola-ku-honua*.

Adam and Eve.

Long before the foreigners, like Captain Cook, came to these islands, the Hawaiian priesthood knew of the story of the Hebrew genesis.

Where did this knowledge come from?

Pastor said, "And, I must prepare to do battle against the evil one again. This will be my last meal as I will fast to become a worthy soldier of Christ." Kanaloa was equated with the Christian devil, Lucifer.

Legends of strife against Kane have been passed down through generations. These legends place Kane and Kanaloa in opposition as the good and evil forces that effect mankind. Some ancient Hawaiians believed Kane and Kanaloa are actually the good and evil wishes of mankind. When Kane draws the figure of a man in the earth, Kanaloa makes one also; Kane's lives but Kanaloa's turns to stone. Kanaloa becomes angry and curses man to die. Like a toddler, he rants and raves. Unfortunately, unlike a young two-year old, Kanaloa could do great harm.

Kanaloa was the personification of the evil spirit, the origin of death, and the prince of Po. Once an angel, his disobedient spirit lead him to become a fallen angel who was conquered, punished by Kane.

Satan was always striving to precipitate the apocalypse. He wanted the second coming of Jesus Christ. With eagerness, Satan welcomed the final war against Him.

In today's modern world, evil was running amok. It was all part of Satan's plan.

"Tomorrow, we must make the offering. Puna will prepare the house of mana so we can make offerings to Kane."

An offering to Kane begins with setting up a sacred stone pile. Within the walls of the heiau, a family alter called Pohaku-o-Kane (Stone of Kane) must be erected in the shape of a single conical stone, anywhere between 1 foot and 8 feet in height. The stone must be sprinkled with holy water, prepared by Kupuna or Pastor. Then, the stone would be covered with a piece of bark cloth during the ceremony. The Kane stone is an emblem of the male organ of generation. During the former battle against Satan, an angel had provided holy water to Pastor which ultimately defeated the evil one.

Maybe another angel would visit him again via celestial travel.

Suddenly, the front door of the sanctuary was opened and a wailing woman entered the House of our Lord. Pastor rose to attend to this parishioner who was in apparent distress. Entering the church, Pastor saw Mrs. Kapono, dressed in black, sobbing at the foot of the altar.

He approached her gently and, with great difficulty, kneeled beside her. "Sister, may I be here with you?"

Her face was pinched and her red eyes were swollen. Mrs. Kapono reached out to Pastor, hugging him and sobbing into his chest. "First I lost my daughter and now I'm going to lose my grandson!"

"What has happened to Peter?" The son of Amos was a hero in the community. "The farm house, the barn, the crops………. all gone. Destroyed by lightning bolts that

caused fires in the valley. Peter ran into the house to get Melissa out and was badly burned," wailed the distraught grandmother. "I cannot lose that boy."

"Then we shall make sure that that doesn't happen. Let us pray." And so, they prayed for the intervention of the Lord to save this special boy who was already blessed.

As they prayed, the noise of pueo filled the night. You see, passed relatives, now spiritual guardians, could incarnate into several animal forms, most often the preferred pueo or owl. The sacred

Hawai'ian barn owls had gathered on the church's roof, lifting their voices in unison. Their Winnie-the-Pooh faces were surveying their island home. The pueo had had a cloak of feathers in shades of brown and white. The short-eared owl's large, yellow eyes were just like Pooh's. An endearing look. And now their sound was like that of an army of warriors preparing to wage war. Satan's soldiers are the sinister Night Marchers.

The loud voices of the aumakua could be heard in the dead silence of night. Ancestral spirits had arrived.

A Hawai'ian Chant Relating to the Trinity and Creation

"Kane of the great Night,

Ku and Lono of the great Night,

Hika-po-loa the king.

The tabued Night that is set apart,

The poisonous Night,

The barren, desolate Night,

The continual darkness of midnight,

The Night, the reviler.

O Kane, O Ku-ka-pao,

And great Lono dwelling in the water, Brought forth are Heaven and Earth, Quickened, increased, moving, Raised up into Continents.

Kane, Lord of Night, Lord the Father, Ku-ka-pao, in the hot heavens, Great Lono with the flashing eyes, Lightning-like has the Lord Established in truth, O Kane, master-worker; The Lord creator of mankind:

Start, work, bring forth the chief Kumu-honua, And Ola-ku-honua, the woman;

Dwelling together are the two,

Dwelling in marriage (is she) with the husband, the brother."

(His Hawaiian Majesty King David Kalakaua. The Legends and Myths of Hawaii: The Fables and Folk-Lore of a Strange People. Charles E. Tuttle Company: Vermont, 1974, p. 36)

*First edition was published in 1888.

Chapter 15

He hoa'iki n aka po.

(A night revelation; a revelation from the gods in dreams).

That night, Kimo had another *pokii* dream. Once again, his father came to him in a dream state to offer guidance, father to son.

And in this dream state, he was once again in the sacred valley. It was the ancient home of the gods.

As he traveled along, he would stop and enjoy a guava or passion fruit. The clear sky was azure blue. There was plenty of warm sunshine and cool trade winds were blowing. He saw the shadow of a Hawai'ian barn owl overhead and he saw it was leading the way up to the sacred cave, one that he had visited in the past on several occasions. The Mana Cliffs.

Times in which he had needed his father's wise counsel.

He began to find his way up the mountain, seeking higher elevation. The air became cooler, quite refreshing really. When he reached about one-third of his way up, he stopped at a babbling brook and sat down and drank deeply from the cool fresh water, cupping his hands.

Like a dog, he dunked his head into the refreshing awa water and then shook his head vigorously, spraying water droplets into the wind.

Awa water is important to the god Kane because the gods are awa drinkers, empowered to engage in water-finding activities during drought. Legends claim that awa water is the principle food of the great gods. Pure water sustenance deemed to purify the soul.

Conversely, awa water is like poison to Kanaloa and his malicious *mu* spirits. Legend has it that in one ancient battle between Kane and Kanaloa, Kanaloa was easily defeated when his spirits rebelled against the edit to not drink the awa water. Immediate death had ensued. At that time, Kanaloa was known as *Milu*, Ruler of the Dead.

Milu was the ruler of the dark underworld. He became the lord of the dead in the realm of darkness. He lived beneath the earth and founded his kingdom in the firey pits of hell. His power grew over the centuries and he became known as Kanaloa. Over the centuries, he had been given many names: the evil spirit; the origin of death; the prince of Po; and the fallen angel who was conquered and punished by Kane.

Kanaloa, who opposes the light in the heavens where divine entities live in peace and harmony, seeks to return the earth back into Po – into chaos, destruction, and, ultimately, darkness. Once the earth had been steeped in death and darkness, he would try to destroy the heavens. The heavens were celestial places that Kanaloa despised. After all, he had been kicked out of there. His grudge ran deep.

Because of its importance, the location of the awa water was a secret, passed down through generations, from Kahuna to Kahuna.

Aina-wai-akua-a-Kane. The land of the divine water of Kane.

Next, he stripped out of his clothes and washed himself from head to toe with the milk of a coconut. After drying off, he rubbed himself with coconut oil. While doing the purifying ritual, he chanted a prayer to Kane:

"O Kane-of-the-great-lightning, O Kane-of-the-great-proclaiming-voice, O Kane-in-the-mist, O Kane!"

More mana, more sacred power.

He redressed and headed to the cave, having prepared himself in the appropriate manner.

Ancient rituals were imperative to a successful coming together of the living and the dead.

Rising to continue on his mission, he saw the Winnie-the-Pooh owl waiting on the branch of a nearby tree. He blinked twice and smiled. Honestly, Winnie-the-Pooh *grinned*. Then, he soared upwards and took the lead position once again. He possessed a large wing span, his shadow marking the way.

Sounds of mynah birds chattering could be heard all the way up. They were excited about something! Goats greeted him on the way. Baby pigs squealed with delight. He felt like Dr. Doolittle.

Several hours later, he finally reached the end of the journey. The owl's shadow was gone.

Kimo approached the sacred cave. An old friend was standing at the mouth of the cave. It was the White Bird of Kane! The large, white bird stood three feet tall. Big Bird had red-tipped feathers, like a headdress of a royal king, around his face. Amazingly, the White Bird of Kane had cobalt blue eyes, as Kane is the god of fresh water and all things necessary for life. The White Bird of Kane was an angel sent by Kane. Truly a messenger sent from the heavens above. Through telepathy, the bird transmitted a message to him: *The fisherman must make the offering of King Kamehameha's shark tooth.*

With that, Big Bird left, wandering down the mountain path to the sacred valley, leaving behind a white feather on the dirt path. Kimo picked it up and put it in his pocket. Then, Kimo prepared to enter the sacred cave. This place was special because it provided a spiritual opening, similar to the one Jesus sought in the garden in Gethsemane on the Mount of Olives the night before his death.

The opening of the sacred cave was covered by vines growing on the cliffs. The cave had a long tunnel which eventually became larger. Kimo walked deep into the cave, the air becoming increasingly dank. Finally, the cave leveled out into a large underground room. In the center of the room, there was a freshwater pool of water. The water had a greenish-blue hue as it was a sacred, mystical cave. Images arose from this green water.

In front of the pool, there was a *kilohana stone*. A black stone that marked the spot where Kimo would kneel and *pule* (pray) to his aumakua – his deceased father. A kilohana stone is part of the requisite rituals of interfacing with a passed relative. Out of his pocket, he took out a wooden figure. It was a carved aumakua that his father had made years ago. It possessed a red feather, making it sacred. This type of wooden aumakua was used for sorcery.

Aumakua worship is an ancient Hawai'ian practice. Throughout centuries, Kahuna (male) and Kupuna (female) have practiced the art and skill of aumakua worship. Through the application of the particular ritual at exactly the right time and place, aumakua worship is used to create the spiritual opening which generates the connection between the living and the dead. Part of the mystic that was so much an integral component of this ancient civilization.

The mana of the aumakua was most powerful when made by a Kapuna and Kimo's father had been a High Priest. This wooden figure could create strong magic. He placed the statute in front of the kilohana stone. Kimo knelt down on the kilohana stone and began to pule to his aumakua. He bowed his head and closed his eyes as he prayed:

"Oh aumakua, give me strength, the knowledge and the courage to defeat our enemies who have returned to destroy our island and our people. Show me the way to save our people from Kanaloa, my sacred aumakua. In the name of Kane, I respectfully ask for your hand in this time of peril. Oh aumakua, please hear my petition on behalf of my people."

Suddenly, a fragrant breeze, perfumed with *awa puhi* or white ginger poured into the cavernous opening. It is an odor that is associated with the gods. The welcome breeze blew through the cave, eliminating the dank smell. The sound of wind chimes announced the presence of spirits from the other side.

Spiritual ancestors, his aumakua had arrived.

A light started to emanate from the pool of water. From the deep dark water, the light grew brighter until it illuminated the pool of awa water. Like steam from a sauna, a mist arose out of the water. The mist took shape and he saw the familiar face with the strong features of his father. He was in the loving presence of his beloved father.

There was an immediate father to son connection.

He could hear his father's gentle voice inside his head.

Telepathy talk.

"My son, use the talisman to defeat your enemies. You will know the right time. Trust in that, my protégé, my loving son. You make me a proud father and I honor you."

The mist dissipated and, just like that, his father was gone. The fragrant odor had disappeared and the wind chimes failed to ring anymore. The spiritual opening was closed. The dank smell had returned.

Kimo began to rise from the kilohana stone when he noticed something beside the wooden aumakua statute. It was a shark's tooth on a twine rope. It looked old. Kimo picked up the amulet and put it in his pocket.

Rising, he turned and left the cave. He departed from the sacred and secret place.

He began his traverse down the mountain path. There was no owl to lead the way this time. The sun was very bright and he was getting hot as the morning progressed. He would soon arrive at the brook where he could cool off and….

Damn! Someone was singing…... and then Kimo woke up. It was his cell phone. Kekela was calling. Now what?

Reluctantly, he answered.

"Wait a minute. Hundreds?" Kimo rubbed his eyes. "Okay, I'll be right there."

Kekela told him that there were hundreds of dead fish washing up on shore. He also told him that it was a very bad omen.

Very bad indeed.

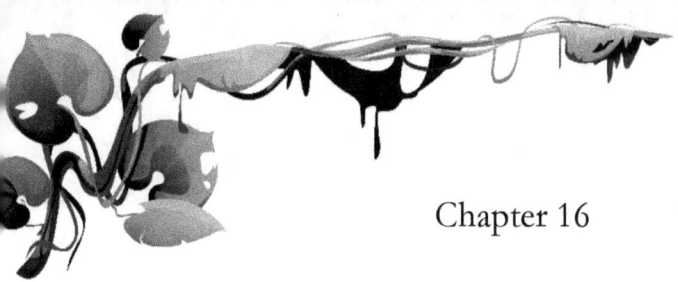

Chapter 16

Mata-kere-po

(Blind eyes)

Kekela was right. He was the blind man who could truly see. There were hundreds and hundreds of dead marine life. Fish and sea turtles, some large fish like ahi and marlin. Dolphins, barracudas, moon fish, and sting rays. All dead. The smell of so many dead fish was overwhelming.

Kimo recognized right away that something very ominous was on its way towards Nardei.

The dead marine creatures were indications of a pending, deadly force. Well, the island's people knew about the force or mana and their gods and aumakua would ignite that commanding power to defeat their enemy.

The sheriff had just arrived. He stepped out of his car and walked over to Kimo, holding his nose. After the former sheriff, Joe Taba, was killed during the period of the great tribulation, his nephew, Keoni, became the town sheriff. At 6 feet and 3 inches, he walked tall in his hat and boots. Quite a good looking fellow. In fact, Keoni was the most eligible bachelor in town. Part- Caucasian and part-Hawaiian. A handsome hapa boy. Also, a ladies' man breaking hearts in his wake, like George Clooney.

"Kimo, this is a big, stinkin' mess. I'll have some men come out and salt these dead fish. Damn! It smells like hell!" Salt was both a purifying element as well as a facilitator of decom position that helps to erode the putrid odor.

"I'll have some of the county workers come help," offered Kimo, as mayor of the town.

"Thanks. So tell me Kimo, what do you think is going on? Burning fires, a blight, a strange sickness and now this." Sheriff Keoni Apune was nervous. It showed in his face, all pruned up. "Seriously, Kimo, are we in for another period of tribulation? Is this the devil's work? Or is related to climate change?"

"Whatever it is, it's not good. Might even be deadly," responded the mayor.

There could be no delay to make the offerings to Kane at the heiau. Disaster was anywhere between 24 and 36 hours.

Kekela had told him when disaster would strike.

The blind man who had visions. Consistently, his prophecies were never wrong. Kimo took out his cell and called Kupuna Hannah. After three rings, she picked up.

"Kimo, I am already making the necessary arrangements at the heiau. Puna is with me."

"How did you know what I was calling about?" he asked. He got it, of course. "Never mind." Is everyone in town telepathic? Everyone seemed to be psychic, except him, of course.

"I will go see Pastor and ring the church bell to alert the town," said Kimo.

When Kimo and Kekela arrived later at the heiau, Kupuna, Pastor, and Kate were attending to the requisite preparations. They planned to hold the ceremony in several hours.

Kate had worked the night shift at the Nardei Community Hospital as the mysterious disease claimed more victims. On top of that, another terrifying disease had emerged. Several children had come in with a sudden-onset seizure disorder. Just a few hours before, the children had been fine. Two or three hours later, they were all dead from massive seizures that destroyed their brains and they had lapsed into comas. Was it some type of a rapid-onset meningitis?

Kimo knew how hard Kate took the death of children. She was a mother herself.

Despite that, she was helping with the pre-ceremony activities. Her generous spirit was just one of the many things he loved about her so much. And with every passing day, he loved her a little more.

"Kate, you're a real trooper!" said Kimo as he warmly smiled at her and sweetly kissed her on her lips. Her captivating, blue eyes shone brightly.

"I've missed seeing you," she sighed.

"I've been missing you too." Kimo hugged her to his strong, well-muscled chest. He could smell the mountain-green apple fragrance of her shampoo in her strawberry-blond hair. To his embarrassment, his maleness grew hard and pressed against her.

She looked up with a sly smile on her face.

"I see you *do* miss me!" Her radiant smile lit up her face. There was a twinkle in her eyes.

"What can I say? I adore my wife." He stepped away from her and chuckled. The laughter broke some of the tension.

Pastor was approaching them, walking slowly with his cane. Pastor's gray hair had grown longer and he had tied it back with a rubber band.

"Aloha," he greeted them, hugging each of them as Hawai'ian custom demanded. He had seen Kimo earlier at the church, where they had rung the bell and the people of Nardei had responded. The announcement for the ceremony to make offerings to Kane was made. Evoking the name of Kane, the equivalent of the Christian God, was sobering. They would be there, if not sick.

They would be there because they understood what was at stake.

"Mason, aloha again," responded Kimo, hugging him again. Pastor wasn't as frail as he looked. "What can I help with?"

"Son, you must tell us that you know the person who must make the offering of the sacred talisman to Kane. Did your aumakua reveal the information?" asked Pastor. He leaned heavily on his cane.

"Yes, Mason. I know who must do it. As a matter of fact, I'm on my way over to his hale right now." Kimo understood that they must follow the aumakua's directions to the letter.

"Then go and God speed." Pastor wearily went and sat in a chair under a shady chair near the heiau's entrance. He sat down and wiped his sweating brow with a white handkerchief. This day would be long. He would go home and rest for a while. He smiled to himself as he cooled down.

He was well aware of who was supposed to make the offering and he knew what the sacred item was that would be offered. An angel had visited him in a dream and shared that knowledge as well as so much more.

He was in the know. Celestial enlightenment.

Kekela was making a sacred stone pile. On top of the stone pillar, he would affix a carved image symbolic of the god Kane, god of Creation and god of Nature. The carved image was a flock of birds flying amongst the clouds at the top of a mountain. *O Kane! god-of-the-heavens- and-earth. O Kane! god-of-the-forests-and-trees.*

Kekela asked Kupuna, "Kupuna, where is Puna?"

"He is collecting the necessary plants for the ceremony."

"Ah yes. The god-of-earth requires his sacred plants be present in the heiau when the offerings are made, otherwise Kane will not hear our petition."

Meanwhile, Puna had traveled to the high grounds to gather the requisite plants of Kane for temple decoration. The cool mountain air was refreshing after being near to the fires that were lite to thwart the blight. For days, the sky was smoky making it difficult to breathe. Up in the mountains, the scent of fragrant flowers was a nice change.

Kane has many names that can be enumerated in many subordinate forms, which the one god who embraces them all, is worshiped. The form plants of Kane include the fragrant myrtle (maile), the ieie vine or climbing pandanus, the sacred lehua and dracaena trees out of which the carved image of Kane was carved.

The guardian spirits are invoked to return and possess the plants.

As Puna and Luke gathered the tropical plants, Puna rendered the chant required while picking the Kane's plants:

"O Kane! god-of-the-forests-and-trees! Produce sacredness, produce freedom, freedom for me, a man," prays Puna ask he plucks the leaves and vines.

Puna worked in earnest to collect the right plants, to evoke the names of Kane's sacred plants, and to chant the correct prayer for the gathering ritual. All efforts were made to assure that the Hawai'ian religious practice of temple worship was conducted the very same way as always, over the centuries of time, from the beginning of time. Polynesians were one of the first civilizations on earth.

They would endure.

While Puna and Luke worked diligently to gather the decorative plants, two red eyes glowed from under a fallen tree branch. Up above, high on a tree branch, a pueo watched the serpent.

The war of good versus evil, as old as the ages, was underway. Game on.

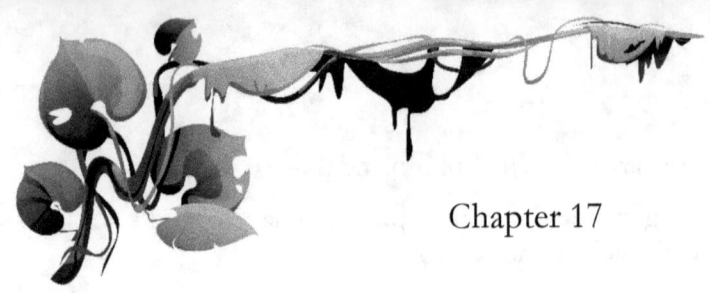

Chapter 17

Ua kapu ke ola na Kane

(Life is sacred to Kane)

Later that afternoon, the people of Nardei gathered at the heiau. At the entrance to the temple was an aggressive-looking, grotesque wooden sculpture called a *luakini* sculpture.

Craggy eyebrows hung over bulging eyes making its short nose disappear. A protruding forehead sat low on its distorted, red face. The mouth was set in a pulled-back leer displaying sharp, chain-saw teeth. A large, erect penis was disproportionate in size to the rest of the figure. It was a frightening statue that warned evil entities to stay away.

Kapu.

Forbidden.

All of the appropriate preparations had been made. The Kane plant decorations graced the sacred temple. White tapa cloth covered the erected platform where offerings to Kane would be made. White tapa is considered sacred.

It was now a holy temple.

Kupuna Hannah was adorned in white tapa too. Kupuna's robe was pure white, undyed, and undecorated. Around her neck, a ti lei hung. It was the required attire for Kupuna to lead the Kane-offering ceremony.

She looked out at her people, young and old alike. There were so many familiar faces. Their faces intently focused, yet fear shone through around the edges. A newborn baby cried loudly as though he was the voice for their fear. But there were also faces that spoke of courage and determination. Pastor, Kimo, Kekela, Ray and Puna to name just a few. Lili, Kate and Kapukini stood side-by-side, fearless and poised. Many would soon follow suit.

Tradition dictated that the ceremony open with an old Hawai'ian prayer to Kane. The prayer

acknowledges Kane as the father of all living things, a symbol of life in nature. Kane represents the god of procreation; the creator of life. Hawaiian legends assert that man was made in the image of Kane.

Legend claims that Kane formed three worlds: the upper heaven of the gods, the lower heaven above the earth, and the earth itself as a garden for humanity with the latter being furnished with sea creatures, plants and animals.

Hannah began to chant. The people joined in, lifting their voices to the heavens above. Then, Hannah raised her arms toward the skies and offered the traditional prayer:

"Green are the leaves of God's harvest fields.

The net fills the heavens-Shake it!

Shake down the god's food!

Scatter it, oh heaven!

"Life to the land!

Life from Kane, Kane the god of life.

"Life to the people!

Hail Kane of the water of life! Hail!" *

The crowd whispered, *Amene.*

(E.S. Craighill Handy et al., 1979. Ancient Hawaiian Civilization: Religion and Education, Charles E. Tuttle Company, p. 50).

Hannah lite a torch and placed it near the erected platform that was the mana or power house for Kane. Kimo made the first offering. He laid down *aholehole* or whitefish. This was Kane's favorite fish, marking a good start to the ceremonial offerings. Kekela followed and placed *awa root* on the white tapa cloth.

Kane is an awa-drinker, mixing the potent root and water to make an intoxicating beverage. *Awa-iku* are the beneficent spirits made from the mixing of water and awa. It is believed that they are messengers for Kane who ward off the influences of the *mu* or evil spirits, those of the Great Serpent Kanaloa, who seeks to destroy those who are life-givers. All those who worship Kane or the Lord.

Awa water was holy water.

Hence, Kanaloa hates awa water in the same way that ants hate Raid. Awa water was toxic to both Kanaloa and his agents.

After the initial offerings, bananas, pineapple, papayas, lichee, sugarcane, poi, flowers, dried fish and a variety of herbs and roots covered the white, tapa cloth.

As the people moved through the line and deposited their sacred gifts to Kane, the sky darkened, and ominous black clouds filled the sky above the heiau. Thunder rumbled overhead. Soon, lightening pierced the dark sky. Kane seemed pleased with the offerings. And yet, the most important offering had not been made. The appointed giver of the sacred offering had not come forth to lay it on the white tapa on the platform.

Ray had been standing to the side of the crowd. He was dressed in a traditional, white tapa shirt and wearing a ti lei. He announced that he was the giver chosen to offer the sacred gift to Kane.

The one that seals the deal.

Moving forward, he approached the mana platform. Folks stepped out of the way. When he finally stood before the mana platform, he pulled out of his pocket, the amulet. The shark's tooth on the old rope that had once belonged to King Kamehameha. A powerful talisman that was sure to please Kane. It was placed on the white tapa cloth. Ray got down on his knees and chanted:

"These are the offerings for you, oh Kane,
Where flows the water of Kane?
Deep in the ground, in the gushing springs, In the mountain streams,
In the ponds and rivers in the valley, A water of magic power we seek,
O Kane, give us this life!"

The crowd said, *Amene.*

(E.S. Craighill Handy et al., 1979. Ancient Hawaiian Civilization: Religion and Education, Charles E. Tuttle Company, p. 50).

Out of nowhere, thunder boomed loudly and lightening forked the sky and spiked the ocean. The god Lono was pleased.

Suddenly, the skies opened and a heavy rain fell. Kane, the god of the water of life, was signaling his pleasure with the ceremony. He who could influence the weather from the heavens above. Evidently, the gifts at the mana house had been well received. The crowd chanted, "*E Kane-i-ka-opua.*" O Kane-of-the-clouds-on-the-horizon.

The ceremony closed with Kupuna blessing the people that she loved so dearly. Their fate now rested with the gods.

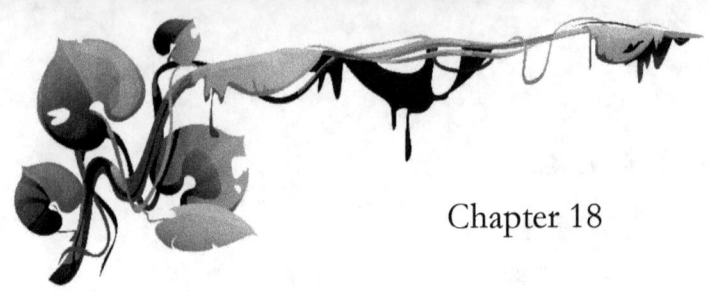

Chapter 18

Ka Ahaaina hope

(The Last Supper)

After the earlier rain, it was a cool night. A cloud-covered moon hung in the dark sky like a dirty, light globe. Kimo, Kate and the rest of the gang were having their last meal together before they would depart to ascend the mountain and find safe harbor in the caves at the Mana Cliffs tomorrow morning.

"Daddy, are we going to have a picnic on the way up the hill? Please!" asked little Hannah.

Her face was covered in barbeque sauce. Barbeque chicken was one of Hannah's favorite meals, depending when you asked her.

"Sure, Hannah. After all, we need to eat." Kimo smiled at his precocious daughter.

"Maybe you and Hina can help me make the picnic lunch after your bath. What do you say?" asked Kate. She knew that both her girls were anxious about leaving their home. A distraction before bedtime was good. Despite usually having a hearty appetite, she noticed that Hannah had hardly eaten a thing tonight, despite her messy face.

Hina looked up from her plate and nodded. She appeared frightened with wide-eyes and a furrowed brow. Because she was mute, she didn't have the release from anxiety that comes with the verbal expression of one's fears. She could not vent her feelings. For Hina, everything was bottled up inside. The question was: *When would Hina explode with voice?*

"We've gotta be serious about this!" chimed in Luke. The adolescent boy was flexing his manhood muscles. "Can you pass me some rice, please?" The growing boy ate like a man – a giant of a man. One with a wooden leg.

"It is serious Luke but it's important that we stay calm," responded Kimo. "Right Kekela?"

Kekela had joined them for this last supper. His face was covered in barbeque sauce too. "Why, yes my man. We warriors always remain calm and in control. Brave are we." He thumped his chest. Pua sat under his chair, awaiting food donations.

Hannah laughed and thumped her chest. "I'm a monkey!" Luke and Hina rolled their eyes.

Pua barked.

"Uncle, we shall saddle up ole Duke in the morning to take you up the mountain. Save your leg," offered Luke who adored his uncle who had overcome so much.

"That won't be—" Kekela was cut off.

"Son, that would be great. Get Duke saddled up by dawn." Kimo was proud of his son who was evidently turning into a nice young man. Surely, he was a son to be proud of.

"But…. what about Pastor? He'll need a ride up the mountain," asked the ever-thoughtful Kekela.

"No worries, bra. I got it covered." Kimo knew that Pastor would probably stay at the hospital with the patients who were not able to make it to high ground. "Hey Luke, can you pass me some of that finger-lickin' chicken?"

"Kate, another wonderful dinner," said Kekela. "Might be awhile before we get a good, hot meal again. Can a man hope for dessert?" He grinned. She always made something to appease his sweet tooth.

"Okay, I give. What's the dessert on tonight's menu?" asked Kimo. He knew it was Kekela's favorite. Haupia or coconut pudding.

"Like you don't know, Dad!" said Luke with a goofy look on his face. "I'll have some pudding too! I still got room."

"Luke, you always have room!" laughed Kekela. He'd always been able to eat a lot too yet he remained thin.

Hina looked up, smiled and nodded. She wanted some pudding too.

Little Hannah seemed uninterested. She began fussing. Kicking her feet against the table.

"Don't you want some pudding, honey?" asked Kate. What had gotten into her? "No." Hannah was out of sorts. She looked a little pale.

"Do you feel okay?" asked a concerned Kate. Her daughter was rarely grumpy. She leaned over and felt the girl's forehead. Hannah's forehead was hot with fever. "Oh, no. She's burning up! Hannah's got a fever!"

No sooner said, Hannah threw up. Clearly, Hannah did not feel okay.

Kate picked up the young girl and carried her upstairs to the bathroom. The girl was crying and sobbed, "Mommy, I don't want to go to the caves!" After cleaning her up in the bathroom, Kate took Hannah's temperature. She was alarmed to see her fever was 103.2 Fahrenheit.

Hannah needed to go to the emergency room.

Right now.

Kate dressed the child in warm clothes. She hurried downstairs.

Kimo looked up and saw the harried mother and child. He stood up abruptly. "What's wrong?"

"Hannah's fever is over 103!" exclaimed Kate. "She needs to be seen in the emergency room.

I'm taking her right now. You put the other children to bed." With that, she grabbed her car keys and hurried out the door.

The sky was dark, with only a cloud-covered moon in the sky and no stars present. Without the illumination, it made the drive more difficult. Kate felt the car drive over some bumpy objects on the road. She slowed down and saw in her bright lights a green mist. But she also saw something unnerving. There were hundreds of dead frogs, mice, rats and mynah birds and, who knows what else, all over the road like spilled rubbish. Hannah saw too and began whimpering, "Mommy, mommy…they're all dead! The birdies!"

"It's okay, honey. Sh….." Kate said in a soothing voice.

"Close your eyes, you're fine."

Kate's heart pounded with fear. There was sweat on her brow and her mouth felt like it was stuffed with cotton. It was hard to take a deep breathe. She was spooked by the dead animals that were littered all over the road. It was going on for miles! And, what if Hannah had the same thing that had already proved fatal for three children? She gasped out loud with that thought.

"Mommy?"

Kate settled down and said, "I'm fine, little pea. Close your eyes."

As Kate approached the road to the hospital, she saw a bright streak of light up the dark, night sky. A comet!

She hoped it was a good omen as she drove to the entrance of the emergency room.

Hannah stirred.

"Open your eyes now, honey. We're at the hospital." Kate took her out of her booster seat and rushed through the doors. Kimo had called ahead to alert the staff. Little Hannah's eyes were closed. Kate carried her directly into the examination room. Dr. Fukina wasted no time to begin his assessment. The nurse was already checking Hannah's vital signs. Hannah was barely conscious. She moaned and complained of nausea and a headache. She was so pale.

"Heart rate is elevated at 130; respirations shallow at 14; blood pressure low at 72/37," the nurse spoke loudly to the doctor. "Fever of 103.5 Fahrenheit."

"Lactated Ringers at a rate of 100 mls. per hour; a heart monitor and get me her oxygen saturation level," ordered Dr. Fukina. "CBC, UA, and a spinal tap tray. Tylenol 500mg. per rectum stat."

As Dr. Fukina examined Hannah, he noticed that her right eyelid was drooping. Her neurological exam was altered. Her pupils were dilated too. Not good. Did she have a stroke? Did she have a brain bleed? Or was it meningitis as he strongly suspected it was? The results of the spinal tap would tell the true story. As they say, the proof is in the pudding.

Hannah began to thrash in the gurney bed. She was clearly agitated.

"Big Bird! Big Bird!" she cried out. She was hallucinating. Another symptom of an altered mental status.

Immediately, Kate was by her side, speaking to her in a gentle voice.

Kimo rushed into the examination room. "How is she?" he asked of Kate.

"I don't know!" she cried out. Kimo looked Dr. Fukina.

"I'm going to do a spinal tap right now. That'll tell me a lot."

"Will it hurt?" asked the concerned father. He thought he already knew the answer and he didn't like it one bit.

Kate was the one who responded. "Yes. It will and let's hope that she's responsive to that pain."

Kimo sighed deeply, he would need to stay in control although, right about now, he would like to lay his weary head down on a soft pillow and cry until no more tears were left.

"I'm going to ask that you and Kate wait outside," said the good doctor.

Reluctantly, they left the room and waited nearby in the unit's sitting lounge area. Their anxiety was palpable. Kimo held on tight to Kate. She was shaking. Pastor appeared in the lounge. They greeted each other with hugs and tears. He had been in to see Peter. Apparently, he wasn't doing so well. The burns were serious. The waiting was like an exercise in torture.

Finally, Dr. Fukina appeared. They rose.

"Is it meningitis Dr. Fukina?" asked Kate as her heart pounded in her ears making hearing difficult. She held her breathe. Kimo held her.

"The fluid was clear Kate," replied Dr. Fukina. "No evidence of meningitis."

As much as that was music to her ears, Kate asked the next obvious question, "Then what is it?"

"I think it's some kind of poison."

"*Poison*! My God, what kind of poison?" she demanded. Her face was a mask of utter terror.

Images of dead animals flashed in her head.

"My God! Who can stand this? Poison....what kind of poison?" Kimo echoed Kate in despair.

He sought out the hand of Kate and held it tightly.

"I'm not sure. Maybe a toxin from a parasite," he explained. I'm going to treat her aggressively with several antidotes and also with a couple of big hammer, broad-spectrum antibiotics. Also, I'm going to run an intravenous drip of steroids."

"Okay, doctor. That's seems like the best course of action. It's not like there are a lot of options," Kate responded gloomily. She looked like she had aged 10 years in that very moment. Kimo was silent.

"I am sorry Kate. I must go now but I will be praying all day." Kimo's eyes shimmered with tears.

Dr. Fukina admitted Hannah to a room on the pediatric unit. She would need to stay in the hospital. There would be no trip up the mountain for her. That meant that there would be no trip up the mountain for Kate either. And, reluctantly, Kimo would take the rest of the family upwards to safety in the morning, leaving his wife and daughter behind.

He left the hospital with a heavy heart and an uncertain future.

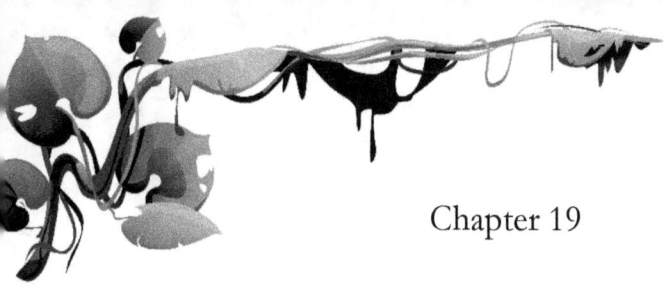

Chapter 19

Kahuna ho'ounauna

(Sending sickness or trouble)

Ray had seen the comet the previous night. He believed that Kane was giving them a celestial sign of his steadfast commitment to his Polynesian people. Just as Haley's Comet had back in 1758, on the very day of the birth of King Kamehameha. In ancient Hawaii, legends spoke of a day when a great king would come and unite all of the Hawaiian islands. Kahunas from the earliest times had claimed that a great unifier would be born on the day of a great comet.

Signs like comets were guideposts and could be found everywhere. You just had to know where to look. This morning he decided to go out to sea and examine the signs in the ocean waters and the heavenly skies. Was there evidence that a tsunami was approaching?

Of course, David had wanted to come but Ray was firm on that issue. He told the boy that he must go up the mountain to the safety of the caves with Kimo and Kate, as well as Uncle Kekela and the rest of the gang.

"Go ahead, dude. I'll meet you up there," reassured Ray.

"But, Uncle! Maybe you shouldn't go out to sea. There's bad things out there!" lamented the trembling boy. He was trying very hard not to cry. David was silent on the ride over to Kimo's house. Both were shocked at seeing the dead creatures everywhere.

Definitely not a good sign.

When they arrived, Kimo came out to greet the carrying two hand-held radios. He looked tired and haggard.

"Kimo, I've brought the boy. I'll head out to sea shortly and report back in," said Ray.

Kimo nodded and handed Ray a radio.

"What's up, Kimo?" asked the intuitive fisherman.

"It's little Hannah. She's in the hospital. It looks serious." Kimo went on to explain that she had fallen into a coma last night. "Kate's with her now."

"I'm so sorry to hear that, bra." He knew that it meant Kate would be staying back at the hospital.

"Is she gonna be alright, Uncle?" asked David. He called Kimo uncle too. David was very fond of Kekela so he was happy to see him. They had a strong bond. Kekela knew firsthand about David's past encounter with Kanaloa and the sheer terror that the boy had experienced at the mercy of the evil serpent.

"I sure hope so."

"Well, I best be going," declared Ray. He hugged the boy he loved so much and watched him exit the truck. He briefly wondered if he would see him again. Kekela hugged the boy to him.

Ray headed down to the harbor where the boat was docked. Within 20 minutes, he was out at sea. He didn't have to go far to see dead creatures all along the shoreline. The numbers were overwhelming. The odor of death loomed in the air. Dead birds floated in the water.

Bad signs. *What was to come next?*

Just above the horizon, there was a green mist that was eerie looking, like something out of a science fiction movie. It was a rather substantial size suggesting that there was something even larger behind it.

He looked at the water along the shore to ascertain if there was a strong tidal pull that always precedes a tsunami. A tsunami carries enormous energy that pulls the water from the beach out to sea. There was no evidence of that. That meant they had some time – maybe, a couple of hours- before the wave came on shore.

He turned the boat towards the horizon and sped towards it. He felt a sense of both fear and urgency. It was time to investigate the green mist. What the hell was it?

Silently, he prayed.

As he got closer, the odor of some kind of an electrical burn filled his nostrils in an uncomfortable way. The area contained within the shroud of green fog was dense with dead sea creatures. It was a thick, slow-moving carpet of stinky, dead fish and mammals. It was also heart-breaking for this Hawaiian fisherman who cared about the aquatic environment.

Even outside the mist, there were hundreds of dead birds, cresting up and down in the ocean waves. So many dead wedge-tail, shearwater sea birds! A species of birds that was already at-risk for becoming extinct. What a loss!

Ray stayed outside the shroud, looking at the green particles that hung in the air like bugs hovering over a warm light. *They were deadly. They carried pestilence.* He intuitively knew that before the sorcery-god appeared!

The green particles moved around like busy bees in a hive forming a shape. It was a familiar shape and Ray knew it well.

Haumea!

In her sea-monster form!

Legends told of the sorcery-god Haumea, who was associated with Kanaloa. Sorcery-gods are possessed by demons, embodied in evil spirits. These evil-intended sorcery gods engage in several practices: *the kahuna anaana* (praying to death*); the kahuna ho'ounauna* (sending sickness or trouble); and *the kahuna kuni* (divination by burning).

The head was like a dinosaur's with gills and a large body covered in reptile black, shiny scales emerged out of the swirling green mist. Her long tail swept through the water like a large rudder on a ship. Glowing, yellow eyes acted like bilateral telescopes giving Haumea superior visual acuity.

In addition, this sea-goddess had special powers but only at sea. But, at sea, she was very dangerous. She could spew poison at his enemies and dissolve them with her vile toxins.

Sorcery sea-goddesses were like monsters in every way.

The boogey man we all fear.

It was clear to Ray who was behind all of their troubles. Kanaloa, once again. To end their difficulties, they must defeat the great serpent. He would have to be returned to the firey pit from whence he came.

Haumea rose upright from the ocean and roared a fire of green mist at Ray. Her reach was at least forty feet. But Ray had anticipated this action and he already had reversed the boat at top speed.

Boom! He was outta there! He turned the boat to the right to speed away as the sea- goddess focused in on Ray's boat with his left telescopic eye. He employed his tail as a rudder and sped after the fisherman. It wasn't long before Haumea caught up to Ray. She was within 50 feet of the boat.

Within striking distance.

Ray couldn't out run the evil sea-monster and so he began to pray because his death seemed imminent.

"Oh Kane, Oh Lord, forgive my sins. I have tried to be your servant but sometimes I fell short.

What can I say? I have messed up plenty….. I ask for your mercy…"

Kaboom!

Suddenly, the clouds in the sky darkened and thunder pounded like a loud drum announcing the presence of Kane. The dark clouds parted and hail stones the size of baseballs poured from the sky above beat down on Haumea. Lightning struck the sea-monster's back twice and the scaly skin sizzle. The smell of burnt meat on the barbeque filled the air. Clearly, the reptilian flesh was badly burned. Haumea roared in pain, her voice angry and agitated. Green mist rolled off her back. Haumea's scream was the voice of an evil monster as it dissolved back into the green particles, much like the Wicked Witch of the West when water was poured on her.

And like Dorothy and the gang, Ray was heading back to the emerald city.

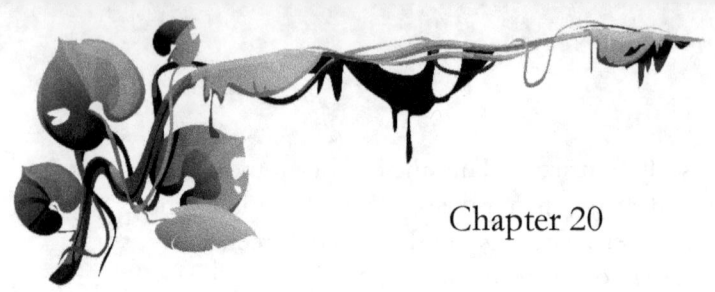

Chapter 20

Pa 'ahana

(Busy and hardworking)

Lili had finally gotten to the first two autopsies – Gladys and Earnest. They could offer up very little information because the bodies were so badly decomposed. In fact, the remains were liquefied. Whatever this disease was it was aggressive and fast-acting.

And all-consuming.

Given the lack of body materials to work with, Lili would need to examine more recent corpses that had been brought in with the same symptomology and pathology. Two days ago, Calvin and Nadine had been brought in after the sheriff discovered them dead under a large mango tree that had survived the fire on their farm. Animals had messed up the bodies pretty badly, according to Sheriff Apune. "It ain't pretty," he had said.

But, not right now. She was too weary and still had patients to see. A little boy with symptoms similar to Hannah's presentation had been admitted last night in serious condition.

She decided to take a break, drink her daily dose of the god-awful noni drink, and rub her achy feet. She would even afford herself the luxury of spending a few minutes thinking about Puna. She had seen him briefly last evening. They meet at the pavilion in town. The dead fish made the beach off limits. He had already arrived when she got there and he was sitting at a picnic table. He looked as handsome as ever in a dark t-shirt and jeans.

"Puna," she whispered. Immediately he turned and saw her. Her hair was disheveled and her clothes were in need of an iron. Her profound fatigue was evident in the dark circles around her eyes. She looked ready to collapse.

He rose and rushed to her. "Lili, I've been so worried about you!" She fell into the comfort of his arms. She began quietly crying. Her body was shaking as she released some of the overwhelming tension that she had been experiencing. Puna held her close and caressed her dark, long hair. He would probably never know the true extent of the horrors that she had witnessed at the hospital over the course of the past week.

"Lili, I can't stand to see you like this," he said, concern etched on his face.

Lili looked up into his dark eyes, "I need you Puna."

Puna leaned down and kissed her deeply. When they paused, he confessed his love for her.

"That's good because I need you too. I love you Lili, with all my heart."

They held each other like that for a while. Two hearts beating as one. She told him she had things to tell him about her past. He just silenced her with another kiss and murmured, "Not now."

Lili felt her cell phone vibrate. Coming out of her reverie, she saw that it was the nurse calling

from the ICU. She prayed that little Hannah wasn't worse or.... She wouldn't go there! "Yes, what is it?" she asked.

"Hannah's lab work and test results just came in. I thought you would want to know."

"Yes, of course. I'll be right up." She snapped the phone shut. Reluctantly, Lili stood up. For the second time in the past week, she vowed not to let this child die. No child would die on her watch!

She walked down the hallway to the elevator. The door opened and, much to her delight, Jessie and her mother were on board.

"Surprise, surprise!" said Mrs. Alexander. But the real surprise was her hair. The former brunette was now platinum blonde. What a change! And, perhaps not for the better.

"Good to see you two. How's Jessie?"

"She's doing great, Doc. We came to pick up some insulin at the pharmacy," she explained.

Then she registered the look on Lili's face. The hair! "I changed my hair or rather, my wig." "Oh, I see," said Lili except she didn't get it. The color was all wrong for her.

"Mommy, are we gonna go see the puppy?" said a young, sweet voice. "Yes. In a minute."

"You know, Doc. Chemo. Under this hair, I'm as bald as an eagle," she explained and laughed. "Stage 4 breast cancer."

"I'm sorry to hear that," replied Lili quietly.

Then the door opened on the floor where the pharmacy was located. Mother and child exited the elevator, smiling and waving.

Lili got off the elevator and went to the nursing station in the ICU. Kailey Kanaka was the nurse who had called her and she handed Lili the results from the tests that she had printed out.

Lili looked at the blood work first. Increased WBCs and differential to the right. Neutrophils were also at high levels. Some infection was raging in the body. Slight anemia. Increased coagulation time noted as well. P.T. and P.T.T. abnormal.

Next, she reviewed the MRI. It showed that her liver and spleen were grossly enlarged. Her immune system was trying to defeat a potent offending organism. But what was it? She had begun Hannah on two different, intravenous, broad-spectrum antibiotics last night. She didn't know if they would help. Only if the offending microorganism was a bacteria would they be effective.

But something was nagging her about this presentation. The drooping eyelid and some of the children's verbal complaints that they had lost their sense of taste. She had seen something like this before. Post Katrina in Bernard's Parish. She'd been doing an internship in community health and it had been quite the experience. Some children had become infected with a rare amoeba

– N. fowleri. It's a very, tiny, microscopic microorganism. It is a brain-eating water parasite.

Normally, this organism eats bacteria found on any type of vegetation, but, if there is no vegetation, it will find a way to get into humans to use their brains as a food source. It seems as though they find brains a tasty treat. N. fowleri cannot live in salt water. Only in fresh water, like puddles or pools of water. They prefer hot weather and can't survive in cold temperatures so they are found in the southern parts of the country. Or, in hot, tropical zones.

In New Orleans, they had tried many drugs to eradicate it once it had entered the person.

All, without success. Many people have antibodies to N. fowleri and they are able to fight it off. Others were not so lucky.

Could this possibly be the same organism? Lili thought that it might be so.

An idea struck her! What if she put little Hannah into a state of hypothermia? Would that kill the deadly amoeba?

She would talk to Kate right away. It was worth a try. There really were no other options. And time was running out.

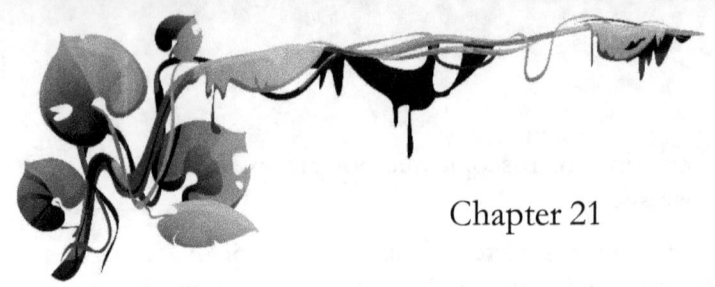

Chapter 21

Aina-wai-akua-a-Kane

(The land of the divine water of Kane)

Ray had tried to radio Kimo but was unsuccessful. There was too much static in the air. He planned on heading up the mountain upon his return to land. He was convinced that something evil was coming on shore. He thought that going up the mountain to where there was a wooden cross, erected by the first missionaries and that had endured through many centuries, would be their best hope. The caves were nearby. It was sacred ground.

He was anxious to see David. Given that the evil one, Kanaloa, was behind all their misfortunes, he worried about the boy. In the past, the serpent had singled David out and tried to capture his soul. He had failed to do so. He might try again. Kanaloa was a tenacious bastard.

After securing the boat at the dock, Ray went home to change clothes, pack his back pack and head to the Mana Cliff. He had bought two dozen of David's favorite candy – peanut M & Ms – which he now put in his pack to surprise the boy. And, to distract him too. The next few days would be scary, to say the least.

As Ray started out on the path that led up to the cliff, a Hawai'ian barn owl flew overhead, exhibiting his incredible wing span. His Winnie-the-Pooh face was soft and compelling, like a familiar friend. He was acting as a guide, leading the way. He was also acting as Ray's protector.

Ka pueo kani kaua. The owl as protector in the battle.

Ray traversed up the path following the owl. It wasn't long before the owl was talking to him in his head, using telepathy. *Brother, you are right. Run to the cross!*

"Is that you, Joe?" responded Ray in his head.

Who else would be lookin' after your sorry ass?

Now Ray knew with certainty that it was his deceased brother Joe – his aumakua both guiding and protecting him. Just as he had done on this earthly realm.

"Joe, what else should we do?" asked his little bro.

Remember what worked last time during the days of the great tribulation.

Ray wasn't here then. He was on Oahu. He wasn't really certain what had truly saved the day. The owls? Perhaps, their passed spiritual ancestors. But he knew that Kimo would know for sure.

The owl took off in flight up to higher ground. Soaring above, the bird's large wing span cast a shadow as it progressed upwards towards the heavens.

Ray continued to climb for several hours, finally stopping and resting beside a clear, babbling brook, trickling along over smooth stones and forming a deeper pond at its lowest point. One had to know the exact location of this place as it was off the beaten path. It was an oasis that was well hidden in a small valley.

It was, in fact, a sacred place. In human form, Kane had lived here. This special location, unknown to most, possessed physical, emotional, and intellectual characteristics. Upon entering this place, one experiences peculiar sensations or feelings which can be attributed to the mana imprint from its previous visitors throughout the ages.

The water was fresh, crisp, and cold. Ray drank from the brook until his thirst had been satisfied. And satisfied he was! This was awa water, the water of Kane-the-awa-drinker.

Unbeknownst to Ray, this holy water would fortify him in amazing ways. It was the magic of awa water.

As part of a purifying process, Ray sang a very old Hawai'ian chant that spoke to the awa- drinking propensity of the god Kane:

Ua moana a Kane I ka awa, Ua kau ke kaha I ka uluna, Ke hiolania la I ka moena, Kipu I ke ke kapa a ka noe.

"Kane has drunk awa, He has placed his head on a pillow, And fallen asleep on a mat, Wrapped in a blanket of mist."

(Hawaiian Mythology: Part One: The Gods V: Kane and Kanaloa)

Apparently, awa water was very intoxicating.

He pulled off his hiking boots and placed his hot and tired feet in the water. It felt like heaven! This water had curative powers and when Ray finally did get out he felt like dancing!

Overhead, Ray heard a noise. He looked up in the trees and saw the owl-that-was-Joe again.

It brought him a sense of security and comfort he'd need in the hours and days ahead.

He was drying off his feet, when he felt something hit him on the back. It was a hard, kukui nut. Another struck his head. Once again, he looked up, carefully. It was the owl-that-was-Joe throwing the nuts at him. So Joe!

"Okay, you got my attention so stop with the nuts!" said Ray in his head.

Follow me.

Hastily, Ray threw his socks and boats back on and followed the-owl-that-was-Joe into a lush flower garden. The fragrance of tropical flowers was intoxicating. White and pink plumeria, red and white ginger, hibiscus, pikaki, varied colorful orchards and so many ornament plants! The owl-that-was-Joe was waiting there, sitting patiently on the branch of a banyan tree.

"Okay, I'm here. Now what?" asked Ray.

Another nut! It had been thrown several feet ahead of him, so therefore, he walked forward.

Suddenly, he saw a *kilohana* stone in a flower bed, surrounded by lush flowers. It was a sacred garden. A kilohana stone is a kneeling stone used for praying to one's aumakua and Kane. The smooth, black stone marks the spot where one should pray to deliver and receive a message from the celestial heavens. And, so Ray, knelt on the stone, bowed his head down to the earth and his eyes closed. He prayed,

"Oh aumakua, give me the strength, the knowledge, and the power to defeat my peoples' enemies. Hear my prayer, oh Lord. Help me to defeat the evil that has returned to our island home. Oh aumakua, in the name of Jesus Christ our Lord, give me the will and courage to defeat the darkness, Amene."

A vivid picture of a white bird with bright, blue eyes filled his head, as though he had ingested a hallucinogen. The three-foot high white bird had red-tipped feathers around his face, rather like a headdress. Of course, it was the White Bird of Kane!

The bird floated down from the heavens, ascending on a white, luminous cloud. He had come to transmit a message: *Kani ka moa I ka 'ipuka, he malihinin kipa. When a cock crows* at *the door, a guest is to be expected.*

Abruptly, the vision ended. Opening his eyes, Ray saw that there was a koa wood box with a strip of white tapa cloth wrapped around it, tied with the leaf of a dark, green ti plant. He understood that the combination of koa wood and white tapa cloth was a symbol of peace. A heavenly gift.

Ray unwrapped the ribbon ti leaf, and then he removed the tapa cloth and lifted the box free from it. He set it back down on the dark dirt. There was a carved image on the top of the beautiful, koa box. It was a tau. The Hebrew symbol of the true believers of the Lord. Slowly, he lifted the lid on the box. Inside, the box was lined with deep, dark, blue velvet. There were three ocean-blue, glass bottles lying in the box. He gingerly picked one up. The bottle had an imprint of a fish symbol. He felt a warm vibration. Immediately, a feeling of calm overtook him.

Replacing the bottle in the wooden box, Ray returned to the place by the brook where he had left his back pack. Carefully, he put the box into his already overstuffed bag and zipped it up tightly. He filled his large, water canteen with the awa water and then headed up the mountain, staying on the narrowing path.

As he climbed upwards, a black snake with yellow spots emerged from the vegetation, it's red eyes glowing with hatred. It moved stealthily behind the unsuspecting Ray.

However, following the snake, the owl-that-was-Joe flew quietly behind.

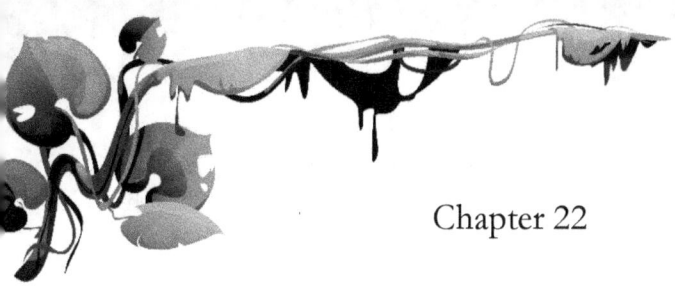

Chapter 22

E Make ana ke keiki

(The child is dying)

Pastor Kua entered the hospital room where Peter was on strict isolation. This protocol required that he put on a hospital gown, mask, hair cover, gloves and booties over his shoes. They were trying to avoid the often fatal complication of infection. With the severity of the burns and the large surface area involved, Peter was at high risk for contracting an infection.

Peter had been placed in a drug-induced coma because the burns were so severe. The boy was covered in dressings from head to toe. Since he had no skin, he had no first-line defense against microorganisms. He was hooked up to several different resuscitation fluid infusions, including antibiotics, which ran through a central line. Heart and oxygen monitors beeped steadily.

Amos was sitting at Peter's bedside, looking stoic as always. He was engaged in prayer. Amos believed in the power of prayer because he believed in the Christ Jesus. He understood that in the end, it would rest with Him. Pastor Kua walked over beside Amos and gently placed his hand on the grieving father's shoulder and joined him in prayer. Together they prayed for a miracle.

They were interrupted when Lili walked into the room.

Sadly, she had come to deliver bad news. She had just reviewed his latest lab work and it showed that he was in a state of academia. His pH level was only 7.8., barely compatible with life. Metabolic acidosis was usually an irreversible, fatal condition. He was already on life support.

"I'm so sorry, Amos," said a solemn Kate. This family had already seen so much tragedy.

Amos took in the news quietly and just shook his head in acknowledgement of receiving the information. And still, his faith did not waver. He continued to pray.

Lili had more bad news to deliver so she headed down to little Hannah's room. Kate would be waiting. Little Hannah's labs and scans had come back and there was evidence that the parasite was attacking her brain. They were out of time.

Kate stood when Lili entered the room. Immediately, she could tell by the look on Lili's face that the news was grim.

"Oh God, she's dying isn't she?" Kate trembled with the articulation of her greatest fear. "I'm afraid so, Kate," responded Lili in a quiet voice. "But, I have an idea."

Lili told Kate about her theory of inducing a state of hypothermia that is maintained for 36 hours. It would take that long to kill the warm-blooded parasite. It was a scary proposition, riddled with high-stake risks. There were so many life-threatening adverse reactions including a heart arrhythmia, a blood clot, a serious infection and the risk of bleeding out when normal temperature is returned to the body. All in all, a high-risk procedure.

There were zero options.

"Oh Lili, I know we have to try or she'll die anyway. And soon." With tears in her eyes, Kate said, "Yes, try it. Please save my baby."

"I'll get the necessary equipment and get started with the procedure then, without delay."

Lili turned and left the room.

Kate sobbed but she knew this was the right thing to do because it was the only thing to do.

That, and pray.

And, as if on cue, Pastor Kua entered the room, dressed in the isolation garb. He walked over to Kate and held her while she cried it out. Once again, he was there for her during a time of enormous pain and worry.

They began to pray.

The temperature in the room dropped precipitously. An apparition of a young, cherub boy with curly, dark hair, floating down on a white cloud, appeared. His face was that of an innocent, pure child of God. Gazing upon that special face made one feel soothed and comforted, much like a baby swaddled and nursing in the arms of its mother.

"Mason?" stuttered Kate. Was she hallucinating now?

"It's okay. I know this boy – this angel. His name is Jacob," replied the pastor.

The boy-angel-named-Jacob floated down towards Hannah's small body in the bed. He reached out and touched her forehead, making the sign of the cross. Then, he gazed upon Kate's face and the Holy Spirit shone brightly and warmly from his eyes. Kate was filled with both wonderment and peace for the moment.

"I believe that Hannah will live now. For divine intervention is at hand," said Pastor with a calm voice of reassurance. This wasn't his first experience with angels. "So that was real?" asked Kate, hope like honey in her voice.

"It was real and it was divine." Pastor was a model of utter confidence. He knew what he saw because he had seen it before. And, so had Kate.

Kate let out the deepest sigh and crossed herself. Relief. She felt relief but no doubt.

"Thank you, Lord. Thank you. I trust in you, Lord," she whispered.

Kate walked over to Hannah's bedside and looked down into the angelic face of her daughter. She looked peaceful. Then Kate saw it.

There was a red, Hebrew tau sign on little Hannah's pale forehead.

The sign of Ezekiel, drawn in a crucifix, was in the center of the girl's forehead and it was pulsating. Like a living force. And so it was.

A divine, living force had blessed little Hannah. A child that belonged to the Kingdom of God.

"There is nothing to fear anymore Kate," declared Pastor.

"I know." She wept with that declaration. Her fear dissipated.

Lili knocked on the door and entered the room wearing a protective, sterile suit. The ever efficient nurse, Kakalina was right behind her. She too was dressed in the sterile, required attire and she was carrying a sterile, surgical tray. They would be making an incision into the large vein, the inferior vena cava, to implant an endovascular cooling device. No anesthesia would be necessary as little Hannah was in a coma. Local anesthesia would be utilized because, hey, no one really knows if patients can feel pain in a coma. The jury was still out on that matter.

Kate was waiting outside the room while they performed the procedure to insert the cooling device. Pastor Kua was by her side.

Inside the room, the doctor and the nurse began. Kakalina exposed the girl's small right thigh and cleaned the inner aspect of it with betadine. This was the location where the doctor would make the incision to insert the cooling device in the vein. After the area was clean and dry, an injection of lidocaine was given at the incision site. Just in case.

A combination of buspirone, meperdine, and a cutaneous warming blanket were used to reduce the discomfort of shivering. They expected her to reach the target temperature of 33C or 79 F in about 3.5 hours. They will maintain that temperature for a total of 24 hours, from the time of the initiation of inducing a hypothermic state, and then, rewarmed in the next 12 hours.

They had begun.

Now they would wait for the next 36 hours.

Kate came into the room now that the sterile, surgical component was completed. Pastor followed behind her. They would keep vigil for the next day and a half.

Right away, Kate approached little Hannah's bed.

Lili had taken off her face mask and eye goggles. She looked at Kate's face. She seemed unaffected by the red, pulsating mark on the girl's forehead. So, what did she know?

"Kate, you don't seem surprised to see this strange mark on her forehead," said Lili.

Kate made eye contact with Lili. "No Lili, I'm not. The mark is the Hebrew tau sign. It was put there by an angel."

"Well, since I know that you are not psychotic, I just might have to believe that," replied a curious Lili. Clearly, something extraordinary had transpired here.

"I saw the angel too," declared the Pastor. "There is divine intervention involved here, Lili."

Lili turned towards Pastor Kua and saw the truth in his face. She was getting help from an angel and she was suddenly, much more optimistic about little Hannah's odds.

A green lizard blinked from the corner of the room.

This wasn't just any ordinary lizard. It was a god-lizard. Ancestral spirits used not only owls as vessels to house their spirit, the use of lizards was common too. Kate had encountered these god-lizards before during the great tribulation. So, when it spoke to Kate, she wasn't as surprised as one might think. Of course, the lizard used telepathy to convey its message: *Fear not, angels are hovering near. They are close by, in daylight and in darkness.*

Kate smiled as she heard the god-lizard's words of reassurance.

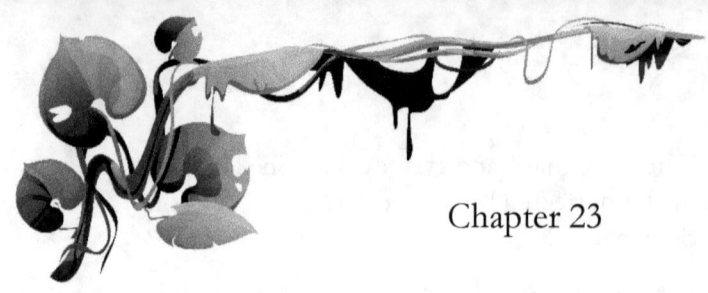

Chapter 23

Laulima

(All hands working together)

Ray pushed on. Hour after hour in the hot sun, he climbed higher and higher up the mountain which grew steeper and steeper. He could reach out and almost touch the clouds. And soon, as dusk approached, he would be near to the night stars. As a fisherman, he used the stars to navigate the ocean waters.

He stopped and rested under the shade of a tree. He ate two protein bars and drank from his canteen. He wanted to close his weary eyes and sleep. Ray felt exhausted, both physically and emotionally. However, his spirit was filled with a sense of calm. He had witnessed supernatural events in which there had been both forces of good and forces of evil.

His people were expert warriors against evil entities. Tried and true, as a matter of fact.

Since the days of Captain Cook and his malicious men, the island men had battled evil entities in many forms. Because of the battle during the days of King Kamehameha, they were both seasoned and expert warriors.

Being a true native warrior, Ray rose to finish the arduous journey to sacred ground.

The owl-that-was-Joe returned to guide Ray on the final leg of his journey. And, where was Kanaloa? He stayed back. He was not ylet ready to enter sacred grounds. This was not the time.

As the stars emerged on the night canvas, Ray reached the sacred caves.

He heard familiar voices inside.

Upon entering the cave, voices quieted.

"Uncle Ray!" exclaimed an excited David. Looking dirty and disheveled, he ran up to his uncle and hugged him tightly. He smiled brightly.

"David, my boy! How are you doin'?" He hugged the boy to him and messed up his hair. David pretended he didn't like it.

"Uncle, what did you see out on the ocean? Is a tsunami coming?" David's eyes were wide.

"Ray, you're back," said Kimo as he approached his bradda. He hugged him warmly and patted him on the back. "I too want to know what you discovered, but let's get you fed first."

"Puna, get Ray a plate of food," requested Kimo.

"Sure Kimo," replied Puna. He laughed and said "One loaded plate of grinds comin' up with today's special!" Same as yesterday's special.

Puna had been working in the kitchen helping Kapuna Hannah to prepare the noni drinks. Hannah continued to supervise the ongoing noni production although they were unclear as to the reason why their ancestors had directed them to partake of it on a daily basis. They just knew that their Kapuna had declared that they must do so. And so they did.

Mrs. Tanaka, the principal from the local high school, had brought some of her students along to help with the processing of the noni plants to noni juice. Tanti, always joking, was there also. Tanti and the students were feeling calmer around their beloved Kapuna. Some girls harbored a secret crush on Puna. Except for Alemea, of course, who had a not-so-secret crush on her Romeo, Luke. They were a cheerful group as they worked together. It was nice to hear laughter again.

Puna went to their makeshift pantry and prepared a plate of local foods. Dried fish, seaweed salad, rice, and avocado. They were short on poi with the damage to the taro crops. There were plenty of local fruits including pineapple, mango, kiwi, and papayas. Ray was sitting down at a table, weary from his journey. Kekela also sat quietly at the common table. Ray reached out and grabbed Kekela's shoulder.

"Kekela, good to see you bra," greeted Ray.

"Be sure to tell him about Haumea," responded Kekela. Once again, the blind man had seen the truth of what had transpired.

"Here, Uncle Ray," said Puna, handing him a plate piled high with food.

"Mahalo, bra," responded the tired fisherman. Gratefully, Ray took the plate and dug into it.

"All right," said Kimo. "Ray and I need to have a talk, folks so, please leave us be." He told Kekela to stay put. David resisted leaving the side of his Uncle Ray. With reassurance that he was not going to leave, the boy left and went to see Kapuna Hannah who was in a nearby cave. Ray had given David a pack of the M&Ms he so enjoyed.

Ray recounted his encounter with Haumea and the strange and dangerous green mist. He told him that it was true.... Kanaloa is behind their bucket of woes. More importantly, he told Kimo about Kane's intervention.

Kane was with them.

"I've seen the mist on the horizon, getting closer and closer," said Kimo. "It looks like something out of the twilight zone."

"There's something very toxic inside that mist. Something deadly," replied Ray. "Like some kind of poisonous particles."

"It's a type of pestilence," stated Kekela.

"What kind?" inquired Kimo.

"Can't really say for sure."

"You can't say or you don't know?"

"Both." Kekela may be a man of great vision but he was also a man of few words.

"Can we destroy it?" asked Kimo. He was very concerned.

"No, *we* can't, but…"

"But Kane can," finished Ray.

"It is a test of our faith," said a familiar voice.

"Kupuna! You surely know of these things," said Kimo, seeking her wise council.

"Yes I do," said Kapuna laughing. "Right Kekela?"

Smiling he replied, "We will prevail if we remain faithful. Without faith, we cannot defeat Kanaloa. Our faith will empower Kane to send the devil back to where he belongs." That was a speech for Kekela.

"Is a tsunami headed our way Ray?" asked Kimo, shifting gears.

"I saw nothing to suggest that but, I already know, it's coming."

"Ray, you must be exhausted. Why don't you go sleep on a cot back in the cave where the lantern glows," suggested Hannah. Gratefully, Ray accepted and wandered to the sleeping area in the back. He was fast asleep as soon as his head hit the pillow.

Outside, an owl hooted.

Two, red eyes glowed from under a nearby bush before the snake slithered away.

O Mists Creeping Inland

Awake, O rain, O sun, O night,
O mists creeping inland,
O mists creeping seaward,
O masculine sea, feminine sea, mad sea,
Delirious sea, surrounding sea of Iku,
The islands are surrounded by the sea,
The frothy sea of small billows, of low-lying billows,
Of up-rearing billows that come hither from Kahiki.

(Luomala, Katherine. *Voices on the Wind: Polynesian Myths and Chants.* (1986). Honolulu: Bishop Museum Press, p. 40).

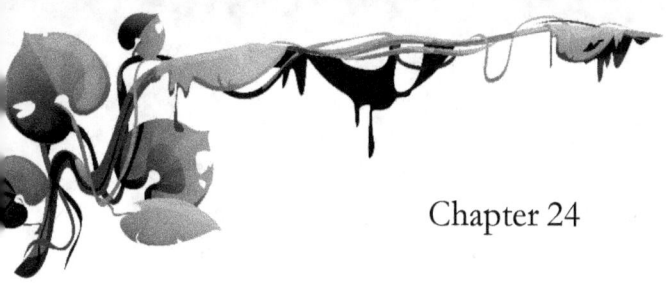

Chapter 24

Na-maka-o-ka-hai

(The water spirit in her fish form)

The green, god-lizard remained on guard in the corner of Hannah's room.

While in her coma, little Hannah shivered in the bed under her warming blanket.

After the first 4 hours, little Hannah had reached her target temperature of 33 degrees Celsius or 79 degrees Fahrenheit. She would spend the next 20 hours in that hypothermic state. So far, her vitals had dropped as expected but they were holding stable.

The red, tau sign on the girl's forehead continued to pulsate.

Kate and Pastor stood vigil, hoping and praying. Neither one of them had slept in over 30 hours.

There was a gentle knock on the door. Amos opened the door and walked quietly into the room. He looked so tired, a fatigue so profound that sleep alone could not remedy. He had aged markedly in the past few days.

"How's the girl?" he asked.

"Hanging in there. We're hopeful," replied Kate.

"How's Peter doing?" asked Pastor. He could feel the grief coming off Amos like a waft of cigar smoke.

"I've decided to take the boy off life support." He paused. "I came to ask you to administer his last rites. Can you do that for me, Mason?" Amos held back his pain. Tears shimmered in his anguished eyes.

"'Course," replied the Pastor. He too had tears in his tired eyes.

"Can you come in about an hour? His sister and grandma are in with him now. Saying good- bye. Grandma's performing an old Hawai'ian chant that ensures the cleansing of the boy's spirit."

"Sure," said Pastor and he bowed his head and began to pray. He would pray until it was time to send this sweet and gentle boy into the loving arms of the living God. Kate was weeping as she sat by her daughter's bed. She was not able to imagine how Amos could be so strong and courageous to make that choice. To end his son's suffering.

Would she be able to be that strong? She surely didn't want to have to find out.

Amos was a man of great faith.

Nobody noticed that the lizard blinked three times. Amos left in a cloud of sorrow.

Pastor sat quietly praying for the soul of his faithful servant, Peter. Kate kept vigil at her daughter's bedside. She rested her weary head on her arms as she leaned on the bed. The rhythmic beat on the heart monitor was hypnotic and soon Kate was sleeping soundly.

She slipped into a pokii dream. She began to dream of being at the beach on a sunny day with her family. Always a happy time. Everyone was there, including Kekela. He was entertaining the children at the water's edge by throwing a bright, yellow ball in the water for Pua to catch. The dog jumped, leapt and frolicked in the shoreline, chasing the ball. Little Hannah and some of the other children at the beach laughed with delight.

Pua was an entertainer.

Amos and his family had joined them at the beach on this beautiful, sunny day. Peter's dog, Max, frolicked in the shoreline. Hina threw him a stick to fetch, over and over.

Peter was out in the small surf with his boogie board catching a few small waves. His blonde hair shone like gold in the sunshine.

Given that both his parents were Hawai'ian, where he had gotten the blonde hair was a mystery to the family. Perhaps it was a throwback to the days of Captain Cook.

His younger sister, Melissa, watched from the shoreline. She adored her older brother. Peter was her hero. Grandma sat with Melissa, braiding her long, dark hair, before the girl went snorkeling in the calm waters. Hina was already in the water exploring the ocean life.

The smell of a barbeque grilling some meat filled the air, making stomachs groan. Other local foods like kim chee and pickled mango were also scenting the air. It was a peaceful day in paradise and life was good.

Suddenly, the sky began to darken. Thunder rumbled in the background as the day turned on a dime. The wind picked up and storm clouds gathered in the sky. Clearly, a storm was brewing.

The waves grew in size and became choppy.

Peter was taken aback by the rapidly changing ocean waters. He knew it was time to come in. He prepared to catch the next wave and paddle into shore. As the wave rolled in, Peter began to kick and kick until he caught the wave……..and so he did. He was headed for shore.

Swoosh!

The water began churning. A whirlpool of white suds created a vortex.

A form began to emerge from the white water. It was a woman with the face of a rat. She had beady, red eyes and formidable, sharp teeth that could do real damage which gave her a predatory appearance. It was *Na-maka-o-ka-hai*, the water spirit in her fish form!

Hawaiian mythology claims that the gods and goddesses are able to take on many forms, like a human, or a fish, or a tree, or even a vegetable! These forms are called *kino lau* or many bodies.

Na-maka-o-ka-hai was Pele's oldest sister as well as her most bitter enemy. It is said that these two daughters were born from the same mother. Na-maka-o-ka-hai, the sea goddess came from the mother's breasts and Pele, the fire goddess, came from the mother's thighs.

The sea goddess has three supernatural bodies: a fire, a cliff (pali), and a sea. She possesses the power of flying; of coming to life again after being cut up into bits and of reducing other to ashes by turning her magic skirt (*pa-u*) upon them. As the sea goddess, she was able to grow gills and fins, and therefore, stay under water for long periods of time. Moreover, she was able to stand on a wave, even a very small one. Na-mak-o-ka-hai could change the water currents and create dangerous situations, drowning her victims if she chose to do so.

Na-mak-o-ka-hai liked young boys like Peter. She hoped to devour him, heart and soul. This was her fishing expedition and she hoped to lure him into her sea.

This once well-intended and compassionate goddess had given her soul to Kanaloa long ago. After a nasty and contentious fight with Pele over a lover, Na-maka-o-ka-hai had sold her soul to the devil in a revenge-seeking rage. The malicious plot to steal the lover from the younger and more beautiful Pele had worked. She had prevailed and now she possessed the young, male lover from the lineage of the shark-god costing her a fall from grace from Pele and her other siblings. Na-maka-o-ka-hai had brought shame upon her family. Consequently, they had disowned her.

She had been spurned.

She planned to use her pa-u against him. Catching a wave, she would rise up and point a light ray, emitted from her magic skirt, which would completely render him powerless. Then, she would possess the virgin boy. It was his soul that she desired. Taking over the boy's soul, her power would increase dramatically. Souls were power houses, energy generators.

Peter was being sucked up into a vortex of a whirl pool, drawing ever closer to the sea- goddess. Ever closer to the paralyzing pa-u.

He knew he was in great peril.

Even though Peter knew the end was near, he was unafraid. He prayed in anticipation of seeing the Father.

Na-maka-o-ka-hai was smiling gleefully as the innocent boy drew near to her. This one was so pure.

She must have him!

She reached into her magic skirt to feel the pulse and heat of the paralyzing light spear. Her hand found the warm wand. It was revving up, getting hotter by the second.

Peter allowed himself to be pulled further into the sea-goddess's grip. He was ready to face his maker. He would die for his Lord before he would allow this sea-devil to soil his soul.

But his maker was not ready to receive Peter into eternal life.

An angel was sent to intervene on behalf of Peter. It was not his time. He had much to do yet.

This angel was familiar. She was a beautiful, young Caucasian woman with golden hair. Her eyes were aglow with the light of the Holy Spirit. This light was the brightest in the universe and the pa-u was no match for the power that comes from the glorious heavens above.

The angel pointed her eyes at the eyes of the evil goddess. Rays of brilliant light flashed. Na-o-maka-ka-hai exploded. Spontaneous combustion. Her particles rained down like acid rain, dissolving in the ocean waters.

Peter was gazing at his angel of mercy. He had been saved!

The angel had a message to deliver to the boy: *You are destined for great things. You will live a long life in your walk with the Lord. Always persevere in your toils. Never give up and you will be rewarded by your Father.*

The sun began to shine once again. The storm had passed. Peter began paddling to shore as the seas calmed. He was safe.

Max, waging his tail, greeted him on shore. Now, he was also blessed.

As he paddled closer, a shark with red, glowing eyes began to swim circles around him...

Kate woke up in a cold sweat, her heart pounding.

She looked at little Hannah who lay still in the bed. How long had she been asleep? Where was Pastor?

Then she remembered and came fully awake with a start. Pastor was giving Peter his last rites!

She ran out the door and rushed to Peter's room. Opening the door, she saw Pastor praying over the boy. Amos was with them.

"Stop!" she cried. "You must not read him his last rites. He's not going to die. You hear me?"

"My God Kate! What has come over you?" asked Pastor. He felt bad for Amos. What was Kate talking about? The boy was not going to survive his injuries. They were too serious. He sincerely hoped she wasn't going to offer false hope. Amos and his family had already endured so much pain.

"Pastor, I would never say such a thing if I wasn't sure." She rushed on, "I had a dream and an angel came and said that Peter would live.... that he *must* live." She paused. "It was a prophetic dream. Peter is destined for great things. Great works for the Kingdom."

"How can you be so sure Kate if it was a dream? How can you be certain?" asked Pastor.

"Because the angel gave me this to give to you, Mason," she said quietly. She pulled something out of her pants pocket and handed it to Pastor.

It was a gold key.

Amos finally spoke, "Is it *the* key?" He knew that, through a dream, the kingdom had provided a gold key to return Kanaloa to the pits of hell during the dark days of the tribulation.

Pastor was examining the key. As he held it, it began to vibrate and get warm. It was the right key.

"In the name of all that is holy, I swear that this is the divinity key."

Amos got down on bended knees and began to both pray and weep for the truth had been revealed. His son would live.

Code Blue! Code Blue! Room 404.

That was little Hannah's room.

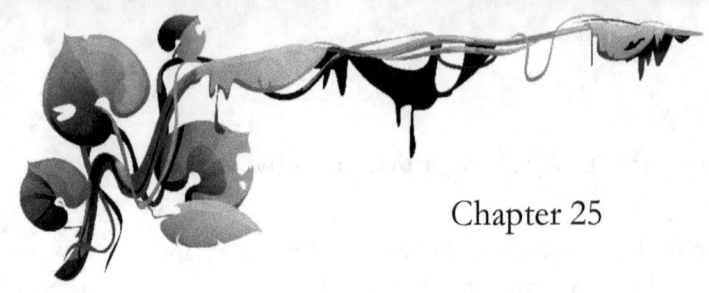

Chapter 25

Kanaloa

(The Great Serpent)

Lili was in the emergency room examining a four year-old boy named Billy who seemed to have contracted the brain-eating water parasite. The disease progression was much farther along than little Hannah's was when she was brought in. Of course, her mother was a nurse practitioner and she understood the importance of early intervention. Because of that, she harbored a great hope that Hannah would survive.

And then she heard the code blue.

Running to Hannah's room, she kept saying, "No! No! I won't lose this child!"

On her arrival to the room, she saw that Dr. Fukina was already there leading the resuscitation. Little Hannah looked blue.

The red tau sign had disappeared.

"Another cc. of epi," he called out to Kakalina. She was an excellent nurse in a code situation, being a cool-calm head and quick-thinker in stressful situations.

"Get ready to shock her."

Another nurse got the defibrillator ready to shock the girl's heart in the hope to restart it.

The heart monitor remained silent.

"Getting ready to shock the patient. Stand clear," commanded the nurse. Then she applied the electrical shock. This nurse was a recent hire and very efficient and effective too.

No arrhythmia. Flat line. Continue CPR.

"Another cc. of epi," ordered the Dr. Sweat caused his face to shine under the fluorescent lights. "Then, shock her again."

Kakalina injected another dose of epinephrine into the girl's IV.

Again, an electrical shock was delivered. This had to be it. Everyone in the room held their breathe.

Beep. Beep. Beep. Beep.

It was a symphony to everyone's ears. The heart monitor showed that Hannah was back in a stable arrhythmia. The girl was not lost, but it had been close.

"Thank God!" exclaimed Kate and then she broke down and wept. Tears of relief dropped like pennies from heaven.

It seemed as though her faith was being tested this long night. She wondered what Kimo and the other kids were doing right now. She missed them all terribly. Without Kimo, she felt off balance. Adrift.

Where was her anchor?

Pastor had left the room to get them each some food and a cup of coffee. There was still more waiting to endure. They would need their strength. He already felt like he might just collapse so great was his fatigue. But, he needed to be strong for Kate. She was like a daughter to him. He was Hannah's godfather.

Kate gathered herself together. Taking a deep breath, she looked around the room. Then, suddenly it struck her. The lizard was no longer in the room. Where had the guardian god-lizard disappeared to? Something had run a foul in this room when she had left. She vowed to not leave Hannah's side again.

The steady beep of the monitor was a reassuring sound that helped calm her.

Kate took this moment to reflect on the amazing, divine events that had occurred over the course of the long night. Yet, it still was not over.

The vigil continued as the-owl-that was-Joe sat perched on the branch of a jacaranda tree that was in full bloom with bright, yellow blossoms. The owl as the protector was standing by.

Another vigil was taking place down the hall in Peter's room. Amos kept watching for his son to improve but, so far, his condition remained the same. Amos's faith never wavered. He patiently waited for his miracle to occur.

Peter lay still in his coma, wrapped in gauze from head to toe. Most of his face had been spared. His pale, young face looked peaceful as he lay there in bed hooked up to several intravenous infusions and heart monitors.

Amos had been up now for over 48 hours and he was losing his ability to focus. He was drinking a coffee, but it wasn't helping. The sense of utter exhaustion was overwhelming. No amount of coffee could address this level of fatigue.

Amos's eyes closed. The empty cup in his hand fell to the floor. So weary, he started to doze.

"Amos. Rise and shine. You got company," said a voice.

Amos jumped. He was awake now.

There was a foul odor in the room. The smell of death and decay was pungent.

"Who's there?" inquired Amos. Maybe he was hearing things.

Two, red eyes glowed from under a chair in the corner of the room. The snake that was the great serpent, Kanaloa, had arrived.

"You're losing it Amos," said the yellow-spotted, black snake as it slithered from under the chair. "Truly. Did you not think I would come to prevent any divine int ervention?" Kanaloa chuckled. As he did, his red tongue protruded out and flickered. "I live to disrupt miracles." He laughed again, so pleased with himself to have gotten so close to the kid that the Almighty wanted to save for important work. He would change that plan.

Right here, right now.

"So, there is something special about your boy, Amos." The serpent hissed. "You have kept this well hidden from me." He hissed his displeasure.

The snake slowly moved closer to the boy's bed.

"Get away from him!" yelled Amos as he rushed towards the snake.

Laughing, Kanaloa stuck out his red, piercing tongue and a flash of fire shot out, like a torpedo.

It made its target.

Kanaloa loved playing with fire! After all, he reigned in the fire pits below the earth as Milu, lord of the dead.

Amos squealed with pain as the fire consumed the flesh on his thigh. He quickly patted it out. A raw, red wound lay gaping open. The nauseating smell of burnt flesh wafted in the air.

Nonetheless, Amos moved towards the snake, ready to kill it with his bare hands if he had to.

He would not allow Kanaloa to interfere in God's divine plan for his son.

The snake-that-was-Kanaloa just looked at Amos and said," You're pathetic. You and your God."

"Where is your God now?" asked the serpent as he shot another flash of fire at Amos. "Hmmmm…where is he now, Amos?" He broke out into hideous laughter that sounded like a garbage disposal grinding slivers of sharp bones.

Amos's chest was struck and the damage was severe.

"He is with me always. My heavenly father is present." Amos collapsed on the floor holding his chest. The smell of both burnt flesh and burnt hair permeated the air. To Kanaloa, the odor was sweet.

Amos lay curled up in fetal position on the carpeted floor, holding his severely burnt chest.

It was over. He was unable to go on.

The serpent had reached the head of Peter's bed. He detached the delivery apparatus on the oxygen set-up, leaving the oxygen to flow freely into the room. He increased the amount being delivered to maximum. The oxygen began filling the air in the room.

A flash of fire ignited the room and it went up in a whoosh. Amos, barely alive, was praying out loud with his last breathe. And then there was another whoosh!

Water drops fell from the ceiling as the sprinklers came on.

As they hit the snake, he immediately was destroyed by spontaneous combustion. Kabang!

Incinerated.

The water was no ordinary water. It was awa water.

The awa water poured over Peter, drenching his body and saturating the bed. When it stopped, the bandages had been washed away by the water. Fresh, new, pink skin like a baby's covered the once damaged body. Holy water had cleansed the boy and caused his skin to grow anew. He was healed.

On the floor, Amos lay dying. Before he passed on, he saw his son's body restored. He smiled. Peter called out to him, "You have taught me well, my loving father. You are free to go to Him."

With that, Amos drew his last breath.

Removing the rest of the oxygen equipment, Peter inhaled his first new breathe deeply. He would have to grieve for his father later.

He pulled out the rest of the IVs and got out of bed. His legs were a little unsteady. He couldn't find any clothes so he just put on a couple of hospital gowns.

Kanaloa was not gone. He had managed to transmigrate into another vessel. Without the key, he could not be destroyed. Peter had been given the golden key for safe keeping. After all, Pastor's physical ailments made him vulnerable to Kanaloa.

Peter knew it was time to begin his work.

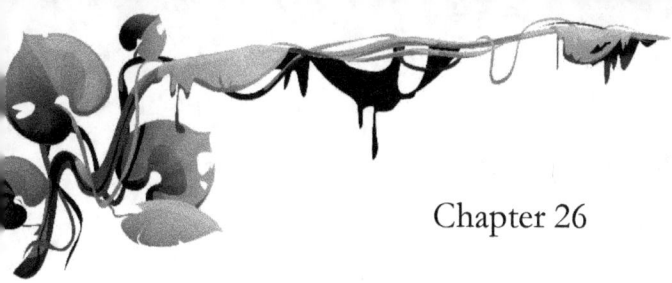

Chapter 26

Wai Hoano (Holy Water)

Ray slept soundly for 13 hours.

Upon rising, Kimo approached him with a cup of hot coffee. They sat at the table while Puna prepared some breakfast.

"I can't remember a coffee that tastes this good," said Ray with pleasure.

"I second that, bra. Ray, there's more to tell, isn't there?" asked Kimo. Max, the poi (multiple breeds) dog, was with him. He was a medium-sized dog that was gray and black with some white patches. He was a handsome dog in his own way. The dog had a great disposition.

"Who's your friend?" asked Ray.

"Max. He's Peter's dog. We're watching him." Max wagged his tail in a greeting.

It was time to get down to the business at hand. "Yes, my friend, there is more to say." Ray told him about his communication with the owl-that-was-Joe.

"Kimo, Joe said we should do what was done last time, during the days of the great tribulation, to defeat Kanaloa. So, what worked?"

"Three things were necessary to defeat the evil one. Holy water, a special gold key, and a demonstration of our faithfulness," claimed Kimo.

"I have the holy water." Ray told him about the bottles of liquid in the blue glass bottles. He told Kimo that they needed to listen for a cock to crow. It will be the announcement of a guest, apparently a friendly visitor.

"What about the key? How do we get that?" asked Ray. "Through divine intervention," Kimo responded.

"And how will…" Ray didn't get to finish asking the question.

"Faithfulness. That's how Ray." Kimo understood that steadfast faithfulness by his people was what allowed the Lord to hear their petitions and provide divine intervention when they faced Kanaloa last time. Kanaloa didn't take defeat well. So he had returned with a mean hunger to be victorious.

There would be no mercy.

After all, Kanaloa knew what was in the green mist. He welcomed its arrival onto the island.

Puna served them a breakfast of fresh, local fruits, including cottage cheese inside half of a papaya, boiled eggs and some of the last taro bread that was available. A small generator allowed them to have a small refrigerator.

Kupuna Hannah, Kekela, Puna and David had joined them. After greeting each other, they all

wanted to hear about Ray's surveillance when he journeyed out to sea.

"After we eat, Ray can fill you in on his journey. But before we eat, let's pray," said Kimo. Thy

joined hands. He bowed his head and prayed,

"O Heavenly Father, O Kane, we praise you, we worship you. Please hear our petition to save our island and its people. The people of Nardei have been faithful servants, O Lord, O Kane. We will maintain our faithfulness through prayer and the reading of the Word. Thy will be done. We submit to you, the Almighty God. Amene."

The good people of Nardei began to chant as Hannah led them in an old Hawaiian prayer to the god, Kane.

"Life to the land! Life from Kane, Kane the god of life.

"Life to the people!

Hail Kane of the water of life! Hail!"

They dug into their food and ate in earnest, eager to hear what Ray had to say. However,

David's curiosity got the best of him and he blurted out questions. Was it curiosity or was it anxiety? David's a very mature boy but he was still a child.

Kekela sat beside him and quieted the boy in his gentle way. Kekela was so tuned into children. They haven't developed a repertoire of defense mechanisms like denial or being deceptive. With Kekela's psychic skills, he read them very easily. He said children have open minds and open hearts, unfettered by hate, lies, and treachery.

However, before David pounced again, Kekela spoke up. And, when he spoke, others listened.

"My friends, the key is secured. Pastor has it. Just like last time."

"Mason remains at the hospital. Someone will have to bring both him and the key," announced Kupuna Hannah. The next move was clear. The key and the man of God were needed to fulfill their destiny.

"That's right Kupuna. This was revealed to me also. Puna must go and fetch him," Kekela announced.

Puna bowed his head and told his God that he would do his bidding. Mission accepted.

Both Kekela and Kapuna knew that his father who had passed many years ago would be his owl-as-protector; owl-as-guide. The owl-that-was-Kai would be Puna's salvation.

Or not.

Outside the cave, a noisy ruckus could be heard.

They went outside the entrance of the cave to see what all the noise was about.

Immediately, they saw a dead rooster who had been decapitated. Was this the cock that was ordained to crow when a special guest arrived?

Did this change their chances of defeating Kanaloa? More importantly, would it diminish their faithfulness?

(Ancient Hawaiian Civilization, p. 50)

Chapter 27

Aloha

(Have mercy)

Lili had just completed the autopsies on Calvin and Nadine. The results of the examination were puzzling. She was perplexed and was trying to sort it all out.

She was sitting at her desk, pondering about the data from the autopsies. They too had shown evidence of a massive infection that rapidly liquefied the internal organs. She'd never seen or heard anything like it. The gastrointestinal system and bone marrow were completely ravaged. Some of the other organs were not completely liquefied and she was able to observe small, gnarly tumors on the inside walls of some organs. How did an infectious process lead to such a mutation in the cells? These were no normal tumors. No, these gray-black, wart-like tumors reflected an extreme case of cell mutation.

Was that it? Was some kind of toxic agent creating these mutations? Like agent orange?

Mutations in Paradise.

In the hospitalized patients that had the same illness, Lili noted that the later symptoms included red, itchy skin. Maybe from the irritation of the deadly toxin. She had also observed bloody vomit and stools. That was from the tumors. Tumors bleed. So, at the end, the patients were hemorrhaging internally. She got that. It also explained the low blood pressure that finally bottomed out. It also provided the explanation for the profound anemia found in every patient's lab results. That, and the absolute destruction of bone marrow.

Lili understood this much: *the toxin was fatal.*

She understood more now, but still, the puzzle remained. Maybe the tissue samples that she sent to the laboratory in Honolulu would yield some results soon. That is, if the island doesn't get obliterated by a giant tsunami.

Lili sighed. She was so tired and so distressed by this illness that was proving to have a hundred percent mortality rate. She had already lost so many patients.

The dam burst.

Lili laid her head down on her desk and wept. She shuddered as she released all her pent-up discouragement and grief. When her tears were spent, she went to the bathroom and washed her face. Looking in the mirror, Lili thought she looked pale and gaunt. Older too. Did she actually see a few gray hairs?

Another deep sigh. She would get another coffee, already her third cup and it was only eight o'clock in the morning, then go upstairs to see her patients. Little Hannah would be her first patient on her daily rounds. Little Hannah was handling the hypothermic state much better and in six hours they would begin the warm-up process.

After that, in twelve hours the whole process would be completed and the real question was: *would it work?*

The crying had been therapeutic for her and by the time she hit the elevator, Lili held on to her faithfulness and uttered a prayer. She needed to understand what was killing her patients. Maybe some divine intervention could be dispensed.

Up in Hannah's room, Kate was watching her daughter who continued to shiver despite the countermeasures against the cold. At times, the little girl whimpered. That was heart-wrenching for Kate. She felt so powerless.

Kakalina had just left the room after changing her daughter's gown and linens. She'd not bathed her because of her decreased temperature. Hannah moaned when moved in the bed. When the little girl moaned, Kate's heart broke for her vulnerable baby daughter.

You got the power because I got the power!

"Who said that?" asked Kate as she quickly looked around the room.

You ain't lookin' close enough, little darling.

Kate thought that she was probably experiencing auditory hallucinations from profound exhaustion.

You ain't hearin' voices. Look over here. In the corner. It's Uncle Bert.

Uncle Bert? It did sound like him. Kate looked in the corner nearest to Hannah's bed.

A large lizard sat in the shadows.

"Uncle Bert?" Kate said in disbelief. "Is it really you?"

Well, who was you expectin'? Bruno Mars?

"Okay. It *is* really you."

Lookin' out for my favorite girls, Kate. By the way, you're smellin' pretty ripe there girl. Might want to hook-up with a bar of soap and some water! Hey, what's that red mark on Hannah's forehead? Is it pulsating? I don't know about that. It's kinda creepy.

"Never mind that now. What can you tell me Uncle Bert? Is she going to be okay?" "Who are you talking to Kate?" asked Lili. She had quietly entered the room.

Kate spun around. Oh brother! Busted! She was talkin' crazy talk.

"I don't know. I guess I was hallucinating!" she joked (she hoped). Her rosy cheeks gave away her embarrassment.

Lili laughed, "God knows that I've been there. Exhaustion can play tricks on your mind." Kate's eyes drifted to the corner.

The lizard that was Uncle Bert was gone.

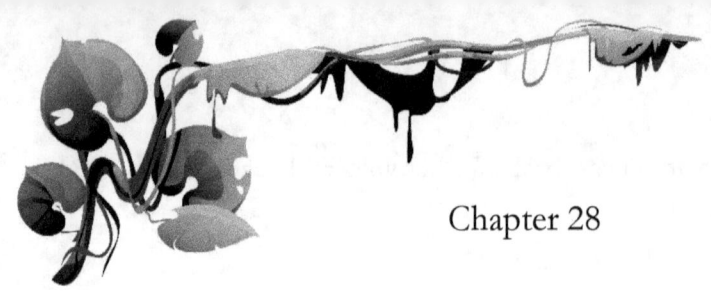

Chapter 28

Ka pueo kani kaua

(The owl as protector in the battle.)

Puna prepared to traverse down the mountain.
The mysterious green mist could be seen on the horizon. It was getting closer to the island.

There was no wind. The utter stillness in the air was often a precursor to an approaching tsunami. The air was heavy, making it difficult to breathe.

Time was running out.

Puna's back pack carried protein bars, nuts and trail mix, dried fruit, noni drinks, extra clothing, a sharp-edge knife and a small, wooden statute with a red feather. This aumakua figure was very special. His father, Kai who was a Kahuna, had carved this warrior-style aumakua. The red feather can only be placed on an aumakua figure by a High Priest or Priestess. In doing so, the red feather made it sacred.

It was Puna's rabbit foot.

Kupuna Hannah held back her tears until her son had departed. Everyone had gathered around him and prayed for his safe return. A Hawai'ian *pule*.

Little Hina hugged him tightly and tears flowed down her cheeks. Luke embraced him and wished him well on his mission.

David, putting on a brave face, said," Here Puna. I made this for you." He pulled a carved wooden cross out of his pocket.

"Did you make this?" asked Puna.

David nodded and his chin quivered. He tried so hard not to cry but he was not successful.

When Puna hugged the boy, he sobbed into Puna's chest. He was a sensitive boy.

The gift was a reminder to maintain his faithfulness.

Puna exited the cave and set out on his journey. Immediately, his owl-as-protector-Kai emerged from the tall trees and led the way. He was guiding his son to the awa-water brook. A sacred place.

The trip down to the brook took several hours under the hot, tropical sun. There was not a breeze in the air. When they reached the shaded oasis, Puna was more than ready for a break. It was a pit stop to fuel up on fluids and food. The humidity made the journey arduous. His owl-as-protector-Kai rested on a branch of a nearby ironwood tree. Always watching, ever vigilant.

Puna drank greedily from the awa water. He took off his hiking boots and socks. Dipping his feet into the cool brook water, he immediately felt refreshed. He dried his wet feet and sat back, eager to eat something. His mind drifted to Lili.

He took out a large protein bar and a bag of Kate's homemade trail mix that consisted of macadamia nuts, dried pineapple and papaya fruit, coconut, and crushed taro chips. He added an avocado that he picked up on the way down the mountain to his meal. Keeping his promise to his mother, he drank his daily dose of noni juice. After his hunger was satiated, he lay back against a tree and closed his eyes. He thought of Lili and smiled. Tonight, he would see her.

Soon, he dozed in the cool shade.

Squeak! Squeak!

Abruptly, Puna awoke. *Squeak! Squeak!*

Puna heard the squeal of wild, baby pigs. They could be dangerous, even as babies. Their protective mother pig would definitely be murderous to a man in her turf, near her newborns.

After grabbing the knife from his back pack, Puna stood up and struck a warrior pose. Ready to strike if needed.

Squeal! Squeal!

They were close. Their squeals were very loud now. He could hear their hooves striking the ground and see the dust they kicked up with their sharp-clawed hooves. They were very close.

When the first baby pig broke through the brush, Puna looked with horror at the noisy, not- really-a-pig animal. No, this was a strange, vicious creature.

The animal's skin had sores all over his torso. They oozed yellow-green mucus that looked and smelled like a bacterial infection. The pungent smell of disease.

A foul, putrid odor.

The pig was only three feet tall. It had very short legs that had very large feet that contained sharp claws with pointed, long, black nails. The face of the creature was rodent-like, with beady, red eyes. It's mouth was large with protruding, razor-sharp teeth that could easily shred a neck in seconds. When it came upon Puna, the creature froze and assessed the danger.

Likewise, Puna assessed the creature.

It was Haumea!

Through telepathy, the owl-that-was- Kai conveyed this message to the boy.

This was one of the female forms of Haumea. She had several female versions of her spirit.

As the legend goes, Haumea, in her female form as the sister of both Kane and Kanaloa, came with her two brothers from overseas to the chain of Hawai'ian islands. She serves the dark side. Today, she was serving Kanaloa.

Through rebirths, Haumea changes herself from old age to youth and returns over and over again to marry her children and grandchildren. She is capable of transforming herself into a growing tree. Upon entering the tree, Haumea became *Kamehaikana,* meaning "the tree of changing leaves."

Being knowledgeable about Hawai'ian mythology, Puna grasped all of that in a minute.

These baby creatures could easily kill under the command of the evil goddess.

He prepared to defend himself as the second baby creature came on the scene. Then, another. He was surrounded by the vicious creatures. And where was the mother pig?

Maybe they were waiting for mama before they began aggressing towards this Hawai'ian warrior. Fire shot through their nostrils.

Son, the water. The awa water.

Puna understood and began looking for some kind of vessel to scoop up the water.

Under the tree.

He slowly advanced over to the Ironwood tree. Underneath the tree, at the base of the tree was a large and deep ironwood bowl. Kai hooted.

The three, not-pig creatures were squealing at top pitch as the ground shook with the noisy arrival of the Mama Pig.

Puna grabbed the wooden vessel and stood in the cool waters of the brook. Come and get me, you bastards!

The first pig wanted to show off to his mama and he dashed into the brook, eyeing Puna's vulnerable neck. As his first foot entered the awa water, he immediately began squealing loudly in an even higher pitch. Steam rose from the water. The pig tried to back out of the water but his foot was stuck in the mud. Puna filled the wooden bowl with water and flung it into the face of the animal. Piggy number one fell over dead, dissolving into a cloud of steam.

Little piggy number two decided to approach the enemy man in a different manner. He decided to set a fire and smoke Puna out of the water that acted like a deathly repellent to the creature. The pig gathered up some ironwood branches and twigs, leaves and bark.

Once the fire wood and starter components had been piled up, the piggy number to let out a small roar and shot fire out of his nares.

Swoosh!

The fire started easily and, as planned, it began to spread.

Snap, crackle, pop!

As the vegetation burned, one tall tree stood tall, unaffected by the burning embers. It was Kamehaikana. The tree of changing leaves had transformed its leaves into poisonous darts that she could thrust with great precision, like little spears. Once Puna was forced to leave the now smoky brook, she would shoot him with multiple, toxic spears that would cause an agonizing death.

A death so cruel it would test his faith.

Stay in the brook, son.

Despite the smoke and heat, Puna covered his lower face with his t-shirt; unsure of what would happen next, yet trusting in his father's directives.

The sound of many owls filled the air as dozens of pueo swooned down into the awa water and drank deeply from the brook. When all had filled their beaks, they surrounded the tree that housed the evil goddess dispatched by Kanaloa. The owl-that-was-Kai hooted. It was time to act like fire hoses and drench the tree with the awa water.

Dozens of owls sprayed the tree.

On contact, a pained scream shattered the day. A whirlwind of white particles emerged from the dying tree, swept away on a tropical breeze. Haumea had fled. For now, that is.

The third little piggy had been killed by the fire. Their mission had utterly failed.

Kanaloa would be displeased and would probably dispatch her again.

The blue sky had turned cloudy, storm clouds gathering. The sky opened with a heavy downpour, dousing the fire with rain. Puna figured that Kane or Lono probably had a hand in that.

The pieces of this chessboard were moving very quickly.

Chapter 29

'olelo ko'u makua a pau e kama'ilio mai ia'u

(My amakua speaks to me)

Kate could hardly contain herself. She felt inclined to bust out laughing hysterically. Uncle Bert was somewhere nearby. And Uncle Bert was a lizard.

Kate dug her fingernails into the palm of her left hand to prevent herself from laughing.

Lili examined Hannah and made notations in her chart. She seemed pleased with Hannah's condition. They had begun the warming-up phase. Hannah was warming up nicely, like a loaf of bread in the oven. Despite that, the little girl still shivered. Most importantly, her vital signs were stable.

She hoped that the hypothermic state had destroyed the brain-eating parasite. They would soon know.

Kate looked around the room in search of Uncle Bert. She didn't see him. Maybe she was losing her mind after all. She missed Kimo so much. He would tell her if she had lost her marbles. She yearned for her other children too. Hina, Luke. She prayed that the family would be reunited soon.

"Earth calling Kate," called out Lili.

"Sorry. I'm so tired that my mind wanders. I was thinking about Kimo and the kids." "I know. It's hard to be separated from loved ones right now."

"Like Puna?" asked Kate. She could see the fatigue in the young woman's face.

Lili sighed deeply and said quietly, "Yes. Like Puna." Her throat constricted. She swallowed and continued, "Hannah is doing well. We will just have to wait and see if it affected the parasite and the subsequent infection in her brain." Lili smiled. "I'm optimistic Kate."

"Any news on the tsunami?" asked Kate, as she rubbed her eyes. Her blood-shot eyes burned with the need to sleep.

"Some say it's fast approaching. What I do know is that green mist *is* approaching. And, I think it is dangerous," replied Lili. There was fear in her voice.

There was a knock at the door and Pastor entered. He slowly walked over to Kate and embraced her. He then walked over to little Hannah who was still under the influence of the heavy sedation. She shivered periodically. He prayed over his beloved godchild.

When he was done praying, he turned to Lili and said," Puna will be here later today, my dear."

Lili looked startled. "What?! How do you know this?" "An aumakua told me."

"But why?' asked Kate, jumping into the conversation.

"He has come to fetch me and the key," he replied. "But I no longer have the key. I gave it to Peter."

"I see," responded Kate. "Like last time."

"Exactly. So, I will be leaving in the morning to go up the mountain. The battle will take place in the sacred place. On sacred ground, near the cross." The rugged cross stood on a nearby hill beside the sacred caves.

"I don't understand," said a confused Lili. She was far too tired to track this conversation.

Both Pastor and Kate explained the circumstances surrounding the gold key and how it was instrumental in defeating Kanaloa during the days of the tribulation.

"I still don't understand how you know that Puna is coming to get you and the key," declared Lili.

"Well, …..."

Code blue! Code blue! Room 317!

"That's Billy! Oh my God!" cried Lili as she turned and rushed from the room. Obviously, the patient in trouble was one of her patients.

"I hope it's not another child," said Kate, looking over at her own daughter, resting quietly.

"Let us hope for divine intervention." Pastor knew that the four-year old boy was in critical condition. He too had contracted the deathly amoeba. His brain had already been seriously damaged.

"By the way, Mason, what aumakua told you?"

"Why, it was *your* aumakua. Uncle Bert told me," he replied and smiled.

Kate burst out laughing. She'd just fallen into the rabbit hole.

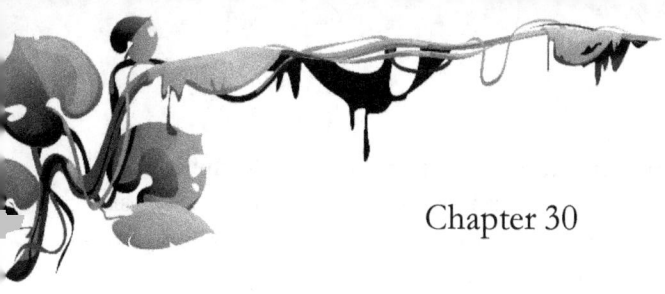

Chapter 30

Mahalo Ke Akua
(Thanks be to God)

While little Hannah awaited her fate, Kupuna Hannah had just finished her breakfast with the others. She rose from the table and stumbled in her steps.

Suddenly, she collapsed onto the floor, like a felled tree.

"Oh no! Hannah, are you okay?" asked Ray as he rose from the table and rushed to her side.

Kimo was already there.

Kimo turned her on her back and checked her breathing. She was breathing okay and her color was good but she was clearly out cold. What had happened to her? Was she sick? He felt her forehead. No fever.

"She seems okay. Just out cold," verbalized Kimo. He was uncertain what was wrong with her, but he knew it scared him. Terribly.

"What happened to Kupuna?" asked a concerned David.

"A spell has been cast on her," stated Kekela, in a matter-of-fact voice.

"What?" responded Kimo. A spell? Really?

"An evil spell cast by Kanaloa," said Kekela. No one doubted the blind man who could truly see.

"What can we do, Kekela? Anything?" replied an alarmed Kimo.

"Fortunately, I am familiar with the process to undo the spell but we must act right away. As more time passes, the deeper she will slip into a dark realm that she may never escape." "Then, let's get on it. What must we do?" said Kimo, assuming the leadership role.

"First, we must gather a very special flower, the jewel orchid. It is also very rare. It is only found in mountainous areas in the tropics. These orchids grow in high altitudes, in diminished light, cool air and in a slightly damp place," instructed Kekela. "You must go to the small, forested valley just down the mountain path – about three-quarters of a mile, and then turn left when you come upon the haiku forest. There is a worn path beside the tall ironwood tree. Follow it for a bit and then you will come upon a small stream and the rare orchids."

"I can go, Uncle!" exclaimed David.

"Yes, you can go with Luke, okay Luke?" The father was demonstrating his confidence in his son.

Happy with something to do, Luke readily agreed.

"Hina, you can go and help too." This pleased the quiet girl who sorely missed her mother.

"Take your cousin's dog with you. Peter won't mind," advised Kimo. The poi dog was part

Blue Healer and had a great nose. They would never get lost with Max along.

"What else Kekela?" asked an anxious Kimo. He wished Kate was here.

"Yeah, what can I do?" chimed in Ray, fear radiating from his body. He prayed for guidance and promised to remain faithful. The fear began to dissipate.

"Kimo, you must go bathe in the awa water to prepare to offer the appropriate chant. Beside Hannah's cot is her pule mat. Take it with you and dip it – all of it – into the water, then bring it back."

"Okay. I can do that but I don't know the proper chant."

"Fortunately bra, I do." Kekela smiled. "Ray, you must prepare Hannah's room by burning sage and praying over her. Guard her starting right now."

"Okay. I'll go and attend to her now." Faith intact, he turned to go. Kekela warned, "Do not leave her side. Not for one moment."

"Got it. I'll stick to her like glue." With that, Ray turned and left the main cave and went to the sleeping quarters nearby." No matter what, it was imperative that Hannah be pulled from the clutches of Kanaloa.

"How is Hannah? I mean, you're tuned in with her, right?" inquired Kimo.

"She has slipped no farther into the darkness. At some level, she is fighting it," said Kekela. "You know, Hannah. She is a force to be reckoned with."

"I shall go get the mat and head down the mountain now," declared Kimo. He left the room to gather some things he would need to perform a proper cleansing bath. A ritual of the appropriate purifying process.

Kekela didn't share with the others the dream he had last night. He saw a bloody battle on the sacred grounds on the Pali Cliff. Strange, in the dream the mountain changed both color and shape, rocks falling from the mountain cliff. The side of the cliff became red. The night moon was a crimson-red moon. Ahead, there would be a battle in which the struggle between Kanaloa and Kane would be epic. Some would be lost. Sadly, it is the cost of war.

Some would trade their souls to remain in the flesh. A life based on an eternal debt. A life of unending, unrelenting, and unbearable hell.

Chapter 31

'olelo 'aka'aka ka Popoki

(The Cat Smiles)

After a fit of uncontrollable laughter, Kate sat down.

"As in, Uncle Bert-the-lizard?" asked Kate. *I must be in Wonderland.*

"Why yes, my dear. You've surely met him. He's quite a character." Pastor had a twinkle in his eyes.

Mad Hatter, perhaps? Had they met at a tea party? Kate wondered and decided that she had passed into Disneyland…as in not grounded in reality anymore.

"Am I really sane at this point? Tell me the truth, Mason."

"You are as sane as the rain in Spain, Kate. The world around us has changed into a supernatural one," explained Pastor. "Take Uncle Bert – he's certainly out of this world."

"Are angels nearby like in the dark days of the great tribulation? Is Bert really one of them? 'Cause he wasn't such an angel in his mortal life. I mean, he had a lot of ……. vices."

"He sure was one hell of a sinner. I grant you that. Of course, that was before he repented and embraced the Lord. Near the end, he had changed his ways. He died on an operating table. He was donating a kidney for his granddaughter who would die without it. She had a cancer called Wilm's tumor."

"Did she live?"

"She did Kate. She's a healthy, growing, precocious kid."

"Son-of-a-gun! He really did change." Kate understood why Uncle Bert was looking out for her little girl now.

"And what about the tsunami? Is it coming?"

Mason nodded his head. "Yes, it is coming." He would not deny what he knew to be true. "When you reach the caves, tell my family….," she began sobbing. "Tell them I love them…please… I love them all so much." Kate released all of her fears and tears.

"They all know that Kate. As you know, they all love you so very much. But do not abandon all hope. I didn't say that we can't stop it. You must remain faithful Kate." Pastor seemed calm and confident. "But, I must leave right away, at dawn's break, to get to the sacred grounds.

Time is of the essence."

Little Hannah muttered as she continued to proceed in the warm-up phase of her hypothermic state. The sound startled both Hannah and Pastor. They both laughed as they realized that the girl was exhibiting brain function. Joyful sounds drew Lili to the room.

"What's going on?" she asked as she entered the room.

"Shhh. Listen for a minute," Kate urged. She was grinning like that cat that swallowed the canary.

Lili paused. She tilted her head to listen. She could hear the steady beep of the monitors. And then Hannah muttered something again.

Lili drew in a sharp breath. And then she released it and continued to smile.

"Yes, it's a very good sign," said Lili. It felt good to smile. It felt even better to hope.

For a moment, Kate, Pastor and Lili shared a powerful connection that served as a reminder that faithfulness is rewarded. The connection was so powerful that the accumulation of their joy created an energy that allowed the smile to linger.

Just like the Cheshire Cat who sat in a perch in a tree, directing Alice to the March Hare's house. The smiling Cheshire Cat happily offered the directions to Alice and her friends. The Cheshire Cat's smile was so vibrant, it lingered even after they were gone. The smile floated in the air like a wistful cloud. This had prompted Alice to remark that she had seen a cat without a grin but never a grin without a cat.

The imprint of the mana or power created by the synergy of their expression of their mutual joy had produced a grin without a cat.

Pastor spoke, breaking the spell. "My dear Lili, Puna will arrive in several hours. May I suggest you get a shower and put a little make-up on that pretty face of yours? *Fatherly* advice, you could say." He chuckled, rather amused at himself.

Suddenly, thunder boomed. Piercing lightning flashes followed, spiking the earth.

Kate shuddered. The storm was beginning. What would arrive? Was the mysterious mist here? Would it ultimately poison everyone?

Again, the sky lite up and thunder clapped. It was getting closer. Pastor prayed over the little girl as Kate waited for her young daughter to fully wake up.

Would she be cured of the deadly microorganism? Would she have any brain damage? Would her memory be intact? Would she know Kate and the others?

Would her little girl still be the same little girl that she was before this bug had invaded her brain?

Little Hannah mumbled again. Kate prayed too.

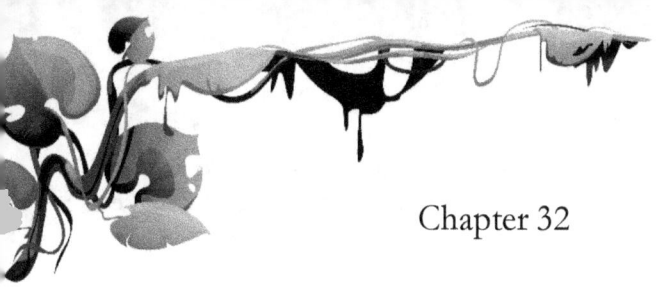

Chapter 32

Ka I ke kino

(Smites the body)

Lead by Luke, the children and the ever-obedient Max, left the caves and followed the pathway down the mountain. The late morning sun was high in the blue, cloudless sky. The notion that a storm and giant wave were coming seemed impossible on this bright, sunny day.

As they walked down the dirt path, David chattered away, sharing all kinds of information he had gleaned earlier from the internet on tsunami events. Since Hina did not speak, David was accustomed to filling the void. Luke was at the front of the motley crew, looking at everything, ever vigilant. Eventually, they came upon the haiku forest and, as directed, they followed the worn path until they reached the tall, ironwood tree with its gnarly branches. They seemed oblivious to the owl perched on a branch of the tree.

However, the owl was well aware of them.

"How much farther is it?" asked David, always impatient. He was hot, thirsty, and hungry. "I don't think it's too far now," replied Luke. He too was thirsty. He could see that Hina was

weary already. Her t-shirt was soaked with perspiration and her face flushed with the heat of the day. She looked very sad.

As they continued down the narrow, worn path, surrounding trees provided more shade, offering some relief from the heat. The gang was quiet, including Max. He marched on. It wasn't too long before they came upon the small stream. Max quickly ran into the cool stream and drank greedily from the waters. Right behind Max, the children took off their socks and shoes and followed suit. They drank the refreshing, cool water too.

"Luke, I'm ready for some food," declared David. Luke had been carrying the heavy backpack. "I'm starved! In fact, I could eat three hamburgers!"

"Alright already," said Luke. "And you know there's no burgers, right?" He left the cool stream and sat down under the shade of a tree. He took out their snacks. There was pineapple and mango, dried fish, taro chips (some of the last), beef jerky, and crunchy, seaweed salad.

Sweet and sour cherry candies had been added as a special treat.

David was quiet as he ate. The birds were chirping and the insects were buzzing over the stream. Summertime sounds. Happy sounds.

"I guess the orchids are nearby," stated Luke. He was finished eating and was now thinking about the task that they had come here for, the jewel orchids. They must do their best to help Kupuna Hannah.

"Where?" asked David.

"You stay here with Hina and I'll go find the location of the orchids." Luke stretched and then stood up. Max stirred and got up to follow his new master. They saw the continuation of the path and ambled down into a lush area of vegetation.

Suddenly, Max started barking like a mad hatter up into the branches of a nearby ironwood tree. What had got him so riled up?

Luke walked over to the tree. "What are you goin' on about Max?"

Max just barked more vigorously.

Luke looked up into the branches in the tree. He saw a large, eyes-wide owl perched on a branch.

The owl blinked.

Ka I ke kino.

Luke heard the voice of Amos. *Ka I ke kino. Smites the body.*

Luke understood the meaning of this Hawai'ian proverb. It is said of the evil done to others that rebounds and hurts the person who started it. In this case, Kanaloa had started it. His karma would hopefully be the end of him.

Son, you must collect the jewel orchids quickly. Evil is close by. I will protect you.

It really was the voice of Amos and, with great sadness; Luke realized that Amos was dead.

Now, he had returned as an aumakua. The owl-as-protector.

Max knew it was Amos too. Where was Peter?

Out of the corner of his eye, Luke spotted the vibrant, colored orchids to the left of the tree where Amos had taken up residence. What he didn't see were the two, red eyes glowing from under a bush to the right of him. Hiding in the darkness. Watching, waiting.

Quickly. Amos had told him to make haste in collecting the brightly-colored, rare flowers.

"Come on Max. Let's go get the others and pick the flowers," said Luke. He and Max turned away from the tree (and Amos), and returned to gather up the other children.

The boy who was claiming his manhood and the dog who was acting as a guardian hustled back to the spot where they had left Hina and David. A man and his dog.

Upon seeing Luke and Max, David jumped up and shouted, "We saw an owl and it talked to us!" Hina remained seated under the shady tree. Pining for her mother and little Hannah, Hina was suffering with depression and anticipatory anxiety. What would happen in the days ahead?

"Honest Luke!" declared David. He ran up to Luke. "It was Uncle Joe!"

"I believe you. What did the owl.... What did Joe say?" replied Luke. He appeared serious. "That we should hurry up....so let's go!" Hearing this, Hina stood up. She walked over to Max and petted the dog. Max licked her face, making her smile. This, in turn, made Luke smile. He was worried about his little sister.

"You're right David. Let's go get the orchids and head back."

While the children collected the flowers, Amos, the-owl-as-protector, stood guard. Amos was well aware of the nearby snake.

A snake in the grass.

Evil lurking about, waiting with great patience, to strike.

Chapter 33

Na Puke Wehewehe

(A death shroud)

While Pastor and Uncle Bert-the-lizard-as-protector watched over little Hannah, Kate stepped outside the hospital doors to catch a breath of fresh air. The day was hot and the air was heavy, the smell of smoke in the air. In addition, the air was pungent with the smell of dead animals rotting like apples on the ground. Looking out towards the ocean, Kate could see the approaching green mist.

The mist that Lili had described as toxic. *Deadly.*

A green shroud of death.

Kate felt overwhelmed by all that had already transpired and that which was about to unfold. Would Hannah be saved only to die in a deadly, green fog or from a destructive tsunami? Would she get to see her other two children again? And, what about Kimo? Kate sighed. There was so much uncertainty. She could only focus on her youngest daughter at this point. Little Hannah would be out of the induced hypothermic state in four more hours. What would her brain function be like? It was difficult to know what condition her mental status would be. The waiting was so hard.

Behind her, she could hear an EMT vehicle pull up to the emergency room, its siren abruptly silent upon its arrival. More and more people were falling ill with the mysterious ailment. The local funeral home was doin' a lively business. They had been conducting about four or five funeral services a day.

Kate could hear all the chaos in the emergency room as more people arrived. One young couple brought in their six-year old son who had the same affliction as Hannah. She prayed that the hypothermic state had worked to destroy the brain-eating parasite. For the sake of her daughter as well as the sons and daughters of the island's people, Kate truly hoped that this intervention would be the answer to all of their prayers.

Soon they would know.

A young, beautiful nurse came over and stood near Kate. Tall and fit, she was the picture of Hawaiian beauty, her long, shiny black hair swayed when she walked. She smiled and nodded towards Kate. Then, she took out a cigarette and lighter and fired up. She was on a break. Kate didn't recognize this nurse. She knew that they had recently hired some new grads.

As Kate reflected on the circumstances at hand, she heard wind chimes. She recalled that, during the days of the great tribulation, the sound of wind chimes signaled that divine entities were nearby. Angels waiting in the wings. Indeed, these were supernatural times.

Kate returned to keep her vigil by her daughter's side. As she entered the room, she heard

Lili and Pastor talking about arson and murder.

"The whole lodge was burned to the ground. 'Course, there are no more firemen in town and even if there were some guys around, the roads are so littered with dead animals….some of 'em large…. they couldn't get there anyways," said Pastor. "So, everyone perished."

"I heard that the bodies were reduced to bone fragments and ashes," replied Lili.

"It was started by some locals. They blame the tourists for bringing the disease, death and destruction that is plaguing their native home." Pastor shook his head in sorrow. Evil was afoot on their island, from the turquoise-blue ocean waters to the green, lush mountains. A hard battle lay ahead. That was the nature of trials and tribulations. It has been that way since the beginning of humanity.

Lili understood this too. She knew her people's history. She asked, "Pastor, in the end, will we prevail?"

"It depends on our ability to remain faithful. Clearly, the men who set out to harm the people at the lodge have abandoned their faith, becoming barren in hope and trust." Pastor was wise, knowing that some had already lost the battle against Satan, the great serpent known to Hawaiians as Kanaloa.

"I will remain faithful.... whatever the outcome," affirmed Lili. Pastor walked over and gave her a hug.

"Puna will arrive soon." Pastor hugged her tightly again. Despite her extreme fatigue, Lili was still a striking woman. Her flawless, cocoa-colored skin, her long, black hair and her large, dark eyes exemplified the beauty of the island's women. At the mention of Puna's name, Lili's cheeks flushed red and there was a twinkle in the dark pools of her eyes.

Kate chose that moment to enter the room. And, little Hannah chose that moment to mutter, "Mommy?" Kate rushed to her daughter's bedside. She was silent, sleeping soundly as she continued to warm up and return her body to its proper temperature.

Kate broke out in tears. They were tears of joy.

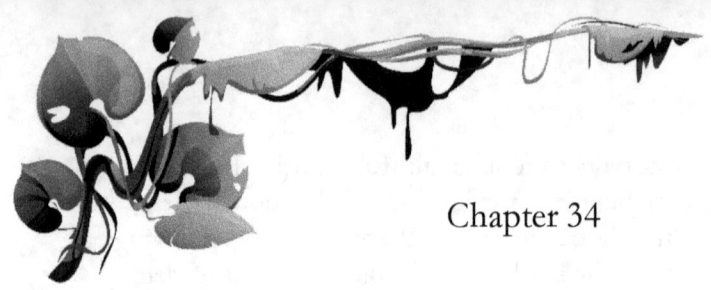

Chapter 34

Ke ahi a me ka pepehi kanaka

(Arson and murder)

Weary from their journey, Luke, Max and the gang returned to the safety of the sacred caves. Kimo was waiting for the children to return safely. He was aware that Kanaloa was in close proximity. He could hear David chattin' away like a noisy mynah bird as they approached the cave.

It was Hina who raced in first, quick as a cat. Rushing up to Kimo, she threw her arms around her father's waist. She was shaking and crying. Kimo picked the girl up and soothed her with his voice. He had a gentle voice, calming in tone and wise in words. He had a special ability to inject calm like an administered drug.

"There, there honey. You're okay," he whispered into the girl's hair as he held her close. Her hair smelled like the fragrant flowers. He could feel her shaking like a jellyfish. "Did something scare you?" Hina sobbed. Clearly, she was frightened. Because of her inability to use her verbal skills, it was difficult to know what was going on with Hina sometimes. This was one of those times.

Would she ever give voice to her fears?

David ran up to Kimo eager to talk about their encounter with Joe-the-owl-as-protector. He was oblivious to Hina's apparent distress.

"Whoa partner," said Kimo. He saw that Hina had stopped crying so he put her down.

Besides, she was getting heavy. The girl was growing.

"The owl talked to us but it was in our heads," David rambled on about the aumakua who had come to provide help to his people, including his younger brother, in these days of darkness. Aumakua's were really Hawai'ian angels in their native forms. Their participation was essential to beating this old enemy. Always has been, always will be.

It's only our faith that changes.

"I believe you David," said Kimo when the child calmed down. "These are supernatural times, like in the bible." He knew the boy was feeling anxious.

"Where is Uncle Ray?"

"He is with Kapuna Hannah." Kimo saw Luke enter the cave with Max, waggin' his tail, by his side. He'd fed Max a hearty meal. He was ready for his own meal.

He placed two weaved baskets full of the colorful jewel orchids on the floor of the cave.

"Son, it's good to see you," smiled Kimo. He could see the transformation of his boy into a man. A man of good character. He was so proud of the young man who came and hugged his father.

Like father, like son.

"Did something scare Hina? She was upset earlier." Kimo looked directly at Luke.

"Another aumakua visited me and told me Kanaloa was lurking around," said Luke in a matter-of-fact voice. "Dad, it was Amos."

"Amos?"

"He's dead, Dad."

"You're sure son?" Kimo wished he'd express doubt, a shred of uncertainty.

Kimo paused and took a deep inhalation of air because his lungs felt like they were filled with smoke. It was hard to breathe for a moment. He saw in his son's eyes the truth of his words.

Sadly, he closed his eyes and said a brief prayer and good-bye to his dear friend. As he prayed, tears slid down his face as he felt the loss. He had been like a brother to Kimo. A good man had crossed over to reap his rewards in heaven. Rewards that Amos had surely earned.

Kimo wondered: What had happened to Peter? Was he dead too?

"Dad. There's more."

Kimo braced himself. Was he going to tell him that Peter was now an aumakua too? But instead Peter said, "Amos said Kanaloa is nearby and he will strike soon."

"Yes son. I know." He slapped him on the back and said, "Come, get something to eat." Kimo called out to David and Hina who were talking (relating in Hina's case) to some of their friends. David was quick to share his encounter with Joe-the-owl-as-protector. Hina nodded as he spoke, affirming the tale being told.

Hina stood up and followed her father. Always hungry, David was fast behind her.

They walked over to the dining area. Spread out on the table, there was cooked meat, rice and sweet potatoes. And poi!

"Wow! I'm hungry and this looks so ono!" declared David as he pulled up a chair to the table.

As Luke and Hina took their seats at the table, there was the rumble of thunder in the distance. Max, who was lying at Luke's feet, began barking. In turn, Hina screamed, in fear of the coming storm. Was a giant wave approaching? How soon before it arrived?

Hina flew out of her chair and ran to Kimo. She wrapped her arms around Kimo's legs and buried her head in the bottom of his t-shirt. As he calmed her, he realized that the other children must be frightened as well.

The thunder boomed louder. Hina hugged Kimo tighter.

"Is the tidal wave coming now?" asked David. His dark eyes were wide and the tip of his ears had turned red. Fear was written all over his face. David set down his fork. He was no longer hungry.

"It may be but we're safe up here in the mountains in these sacred caves. No worries." Kimo smiled to reassure the children. Of course, Luke knew better.

Kekela entered the cave.

"Uncle Kekela!" the children said in unison. Hina left her father to hug her beloved uncle who seemed to really understand her. The blind man related well to the mute girl. They communicate via telepathy, which provided Hina with interactive communication. He hugged the girl tightly.

"How is Kupuna?" asked Luke. Kekela turned towards the young man who was going to be a great leader one day.

"She remains in a deep sleep state." Kekela announced, "We will gather around Kapuna at sunset to undo the spell."

"I am cleansed by the awa water. I will go now and pray until it is time to perform the ceremony. It is required." With that, Kimo left the cave.

As he left the dank cave, he was immediately struck by the oppressive heat. There was a blanket of hot, humid air. Often, it was precursor to a tsunami. He also smelt the distinct odor of electricity in the air. He looked towards the horizon and saw that the green mist was fast approaching.

The mist would kill them all if it came upon their island. How could they possibly stop it?

He had no idea.

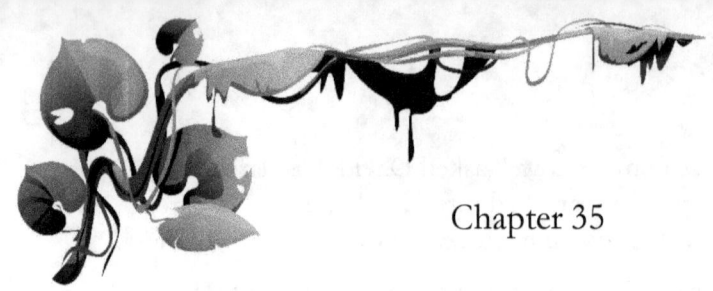

Chapter 35

He po Kane keia, he ma 'au nein a 'e 'epa o ka po.
(A joyousness is in the voice of love)

When he saw her, he drew in a quick breathe. She was so beautiful. Someday, she would make a beautiful bride. She hadn't noticed him yet, so Puna just stood still and took in her beauty. His heart was filled with both love and desire. He longed to make sweet love to her.

Lili must have felt his stare on her back, as she stood in the nursing station on the pediatric unit, because she turned and saw him. A bright smile broke out on her face. Her eyes lit up and her heart swooned. Dropping the medical chart in her hands, she rushed into his arms, overcome with her need to be close to him. She was overwhelmed with emotion. Tears were running down her cheeks.

"Lili, Lili, my love. I've missed you so much," cooed Puna. He could feel her crying gently.

"I need you Puna," she whispered. He pulled back and cupped her face. He knew that she had been through so much. She was an extraordinary woman.

"And I need you too, my love." He pressed his lips against hers and, then he probed with his tongue, kissing her deeply. Her body responded as she felt her breasts swell and her nipples became taut. She moaned into Puna's hair. He briefly pressed his hardness against her before he pulled back. This was not the place or the time.

But he would wait no longer to declare his deep and abiding love for her. His ardent desire for her to become his life-long partner.

"Lili, you know that I love you more than life. I want you to be my wife." He could smell the familiar green, mountain apple shampoo she used in her hair. He kissed the top of her head.

"I love you Puna, with all my heart and….."

Interrupted by a familiar voice, they drew apart.

"Pastor, good to see you," said the young man. Pastor embraced the young man who was the embodiment of strength and gentleness. It was this wise young man who had been chosen for an important task. It was he who held the future of the island's people in his sole ability to be successful with his important mission. He could not get distracted. Undoubtedly, Kanaloa would be implementing his own distractions.

"Son, we must leave at first light. "Pastor would sleep for several before their departure. He was feeling very much like a weary, old man. He would drink a double-dose of noni before they left.

Part of the urgency was the fact that Kapuna Hannah was under a potentially deadly spell cast by Kanaloa. He decided against telling Puna about his mother at this time. Let the boy enjoy his girl tonight because tomorrow their fate lay with this brave, young warrior.

"I understand Pastor. Shall we go eat together? Frankly, I'm starved!" After all he had hiked down a mountain today. It was almost past the dinner hour.

"Yes, of course! I have food in a room they have given me. It has a little kitchenette. I bet you wouldn't mind a hot meal, right son? Maybe even a hot shower?"

"You're answering my prayers!" Luke laughed. "Lili, can you take a break now?"

"I'll join you shortly. I must check on Hannah. She will hopefully be coming out of her coma soon." She kissed Puna's cheek and squeezed his hand. "Soon."

Pastor and Puna headed to the stairs and went two flights of stairs down. The room was adjacent to the maternity unit. Upon entering the room, the smell of garlic, ginger, shoyu and sizzling meat wafted out of the Pastor's on-site residence. Beef-vegetable stir fry! And rice! The room was small but it had all the comforts of home, including a shower. Before eating, Puna took a long, hot shower. As he soaped up, his thoughts were about Lili. It would be hard to say good-bye to her in the dawn hours. At least they would have tonight.

His heart bursting with love, he sang Hawai'ian love songs about his island girl.

The Hawaiian people made poetry by putting it to the rhythm and pattern of music. The Hawaiian music of poetry produces images that speak to our deepest feelings and give us great joy. In fact, they also delight! Traditionally, their magical music expresses the nobler of human emotions. Hawai'ian poetry expressed in music represents a transfiguration of life, portrayed with imagination and a representation of both the glories and tribulations of life.

These songs or *meles* move us with their ability to evoke vivid images of great beauty. It is true that the ancient Hawai'ians were naturally a poetic race in which their beautiful surroundings bred in them a feeling for the metaphors and symbolism of life.

Hawai'ians are naturally poetic. It's in their genetic make-up.

After his shower, Puna sat down at the small dining table. A fragrant white-pink, plumeria flower sat in a small glass of water in the center of the table.

While they ate, they remained quiet. However, much was transmitted between the man of the cloth and the young, budding Kahuna. Puna ate with a hearty appetite, eating seconds.

Pastor had saved the best for dessert. Haupia pudding! He loved coconut pudding!

Suddenly, thunder sounded like a booming cannon in the distance. Yes, time was of the essence.

For a period of time, these two great men prayed together. One old, one young. One mentor, one mentee.

O Kane, O Lord.

"Son, let's pule." They bowed their heads again in prayer.

The night sky clapped loudly with thunder. Or perhaps, one of the gods was offended. Was it Lono? Was it Kane?

Joining hands, Pastor offered the following prayer:

"O Kane in heaven; you of many shapes.
Invoke the powers inland, Invoke the powers at sea, Invoke our ancestors,
Invoke the powers to Kuhuna, Invoke the powers to Kupuna,
Invoke the wind (spirit) that is present.
O Kane, be strenuous, be brave, be courageous!
O Kane, be our savior."

As yet, Lili had not joined them. Pastor told Puna to go find his girl, claiming that he was tired and wanted to go to bed. It was not a false claim.

After saying good night, Pastor undressed and slipped between the cool, white sheets of his single bed. The clock on the nightstand read 9:56 p.m. On a full stomach, he quickly fell into a deep slumber.

Outside his small window, a Hawai'ian barn owl watched over him. Pastor knew that it was

Amos even in his dream state. His owl-as-protector.

He fell into a pokii dream.

In this dream, he was sitting atop a large, white horse. It was nighttime and tonight there was a red moon. A total lunar eclipse was high in the starless, night sky. Hawai'ians called it a blood moon. They believed that it was an ominous sign of some kind of approaching danger and also it announced the arrival of a horrible disease or plague. The horse was already out of the barn on the latter.

A blood moon was a bad omen. A very bad omen.

Crimson moon, green mist.

The world appeared supernatural, right out of a Stephen King movie, not only because of its eerie Christmas colors, but also because of the dark, gnarly dead trees that stuck out like scarecrows from a black and green-speckled beach. No animal sounds from the forest could be heard. There were no birds chirping, no animal noises. The earth smelt of rotting leaves (even in his dream). Pastor knew that this was a bad place. He wanted to get out of there. His heart was beating madly in his chest. Was he going to have a heart attack?

He dreamed of a dark and mysterious forest under the red moon. It was up ahead beside a dark pond. Steam arose from the stagnant, black body of water. Or whatever it was. Oil perhaps? Crude, slimy, slick oil. A bath that was surely fit for the great serpent.

At the pond, a man dressed in a black-hooded robe, sat on top of his large, black stallion, while the horse drank from the foul pond waters.

Despite an increasing heart rate, Pastor's horse galloped towards it undeterred. As he got closer, the air held the distinct odor of decay. He recognized the nauseating smell of decomposition. Surrounding the foul pond, he noticed small dead animals littering the area.

As they rode towards the pond, several bird-size cockroaches flew around Pastor's head.

Beady, little eyes glowed red in the dark. They made a loud, buzzing noise as they rubbed their furry, brown legs together. It produced a static, charged noise that continued to ramp up. They seemed to be buzzing a threat or dare.

You're God cannot protect you. Not here.

Pastor ignored them and prayed, evoking the name of Kane.

Kane will be destroyed by Kanaloa.

Pastor continued to pray.

The buzzing ceased. The vile creatures and their verbal assaults were gone.

Upon their arrival to the edge of the stinky smelling pond, the dark horse raised its head and glared at the Pastor. The horse's face was badly deformed. Its mouth was twisted and fangs hung down from its upper, purple-black lip that dripped with the crude oil. A large square jaw gave it a Halloween lantern appearance. The horse had beady, little red eyes that glowed with the fires of oil fields burning. Above his eyes, there were two little, sharp brown horns on the horse's bulging forehead.

Fire burst from the horse's nares. It was part dragon.

Then, the black-hooded man looked up and stared at Pastor. Red, glowing eyes set in the face of a corpse held Pastor in its cold gaze. Old, dried and wizened skin was pulled over the bony facial structures, giving it a skeletal look of a hungry soldier. But one had to ask oneself, hungry for what?

The hooded man grinned like a Cheshire cat.

Mason, soon you will see Napua. You must welcome death.

Pastor knew this voice. It was his old friend. Pastor laughed.

"You cannot trick me, Kanaloa."

It's no trick. Behold.

Shrouded in the green mist, a young woman walked out of the dark forest. She had long, black hair and moved like a dancer. Just like Napua, his beloved daughter, whom Kanaloa had destroyed during the days of the great tribulation. She swayed gracefully, like a hula dancer, as she stood in the faint edge of the mysterious green mist. It sparkled around her like green jewels caught in the rays of the sun. The young woman looked up and smiled. He would recognize that smile anywhere!

It *was* Napua!

Pastor called out to her. But, she had already turned away and was clouded by the green fog. He called out again, begging her to come back. He so missed his sweet Napua. He remembered the adorable, little girl that loved to chase crabs on the beach, laughing with delight! He recalled the day that she won her first hula competition. How proud she had been! Napua had brought so much joy and love into his life; he had been unable to completely come to terms with that loss. His heart was filling with great joy in the places in which joy was vacant.

Sweet Napua!

I can call her back, Mason.

With urgency, he cried, "Call her back then!"

I shall. Right away. Just as soon as you give me that gold key in your pocket.

"What? The key? No. No, I cannot hand over the key." Clearly, Kanaloa did not know that

Pastor had given the key to Peter for this very reason.

What is one gold key worth? Nothing compared to your daughter, Mason. Nothing.

"I must keep the key for some reason, although I can't exactly recall why that is." Pastor's head was filled with the sound of the buzzing noise of the large cockroaches. He was having difficulty thinking. He shook his head.

O Kane, O Lord.

Mason…… why not have your precious Napua with you in the years ahead? In your old age, you'll need her. You have surely earned it, Mason. You've paid your dues.

The sound of wind chimes filled the air in this eerily quiet land of darkness.

Mason snapped out of his muddled state. He could not allow Kanaloa to confuse him.

"You are right, my old friend. I have lived a life in service to my Lord and my people. I will continue to remain steadfast in my love for my Savior."

You have lost your mother, your wife, and your daughter in the name of this glorious service to a punitive god. You are a fool, my friend. I can offer you rewards, not sacrifices. I can give you back your family.

"No. You cannot. No more lies!" With that, Pastor stood tall and steady. The old, skeletal man turned and fled on his horse-dragon. His sour smiled lingered in the air, like the Cheshire Cat.

Suddenly, the sun emerged and the dark landscape turned into a beautiful field of jewel orchids, their vivid colors creating a quilt tapestry. As the sound of wind chimes rang out, an angelic woman with long, golden hair in ringlets, dressed in a jeweled white dress, floated down on a cloud and set herself down right before Pastor. Her cupid face and soft, blue eyes shone with the light of the Holy Spirit.

Heed my warning: one among you is possessed by an agent of Kanaloa. Seek to find the light in those close to you. Watch for a soul turned and darkened by the evil one.

Just as suddenly as she appeared, she quickly ascended on her cloud towards the heavens.

Pastor led his horse through the field of tropical flowers. In the distance, he heard the chatter of mynah birds.... all they do is talk, talk, talk! He saw a small, wild pig run under a shrub. Overhead, the blue sky was cloudless. It looked like a good day for a dip in the...

A loud knock at the door awakened him. It was dawn and Puna had arrived to gather him and take him up the mountain. Other town people would accompany them.

He knew an arduous day lay ahead. Undoubtedly, Kanaloa would make their journey difficult.

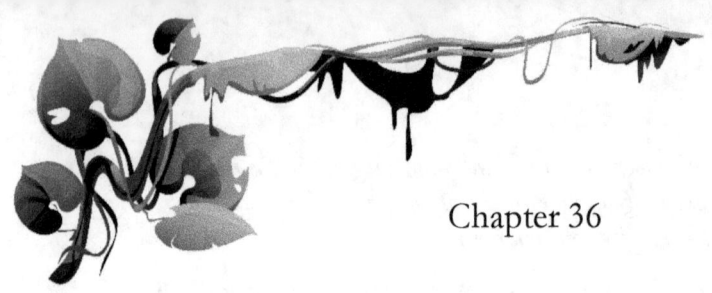

Chapter 36

'Olelo 'a ole hiki ke ho'ololi

(It's never too late to change)

Kate was bone tired but she felt restless as little Hannah's temperature approached normal.

She paced back and forth, wearing out the linoleum. Would she be the same little girl?

Hey, hey, hey, said Uncle Bert. *You're making me nervous! I can feel your anxiety comin' off you like a bad smell!* As a lizard, it was difficult to see Uncle Bert laughing but indeed he was!

His tail quivered and his feet danced. *I already told you Kate, Hannah's gonna be just fine. Mark my words.*

Little Hannah was quiet for the moment. Over the past several hours, she had been muttering intermittently. Twice, she had called out for Kate.

"I hope you're right," said Kate. "I just want my little girl back." Kate's voice breaking up she verbalized her heart's desire,"I want my whole family back." Now Kate's face was wet with tears.

"Mommy, mommy," mumbled Hannah. She remained sleeping peacefully, but this time, her small hand reached out and Kate rushed to take hold of it. She drew it to her lips and kissed it.

"I'm right here, baby."

Bert the-lizard climbed up the rails of the bed. He sat nearby Hannah, standing guard as though he was Napoleon. She wanted to laugh as she thought about asking him about car insurance. Unable to help herself, Kate smiled broadly at him. He was a changed soul.

With gratitude, she knew that he was instrumental in helping her daughter. His great-niece.

Uncle Bert had demonstrated that it was never too late to change. It was all about making a choice.

"She really is going to be okay," rejoiced Kate. More tears slid down her cheeks as she released some of the inner distress that she'd been feeling.

See, just what I said! I told you so. Oh, please don't cry anymore, Kate! Bert puffed out his chest and crossed his arms in an attempt to appear indignant. In his mortal life, no one had taken Bert seriously. Least of all, Kate.

Kate laughed at his attempt at grandstanding but really, did he forget he was a small, green lizard?

I heard that thought! Laugh all you want because..." He was cut off as the door opened and a nurse entered the room. It was time for her half-hourly nursing assessments on her medical condition. Kate recognized the tall, beautiful Hawaiian nurse that she had seen earlier. Looking in the place in which Bert had placed himself on the side rail near Hannah, she saw that Uncle Bert had disappeared.

"Hi. I'm Pua," said the stunning nurse. She seemed older than Kate had initially thought. She took the girl's temperature, checked her vital signs and oxygen saturation, and her level of consciousness using the Glasgow scale. She had either no response or a slow response to imposed stimuli. Her neurological status remained uncertain. It was probably too soon to tell.

"What's her temperature?" asked Kate.

"95.7," replied the nurse. "Another two hours or so before she's at her normal temperature." She smiled at Kate. This Hawai'ian woman was truly beautiful.

"Just two more hours," repeated Kate. *Two long hours.*

Hannah muttered something again. Kate turned her attention back to Hannah. Bert was back on the scene, right beside Hannah.

That nurse was a looker! Curves, ruby lips, and those long legs! She's like a goddess!

"Once a man, always a man, even if the man is a lizard!" replied Kate.

I can still appreciate a beautiful woman.

"And I can appreciate a good uncle," responded Kate.

Ah shucks! Bert did a little dance shuffle.

Boom! Boom!

Loud thunder shattered the night. Windows shook and the lights and monitors flickered.

Hannah muttered something under her breath. Kate soothed her little girl with comforting words. Hannah's eyes fluttered and opened for a brief moment. She was coming out of the drug-induced coma. Kate's heart rejoiced by speeding up, giving her a dose of hope and therefore, a burst of energy. Hope was the fuel that sustained her heart.

Zippity-do-da; zippity-day! Bert was dancin' again.

Kate was reminded that Pastor and Puna would be heading up the mountain in the morning.

Everyone's future rested on their success to make the journey up the mountain to the sacred caves. Both the pastor and the gold key were requisites to defeating Kanaloa. For this was ordained.

The stormy weather that was present had undoubtedly been orchestrated by Kanaloa. The great serpent would have a whole bag of tricks. All of them would be potentially lethal.

Tomorrow would be a very dangerous day for the old preacher and the young warrior man and their motley crew.

They will face great danger, echoed Bert, reading her thoughts. Their faith would be tested.

"Will they prevail? Do you know that Uncle?" Kate longed to know the outcome. Would she see her family again? That was the real question.

Even if I know what the future holds, my dear, I cannot tell you.

"What did you say? You know but you won't tell me…… why Uncle?"

Though now for a little while you may have to suffer various trials, so that the genuineness of your faith, more precious than gold which though perishable is tested by fire, may rebound to praise and honor at the revelation of Jesus Christ (The First Letter of Peter, 1: 6-7).

"As the outcome of your faith, you obtain the salvation of your souls," Kate replied, quoting verse 9 of First Peter. Maybe Uncle Bert wasn't just a caring clown. He had indeed been transformed…. into a True Believer.

Transformed into a living entity that strived to perform good deeds in His name.

Reminded of the need to remain steadfast in her faith, Kate knew it wasn't just up to her.

The collective group of the island people must remain faithful and the arson and murders at the lodge by some of the local men had abandoned their faith. These minions of Satan saw opportunity in the great tragedies that were occurring during these turbulent days. Rumor had it that before they set the fire, they robbed the "rich bastards." Money, jewelry, and credit cards are what they traded for their souls.

Shiny objects, lust for monetary rewards, and the fulfillment of their dark, wicked desires cost them an everlasting life in a heavenly paradise. In their cases, Satan had claimed them, increasing his legions.

In the distance, the horizon was aglow with the neon-green mist, appearing very much like the bright, northern lights seen in northern lands.

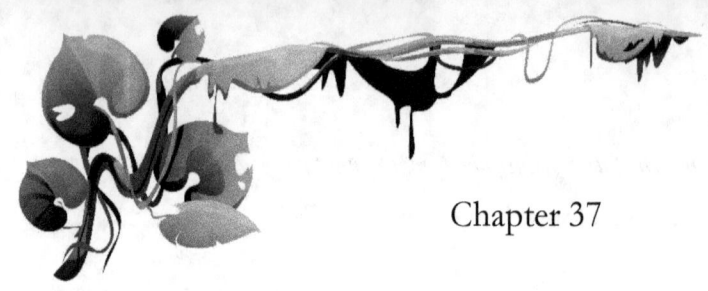

Chapter 37

Alaka'i

(A strong leader)

As the day drew to its end up in the mountain, the sun began to set in the eastern sky, creating a magenta sunset initially. Then the neon-green mist took over and the sky glowed, like emeralds reflecting the moonlight. An almost full moon shone tonight.

The acrid smell of electricity hung in the charged air.

It was time to perform the ceremony to undo the spell casted on Kapuna Hannah. It was an eerie time.

It was eerily silent. No evening noises. No mynah birds chattering away and they so love to talk it up at the sunset hour. No animal sounds whatsoever.

Utter silence. Not even the sound of the wind in the trees could be heard.

Kimo had gathered the people together outside the cave in which the high priestess slept.

Their faces wore the mask of grave concern. Kupuna Hannah was a beloved figure in their lives. They joined hands, bowed their heads and began to pule. Only the voices of the Hawai'ian people could be heard. A prayer to Kane spoke of the peoples' heartfelt petition to lift the evil spell that was cast on their wise and kind Kapuna:

E Kane-i-ka-opua,

O Kane-of-the-clouds-on-the-horizon, Hear our petition,

Heal our Kupuna,

Exorcise the evil demon in her.

Return our Kupuna to her people.

E Kane-i-ka-opua.

Amene.

Suddenly, a flock of noisy mynah birds circled overhead. Clearly, a sign from Kane. Thunder rumbled in the distance.

Kimo asked that they continue to pule while the others performed the appropriate rituals to rid Kapuna of the evil that had a hold on her. Fortunately, Hannah was a woman of great faith. And Kimo was a great leader of his people.

Kimo entered the sacred cave and headed towards the area where Kapuna lay in her deep sleep. The cave was dark and, therefore, lanterns glowed in the darkness providing a soft illumination. Around Kapuna Hannah's resting place, the others were standing, waiting for Kimo. Kekela, Ray, Luke, David, and Hina stood with solemn look on their faces and in their demeanor. Max was there too. He was still also, picking up on the humans' mood.

Beside Hannah's makeshift bed, the tapa matt that had been dipped into the awa water rested. The vivid jewel orchids surrounded Hannah's bed, creating a fragrant odor in an otherwise dank-smelling cave. Sage burned nearby in an effort to ward off evil spirits. The stage had been set to perform the appropriate ceremony.

Kimo stepped onto the tapa matt that had been made holy through the anointment of awa water.

The rest of the group took their places around Kupuna's bed. They joined hands and closed their eyes. They felt a vibrating hum when they connected with one and other. Instantly, their hands warmed. The bond that they had formed was strong.

Kimo cited the proper chant required to rescue Kupuna from the evil spirit residing within her, trying to take up residence in her soul:

There is casting off!

I am casting thee off!

Do not come to possess this spirit again.

For she is Kupuna, powerful in mana,

Let her not be a seat for thee again.

Do not try to know her again.

For she is Kupuna, a keeper of knowledge,

Go and seek some other medium for thyself in another home.

Let it not be she, not at all.

For she is Kupuna, blessed by the Holy Spirit,

I cast thee off for I am weary of thee!

I cast thee off, for I am not afraid of thee!

I cast the off, for I am expelling thee!

Behold my family, stricken with illness.

Thou are taking them.

Thou art a terrible man-devouring god!

In the name of Kane, I cast thee off!

(Adapted from Luomala, Katherine. (1986) Voices on the Wind: Polynesian Myths and Chants. Honolulu: Bishop Museum Press, p.65)

Hannah remained in a deep sleep. She did not stir. The chant was repeated.

A surge of energy filled the room. The air was charged.

Thunder boomed as the storm moved closer. Flashes of lightning spiked into the ocean waters, lighting up the night sky. A strong wind entered into the cave and caused objects to fly around the enclosure. A white plastic bucket flew about, hitting Luke in the head. Grunting, he almost let go of Hina's hand.

Almost.

Coming out of nowhere, a very loud, buzzing noise was heard. A most disturbing sound.

Large cockroaches, rubbing their hairy, brown legs together, flew around the children's heads, attempting to scare them into breaking the circle. None of them landed on this now sacred place. Yet despite their fear, the children did not break the circle that they had created by holding hands. Little Hina cried out and Luke held on tightly to her small hand. Were these mutant cockroaches the pestilence that Kekela had spoken about?

Hina, don't let go of Luke's hand or mine! Kekela transmitted the message via telepathy, as that was how they communicated with each other. *And don't open your eyes!*

Boom! Boom!

The thunder was so close that it shook Kupuna's bed. The ground underneath the troop's feet also shook. It was an attempt to throw them off balance. A failed attempt. However, Kanaloa was intent on not allowing the spell that he had cast on the powerful Kupuna to be lifted. He needed her out of commission if he was to prevail in the battle against Kane and his True Believers.

It was at this moment when Hannah began to stir. She mumbled something that was incoherent. Kupuna was coming out of her deep sleep! She briefly raised her right hand and placed it over her heart. She signaled to them that her heart had prevailed through its love of her people and the Lord.

Rejoice! Rejoice!

The ceremony had been successful!

Smiles graced the faces of the people who surrounded her. People who loved her dearly.

There was virtually no one in their community who did not hold Kupuna Hannah in the highest regard. Her loss was inconceivable.

Brave little Hina had not succumbed to her fears and, therefore, she had not been distracted. But this was not the case with David.

Kanaloa had gotten into his head. After all, he had been in David's head on several previous occasions.

Using his most powerful weapon – discouragement – he found access to David's head.

You know that you are a weak little boy. Like a baby, in fact. Boy, you are a sissy!

Kanaloa continued to taunt the boy. With glee, I might add.

You are nothin' David. A big, fat zero! You will grow into a weak man. Nothin' like Ray. You are a stupid, ugly, weak boy who will amount to nothing. You are nothin', orphan boy! These people only put up with you because they have to – they pity you. They don't really care for you. How could they, you disgusting boy?

David was vulnerable to these negative assertions. He was just a young boy after all. Indeed, he was an insecure, little boy who had experienced too much loss in too few years. Both of his parents had perished during the terrible days of the great tribulation.

Baby David! Baby David! Just a little wuss! Big baby! Big wuss!

Suddenly, David shouted out loud, "I'm not a baby! I'm not a wuss!" His eyes snapped open.

He saw the yellow-spotted, black snake, with the frightening red-glowing eyes, nearby. The Great Serpent.

David released his hand from Kekela's hand as he raised a small, angry fist at the apparition.

The circle was broken.

Immediately, the warm vibrations they had been experiencing in their hands when the circle was intact ceased.

With their eyes open, they could see that Kupuna Hannah lay very still in the bed. She uttered nothing.

She remained in a deep sleep.

David fell to the ground and sobbed, "I'm sorry! I'm sorry!" Kanaloa had successfully employed his most potent weapon. "Kupuna, I'm sorry! So very sorry."

David surely felt discouraged. As did the others.

Fortunately, there was a way to protect against discouragement. And the way was contained in the Word.

If you abide in me, and my words abide in you, ask whatever you will, and it shall be done for you. (John 15:7).

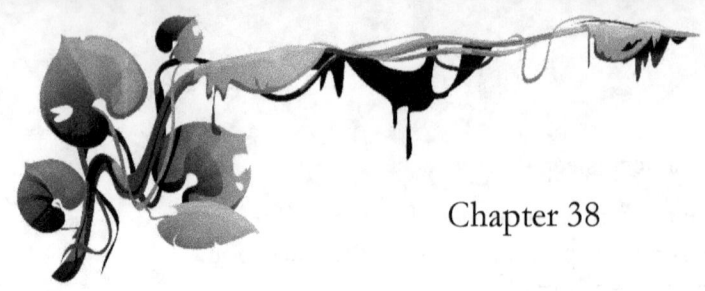

Chapter 38

Hana mana

(A miracle)

While Kupuna Hannah was in a deep sleep state, little Hannah was emerging from her drug-induced coma. Her present temperature was 98.1 F. She was moving her arms and legs in the bed. Clearly, she had some motor control.

A very good sign.

She was speaking more clearly when she muttered something. Kate heard her sweet girl call for her more than a couple of times. She sounded like she always had, before the brain infection. She sounded like her little Hannah!

Another very good sign.

Pastor would be asleep by now. She wanted to share her joy with him but it would have to wait.

Kakalina entered the room, smiling warmly at Kate. She had grown attached to little Hannah and her devoted mother. Before the little girl became ill, Kakalina had always admired Kate's nursing skills. For years, Kate had been a role model among her nursing peers. Trailing behind her was the new nurse, Pua.

"She's waking up." Kakalina moved to little Hannah's bed, examining her and checking the output measures on the monitors. Her heart rate was regular and her blood pressure was normal. Her oxygen saturation was at 100%. Her skin color was no longer blue-tinged, but rather, it was now a pink-hue color. Pink skin, including fingertips and toes, offered evidence of both warm blood and good circulation that was being pumped by a healthy heart.

After auscultating heart, lung and bowel sounds, Kakalina asserted, "She seems just fine.

Absolutely fine! It's amazing! Truly amazing!" Kakalina was bursting with excitement, her cheeks flushed and her dark, large pupils showed that she was on an adrenaline high.

"She's such a beautiful girl. A sweet, innocent little soul," said Pua as she gazed upon the small child. She shook her head and exclaimed, "It's a miracle!"

"Yes it is. It's a real miracle!" beamed Kate who couldn't contain herself. Right at this moment, her exhaustion was forgotten. She felt like she was dancin' on the ceiling! As a matter of fact, she felt like Uncle Bert!

Zippity-do-da! Zippity-day!

"Kimo, our little girl is going to be okay," she whispered to herself. "I wish I could tell you."

A familiar voice answered inside her head. It whispered, *"I will tell him. I promise."*

Kekela would keep that promise.

Hannah stirred some more and, again, her small, pink hand reached out as she called for her mother quietly. Next, the little girl's hand moved more vigorously. She moaned and suddenly, her eyes fluttered and, for a brief moment, opened and looked directly at Kate. Then, she cried out, "Mommy! Mommy!"

"Honey, I'm right here! Baby, I'm right here!" Kate spoke with tears pooling in her azure-blue eyes. Her daughter's eyes were the same color. She was a little version of Kate.

However, Hannah had already closed her eyes and drifted back to sleep. She looked comfortable, in no apparent distress. Her baby girl looked so peaceful.

"She looks so peaceful," echoed Pua.

"Doesn't she?" responded Kakalina, her broad smile lighting her angelic face.

"You must be so relieved, Mrs. Kanekoa," said Pua, grinning from ear to ear.

"Kate. Please, call me Kate." Kate told her, "We're all family here." Certainly, that was true for Kate. She would never have survived this ordeal without the support and generosity of spirit that these caring people had shown. All of them. Kakalina, Lili, Pastor, Amos, who had lost so much, Dr. Fukina, Kekela, and, of course, Uncle Bert....all of them. Her gratitude knew no bounds. Unbreakable bonds had been forged.

Overwhelmed with gratitude, she said to the two nurses,"I feel compelled to say a prayer of gratitude to our Lord. Will you pray with me?"

The smile on Pua's face disappeared and Kate noticed that her smile had never really reached her eyes. Rather, she wore a wicked sneer that gave her a sinister appearance.

Kate felt frightened. What was going on?

"Pray? No, I don't think so!" She laughed. It sounded like a cackle. "That's not who I worship." She leered at Kate, sending a chill down her spine.

Quickly, she turned to Kakalina.

Kakalina was unhooking the intravenous lines and detaching the probes that hooked up to the monitors. The beep-beep sound ceased.

Little Hannah slept soundly, despite the noise and movement at the bedside.

Stunned and confused, Kate yelled, "What are you doing?!!"

Kakalina turned and, with glazed eyes, she looked directly at Kate and in a matter-of-fact voice said, "I'm getting her ready for transport." She looked both crazed and chillingly calm.

Without a doubt, she was detached from her true self as though she was in a dissociative state. What was wrong with Kakalina?

Clearly, something nefarious was going on here. Terror ceased her heart.

"Kakalina, what's wrong with you? Snap out of it!! Are you on drugs? For God's sake, what is wrong with you! Stop!" Kate cried out. "Please, don't take my little girl away!" screamed a distraught Kate. "I'm begging you, leave my little girl alone!"

"I want her!" shouted Pua. "And I will have her!" "Who are you? Why do you want my child?"

"*I am Haumea!*" The sea goddess had taken on her human form. Over the centuries, she had done it many times. Just as she had lusted after Peter's soul that day in the ocean, she now wanted the soul of this young, innocent girl. She had drugged Kakalina and then she had taken over the control of her mind. She now served Pua. The tactic of brainwashing the nurse in order to get access to the child had worked beautifully.

"I am the greatest goddess in the islands!"

Haumea was engaging in the practice called *the kahuna ho 'ounauna* or the delivery of terrible trouble. In ancient Hawai'ian chants, Haumea is described as the goddess of mysterious forms, of eightfold forms, of four hundred thousand forms! Haumea is *kino lau* (many bodies).

"I am here in service to Kanaloa." She did not deny that she worshiped Satan and assisted him in his mission to destroy these weak people.

"Why my daughter?" asked Kate.

"Because she is very special. Kanaloa believes that she is an earth angel. One who is an agent of the Lord here on earth."

"I won't let you take her. You'll have to kill me first!"

"Then so be it."

Kate began to move closer to Hannah but Kakalina stopped her. She already had her hands on the sleeping girl. Had they given Hannah drugs?

With her warrior face on, Haumea moved closer to Kate.

"Kakalina, get the girl out of here. I'll take care of Kate. Meet me at the side door of the morgue. Go!"

"Nooo! Stop! Don't take her! She's my baby!" Kate grabbed for Hannah but it was too late. Kakalina had already picked the limp girl up and headed towards the door.

Kate screamed again. Why didn't anyone hear her?

Haumea prevented Kate from getting to the door by blocking her way. As a goddess, she was physically strong making it easy to hold Kate back. Her grip was like a vice. She whispered the unholy things she intended to do to this earth angel. Acts of cruelty were described to Kate in detail. The intent to damage the pious woman's soul had been successful. Haumea was a cruel woman with a sadistic streak in human force, like the wicked witch of the west. Except she wanted more than Dorothy's dog.

"Noooooo!!" screamed Kate. "Help me! Somebody help me!"

"Hurry up Kakalina! Get the girl outta here!"

But Kakalina was struggling to open the door. She had laid the sleeping girl down on the cold floor as she fought to get the door open. She did not stir.

"I can't get the door open!" grunted Kakalina, her face getting red. She pulled on the doorknob with all her might, but, to no avail. Perhaps they had been locked in.

"Open the fucking door, Kakalina!" screamed Haumea. She was also short-tempered in her human form. A quick-to-anger personality type.

"It won't budge," stated Kakalina.

Wisps of white fog began to drift up from under the door. The sound of wind chimes floated up too.

As it drifted upwards, its tendrils reached out to little Hannah. The tau sign reappeared on her forehead and began pulsating again.

Suddenly, the door opened.

A young, blond man entered the room.

"Peter?" asked Kate in disbelief. He was whole and healthy!

"Yes, Aunt Kate, it's me," responded Peter.

Haumea turned on a dime. When she saw the young man, she knew he held the great power of white light. She could not defeat this holy man. Not even her pa-u, with its white rays that emitted a paralyzing and deadly effect, could match the light that this man emitted. He had been blessed with God's grace.

She conceded defeat.

But, it was too late for that because Peter had already thrown awa water on her and she dissolved into a puddle of ashes. A foul odor emanated from the puddle.

Unfortunately, Haumea's spirit had already fled.

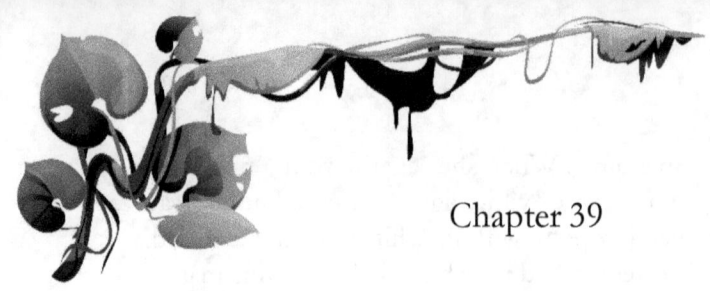

Chapter 39

Loa kea la e hele 'ia.

(Long the path being traveled)

As the dawn broke, Pastor and Puna left for their arduous journey. It was a tender farewell that brought tears to the three who cared deeply for each. One man, as a father, the other man, a lover. Lili sighed.

The day was overcast. Despite the early hours, the thunder and lightning persisted in the early morning hours, making the clouds shimmer with silver. The air was heavy with moisture. In the near distance, the green mist rose up from the waters like steam.

The dawning of the day was a forecast of the remaining hours that lay ahead.

Pastor was riding on a donkey that also carried their provisions, including awa water. Puna, lead the way.

Under gray skies, they headed up the red dirt path. Their very own yellow brick road.

After several miles, they came upon a group of wild, baby pigs crossing the trail. Right away, Puna was on alert for the appearance of Haumea after his last encounter with the malicious goddess and her vicious pigs. He looked up at a nearby breadfruit tree, her favorite haunt.

Haumea was nowhere to be seen.

She who had so many, mysterious forms could be anywhere. She could be up in a tree, in the ocean, but, certainly not in the sky. It was far too close to the heavens. She could be in human form, or as a breadfruit tree, or an animal, or as a vegetable. Basically, she could be anywhere and be anything!

Puna remained ever vigilant.

Wherever she was, Haumea was engaged in the practice, *kahuna ho'ounauna*, or making trouble or causing sickness. And she always acted in the service of Satan.

They paused on the path to allow the pigs to pass.

"Pastor, you thirsty?" asked Puna. He could see the sweat pouring off the older man. The day was hot and humid. The air was still, with no noticeable breeze to offer some relief. Puna started feeling really itchy.

"I could use some water," he replied. He wiped his brow, slick with perspiration. He wore a large sombrero-style hat. Puna grabbed a water bottle out of the back pack that was also being hauled by the dutiful donkey.

He handed the pastor the water bottle and pastor drank with great thirst.

"Thank you, son." He smiled at the handsome, young man. He would be a good husband for

Lili.

It was Puna's turn to drink. When he had quenched his thirst, he said, "We will take a break up ahead at the pond and find some shade."

"I hope that includes some of the food that Lili prepared for us, back at the hospital." Pastor was known for his appetite. The church ladies were always dropping off casseroles, dinners, cakes, puddings, sweet bread, fresh fruits and vegetables and fresh fish after a big catch.

Puna laughed. "Of course, Pastor. After all, we need to keep up our strength. The long day looms ahead."

What else loomed ahead?

As they continued on their way, they were quiet. The noises of insects buzzing around, birds chirping, and chickens clucking were the only sounds to be heard this morning. Soon, they came upon a grove of Norfolk Island evergreen trees and a small pond. It was a good place to rest and eat, since Pastor was clearly hungry. Beside the pond, was a grassy bank that offered shady place on the hot day. They would rest in this spot. Truthfully, Puna was really hungry too!

After getting off the donkey, Pastor took it up to the pond where it drank mightily. Then he tied the animal to a tree that also offered shade.

Wearily, he sat down under the tree. Puna was getting the backpack off the donkey's back.

He too sat down.

"Well, Pastor…. I think we got some taro bread and cooked meat, and some seaweed salad…oh, and some dried fish." Puna smiled at the older man, with his deep-lined face and dark-weathered skin, covered in age spots, after years of living in the tropics. Pastor has lived a difficult life, yet he has always remained a man of God.

As a boy, he worked in the sugar cane field which was hot, labor-intensive work. He was raised on the plantation by his mother and grandfather. His father had died of a fatal case of appendicitis when Mason was a young man, around Puna's age.

"Sounds good, son." Pastor took out a handkerchief from his shirt pocket and wiped his wet brow. "Got any cake in there?"

"Lili wouldn't forget your sweet tooth." Puna laughed. "There's banana cake and lilikoi mochi." Mochi is like sweet candy that is similar to toffee. Very tasty! Of course, it was one of his favorites.

"Any kim chee?" Pastor loved pickled cabbage.

"She didn't forget that either." Puna took out the food items, two plastic plates, and chopsticks. After filling up their plates, they ate quietly.

The sun was breaking through the gray dawn. The thunder and lightning was long gone. It was very peaceful, much like the calm before the storm.

Each had that unspoken thought.

Each knew a storm was coming.

Each sought refuge in unspoken prayers.

Puna reached into the backpack and took out a thermos of coffee. Pastor beamed.

"It must be time for some of that banana cake!" Puna passed him a cup of black coffee and a piece of Lili's delicious cake.

"Your Lili is quite a woman, Puna!"

"Yes sir. You don't have to tell me that. I know I'm a lucky guy." Puna sighed as he thought about his woman, his soon-to-be wife.

Pastor set his cup and plate down, satisfied and somewhat sleepy. He closed his eyes for a moment. Just to rest, of course.

Immediately, he fell asleep.

And, immediately, he had a *pokii* dream. A familiar friend appeared on the path as they climbed higher towards the sacred caves. Amos, who rarely smiled while on this earthly plane, smiled widely and waved. He lumbered along as only Amos could, but without his slight limp that was an injury from the Vietnam War.

"Amos!" greeted Pastor as he approached. "Pastor, good to see you, my friend!"

Pastor looked at Amos and saw that his eyes glowed with a radiant, brilliant white light. The Holy Spirit shone within him.

I lele no kalupe I ke pola.

Pastor thought of the warning being offered: *Do not ignore small things.*

"I'll be watchful," replied Amos.

Umi ia, I nui kea ho.

Pastor grinned. Amos had encouraged Pastor and said, *Hold on and take a long breath.* He grinned warmly at his friend again. It would appear that heaven suited him.

Amos turned around on the path and began to recede down the mountain until he seemed to just disappear. The thing was his wide-beamed, 100-watt smile lingered like the Cheshire Cat who was there no more.

Pastor felt something crawling up his leg. It caused him to wake up. In fact, up in the bottom of his trousers he could feel several bugs heading north. He hoped it wasn't centipedes. Their stings were painful and lingered like a bad toothache.

Sure enough, he was bitten. And, it was a doozy! He yelped and became fully awake.

Then, again…a nasty bite! Yiks!

Puna, who was over by the pond, turned around. He was trying to put the cool awa water on his back where he had several centipede bites.

"What Pastor? You okay?" asked Puna. He rushed over to Pastor who was yelping some more. He was hopping around and screaming!

"What's goin' on?"

"Centipedes! There's more than a few in my pants!" he cried out. "Take your pants off!" exclaimed Puna. "Take 'em off!"

As Pastor dropped his trousers, dark, brown-black beetles were running up and down both of his legs, leaving bloody trails in their wake. They were unusually large. He noticed their long legs. But, he was terrified by what he saw next. They were sinking their gnarly mouths into Pastor's legs as though he was a dinner of legs of lamb.

What the hell were these creatures?

"Is it centipedes?" Pastor asked gasping, as he whisked them away, off his bloody legs. "No, It's not. It's beetles!" Puna had never seen beetles attack a human. He'd never heard of it either. These bark beetles, that had infested the evergreen trees, were gnawing on

Pastor's legs! There were small gashes up and down his legs, a series of bites exacted.

Eating the flesh of his legs!

These beetles had become little cannibals!

He took of his t-shirt and began hitting Pastor's legs to get them off but they were sturdy, little pests who seem to have some kind of teeth that they were using to chew through the skin and, then, into the muscle.

Finally, Puna was able to get them off the old man whose legs looked like a set of bones that dogs had gotten a hold of.

There were deep gnashes on both of his lower legs. They were worse on the left side and Pastor would need to stay off his legs as much as possible. Normally, he would need to get stitches. Not today.

The needed medical supplies, including antibiotics, were available at the caves. Everything depended on them making it to the caves. They must keep on, despite set-backs like this beetle attack orchestrated by Kanaloa.

"Wait Pastor! I'll go wet my t-shirt and clean you up." Puna stared in disbelief at the damage that these aggressive beetles had inflicted.

It looked bad. There were broken blood vessels that would lead to massive bruising and the subsequent risk of traveling blood clots, especially in an elderly person who was riding a donkey for hours in the hot sun.

He walked down to the water's edge. Dipping the shirt in the water, he heard Pastor yell.

"There's more! There's a whole army of them coming! Pastor pointed to the right of Puna.

Puna looked and saw hundreds of the beetles marching out of the grove of Norfolk Island evergreen trees and marching towards the slope of the streambed banks. They were like an army of beetle soldiers approaching.

Their deadly weapon was a mouth that was able to cannibalize a man. When a blanket of them covered a man, they consumed a human in less than 5 minutes.

In the sunlight, one could see microscopic flecks of green on their dark, hard-shelled forewings, called elytra, which serve to protect the delicate hindwings beneath them. This was the place where they were vulnerable.

Their mouth parts had changed.

They had very large, wide mouths lined with sharp, small fangs. Rat-mouths. Their small eyes glowed red. Rat-eyes.

Usually, predatory beetles attack other vertebrates in the vegetation and soil. Parasitic beetles may live on other insects or mammals. But not humans.

Never humans!

Unless, of course, they were dead humans. Beetles are used by forensic entomologists to determine the time of death in homicide investigations. Beetles do consume dead humans, but not live ones.

Until now.

Puna turned and rushed up the bank to gather up Pastor and their provisions. Pastor had put his pants on over his bloody legs that were beginning to throb. He had trouble bearing weight on them.

He didn't think that he could go on.

Puna ran up and scooped the old man up and placed him on the donkey. He untied the ass and slapped him, sending the donkey and his passenger up the mountain. Pastor protested all

the way, wanting the boy to run ahead. But the brave warrior knew that that the Pastor must be safe at all costs.

Pastor remembered something important. He needed to get the gold key from Peter!

"Son, you must get the key!" he called out. Puna ignored him as he understood that the preacher was as important as the godly, gold key. Both were needed.

The beetles marched on at a faster pace, their increasing mass giving them momentum. Faster and faster, they moved on.

Puna cried out, "O Kane, help us against these pestilence! Sent from the devil himself!"

He began to chant, *E Kane-i-ka-opua. O Kane–of-the-clouds-on-the-horizon.* Help us! Thunder rumbled like a runaway train. The gray, heavy clouds darkened.

Large, hard hailstones fell from the sky, like a torrential downpour during a tropical storm.

They beat down on the band of beetles, yet their hard shells seemed impervious to the golf-ball size weapons. Or so it seemed.

Until, the smoke began to rise off the backs of the mutated creatures. They were sizzling like bacon in a frying pan. The noxious odor of burnt rubber filled the air.

The hail was formed out of awa water. It was the work of the *awa-iku,* or the spirits of Kane, who perform good deeds on his behalf. They had been dispatched by Kane to act against the *mu* spirits or evil entities that Kanaloa had clearly dispatched to foil the strategy by Kane to send the evil one back to the pit where he would be locked up for another fifty years. These two agents of Kane were essential to that plan in accordance with the scriptures.

Awa water delivered by the awa-iku was no match for the mutated, destructive pestilence. Awa water had defeated Kanaloa in the past and so it would again.

Praise to Kane!

The cloudy skies cleared up and the sun came out.

A rainbow graced the sky and God's promise remained.

Ka 'onohi wai anuenue. The rainbow patch, water, rainbow.

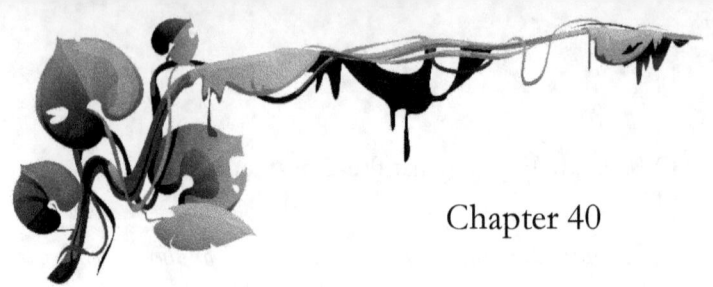

Chapter 40

He kua anoano mehameha kanaka ʻole.

(A lonely, awe inspiring god: not a man)

Gathered inside the hospital cafeteria, people surrounded Peter, clamoring to see and touch him. Word of his miraculous recovery had spread like wildfire in taro fields affected by drought. Quickly, folks had gathered around him as whispers of the second coming were murmured.

Peter stood tall, healthy and whole in the back of the room. His blond hair was no longer burned but rather, it shone like the sun touching a field of wheat. His handsome face was healed and his hazel eyes shone brightly. Love shone in those eyes. His beautiful smile, so much like his mother, radiated from his open and inviting face, giving joy to all who were in attendance. The Holy Spirit was present because the room was filled with True Believers who had demonstrated steadfast faithfulness during these dark days.

Hence, the room became a holy place.

Furthermore, it was no coincidence that they had come together at this particular time and in this particular place.

Proudly, Peter's grandmother stood beside him, dressed in gratitude and joy. Her long, gray hair was in a braid on top of her head. It was obvious where Peter got his hazel eyes. She looked older than her 64 years from years of hard labor in the sugar cane fields. Despite her recent grief over the loss of her son, Amos, she carried herself with pride, standing tall and erect. The cotton dress she wore was crisp and clean, despite the torrid heat of the day.

"Peter, tell us! Are you the second coming of Christ?" asked an older Chinese-Hawai'ian man who had worked at the hospital as an accountant for decades. He was close to retirement.

"No, Mr. Wong. I am not our Lord."

"But, you were healed by Him, right?" asked a nurse named Laenihi from the I.C.U. The room was so quiet you could hear a pin drop. "Isn't it true that God performed a miracle?"

"Or was it an angel?" shouted another. "Did an angel heal you, son?"

"It was the Almighty!" The group was getting all worked up. "It was the Lord! He performed a real-life miracle!" Voices rose in exaltation.

"It is a miracle performed by Him," wept an older woman as she crossed herself. In her arms, she held her newest grandchild. She whispered blessings upon the child.

"That is for you to decide," responded Peter. Dissatisfied with that answer, the people in the room began to mutter amongst themselves.

"But, you must know. Did you see God?" yelled a woman in the back of the room. "Tell us!"

"You must look inside yourself and seek the answer for yourself. I am but a mortal man who was blessed by the grace of the Holy Spirit." Peter knew that enlightenment came from a solid foundation of faith and prayer.

"Mrs. Kapono, tell us! Is Peter divine?" urged one patient, Mrs. Rapozo, who was one of the Kapono's neighbors. He had snuck down to the cafeteria to get some coffee.

"He is my grandson and he is healed," she asserted. Some began to sing praises to God.

Others engaged in fervid prayer.

"Praise Kane!" they shouted. Some fell to the floor while others wept. They believed that they were in the presence of the divine.

A swell of hope and gratitude filled the room.

Faith was strengthened through the manifestation of its reward.

"Quiet down!" prompted Peter. "I have things to tell you. And time is of the essence."

The crowd went still.

"The time has come, once again, to be united in our faithfulness. The Lord's presence is evident in my healed body and in the embrace of the Holy Spirit which has touched me. Heed my words." Peter looked out at his people. They were agents of Kane who, like a chalice cup being filled with wine, were being filled with the Holy Spirit. The mana created by the abundance of energy in the room bore the fruit of unwavering faithfulness.

"Let us join hands and pray as we prepare to go into battle with Satan. Pastor will need our mana if we are to win."

As they prayed, more awa-iku swept around the hospital, like butterflies floating on the winds of mana, awaiting assignment from their Higher Power. Like Peter Pan, the spirits roamed freely to thwart any evil remnants lingering in the area.

Their faithfulness had drawn these ethereal spirits to them. Guardian angels had been deployed by Kane.

Peter spoke again, "More than prayer will be necessary to support Pastor and the others. There is a problem that requires our honoring our traditions." He paused and looked out at the town folk in the quiet room. "It's Kupuna. Kanaloa has cast an evil spell on her. She remains in a deep sleep, lost in the darkness. She is caught in Po."

Murmurs of concern swept the room.

"What can we do?" shouted Mrs. Rapozo, tears in her eyes.

"We must save Kupuna!" cried another.

The noise in the room grew louder; the people were deeply upset about Kupuna Hannah.

Their love for her was a palpable phenomenon.

Peter raised his hands to quiet the group of people who had gathered. More individuals had joined the group.

"A ceremony to break the spell that was cast but it failed because of two things." He paused. "First, offerings to Kane alone had not been enough. We must set up a house of mana to pay homage to the Fundamental Supreme Unity – the trinity of Kane, Ku, and Lono. This must be done right away."

The crowd nodded their understanding.

Hikapoloa. The united will of the gods.

"I can build the hut for the mana!" cried an old-timer fisherman named Ku-ula. His genealogy originated with the deity that controlled the fish in the sea. This god transformed into human form and took a wife. They had four children – two sons and two daughters. Ku-ula devoted all his time on his vocation, fishing. After all, he had a family to feed.

First, he constructed a fish pond near the shore where the surf breaks, and he stocked it with a variety of fish. His fish pond became plentiful and so he built more. He also built a house of mana to the triad of gods that constituted the Hikapoloa.

Hawaiian folk tales claim that when Ku-ula made all these preparations, he firmly believed in the existence of God, as the Supreme Being, and the Holy Trinity.

Ku-ula taught his sons the art of fishing. Over the years, they developed the skills to build fruitful fish ponds. They always remembered to give thanks by making the appropriate offerings to the Hikapoloa. These included the gourd of Lono, the plants of Kane, and a sacrificed pig for Ku.

Peter knew that he had drawn the right card.

The architect or builder. Homage to Ku.

"Ku-ula, I thank you. Take your two sons with you to help with the work."

"I will only need one of my sons. You can take the oldest boy up the mountain to the sacred caves. My son, Pilikana, is a great builder and a faithful servant to our Lord." Apparently, the elder was prophetic too. He could see what lay ahead.

Pilikana was a tall, strong man with a stocky build, well-muscled like Brutus. His head was completely bald. Despite having an intimidating appearance, Pilikana possessed a kind and gentle spirit.

Prayers of thanks to Ku-ula filled the room providing buoyancy to the awa-iku or the spirit messengers of Kane that were floating all around the room of local folks.

Were they playing a role in the drawing of the cards?

"Peter, you said there were two things. What's the other one?" shouted Laenihi.

The crowd quieted. They too wanted to know.

"The other thing is this: the chain surrounding Kupuna was broken. Kanaloa was able to introduce the weapon of discouragement into the mind of one who was young and vulnerable. I will leave soon to go up the mountain to the sacred caves to lead the ceremony. It must be repeated. Three others are needed to accompany me to the sacred cave where Kupuna lays. It must be three individuals who can hold steady by virtue of their history and their faith. These are the individuals that must be a part of the unifying chain.

Like the lion, scarecrow, and tin man, they must have the courage, pure thoughts, and a kind heart to stand up to Lucifer. Who among us is not vulnerable to Satan?" Peter knew that that was a tall order. Would anyone feel certain that they could withstand his onslaught?

"I am a servant of God who can resist the influences of Kanaloa," quietly asserted a young Hawai'ian man, named Maui. He had been named after his great, great, great….. great grandfather. His ancient grandfather had been the son of a demi-god named Maui. He was born as the youngest member of this powerful family.

As a young boy he was capable of performing amazing feats using his supernatural powers, however, he preferred to do tricks and a fool's folly, rather than participating in acts that were good deeds. His parents referred to him as "that nasty joker."

As the boy grew into a man, he began to perform more and more good deeds. In legends, one particular deed stood out as the most prominent.

It was the time that he lifted the sky and made a dark earth bright with sunlight. For many long years, the Hawai'ians had been living in darkness. Apparently, the heavens had fallen down and the clouds could not be separated from the earth.

Before Maui, no one had been strong enough to lift them.

Maui used his supernatural powers to gain the strength to lift the sky and allow the light to shine on the good earth. Some tales describe him as "the south sea superman."

The second card had been drawn.

The originator. Homage to Kane.

"Bless you Maui for your courage," Peter said and he smiled warmly at the young man.

More prayers of gratitude were offered.

"Who is the third person, Peter?" asked Mrs. Rapozo.

Peter looked out at the people who had gathered and said, "Let him speak for himself." "It is I." Another young, dark-skinned, and a very thin Hawai'ian man named Mana, had

called out. His long, dark hair was pulled back in a ponytail. He was a wiry guy who was quick on his feet. Born on a full moon on Christmas night, Mana was said to be blessed.

Mana's namesake was after a young boy who was a long-ago cousin who had been instrumental in saving his family from a terrible drought. After fleeing an evil relative named Umi, the family got separated. The parents fled to the mountains but, the children, ended up lost in a desolate, desert place. The grasses were seared and brown, withered up by the lack of water, under an unrelenting, hot sun. The younger children became sick with dehydration and fever, rendering Mana, the oldest sibling, their only hope to save them.

He needed water!

Mana pleaded to Lono, "O *Lono, cast your eyes upon these stricken children! Bring forth the waters from the heavens, lest my brothers and sisters should die! Bring forth the water of life!"*

In response, the celestial skies opened and rain poured down from above, saving the children's' lives. The water of life had been delivered.

Mana never forgot this blessing and he had served the Lord ever since that fateful day in that valley of death.

The executor and directing of the elements. Homage to Lono.

The third card had been drawn.

However, another man said that he had been told in a dream that he should accompany these holy men as the sheriff, providing them with security. He would heed this directive. Keoni, had a reputation as a courageous man of law and order.

The handsome sheriff stepped forward and stood tall in his state of righteousness. The three cards had been drawn.

And a bonus for the sheriff to guide and protect them!

Chapter 41

He 'ino, he 'ino loa no e!
(Evil, indeed very evil!)

It was a slow journey up the mountain.

The heat of the day at high noon was depleting, both for man and donkey. Fortunately, after the attack of the mutant beetles, they had encountered no further provocations from Kanaloa. Thankfully, there had been no sight of Haumea. Puna took them off the trail and down into a small valley. They soon arrived at a brook that was surrounded by Norfolk Island evergreen trees, they decided to take a break in this peaceful location.

Of course, it was not the brook where the awa water flowed. They would reach there later in the day.

After tying up the donkey, Pastor, Puna, Maui and Keoni rested briefly under the cool shade of the large grove of coconut palm trees. Hopefully, none would fall onto their heads!

"Pastor, let's go cool off in the water!" cried Puna as he pulled off his boots and socks. He jumped up and rushed down a slight slope, then, he stepped into the brook, plopping his hot feet down in the cool water.

"Ahhhh!" He repeated it several times.

He then dunked his head in the water, feeling utterly refreshed as he shook his head afterwards. Max could probably relate.

After taking off his hat and wiping his brow, Pastor was drinking lemon, ice tea that Lili had prepared. After the delicious tea, he decided to set his old, tired feet into the cool water. He removed his shoes and socks and stood up. Slowly, he wandered over to the brook, being careful not to fall. Gratefully, he found a smooth rock to sit on. After all, his behind was sore from all the hours of riding the donkey. In the places where he had been bitten by those mutant beetles, his legs throbbed. As he immersed his feet, he actually thought that steam would rise from the water.

Like Puna, he let out a long,"Ahhhh!"

Pastor washed the areas that were open wounds on his legs. The cool water felt exquisite.

Again Pastor uttered,"Ahhhh!"

Puna laughed out loud.

"Pastor, get your head wet!" Puna was wet from head to toe. "I will, but I'll just sit here and take my time, son."

"I am going to take care of the donkey," said Maui as he got up and wandered down to the brook where the donkey, named Mule, had been tied up in the shade of the coconut groves.

"Okay. I'll go get out our gourmet delights that Lili prepared for us. If I'm not mistaken, I believe I saw some blueberry muffins. One of your favorites." Puna stepped out of the brook and went and retrieved the back pack. "She's quite a woman!" He beamed.

"Yes she is. Don't ever forget that Puna!" Pastor called back.

Pastor enjoyed having his feet in the cool water. He closed his eyes and let his mind drift.

Keoni sat quietly nearby, soaking his own throbbing feet. He was eating a blueberry muffin and Kate's famous trail mix.

He thought of the many travelers who had come before him and had sat on this very rock, soaking their feet in the water. How many had been on an important mission like him? Surely, some had been warriors for the alii. Kings and chiefs alike would seek to find the healing awa water. Perhaps even someone from the royal court had once sat here. Had missionaries visited here in the past? Did any of Cook's men traverse this trail?

And who before him had had to face down Kanaloa? This was cer=[tainly was not the first attack.

In fact, the last time that Pastor had confronted the beast was in the sanctuary of his church.

Out in the open environment, he felt vulnerable.

For centuries, our people have lived here.

Pastor reflected on his boyhood home. He recalled adventures in the mountains and summer fun at in the ocean and on the beaches. Back then, the coral reefs were pristine and snorkeling was always a magical aquatic experience. He had loved to spear fish and ……….

I'm talking to you, Mason.

It would seem that the Lord had a message for him.

Mason, its Amos. Open your eyes and look up.

As directed, Pastor opened his eyes and looked upwards. He was looking at the underside of a newer, stout coconut tree. Sitting on one of its lower fronds, was a Hawai'ian pueo – a barn owl.

It was an aumakua. Intuitively, he knew it was Amos.

The owl-as-protector. Apparently, he had a message to transmit to the pastor.

Ahu kupanaha ia Hawai'I 'imi loa! Wonder heaped on wonder in regard to Hawai'i searching far!

"What are you saying Amos? I don't understand." Pastor had no idea what his friend was trying to convey to him.

A new land must be found for our people. You can no longer remain on Nardei in the days ahead.

"Find a new home? Is that what you're saying?" asked Pastor. Surely not.

Oki no ho'i ka hana a ka Hawai'I 'imi loa! Wondrous strange indeed the doings of the Hawai'ian searching far!

"Amos, you're speaking in riddles, my friend," said a confused Pastor.

Nana i ke kumu. Look to the source.

Amos took flight, his wing-span wide as he soared on the breeze. A mele or song could be heard in the wind. It carried a song about regeneration, rejoicing in abundant harvests and bountiful fishing.

Amos was aware that there were others who needed his protection right now. One of them was his son.

Pastor was reminded of the tale of the Cheshire Cat: *The messenger does not remain, but the message remains.*

He would have to ponder Amos's message later.

Right now, he needed to eat. He stood up and returned to the spot where Puna had placed their blanket and food. He also included their daily drink of noni. Lili forgot nothing. Keoni rested nearby, under a large banyon tree. He was eating trail mix that Kate had prepared.

He sat down, looked and smiled at Puna, "Okay son, I am more than ready to eat! What have we got?"

Puna passed him several containers. He noticed the red, inflamed sores on his legs. If they became infected, the pastor would be in trouble.

"Pastor, I'll find some aloe to put on that after lunch."

Pastor opened the largest container first. Blueberry muffins!

Next, he opened a yogurt container that was filled with dried fruit, shredded coconut and nuts – a trail mix that Lili had thrown together.

The third container was full of dried fish and cabbage, with a little shoyu on it. Puna had placed a plate and chopsticks in front of Pastor.

Pastor loaded up his plate. He started with the muffin and wished for hot coffee.

Two muffins later, he was eating the dried fish and cabbage, wishing for vegetables too.

While he drank the noni, he ate the delicious trail mix. There was dried pineapple and dried banana in it, making it sweet. Despite that, Pastor was still wishing for something else that would satisfy his sweet tooth. Something like lilikoi chiffon cake or mango cobbler. He considered having another muffin but he thought it was best to eat more trail mix. There was shredded coconut in it and he sure loved coconut.

Puna had closed his eyes, resting while he was digesting his food. He felt a headache coming on. Shortly thereafter, he started to experience a burning sensation in his throat. He complained of having heartburn. But then, it began to spread to his stomach. It burned as though battery acid had been ingested instead of their lunch. Puna moaned with the intense pain.

"Son, what's wrong?" asked a concerned Pastor.

"Not feeling so good," complained Puna. He didn't look too good either. He was perspiring profusely and he looked pale. "I think I'm gonna throw up."

"We will rest here for a while," stated Pastor. Was the boy gonna be able to continue on their journey? Or would he have to go it alone?

Puna moaned and curled into fetal position. Keoni was by his side. What if the boy needed medical attention?

And where had Pilikana disappeared to?

Maui was missing too.

Pastor did the only thing that he knew to do. He began to pray.

O Kane! Let this son not perish. Let this son be, instead, a man whose destiny is fulfilled.

After a half-hour, Puna's condition was deteriorating. He was drooling like a baby that was teething. He had violently vomited twice. Now, he was reporting that his vision was blurred. Clutched in his hand, lay the wooden cross that David had made for him.

Now Keoni had fallen into a deep sleep, with very shallow breathing and a very slow heart rate. He lay very still under a mango tree.

Moaning even louder and holding his stomach, Puna was obviously getting worse. Unanswered prayers.

In sympathy with this boy he loved, Pastor felt his own stomach burning.

He decided to walk down to the brook and wet a towel to wipe the boy's face which was slick with sweat. The heat of the day was bearing down on them.

When he rose, he had a dizzy spell. He thought he should drink some more water so he grabbed a cup from their lunch setting. The dizziness passed and he got down to the brook and the accommodating rock. His bare feet in the cool water, Pastor closed his eyes. He listened to the wind which carried *meles* or songs of nature.

He cupped his hands and dipped them into the water so that he could splash the water on his hot face. Instead of feeling cooled down, the water felt like it was burning his face.

What was going on?

Heat stroke?

He dipped the towel into the water and, then, he wrung it out. He touched it against his cheek and, this time, it felt cool.

He rose – no dizziness – and slowly walked up the bank and over to their spot where Puna remained in a fetal position, holding his stomach.

Pastor knelt beside Puna.

He saw that the boy had soiled himself. Bloody, foul diarrhea. Pastor knew that that was a very bad symptom and he began to fear for the boy.

He continued to pray.

Using the wet towel, he cleaned Puna up. Puna didn't moan. His lips were turning blue as he strived to breathe in enough oxygen. He uttered no noise.

Then he used the towel with fresh awa water on Keoni, trying to cool his hot skin down. The sherrif looked so pale, with a grey hue setting in.

Not good. Pastor knew the colors of dying men.

This only served to increase Pastor's anxiety over the severity of the illness that struck the boys so suddenly. He too felt the burning in his stomach and veins.

Kanaloa! This must be the work of Satan!

O Kane, do not let him perish, I beg of you, O Lord!

This was his last thought before he keeled over, falling on Puna's back.

Pastor's last thought was that Kanaloa had won.

Once again, using Haumea at his will, Kanaloa had poisoned the two most important players of his arch enemy in this game of good versus evil. The sherrif was a bonus.

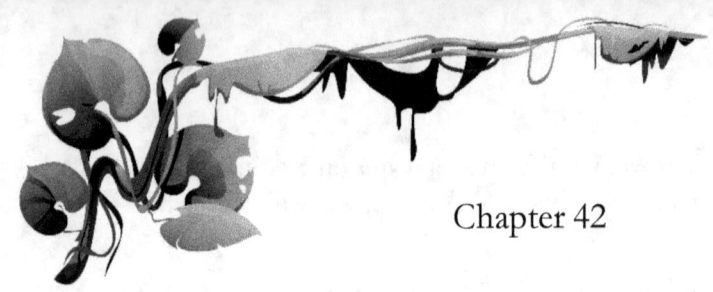

Chapter 42

E lono l kou pomaik'i. Eia!
(Listen to your blessedness. It is here!)

Back at the hospital, the cafeteria was now vacant of the crowd. They were busy attending to constructing the house of mana and gathering the appropriate offerings. Others were attending to the preparations for the Peter and his three-man posy to head up to the sacred caves. They would need to stop and purify themselves at the awa water source.

Pilikana. Maui. Mana. They had become sheriffs for the righteous. They were on a mission to save Kupuna Hannah.

The crowd did not yet know of the miracle recovery of little Hannah. Word would spread on the coconut wireless as other children affected by the brain-eating amoeba recovered using the hypothermic state as a treatment modality. For some, it came too late.

Lili had been the conduit for that particular miracle.

Yet, it had only been hours ago that a nurse had tried to kidnap little Hannah. Who knows what would have happened if Peter hadn't shown up? She was suspicious that there was more to this story.

Lili was so exhausted that she had hit a wall. She was finally being given 12 hours off. Most of that time, she planned to sleep. And, hopefully, she'd have sweet dreams about Puna. She wondered how Pastor and Puna were doing on their long journey up to the mountain top.

Whatever was about to happen, it would occur in the next 24 hours. Success depended on them making it to the sacred caves. Of course, Peter and his men would be following behind them, only several hours' difference in their departure times.

Lili took a long, hot shower and then, she lay down to sleep in the residence for interns. The unit was the same as Pastor's accommodation. She was in great need of sleep so, immediately, she fell into a deep sleep.

Initially, she dreamed of a night on the beach when she and Puna had made love under a starry night. An almost full moon made the ocean water shimmer as small waves had rolled up to the shore. They had slashed around buck naked in the shoreline waves. The night had been magical for her. Soon, the blissful dream turned dark.

It wasn't long before she started having a nightmare. Or, maybe, it was a vision because it felt so real. The scene of the Puna and Pastor had rested and then, enjoyed a lunch under a shady tree. What had transpired indicated that both Puna and Pastor had been afflicted by the same thing.

Lili could see in her dream that both Puna and Pastor were in serious trouble. Pastor lay motionless over the still body of Puna. It struck her that Puna and Pastor had ingested poisonous pokeberries. The deadly berries looked like blueberries.

Pokeberries are native to the islands, growing wild in the forests and along streambeds.

They contained the toxic alkaloid phytolaccine and other triterpene toxins. These lethal toxins irritate the digestive system and can affect the central nervous system, causing neurological symptoms. Triterpene toxins also impair red blood cell formation. They damage the mature red blood cells, eventually starving the body of oxygen. Cells die, including brain cells, and, ultimately, seizures followed by brain anoxia that leads to death.

Lili could see the lunch items on the blanket, including the blueberry muffins.

Someone at the hospital who had helped to prepare the provisions had introduced the lethal muffins laced with pokeberries!

Even in her dream state, her heart rate increased.

There was no remedy for this poison. Death was the inevitable outcome. After suffering through gastrointestinal problems, neurological symptoms ensued. Dizziness would be followed by seizures, then, a coma, and, finally, death. From ingestion until death, this downward spiral took approximately 5 hours.

Were Pastor and Puna already dead or were they in a coma?

She tried to focus in on their chests to look for the rise and fall of their ventilation but she was unsuccessful. There were limits in these pokii dreams.

How could they possibly be saved?

Another kick-up in her heart rate. Her chest felt constricted. Would she lose the love of her life?

Suddenly, in her dream, a Hawai'ian barn owl flew down from a nearby tree and sat down right beside the fallen men. He cocked his head and, with his large yellow eyes, he looked over the two unconscious men, as though he knew them.

E lono I kou pomaik'i. Eia! Listen to your blessedness. It is here!

The voice was unmistakably the voice of Amos.

Amos repeated the telepathic message one more time but Lili remained confused. She had no idea what that meant. And, never mind, she was terrified of what was happening to the two most important men in her life. They were either dead or dying.

The fear that she might lose Puna scared her right out of her dream state. Startled, she woke up wet with perspiration. Her heart pounded and the rush of blood could be heard in her ears.

Taking a few deep breaths, Lili cleared her head and then she pondered the meaning of the pokii dream. It didn't take her long to realize that it was, in fact, a vision.

She shuddered with that thought but she could not deny that it was true. She knew it with certainty. Pastor and Puna really were in trouble – grave trouble.

Once again, her pulse rose dramatically, as she realized that food preparations for Peter and the three men drawn to accompany him on his journey were probably being made right now. How long had she been sleeping? She checked her watch.

Oh no! She'd been asleep for 3 hours!

Throwing off her covers, Lili threw on her clothes and ran down to the kitchen in the cafeteria. A lone, heavy Hawai'ian woman named Mele, who was in her sixties, was cleaning out the fridge. She was famous for her local dishes, especially her lau lau. She was also known for her kindness.

"Is it too late? Have they left?" asked Lili.

The older woman recognized Lili. She frowned at Lili and that was unusual. Mele was probably exhausted too.

"Who, Dr. Lange? Who are you asking about?" asked Mele sharply. "Peter and his men." Lili already knew she was too late.

"They're long gone."

"Well, do you know what food went with them? Were there blueberries or blueberry muffins?" asked Lili.

"I don't know. I'm sure that they got ample food." Mele dismissed her. "Okay. Mahalo Mele." Lili's heart sunk. It seemed that Mele was out of sorts.

Feeling desperate, Lili was at a loss as to what to do. She felt powerless in this moment. Then, she remembered the message that Amos had conveyed.

Someone here is blessed.

But, Peter was gone!

Then, the light bulb went off. Lili knew who she needed to get help from and it was she who had been truly blessed.

She rushed up to Hannah's room.

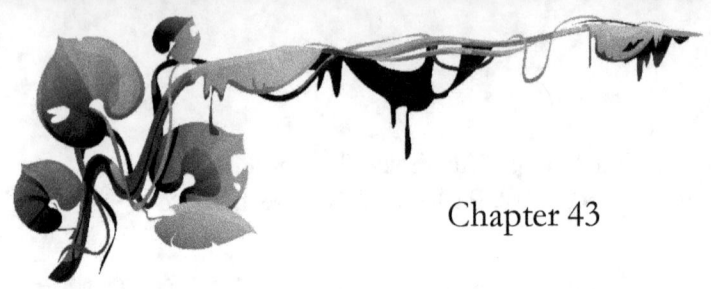

Chapter 43

O kau ke anoano ia 'u kualono

(The great fear settles on me on the mountain).

David had wandered off from the protection of the sacred caves and, at this time, no one was exactly sure where he had gone to mope about his failure in maintaining the hand chain. He had failed Kupuna and everyone else. The boy felt terrible. His faith had wavered. But, David was a resilient boy. He was also a sensitive boy.

Of concern, David was sometimes an impetuous boy. Kimo was more than a little worried about the boy. Ray was out looking for him now. He needed to find and return him to the sacred caves.

Kekela was at Hannah's bedside. Sage burned nearby yet the cave smelled dank. Kupuna remained in a deep sleep. He feared that she would soon drift into a deeper state of darkness, one which was an infinite and timeless night. Offering prayers, he held on to faith. However, he was genuinely frightened because, without Kupuna, they could not defeat Kanaloa. She was an essential warrior to Kane's army.

Hannah was a key player in this game.

Other locals in the caves were sullen. Worry was etched on their faces.

A wisp of the unmistakable stink of fear rode on the winds. The mu or evil spirits planned to carry the fear to the top of the mountain, right to the front door of the sacred caves.

Joe, the-owl-as-protector, and his older brother, transmitted a message to his younger brother:

O kau ke anoano ia'u kualono. The great fear settles on me on the mountaintop.

This is one line from an old, Hawai'ian chant that talks about fear. To understand the full meaning of this old chant, one must recognize that it uses three different words for fear. *Ano* or *anoano* is the religious awe that possesses one, especially when one is alone. A fear of failure sets in. The full chant refers to *weliweli*, or fearfulness that comes with an abiding dread. Kekela dreaded the return of Satan.

Lastly, the use of the word, *Iliilihia* in the chant, is very close to anoano in meaning, but with more of a suggestion that the object of the fear works slowly and almost unnoticed to communicate that emotion to the person. Satan is as sly as a mongoose, insidiously poisoning the individual prey gradually and over time.

Needless to say, fear was one of Satan's weapons.

Iliilihia is the type of fear that Kanaloa instills in people who have any kind of vulnerability in his prey that reflects a weakening of faith and, therefore, hope. If people will give up their faith, it was easy to get them to abandon hope. Such was the case with Kakalina, who had been angry at God for the deaths of the children under her care, and, as a result, she had rebuked Him on several occasions.

She had uttered ugly words to the Almighty without a speck of regret.

She had lost her faith and hope, making her vulnerable to the powers of Haumea. Kakalina had paid dearly for her breach with God and her works for Satan.

She had come down with the illness that had afflicted so many others who had perished.

At first, Kakalina became sick with nausea, vomiting, and bloody diarrhea. Her intravenous fluids kept her hydrated. Shortly thereafter, she began to have difficulty breathing. She was placed on oxygen. Next, she began bleeding from her nose, mouth and other orifices. The blood loss increased to hemorrhaging. Like the others whom she had cared for, she developed the characteristic, red lesions on her skin. Obviously, she had been exposed to the same contagion as Gladys and Earnest, Mr. Worthington, Calvin and Nadine, and so many others.

She was not expected to live through the night.

David may have had a moment of doubt but it did not shake his foundation of love and faith in the Lord. As a result of this failure, he did not abandon his faith, but rather, his faith had been strengthened. David was down at the awa water spot, cleansing himself and, after a thorough bath, he had sat down and prayed for a long time. At times, he wept as spoke about his fears out loud to the Almighty.

The most important thing was that Kupuna Hannah be cured from the spell that had been cast upon her.

Over and over again, David prayed for the restoration of his beloved Kupuna.

It wasn't too long before Ray discovered the boy at this sacred place. The boy looked so sad. "David, we've been worried about you," remarked Ray.

David looked up and said "I'm sorry, Uncle." His face was clean and glowing from his immersion into the rejuvenating awa water. However, the awa water could not erase his sadness. The young man was feeling great regret and sadness.

Ray approached the boy and sat down beside her. "Can you tell me what's going on?"

Looking at the uncle that he so admired, David replied, "I'm a failure, uncle, and you know it! I feel great shame. I hate myself!" Tears fell from his eyes and he wiped his face with the back of his hand. He looked down as though he had warts on his face. At least now the ugly truths were out. He couldn't hide from them anymore. He felt sick to his stomach so great was his self-shame.

Did they not know that Kanaloa had it right? He was a stupid, ugly and weak boy! A big, fat zero. He had repeated it over and over until the words' pierced his tender and vulnerable heart.

"Son, you are not a failure. Honest." "Really?" He clearly doubted that.

"Yes. Most definitely," replied Ray, with love and care in his voice and demeanor. "In fact, you are a really good kid." His smile was seen in his eyes, which crinkled at the edges.

"Really?" He still sounded doubtful.

"David, you've already handled so much in your young years and, as a result, you are developing good character. I mean it. You are a very honorable young man. Your parents are looking down on you from heaven and I know they feel great pride in you, son. I know I do."

"Honest?" There was very little doubt in his voice.

"Honest," Ray said. The sincerity in the articulation of that one word reassured this young man that he was worthy of forgiveness and love.

The boy was smiling. He saw the truth in his uncle's eyes. A deep sigh of relief demonstrated his belief that his uncle had indeed spoken the truth. He trusted Ray. His approval meant everything!

"Shall we return to the cave? Things will begin to occur tonight. Once darkness is upon us."

"Before we head back, let's eat some granola bars and drink our noni drink for today." Ray pulled out these snacks from a pouch he wore strapped over his shoulder.

After eating, David stood up and said, "We better go." David hesitated. "And thank you uncle." The boy ran over and hugged Ray.

"We must pray to Kane before we head back." They joined hands and Ray chanted,

Kane comes with the water of life.

Life through the multitude of the gods! Sacred! Sacred! Life! Life!

Life through the chief! Life through the gods!

(Voices on the Wind: Polynesian Myths and Chants: 1986. Bishop Museum Press: Honolulu, Hawaii, p.67).

As they traversed back up the mountain, David became his old chatter-box persona. He began to speculate about ways to defeat the evil one. He said, "Well, it is obvious that the ceremony must be performed again. Just not with me in it. Another one must be selected."

Ray mused over that. "Of course, you're right." Ray realized that it was really as easy as that.

He began to think about the individuals best suited to participate in the ritual. The ones that had been ordained to perform in these powerful ceremonies, over the span of centuries.

Success in the past had always required the engagement of the correct people. This included the drawing of the twelve to Him.

Ray understood that they must choose very carefully.

Just before they reached the caves, they heard the hoot of a Hawai'ian pueo. The owl-that-was-Kai had signaled that the battle was underway:

'O ka pueo kani kaua. The owl sounding war!

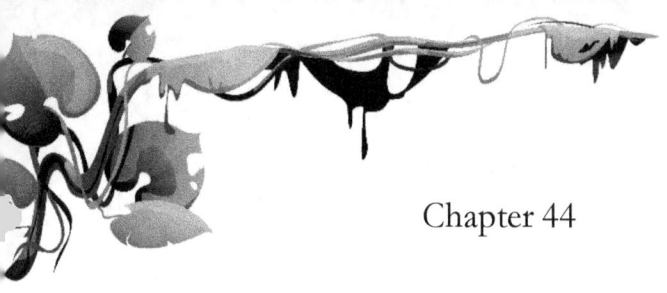

Chapter 44

Mana

(Spirit or power)

Little Hannah was awake and alert.

Kate was asleep in the chair beside her bed. Now that she knew her little girl was okay, she had succumbed to her exhaustion.

Hannah was carrying on a conversation with Uncle Bert who sat on her bed rail in all his green lizard glory.

You're so much like your mother when she was your age.

"Am I?" responded the little girl who looked so small and vulnerable in the bed. She remained pale and weak. Her blue eyes looked like saucers on her thin face. Apparently, she had lost some weight. Some of her pretty strawberry-blond hair had fallen out, leaving a few bald spots.

Child, you look like her, talk like her, and act like her.

"That's a good thing, isn't it, Uncle Bert? You said that you adored Mommy."

I sure do adore your Mommy. And I also adore you, my dear child. Do you know that you're special?

"Special? What's so special about me, Uncle?" asked the young girl.

You have been touched by the hand of Jesus. Bert danced back and forth on the silver railing.

"You know what Uncle? I already knew that. An angel explained everything to me." The not- so-young girl seemed to understand her uniqueness.

So, you will serve Him child? Is that so?

"I live to serve Him."

Uncle Bert was doing the rumba.

Zippity-do-da! Zippity day!

Little Hannah began laughing.

The door opened and Lili walked in.

"Well, aren't you in good spirits, Miss Hannah!" Lili was so pleased to see and hear the child laugh.

"Hi Dr. Lange!" greeted the little girl.

"How are you feeling?" asked the doctor. The question sounded lame, even to her. "Great! Better than ever," replied the miracle child.

"Hannah, I need your help," said Lili as she looked directly into the girl's big, blue eyes.

"I know," responded the girl. "Puna and Pastor have ingested Satan's poison."

Stunned, Lili just nodded, affirming the truth of those words.

"How can you possibly know this?" asked Lili out loud.

"I know, I know. It is because you are divine. An angel here on earth."

"Am I?"

"Hannah, I cannot deny the miracle that I witnessed. None of the other children are being helped by the hypothermia treatment. Only you, only you." Lili moved on to the more urgent matter, "What about Pastor and Puna? Can you help them?"

"Help is already on its way," replied the girl with great confidence. She looked around for Uncle Bert but he was nowhere to be seen.

"Who? Who is going to intervene?" asked Lili.

"Trust me. A friend has been sent to help them." She sounded so mature. Clearly dissatisfied with that response, Lili sighed and left the girl's room. Kate hadn't even stirred.

Back on his perch, Uncle Bert walked up and down the bed railing. He was like a lizard on steroids.

I just hope that help arrives in time. Are you certain about that?

"Frankly, I'm not sure about anything," replied the girl with the enormous weight on her shoulders, but thankfully, she had wings to support her.

Don't tell me that there's a chance that those two men could die before their mission is complete? Uncle Bert's green tail was twitching.

"There are no guarantees in life," said the wise, young girl. "But there are gifts."

And you were endowed with a special gift Hannah. Guard it well.

The girl laughed," I do. I have you after all, Uncle Bert!"

Zippity-do-da! Zippity day!

Uncle Bert-the-lizard began whoppin' it up with his disco dancin' moves. He slipped off the bed rail and toppled into Kate's lap. She woke up with a start.

"Uncle Bert! What are you doin' in my lap?" she asked with a straight face. In fact, she looked rather indignant. "Thought you'd just drop in, did you?" She paused, maintaining her poker face. Then suddenly, she burst out laughing. Hannah laughed right along with her.

You girls are being cruel at my expense.

Both Kate and Hannah rolled their eyes. Kate was totally disheveled, her hair sticking out here and there. She had taken a hot shower just before she had fallen asleep in the reclining chair. She was wearing hospital scrubs. Navy blue scrubs whose pants were too short.

Checking her watch, she saw that she had been sleeping for hours. No wonder she felt stiff. Soon, nighttime would arrive. What would arrive with it? She thought about the green mist and shuddered.

She thought about her husband and other children. She missed them so much.

Then, she looked at her amazing daughter who was not only healed; she had been transformed into someone blessed by the Holy Spirit. She and Uncle Bert were laughing again.

Here was an earth angel talking to a passed ancestral spirit.

An ethereal spirit and an aumakua guardian spirit. The renewal of the relationship of the father figure and the girl that he loved like a daughter, created so much white light or mana that they had used it to assist their two, beloved friends. On the wings of the wind, help was on its way.

Like a speeding bullet.

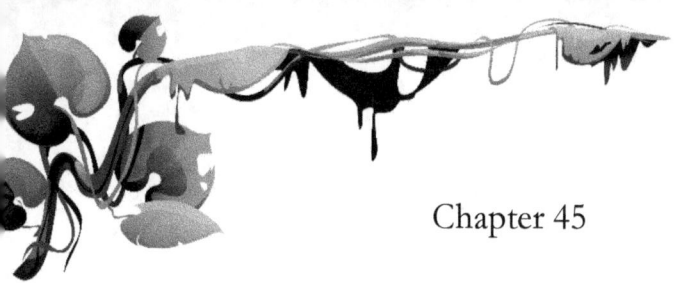

Chapter 45

Loa kea la e hele 'ia.

(Long the path being traveled)

As the midday sun cooled down with the afternoon approaching, the blue sky turned overcast. The air seemed heavy and charged with electricity. On the horizon, the green mist glowed eerily. It served to remind them of the urgency of their mission. Peter had met up with the group of men at the awa water pond. Maui, as promised, had been able to resist the evil workings of Kanaloa.

Unfortunately, Pastor and Puna had separated from the security team. They had taken the donkey and left the pond quickly.

Peter and his three comrades were briskly climbing upwards. After all, they were young men who were very fit. Island lifestyle was all about being active.

Wherever Peter walked, his majestic tread left footprints even on the most hardened ground.

They came upon the first location where Pastor and Puna had taken their first break. The site of the beetle attack. Likewise, Peter and his men refreshed themselves in the cool, fresh-water pond. The grove of extremely tall evergreens was majestic and seemed to touch the gray sky.

Being young, strong men, they were more than ready to eat. Peter and the three men, the three musketeers, sat on bamboo matts and Peter opened the back with their provisions.

Different food items were laid out, including their noni drinks.

First, they prayed. Then, they enjoyed a variety of fresh local fruits and home-made granola bars. Kate had made the granola bars and they included local nuts, shredded coconut, granola, dried mango pieces and dried blueberries. Dried fish and beef jerky provided some protein in their diet. There was also a container that had four pieces of guava cake.

"Wow! This is the best guava cake I've ever had! Mele outdid herself!" declared Maui with his mouth full. "Wish there was more!"

Peter, Pilikana, and Mana agreed.

"The cake is to die for as always, but, Mele ain't herself. Kinda grumpy. Did you notice?" asked Maui.

The others just looked at him and shrugged.

"Lots of folks out of sorts these days," muttered Pilikana.

Who prepared their food? Would they be okay? Had they ingested the poisonous pokeberries?

While they rested briefly after lunch, Peter felt the winds, out of the west, pick up. The winds carried a familiar mele or song.

Ka leo o ka huewai I ka makani. The voice of the water gourd in the wind.

Of course, the water gourd represents Kane. The musical message had been sent by Kane's spirits of goodwill, the awa-iku.

What was their message? Peter listened attentively to hear it.

The mu spirits surround you and those who went before you.

Peter saw the episode of the mutant beetle attacks on both Pastor and Puna. Then, he caught a glimpse of the two men sleeping, under the tree, as though they had been drugged. He wasn't sure if they were still alive. Peter was unable to identify the location. The picture in his head was not clear enough. He felt like his vision was blurry.

With clarity, Peter could see the damaging effects of the mu spirits surrounding the man of God and the young warrior man.

Peter and his posy needed to get to the two, downed men with haste.

He prayed briefly. The song of Kane reminded Peter that the three gods of the Trinity used earth as a footstool. They sang with joy:

Ola ia kini akua ia 'oe. The many gods live through you.

Peter understood the weight being placed on his shoulders. In God he would trust.

As they began their upward journey, Peter and his men noticed that, over the past several hours, the mist had moved considerably closer to the island's shoreline.

Thunder crackled in the dark, ominous clouds. The wind picked up.

Perhaps the god Lono had arrived.

The journey would become more difficult. There were many factions who could affect the weather. Some entities already had done so.

Was the tsunami finally approaching? The toxic mist was moving closer and closer to the island. Was a giant wave behind it propelling it forward?

Peter knew who was behind it.

He prayed to the Lord that he would know what actions to take at the right time. The three within him would lead his thoughts and actions in the hours ahead.

The humid air was suffocating as they moved forward with urgency to locate Pastor and Puna in time. Their location remained a mystery to Peter, with only a vague picture of a babbling brook with green banks and large trees offering shade. He knew that this valley was not on the trail. It would be difficult to find.

Difficult, but not impossible. Nothing is impossible with Him. There were no sounds of nature.

Peter knew this was because the mu spirits were around, riding on the eastern winds. They were waiting for an opportunity to penetrate the posy. However, these three men were godly in nature.

Their attempts were doomed to fail. Of course, Peter was completely impervious to their influences.

Were they impervious to the lethal pokeberries if they had, indeed, eaten them unknowingly?

Only time would tell.

As they walked quietly up the ever-increasing incline, Maui spoke.

"Peter, I have seen this place that you seek to find."

Peter thought of Maui's namesake who had raised the sky to provide illumination of the earth.

"Do you know this place?"

"I do. It is about another two hours away."

"We may not have two hours," moaned Peter. "We must hurry!"

No further words were spoken. The men picked up their pace, with Maui leading the pack. After all, Maui came from a superman lineage. And, the bulk-of-a-man, Pilikana, spoke from his gentle spirit and kind heart, "We must save them! Have Mana run ahead, he is a very fast runner. My heart is breaking with every moment that passes. We have to save them! "

"I agree! I will run ahead," declared Mana. "Maui just tell me where to go."

And so he did.

Maui knew this place despite having never been there. However, his great, great …great grandfather, the Demi-god, had lived in a nearby cave that was located in the foot of an extinct crater. One day, he decided to explore the crater and its other caves. On occasion, he bumped his head on the dark, low clouds. Other times, he cut his hands on the rough lava rocks.

Nonetheless, he pressed on with his explorations until he came to the edge of a forest of tall evergreens. A fresh, cool brook trickled through the forest, its green banks lush with soft grass. It was a beautiful sight to behold.

It was also a sight that generated raw fear — *weliweli* — a fear that is accompanied by a feeling of dread. It was very, very quiet in this disturbing place. Grandfather Maui discovered that, in the other caves, lived the evil mu spirits. They dwelled in the darkness of the deep caves.

The grandfather's memory had been revealed to Maui.

"Peter, when I find them, what should I do?" asked Maui.

"Kiss them. Give them *ha* or the breath of life," he instructed. Peter smiled warmly at Maui, instilling confidence in him. In breath, was the life force.

That was the other thing about the Demi-god Maui. On that great day that he lifted the sky to shine light on the Po, he had finished the job of raising the sky fully up by bracing himself and taking a deep, long breath. With one powerful breath, the sky was thrust upwards to the heavens. Life had emerged after the sunlight fully shone on the good earth.

"I understand."

Maui turned and ran for his life or rather, the lives of others, and he was soon gone in a cloud of red dirt.

God speed.

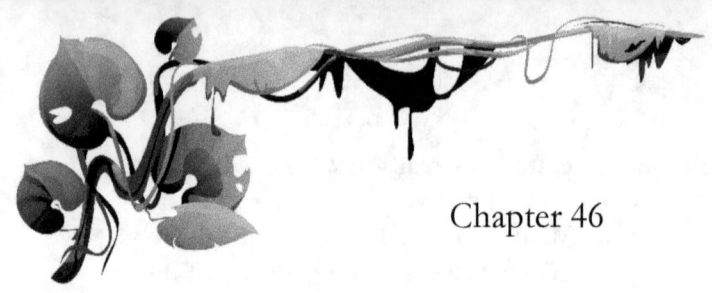

Chapter 46

Ua ho'I ka noio 'au kai I uka, ke'ino neika moana.

(The seafaring noio bird returns to land, for a storm rages at sea)

Sea birds were coming on shore in great numbers, amongst the ever-increasing dead fish.

Noio or marine birds comprise only 3% of all bird species on earth. Many have made the

Hawai'ian Islands their home. Most of the seabirds in Hawaii are noddies.

Black noddies are found on the northern cliffs of Nardei. They distinguish themselves from other species because they have yellow-orange legs and feet. Black noddies vary in color from dark gray-brown to dark inky-black.

Black noddies build their nests on rocky ledges, in caves, or trees. They live to the ripe old age of 25 years of age.

One noddie in particular was returning to the island from the open seas to provide a report to his commander-in-chief. In this case, that would be Kai-the-owl-as-the-protector of the aina or land.

Was a tsunami approaching? Now, they would find out.

The spirit in the noddie bird was an old friend of Kai's. David's father, Duke.

As boys, they had gone to the same school. In the summer, they'd gone fishin' many times.

Neither man felt compelled to talk much. Duke had been the town's postmaster prior to getting the smallpox virus, during the period of the great tribulation, which caused his death.

And his wife's death and almost his son's death too. Fortunately, David had survived against all odds.

The owl and the noddie met on a tree near the sacred caves and the mountainous cliffs where the noddies dwelled.

"First, please tell me what you saw on the other side of that mist," requested Kai. "There is a *mega* wave on its way," stated Duke. "Headed right for us."

"How big?" asked Kai, even though he dreaded the answer.

"The wave front is really steep and about 500 feet high." There was the dreaded truth. Duke added, "The back slope wasn't as steep as the front." As if that, somehow, made it better.

"Wow. That is truly a giant wave," said Kai, stating the obvious. "Yep, bra. It's big alright." His wings fluttered.

More and more seabirds were flocking to the cliffs and caves. They knew what was coming.

"It's probably gonna arrive in the next 24 hours," asserted Duke. "Man, a wave that big could knock out trees and vegetation at elevations as high as 1500 feet." He began making clicking sounds and his head began swerving back and forth, like Stevie Wonder.

"And, what about the mist? Did you learn anything about it?" asked Kai.

"It's like a fog of green precipitation. It has moving particles in it and, here's the thing, they glow." Duke shuddered. "That mist is really scary. Miles of dead creatures, like birds and fish, turtles and other ocean animals, surround the shroud of green." More clicking sounds.

The noise of more noddies finding a safe retreat became louder.

"What do you think it is?" asked Kai.

"It appears to be some sort of pestilence. A very deadly pestilence." "Kane has a lot to deal with!" Kai held onto his faith.

"Amen to that."

"Kai, I worry about David," said the concerned father.

"Of course, you do. And, I worry about Puna whom I fear is in great peril."

"You're right about one thing, my friend. Kane has a lot to deal with," echoed Duke. A gust of wind caused the two bird aumakuas to sway on their perch. The mele in the wind sang,

Auwe! ku'u hoa o ke Ko'olau. Alas my companion of the windward side!

Duke realized that it was time to say good-bye to his dear friend and find safe harbor inside the caves on the cliffs. Kai–the-owl-as-protector and Duke-the-seabird-reporter departed, going in opposite directions.

Kai would not be returning to the sacred caves. He was headed back down the mountain to be at his son's side. His large wing span allowed the owl to glide at high speed on his downhill journey. His son needed him.

He knew that his boy was still alive because they were engaged in telepathic communication.

Soon, father, I will be with you if help doesn't arrive in time.

Help is coming, son. Please hang on!

This Hawaiian owl was wiser that most owls that are used as an aumakua vessel because, in his mortal life, he had been a Kapuna. He realized that he needed to make a stop on his way to Puna and Pastor, who was surely slipping away. When he reached the spot where the special brook flowed with awa water, he looked around for an object to scoop and contain the blessed water.

Awa-iku had conveniently left a small water gourd right beside the brook! Perfect! Sunlight shone on it through the otherwise, dark skies. It was as though the sun deliberately wanted to illuminate the container. Gourds come in many shapes and sizes. This particular one was large and the decoration on the exterior was a painted fish symbol.

This water gourd had been originally planted on the night of Hua, when the moon is shaped like an egg. Legends claimed that a fat-bellied man did the planting. The bigger the stomach, the bigger the gourd!

Therefore, prior to the actual planting, the planter was required to eat a large meal to stretch his stomach and he should carry it as if it were already a huge and heavy gourd. Today as they planted, they still sang the appropriate chant to accompany the planting ritual,

He ipu nui!

O hiki ku mauna, O hiki kua,

Nui maoli keia ipu!

A huge ipu!

Growing like a mountain, To be carried on the back. Really huge is this gourd!

Kai recalled that, as a child, fetching water was one of the first responsibilities he'd been given. He would get up early in the morning, take the long gourd and walk along the trail to the stream. He would fill his gourd, stopper it, and then, walk back home. He would chant a particular song that favored long "o" sounds in keeping with the *hokeo*, the long gourd:

E hano ana, e kani 'ouo ana. It is fluting, it is the youthful 'ouo.

Now, it was his responsibility to fill the water gourd again. His strong and large claws could readily carry a gourd filled with water. Certainly, it was less weight than many of his animal prey.

With remarkable dexterity, Kai filled the gourd with the precious cargo, put the stopper in, and soared to the sky to traverse down the mountain.

He also remembered that, when he would carry the gourd home, it would make a characteristic swishing sound. It was a reassuring noise. When it was poured, it made a gurgling sound. He and his family would laugh and then, repeat the old proverb,

I ola ola no ka huewai I ka piha 'ole. Gurgling indeed is the water gourd under filled.

This proverbial saying is using the sound of the water in the gourd to describe a talkative, empty-headed person. Apparently, Kai and his family were amused by that. Apparently, he had an auntie who was similar to Gladys in her ways. Like mindless mynah birds, all they did was talk, talk, talk!

Gladys had been a talkative empty-head, and look how well things had worked out for her.

She was like an under filled gourd, making a lot of noises, without thinking.

Fortunately, Kai was wise in his ways and the noises that this gourd made would serve to remind him that this was the water of Kane, the water of life.

He huewai ola ke kanaka na Kane ke Akua I hana.

The human being created by the God Kane is a living water gourd.

Was Peter a living water gourd?

Voices on the Wind Ino-ino mai nei luna,

I ka hao a ka makani, He makani ahai-lono Lohe ka luna I Pelekana.

Wild scud the cloudsI, Hurled by the temptest, A tale-bearing wind That gossips afar. Reference, p.3

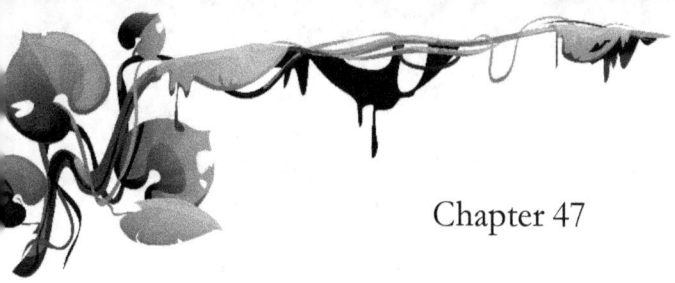

Chapter 47

No Kane, no Lono ka pike I ka lani

(For Kane, for Lono, the shouting in the heavens)

While Maui made haste, Peter and the two other men, marched on. It was mid-afternoon and they still had a long road ahead.

The three men were still feeling good, despite the hot and humid day. Moreover, they were not manifesting any of the symptoms of pokeberry poisoning. Thankfully, they had not been poisoned!

Pilikana had been separated from the group earlier. He had come upon a guava tree bearing the lucious fruit so he decided to pick some. Once again, he had rejoined the motley crew.

After one hour, they stopped to rest briefly at a small stream and drink some water and partake of some food to replenish themselves.

Under a shady mango tree, they sat down on their tapa mats in the shade, stretched out, and unpackaged some snacks. A prayer was said. Then, they each enjoyed some of Mele's sweet Hawai'ian bread, made out of purple sweet potatoes, with some dried fish and goat cheese. In addition, they were lucky enough to find some ripe mangos to eat. Sweet!

"Boy, these mangos are ono!" declared Mana. "Refreshing," agreed Pilikana.

"There's more. Help yourself!" said Peter who was enjoying his second piece of the seasonal, sweet fruit. These Hayden mangos were especially sweet. Never mind that his stomach was acting up. His stomach was acidic, causing it to burn. Gastric reflux. He'd had it before. The mangos would certainly not help the situation as they were very acidic. But they sure were delicious!

Unbeknownst to them, Kanaloa had sent mu spirits to alter the irresistible mango fruit. These evil spirits were dispatched as large black bees and they had injected the fruit with Jimsonweed seeds. The seeds from the Jimsonweed plant (*kikania haole*) have high concentrations of a hallucinogenic compound. In fact, the whole plant is toxic with chemicals that affect the central nervous system. Traditionally, American Indians used this plant for medicines and religious ceremonies. Aztecs used it as a magic, vision-producing drug.

Kanaloa seemed keen on using poisons to disable his enemies. He hoped to incapacitate them physically or mentally. Believing that he could shape their hallucinations to his will, he intended to shake their unwavering faith, especially Peter. That would totally sabotage Kane! Taking out his point man.

As the men rested in the shade of a large hala tree with its yellow blossoms, it wasn't long before the two posy men began to experience the onset of the hallucinogenic high.

First, Mana exclaimed," I just saw a winged-dragon in the sky!" He was frantically pointing to the dark clouds. "Or maybe it was a gorgeous brunette," he chuckled.

In response, Pilikana said, "No bra. It's an angel with wings, not a dragon or a brunette!" A goofy smile grew on Pilikana's face. "She's beautiful, truly beautiful with golden hair and golden eyes. Her wings glow."

"It's a pink dragon," insisted Mana. "And it is *sooo* beautiful."

"You're both seeing stuff in the shifting clouds," asserted Peter. Apparently, he had not been affected by the toxic seeds. As he looked at the two men, Peter thought that they looked kind of spacey. Fatigue must be setting in so he thought it best to get back on the trail before they lost their volition.

Peter placed their filled water containers and the food containers back into the pack.

"It's time to get back on the trail and catch-up to Maui." Peter began to stand up but, suddenly, he felt dizzy. The sun, muted by the clouds, seemed brilliant, causing Peter to sit back down and cover his eyes. The onset of the symptoms varied from person to person, anytime between 30 to 60 minutes. It appeared that Peter was finally feeling the effects of the toxin.

"Peter! There's bugs' crawling on your face!" cried Pilikana. "Little green bugs!"

Peter didn't feel any bugs on his face. Using his hand, he wiped his face. He was aghast!

There were no bugs on his hand but there was a sticky, white, and foul-smelling substance. His hands were covered in this slimy stuff that was causing a serious red rash on his face, neck, and hands. Peter was alarmed.

What was this caustic stuff? Battery acid? His skin was on fire!

His back was also on fire with the red and itchy rash. Like his dog Max, he wanted to roll on his back and squirm back and forth to scratch his back. What he needed was some aloe plant to soothe these nasty rashes.

He should go down to the stream and cool off with water and wash off the nasty substance.

Peter's thoughtful deliberation was interrupted by a scream from Mana who was jumping up and down!

He shouted," Snakes! Look at all these damn snakes!" He continued to dance about as though snakes were at his feet. "God! I friggin' hate snakes!"

Pilikana was also up on his feet. "My God, there must be at least twenty of 'em!"

Peter tried to see the snakes but his vision was blurry and light-sensitive. He really didn't see any snakes. Peter began to think they were losing it.

Sun stroke?

He placed his hand back into the pack to get some water to rinse his eyes, when he felt the unmistakable skin of a snake as it slithered out of the pack. Peter could see that it was a black snake with yellow spots. He could also see that it had red eyes that seemed to glow. Another snake followed suit and slithered out. The snakes were real.

And then, another snake emerged. It suddenly grew in size and its red tongue flickered. It morphed into an old, large snake-demon, with fire on his breath.

The breath of death.

This particular snake spoke to Peter.

I am Milu, ruler of the dead.

"I am Peter. I am with the lamb," responded the agent of Kane. He saw the snake-demon breath fire and he stood back to avoid getting burned.

You have no power here. You are weak, like a kitten. Soon you and your friends will be dead.

Making his point, a small, black kitten rubbed against Peter's leg. Then, a snake lunged, and with laser precision, grabbed it, and ate it whole. The kitten's body was a large lump in the snake's digestive track. Peter could swear that he heard the kitten meow. He had a visceral reaction to that vision, throwing up the snack foods he'd just ingested.

Or was the poison manifesting physical symptomology?

He surely didn't feel right.

The other snakes became frenzied as more black kittens were emerging from the lush vegetation.

Mana and Pilikana were feeling frenzied too. They were practically crying. Both had released their urine.

More black snakes slithered down the mango tree where there seemed to be nests of them. Hundreds of them!

Mana screamed in horror as a snake burst forth, took aim, and struck! He had taken his boots off and his ankle had been exposed. He had been bitten.

How poisonous were these snakes?

Pilikana had also taken off his foot gear and it wasn't long before he too was nailed. He cried out, "The son-of-a-bitch got me!"

Not being a screamer, Peter remained quiet when minutes ago, a snake out of the back pack had readily found his bare arm. Another had found his bare foot. Both areas where he had been bitten were inflamed and painful. The sites were bright red and swollen.

He felt powerless in this situation. Looking upwards to the heavens, he gasped. He was frightened to see an enormous flock of black mynah birds blocking the clouds and the sun. The large dark sky began to emit the squawk of the talkative, air-head birds. These dense creatures rendered them easy targets for the mu spirits to inhabit. It sounded like they were sounding the alarm.

It was an ominous sign. This battalion looked ready to attack.

He turned his attention back to his two companions. With despair, he watched them get several more agonizing bites from these venomous snakes. Then, both of them were down. Literally. They were lying on the ground with snakes slithering over their comatose bodies.

How many bites could they sustain without serious harm?

Peter cried out, "O, all you gods, come to our aid!"

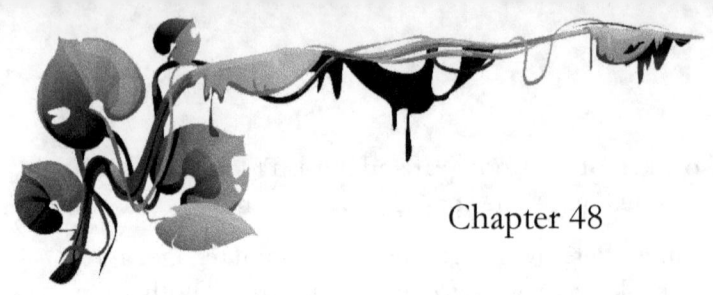

Chapter 48

'Ana'ana

(The practice of evil deeds)

Lili had figured it out.

Mele didn't act like Mele because she wasn't Mele anymore.

Haumea! It had to be her!

Just like she had taken over Kakalina, Haumea had transmigrated into Mele to do her poisonous deeds, after leaving the body of Pua.

She was unrelenting in her efforts to undermine these soldiers of Kane.

Haumea had been in the hospital at that time. She had found an indirect method to do Satan's bidding. She had others of like mind, collect the pokeberries. These were other agents of Kanaloa.

Not all of them were in human form. Some mu spirits had been sent to occupy non-human vessels.

Would one of them be a Jeanie in a bottle?

Perhaps, they'd find another clever way to poison the good humans, weak by virtue of their unwavering faith in loving one another. They foolishly trusted too easily, always seeking to find the goodness in others.

Haumea practiced a form of black magic or sorcery. It was called *'Ana'ana* which is the practice of evil deeds. One type is called *hana'ino*. Evil spirits of darkness become friends of men, preying on their kindness and goodness. Haumea had practiced hana'ino on both Kakalina and, now, Mele.

Lili was sitting with Kate and little Hannah as the late afternoon sun began to set. It had been a gray day and the night would be even darker. The air was pregnant with the need to shed water, the humidity being almost 100%. A storm was imminent, thunder rumbling in the distance. It felt like the dam was going to suddenly burst.

"Hannah, you ready to get up and out of that bed? Move some muscles?" asked Lili. "Afterwards, I'll sneak into the kitchen and get you some ice cream." Lili had had a co-worker bring some from home since she lived just two doors down from Lili's small, plantation cottage.

She wasn't going to take any chances with hospital food. She had already warned Kate. She told her about the poisoned foods prepared by Mele, who was no longer Mele. Haumea was probably sticking around somewhere, bent on targeting Hannah now that she had been ordained by God's grace. Such a righteous being could not stand in the eyes of the evil one.

Little Hannah began acting like a regular 7, (almost 8), year old girl protesting and whining,

"No, not yet. I'm tired. Really tired, Mom." She was no longer Mommy.

"I know you are, honey, but it's really important to get up and move around," encouraged Kate.

Hannah sighed and asked Lili," What kind of ice cream?"
"Rocky Road."

Hannah grinned and replied,"Okay, for that, I will." She threw off the bed cover and sat up to the side of the bed.

"Whoa! Not so quick. Dangle your feet back and forth for a bit. That'll get you blood circulating," instructed Lil.

Come on kid. Take a little stroll. We can move on to dancing later. Perhaps, a two-step.

Uncle Bert was present in his favorite corner. Hannah laughed. The lizard danced a fine two-step, sans a tux and a top hat. *I assure you, I'm like Fred Astaire when it comes to dancing!* "Who?" she asked, smiling from ear to ear.

I mean, I'm like Michael Jackson!

Hannah subsided into a fit of laughter.

"Who what, Hannah? And what's so funny?" asked Lili. Kate was smiling because she knew who tickled the girl's funny bone. She also knew that her little girl missed her father and siblings.

"*Who* else is gonna have ice cream with me?" The little girl indicated she was ready to stand up. Lili stood to her left and Kate to her right. Hannah stood up on shaky legs but each arm was being supported by her Mom and Dr. Lange. They wouldn't let her fall. She really did feel as weak as a kitten. Yet, she took one step, then another, and then, another. It was a few steps later when she told the women, "Let me walk completely by myself. I can do it."

And, she did. She appeared stronger with each step. Little Hannah started laughing again.

"What's so funny? "asked Lili shaking her head.

"I was just thinking I could try the moonwalk later."

Everyone laughed at that, including the star, Uncle Bert. Hannah adored him.

Lili laughed and said, "Child, so much has changed in you."

Hannah sat back down on the bed, her energy spent. She reached under her bed covers and pulled out a small object.

"Dr. Lange, on the way to the kitchen, can you please take this to the little girl in room 401?" asked the girl. She extended her hand and offered a small, undecorated gourd. When she handed it to Lili, it made a swishing sound.

"What should I do with it?" asked Lili.

"Put it by her bedside. And, open the stopper. That's all. "

The little five year-old girl was afflicted with the same disease that had placed Hannah in danger of knockin' on heaven's door. The local, Hawai'ian girl was a school friend's little sister, Kekele.

Kekele had been the star student in her class. Also, she was a gifted hula dancer.

Apparently, this very bright girl, with long, black hair and large, brown eyes, was not responding to the hypothermic intervention like Hannah had. She continued to have seizures. No medications were working to arrest the seizures, which were starving the girl's brain cells.

She would die soon.

The shadows of real death were surrounding her, and the feeling of separation from her body was becoming more and more entrenched as she gave in to it.

Lili knew better to do anything but exactly that which she had been asked to do. She nodded and accepted the small gourd.

The rest was understood.

Zippity-do-da! Zippity day! I love seein' a miracle happen!

Kate wasn't sure why she was not introducing Lili to Uncle Bert. The whole lizard thing, well, she knew about the lizard aumakuas. No, it was about keeping the relationship between her Uncle Bert and her daughter special. Protected.

Of course, who knew how long he would be able to stick around. Lili returned with Hannah's sweet reward.

Hannah did not fail to dig in and, in short order; she was soon lickin' the bowl clean. "Yummy! Thank you, Dr. Lange. That was the best Rocky Road I ever had!" Hannah began wiping her chin with her napkin.

"Now, let me tell you about Puna and Pastor." Hannah looked at both Lili and her Mom. She continued," They are still alive and help is almost there. They will be restored to consciousness very soon."

"You keep saying that help is on the way…a friend. Who exactly is going to save them?!" Lili's voice was rising in volume, her fear getting the best of her,

"The living water gourd of Kane."

233

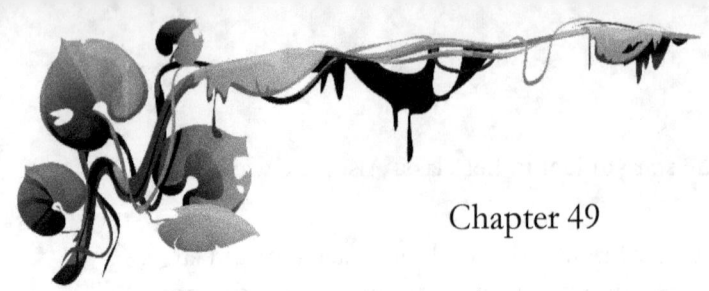

Chapter 49

Kapuna la ʻau lapa ʻau

(Hawaiian physician)

Kimo was making preparations for the long night that lay ahead.

Kupuna Hannah remained in her deep sleep, lost in the realm of darkness.

Luke and the other children and, of course, Max, had been sent to collect more jewel orchids.

Ray had gone along with them as these were very dangerous times. The ceremony to lift the spell cast on Kupuna would be repeated when Puna and Pastor arrived. They could make the difference in the generation of enough mana to exorcise the demon within their beloved healer.

Hannah was a Kupuna laʻau lapaʻau or a Hawaiian physician. Physicians observed rituals devoted to the god Lono, the patron spirit of healing, and they strived to emulate their ancestral aumakua, living their lives in a manner that would make them worthy of receiving mana. Hence, prayers and offerings were made earlier at the House of Mana created just days ago. Legends repeatedly state that when a Kupuna or a Kahuna laʻau lapaʻau was dying, he or she passed on their unique body of knowledge regarding medicines and healing by breathing it in to his or her protégé.

The breathe of knowledge.

Ray thought he had seen his brother, Joe-the-owl-as-protector at the site of the rare orchids. An owl had cast a shadow over the troupe and Ray had felt certain that this particular owl was, in fact, Joe. Ray felt reassured to know that his aumakua was nearby.

Kekela remained faithfully at Hannah's bedside. He was communicating with her by telepathy but, so far, it was a one-way conversation. He was attempting to keep the evil mu at bay.

Kimo had just returned from the awa water brook where he had cleansed the tapa mat and himself. He was ambivalent about whether or not he should allow David to participate. Should he risk it?

Or was it, in fact, now necessary to include David to restore the mana that was lost when he broke the chain?

He sat at the dining table, food items spread out before him. Knowing that others were coming today, the cooks at their camps or caves, killed, cleaned and cooked the chickens that they had gathered and penned. They feasted before the cruel night arrived.

Prayers were offered to the aumakua, and they enumerated those of the heavens; of the east, north, south, and west; of the mountains, the sea, the water, and the land.

After a prayer by the people was uttered, the locals were enjoying the barbeque meat and a variety of sides. Seaweed salad, poi, banana bread, rice, and beans. And, now, so was Kimo.

A fresh breeze was flowing into the cave. The happy sounds of his people sharing good food and good company wafted in on the wind.

It didn't take long before the kids and Max showed up with Ray.

"Dad, is that barbeque chicken?" asked Luke as he sniffed the air. Max followed suit.

Luke didn't wait for a response as he grabbed a plate and sat down. He saw the buffet of foods and smiled. After all, he was a teenager and growing and changing every day. Max waited patiently at Peter's feet, longing for some of the chicken. After Luke had inhaled his food, Max received his own delicious reward.

Then, Max showed his appreciation by offering up a loud belch. In turn, this caused both David and Hina to erupt in laughter. Laughing and crying were the only vocal sounds from the mute girl. Sure enough, she was laughing.

Hina was already sitting beside Kimo. She too had found a plate and brought several more to the table. She loved banana bread so she took two, large pieces of the coveted food.

With mud on his face, David asked, "Uncle, this is awesome!" In an instance, David loaded his plate. "Good chicken…..ummmm."

Ray sat down. "I guess we should eat hearty while we can. Looks good, my friend."

Kimo was eating a mango he'd found on the trail as he returned to the caves from the sacred brook. It was mango season. He'd brought back several for his gang. He thought about Kate.

She made a delicious mango pie. He felt tears well up in his eyes.

His heart ached for her.

And little Hannah. Was she still alive? Pastor will have that knowledge.

He pushed those thoughts out of his mind. He could not think about losing them.

"Ray, it will be a long night before us. We must be ready – on many levels." Kimo wiped his chin with a paper towel, as it was dripping with mango juice. His sticky fingers got stuck in the paper towel, irritating him. He felt short-tempered and resisted the impulse to grunt and shout an obscenity. Now was not the time to lose it. He was troubled by his concerns for Kate and his little girl. He didn't think he had the strength to hear news of his daughter's death.

"Understood. I intend to bathe and pray myself. I know Kane will not fail us!" Ray said with great fervor," In Him, we trust. 'Cause really, there's nothin' else we can do."

"We will all pray together at sunset. Hopefully, Puna and Pastor will arrive by then," said Kimo. He looked at each child to make sure they had heard him. Affirmation all around. Even though they were children, they understood to some degree the gravity of the night that loomed large.

What he didn't tell them was that he had had a visit from an owl. It was his old friend, Joe. He had overheard the conversation between Kai and Duke earlier. Joe–the-owl-as-protector realized that both Kai and Duke were tied up right now with other things so he had taken it upon himself to convey the information to Kimo. Thus, he had visited Kimo at the awa water brook, as he cleansed himself. He told him about the mega wave that was on its way and the approach of the deadly mist. Ray had been right when he said there wasn't anything more that they could do.

The sacred, mountainous caves were at an elevation of 1, 684 feet. Hopefully, high enough.

But what about Kate and Hannah?

Kimo knew intuitively that the key to their success against Kanaloa lay with restoring Kupuna to herself, back in the light of day.

He reflected on the ceremony that they had performed and failed at. Maybe, it wasn't all about David's misstep in breaking the chain and decreasing the power or mana that they had tried to generate. Kimo realized that it was more than just that. It was about the power of words that could render them dangerous, rather than healing.

Words hurt. Curses killed.

All too often as mayor, Kimo had seen the terrible forces that had been unleashed due to careless speaking. Over and over again, he witnessed how words were like poison. He knew that hurtful words are not forgotten. This poison always seemed to be a component of cases of domestic violence or murders for revenge. Jealousy-running-amok cases too.

I ka 'olelo ke ola, I ka 'olelo ka make. In the word, there is life; in the word, death.

He was not a Kapuna. He wasn't even sure he had used the right chant – the right words –and said it in the right way.

Words had power. Incantations worked. A correctly recited prayer rushes to its goal.

It wasn't David who should not participate. It was him!

He was thinking clearly now. It needed to be Pastor to perform the ceremony. Also, they would need the gold key. He prayed for Pastor's safe deliverance.

And soon.

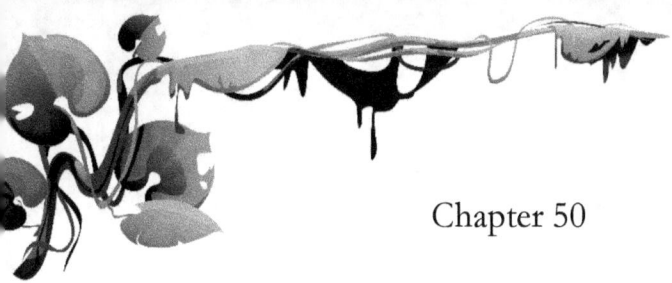

Chapter 50

He uahoa he lima na ka makani
(Ruthless, with hands of a gale)

Pastor and Puna remained unconscious under the shady tree.

When Kai arrived with the gourd containing the life-saving awa water, both men were still alive. But, barely. Their breathing was very irregular and shallow.

Thankfully, he had arrived in the nick of time!

The owl settled down beside the two fallen men. He quickly released the gourd from his grip.

He wasted no time in taking the stopper out. Time mattered.

A black mist arose from the gourd. It had a pungent odor, like a decomposing rat. What had been released was not the Jeannie in the bottle. It was something evil. It was a mu spirit!

Immediately, Kai understood the evil intent of this spirit sent by Milu. Ruler of the dead.

This spirit was the breath of death!

Kai realized that, if inhaled, it would be the kiss of death. He must protect their mouth and nose! Quickly, he grabbed a nearby wet towel and covered Pastor's half-exposed face. He had difficulty reaching Puna's face. He saw that the boy had his face resting in the crook of his arm.

The mu spirit sang a dark mele,

He uahoa, he lima na ka makani. Ruthless, with hands of a gale.

This is said about a ruthless person who strikes and hurries away. That was exactly the nature of this particular mu spirit when it was a mortal.

The mu spirit kept circling around the head of the Pastor, seeking access to offer the killing blow. Kai used his wings like a fan to keep them at bay. But, he feared he could not defeat it as it was able to transform into just a thin, wisp of black smoke, which appeared readily able to escape up a nostril. Kai-the-owl-as-protector cried out, sounding the alarm, and hoping that another aumakua was within reach to hear his cry for help.

Kai heard the Pastor moan. Something within him had been stirred awake and it was his own spirit. It was the breath of life that lived within him. He kept fanning Pastor's face area as the dark smoke danced and darted all around it. At some point, his wings would need to rest.

He let out anther S.O.S. call.

A large shadow was cast over them. It came with a squawk. In fact, it was a familiar squawk!

Duke had answered the call for help. He had in the grasp of his claws a gourd. Its gurgling noise was a reassuring sound. Was it filled with awa water?

Reading his friend's thoughts, Duke answered, *Of course, it is awa water - for your son and our friend here. But, how did you know?* asked Kai. He was still using his weary wings to fan the men. Of course, that was a rhetorical question.

Duke uncorked the stopper in the gourd. Then, with remarkable dexterity, Duke poured the awa water onto the face of the Pastor. He poured the awa water over Puna's face. Some of the water dribbled down on Puna, landing on his dry lips.

Kai dropped his wings and looked at the two unconscious men. He was looking for signs of life.

He was not disappointed.

Pastor's eyes opened. He inhaled deeply and exhaled slowly. Slowly, Pastor tried to sit up. He found himself looking into the large, yellow eyes of a pueo. Immediately, he recognized his dear, old friend Kai.

"Am I dead?" His throat was very dry.

Pastor grimaced as he sat up further. Every muscle in his body ached. In this moment, Pastor felt very old.

You're alright, old man!

"Get off of me!" demanded a perturbed Puna. "What happened anyways?"

"I guess we took a long nap son. I suspect it was against our will." Pastor had moved completely off Puna. When Puna sat up, he saw the owl and he knew that it was, indeed, his beloved father. His aumakua had saved him and Pastor. Duke had already flown away, his mission accomplished.

"Father!" cried Puna. He too was trying to orient himself to the situation and reconcile in his mind exactly what had transpired here. The reality that they had been nearly killed was just sinking in.

"You saved our lives. Mahalo, my dear father," said Puna with great affection. The owl looked directly at his son. *I will always remain close to you and your mother, son.*

Puna remained unaware of his mother's state. Now that Puna was safe, Kai would return to the sacred cave, nearby his wife.

Son, waste no more time. You must get Pastor to the cave before nightfall.

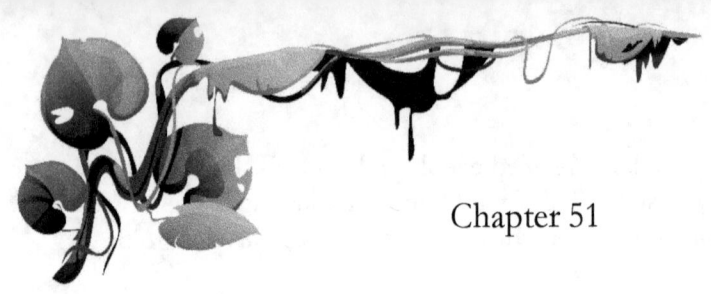

Chapter 51

Lono-'opua-kau

(Lono-of-the-omens-in-the-clouds)

Peter had succumbed to the snake venom just like his fallen friends. He lay still under the tree.

Thunder boomed in the mountains and rain poured suddenly from the dark skies.

Legends assert that thunder and lightning were extremely strong in the old days when they were worshipped by the Hawaiian descendants. It killed their enemies and turned them into stones. In accordance with the old traditions, the thunder and lightning was an expression of rage from an unhappy god in the trinity. Hence, there had been a long history of violent storms.

The god Lono had responded to Peter's cry for help. The water was blessed by Lono and was, therefore, as life-saving and cleansing as awa water.

Similarly, this water was toxic to the mu spirits that roamed around as poisonous snakes.

They all swarmed to the brook, to avoid the caustic rain water. As the downpour persisted, the brook became a fast-moving stream. Soon, it became an overflowing stream that was rushing towards the ocean, sweeping all of the snakes out to sea. The mu spirits had been vanquished.

Peter quickly revived.

Shortly after, Pilikana and Mana woke up and began to check their legs for the snake bites.

Several areas were red and swollen. And, a little sore.

They stood up slowly and looked over at Peter who was already standing up. He was observing the rushing, red water filled with the black snakes gushing down the mountain.

As the two comrades approached Peter, Mana asked, "What happened?"

"I'm afraid that we will have to talk on the road. We need to make haste if we are going to get to the caves before dark." Peter began gathering their belongings. "Besides, we need to catch up to Pastor, Puna and Maui."

"I hope Maui got there in time," said Pilikana.

"Let's go find out," said Mana, fully alert and raring to go.

The soldiers of Kane marched onward, climbing further up the mountain, in the hot and humid air. In addition, the air was becoming more charge with static. As they climbed to higher altitudes, it became more difficult to breathe. Despite that, they went as quickly as they could, picking up their pace.

As they climbed higher and higher, the dark skies over the ocean glowed with the green mist. It was a frightening sight. It was a forbidding sky, charged with something toxic and deadly.

It was mid-afternoon. They were headed to the awa water brook to cleanse and prepare for what lay ahead that night. They spoke very little on their journey, saving their energy. They also remained vigilant, watching for any further mu spirits. Undoubtedly, Kanaloa would have more tricks up his sleeve.

They were approaching the side trail to the secret location of the awa water brook. The narrow trail was about six miles long, running along the side of a rocky cliff, where the roaring ocean waves crashed against the rocks. Sea birds glided in the prevailing winds, floating on the turbulence. Between the noise of the surf below and the squawking of the marine birds, it was difficult to hear each other. Almost impossible, as a matter of fact.

In the practice of 'ana'ana or sorcery, another type of imposing an evil deed was through magical, dark prayers by the evil doers. The prayer was called, *pule 'ana'ana*. This prayer was offered to the evil one before a laborious undertaking, one that was filthy, deadly and dangerous.

Of course, Haumea practiced black magic. She had uttered such a prayer. One hour ago.

What was her filthy, deadly and dangerous intention? What heinous deed had she set in motion?

As the men negotiated the trail on the cliff, Haumea's prayer had been to the mu spirits, "Concentrate on that solid cliff and make it slide into the ocean."

And so, the mu spirits departed for their mission.

There was a shift in the dark clouds and the sun broke through, lifting the men's spirits and penetrating warmth. They were getting close to the brook and its grassy knolls and rich vegetation. By now, they were very thirsty, especially for the rejuvenating awa water. It had been a difficult six miles.

Peter heard it first.

The noise level went up by several decibels. A dark mass blocked out the sun rays. There seemed to be a change in the air's density.

Pilikana and Mana had noticed the changes in the noise, the skies, and the swampy air. They looked toward the dark mass as it came closer into view. It was a large flock of Leach's Storm- Petrel marine birds.

There must have been at least two hundred of the dark, dangerous, predatory sea birds. These medium-sized sea birds were dark, slate gray in color in their upperparts and white in color in their underparts. Other distinctive markings include very dark sides of its neck and underwing margins that are coal-black. The petrel's long, dark bill is hooked like Captain Hook. Its flight pattern is bounding and erratic with frequent changes in speed and direction.

Immediately, the trio recognized these birds as mu spirits. Scary-looking creatures.

On closer inspection, one could see that their normally dark eyes glowed red. Devil-red.

These predatory birds suddenly attacked the gentle sea birds that hung off this cliff that was their home. On mass, they struck out to mutilate the home birds.

The attacks were brutal.

The long, hooked-beaks were like sharp-cutting knives. With their ability to quickly change speed and directions, they could readily slit the throats of the indigenous sea birds. It was a bloody scene as red blood gushed from the home birds' throats as they spiraled down to the sharp rocks and, then, were swept out to sea. Red sea spray covered the men as they watched the gory, horror-scene unfold.

These ruthless creatures were out for the kill.

The home birds that had not been massacred had retreated to their nests in the crooks and crannies of the cliff.

The black petrels began to line up in some kind of formation. They were such a large, dark mass.

Perhaps, an attack formation.

Peter, Pilikana and Mana looked on helplessly. How could they possibly defend themselves against these killing demons?

Peter realized that there was only one way.

As Peter prepared to defend against the evil spirits, the dark-winged devils, lined up in the formation of a V, began to generate a loud, vibrating noise that was painful to the ears, much like a dog whistle is to the affected four-legged friend.

The ground beneath their feet began to rumble. Moreover, the cliff-side began to slowly crumble as though the mountain was tumble down, like the Green Giant. Pebbles and small rocks began falling from the mountain.

Peter shouted over the noise, "Join hands! We must pule 'ana'ana!"

They became quiet and began to pray the magical incantation.

White magic.

White sorcery in action.

Although it was very recent, Peter had been ordained as a professor of 'ana'ana or white magic. He possessed powers that he did not fully comprehend yet. He had not explored the limits of these new gifts. He did understand that these new powers were not to be misused or they would be taken away. In the past, professors of 'ana'ana had used their special powers for their own personal gain. The consequences were fatal.

You see, 'ana'ana can be a virtuous profession. When that is the case, it is called *'oihana hemolele*. The opportunity to become a professor of white sorcery was only given to a humble man who is pure in thought. It is a means of absolution (*he pu'u kalahala*) and a way to dispel troubles. Legends purport that the gods will help such a man until he walks with a cane and his hair has turned white.

The work of learning the magical prayers required the eating of disgusting and poisonous foods. Had the poisonous pokeberries been a part of this process to become a professor of white magic?

It was an ancient prayer that mirrored the Holy Scriptures, Deuteronomy 18:10,11.

"There shall not be found among you anyone that maketh his son or daughter to pass through the fire, or that useth divination (*kahuna 'ana'ana*), or an observer of times (*mea nana I kea o*), or an enchanter (*mea nana I ka mo'o*), or a witch (*mea kilo*), or a charmer (*mea ho'owalewale I na nahesa*), or a consulter with familiar spirits (*mea ninau I na 'uhane 'ino*), or a wizard (*he kupua*), or a necromancer (*po'e ninau I kapo'e make*)."

(Kamakua, Samuel Manaiakalani. 1991. Ka Po'e Kahiko: The People of Old. Bishop Museum Press: Honolulu, p.123).

The noise level began to decrease. The rocks stopped falling from the mountain side.

The dark, ominous creatures fell out of formation. Whatever entity had had control over the mu spirits, no longer did. The flock had darted in different directions and fled the area.

Another defeat against Kanaloa.

One thing that they could count on was that Kanaloa would be infuriated by this latest defeat and he would not be appeased until he was able to succeed at eliminating his enemies.

The long night awaited.

Chapter 52

'olelo Pololi au

(I'm hungry)

Little Hannah's recovery was amazing. She had fully recovered.

Kate had been asleep for the past few hours, catching up on her rest and energy level. She had plans for herself and her daughter this afternoon.

Right after lunch, they would leave and begin the traverse up the mountain trail. They had discussed and they had mutually agreed that, as soon as possible, they wished to be reunited with the rest of their family. Hannah asserted that she was well enough to make the difficult journey. One of the nurses at the hospital had offered them a donkey for the trip for little Hannah. It was her husband who was glad to help. After all, that was the nature of the local people. Mele would attend to the food preparations, including the noni drinks.

They were running out of the wellness drink.

Of course, Uncle Bert was also coming with them. As their aumakua, he was obliged to be a protector. Bert wouldn't have it any other way!

Bert feared the weather outlook. It was 11:00 am. and the skies were already dark and thunder rumbled as the day progressed. The wind was gusting, sometimes up to 17 mph. It would be a difficult obstacle to overcome.

But, lest they forget, they had an angel among them.

"Uncle Bert, you forget that I can read your mind," said Hannah. "We'll be fine. Don't worry.

I won't let anything happen to Mom or you." "I hope so, baby girl."

"Hey, I'm starving. Any chance I can get a burger or an ahi sandwich?" wondered Hannah.

"I'm sure Mele will make you something, especially since she's her old self again. She adores you too, honey."

"Enough to ask for sweet potato fries too?" She had a wide grin on her face. "With mayonnaise."

"Okay. I'll ask the nurse," replied Hannah. She reached for her call bell. "Wait!" exclaimed Bert.

Reading his mind, she declared, "I'll know if she's Haumea or her mu spirits."

Zippity-do-da! Zippity-day!

Soon, a nurse entered the room. She was an older, Hawai'ian woman with her long, silver hair in a regal bun. She was well known in the community as a kind auntie. She taught Sunday School at the family's church. She had taught Hina and David and, more recently, little Hannah.

"Auntie Naomi! It's really you!" Hannah adored this kind-spirited woman.

"Who else would it be, little lamb?" She'd been a nurse at the hospital for twenty-six years.

"Honey-girl, you are a miracle child!" exclaimed Naomi. She rushed over and hugged the little girl.

"I have been blessed," replied Hannah.

"What can I do for you, honey-girl?" asked the cheerful woman. Her eyes twinkled.

Hannah inquired about getting some food from the kitchen.

"Got a sweet tooth? You want any dessert?" It was apparent that she had a sweet tooth. A few Dove chocolates were visible in her smock pocket. Naomi was a large woman who enjoyed her food.

"That'd be great, Auntie!"

"I will go directly to the kitchen now." The kind nurse turned and left to fulfill the request of the blessed child.

I miss eatin' the foods I used to love. Roast pork with gravy, mashed potatoes, lemon chiffon pie, steak and eggs, prime rib, BLT, spaghetti, lasagna, Italian sausage, and macaroni and cheese. Oh, and coconut cake. Cherry pie or blueberry pie with vanilla ice cream....

"Alright already, Uncle Bert. I get it!" Hannah moaned. "You're making me hungry – as hungry as a bear!!!"

Well, just image, I can't eat those things I long for. Right now, I'm eatin' bugs.

"Gross! You're absolutely right, Uncle." She smiled. "I apologize."

Okay, then.

As Naomi entered the room with a tray of food, Hannah sat up eagerly. Once the tray was placed before her, she dug in. Soon, she was making the happy noises that reflected her enjoyment. She ate heartily and that included both haupia pudding and mango cobbler.

Shortly, Kate entered the room.

"I hope I didn't sleep through lunch," she said as she yawned. She pulled an ahi sandwich out of her bag, with taro chips and some of the mango cobbler. She ate with much zeal as she too was starving!

"No, Mom. This was just a snack," she kidded and rubbed her full tummy.

"Seems like it was quite a snack! Somebody spoiled you!" said Kate, smiling. It was good to see that her little girl had her healthy appetite back.

"I had two desserts!" said the girl proudly. "And, Mom? Guess who got the food for me?" "Who was your good Samaritan, honey?" "Auntie Naomi."

"But, honey, that's impossible. Auntie Naomi died several months ago." "I swear Mom. It was her! Ask Uncle Bert!"

Kate saw the green lizard on Hannah's tray table. He was licking the plate that had once held a piece of delicious cobbler. Uncle Bert paused and looked up at Kate.

She did say her name was Auntie Naomi, Kate.

Kate gasped. Stark fear shone on her face.

He grew concerned as he realized the implications. He immediately regretted licking the plate.

Chapter 53

Ku ka lani iluna ke ku'I kapalulu
(The sky stands above, rumbling).

As the day pushed ahead, so did Pastor, Puna and Maui. And, of course, the donkey who seemed tireless, even with his passenger and supplies on board. The beast of burden would need to stop and drink water to cool down and rehydrate the donkey for the remainder of the journey.

A light rain had begun to fall, offering some relief from the hot and humid air. In the distance, the thunder rumbled over the ocean. The green mist was a reminder that something ominous was approaching the island. It helped them to go on.

They became aware of the approaching tsunami after receiving a visit from Kai-the-owl-as- protector. He had told his son what he must do.

Ancient Hawai'ian traditions dictated many mystical approaches to phenomena that threatened their very existence.

"What did your father counsel you to do, Puna?" asked Pastor as he stopped to wipe his brow under his large hat and drink some water as the heat became more and more oppressive. It wouldn't be long now before they reached the sacred awa water oasis.

Maui stopped to listen to Puna's response.

"He said that with the help of the gods, the enemy will be defeated or we will die. It will be a fight to the death or retreat of one side or the other," replied Puna.

"So either we will defeat our enemy or we will die fighting them. Does that about sum it up?" Maui drank deeply from his canteen, as rivulets of sweat dripped down his face. "That's about it." Puna affirmed Maui's assertion. "There's more."

"Okay son, let's hear it," said Pastor as he stretched his legs and sat up in the saddle to relieve his sore bottom.

"We must act as the chief of Kauai did to fight the powerful sea monster that had killed most of his people."

"Refresh my memory, if you would," requested Maui.

"Several centuries ago, the chief was in a battle for the survival of his people. Many had been slain. His son, Kau'ilani who was strong and wise beyond his years, was also a professor of 'ana'ana."

"I've heard about white sorcery." Maui nodded. "I've been told legends about it from my grandfather."

"At the request of *his* father, the son and some men went and cut down some trees and set them into the ground below the cliffs near their mountain home. Then, a feast was prepared. A feast for the gods. At the stroke of midnight, Kau'ilani prayed:

"O gods of the mountains, come!

O gods of the ocean, come! O gods of the South,

Gods of the North, O all you gods, Come to our aid.

The trees are set at the foot of the cliff. Oh, multiple the trees,

Then feast, Bananas are ready,

Breadfruit, and sugar cane. O multitude of gods,

Come to our aid,

Then feast."

(Puku'i, Mary Kawena. 1994. The Water of Kane and Other Legends of the Hawaiian Islands, revised edition. Kamehameha Schools Press, Honolulu, Hawaii, p. 119).

White magic.

"How do you know the magical prayers?" asked Maui. "I am training to be a Kahuna," responded Puna.

I'm not sure I agree with any magical powers, even white magic, but, we must trust our aumakua, especially one as wise as Kai, your Kapuna father," said Pastor.

Thunder rumbled and the wind grew stronger.

"Kupuna is a practitioner of white 'ana'ana," declared Pastor. "We will surely need her."

"Funny, I haven't been able to connect in thought with my mother. Pastor, is something wrong?" inquired the son.

Pastor paused and he knew it was time to tell the son about his mother that he so dearly loved.

"I'm afraid so." Pastor explained to Puna what had transpired that placed his mother into a deep state of darkness. A flash of fear passed over his face. He took a deep breath.

Black magic had been used against her, despite her goodness and faithfulness.

"We must get to her!" cried Puna. "We need to hurry."

With Maui leading the way, they set out, climbing in elevation, ever closer to the sacred water. They expected that Kanaloa would try to sabotage them before they reached the location. Vigilance would be required these next few miles.

They continued to follow the yellow brick road.

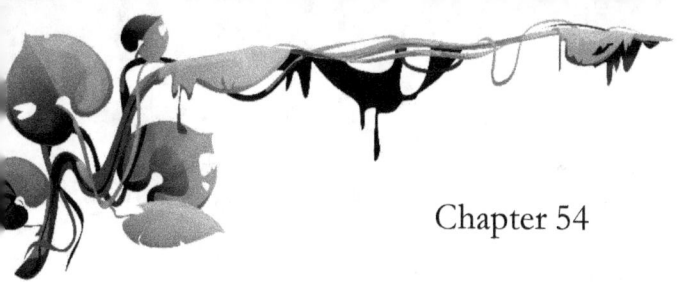

Chapter 54

He ano no ka po pihapiha
(A fear of the night greatly full)

It had only been three days ago since the rebel Hawaiian men had murdered the people (some of them their friends and neighbors, even family members) staying at the lodge. Their arson act had killed any individuals that they had missed shooting to death when they went on their rampage. Apparently, the site was still aglow with burning embers, black smoke rising in the sky.

They were murderers and arsonists. They were now minions in Satan's army.

Overcome by the lust of power and killing, they were eager to kill again.

These soldiers had received new marching orders.

They had been given specific directives from Satan and a cautionary warning to avoid the awa water.

Stay away from that location. Kapu!

Using an alternate trail up the mountain, they were racing off to kill as many people that they could, the folks in the caves. These were more friends, neighbors, and relatives. Not that that mattered because these men were no longer men who possessed s ouls. As sunset approached, they would perform a satanic ritual and become *Night Marchers*. Night Marchers are the ghosts of ancient Hawaiian warriors. On the night of Kane, they are said to come forth, rising from their burial sites to march out to past battles or sacred places.

These mysterious Night Marchers had certain characteristics. They emerged on a certain night of the Hawaiian moon calendar.

Accompanying them was inclement weather including heavy rain and high surf, thunder and lightning, a mist or fog, and heavy winds. As they get in close proximity, one can hear drumming that is distant at first, but then it gets louder. In addition, there was a foul, musky smell associated with their presence. It was the smell of a dead animal that had been decomposing in the hot sun for several days.

These men had sold their souls with the knowledge of the no refund policy offered by Satan.

On closer inspection, these men did not look like proud Hawaiian warriors. Not at all. These men looked like a pack of wild animals because that is what they were now. Animals employed by Kanaloa. This zig-zag trail was slower going so they had left at dawn's break. They moved as jungle guerillas, with stealth, speed, and silence.

The leader of the pack was named Owa. He belonged to the third rank of the ao or the realm of the spirits of the dead. *Kea ao o Milu*, the realm of the ruler of the dead, Milu. He was a very large man that stood over six feet tall. His long, jet-black hair was in a ponytail that hung down his strong, well-muscled back. His chiseled face bore strong features. Romance novels would describe him as the embodiment of being strong, ruggedly-handsome, and sexually-charged.

The flank trail that these men were taking was closer to that area where the lodge once stood and the air quality from the smoke was poor. Hopefully, that might slow these evil soldiers down.

How many supernatural powers did these men possess?

Lead by Owa, they had made good progress. Much like men on steroids, they had almost raced up the mountain. By nightfall, they would surely arrive. They wanted to use the darkness as cover to slip into the caves and use their sharp spears to cut them down, as the Hawaiian warriors had done for so many centuries. But these were not the honorable Hawaiian warriors described in the history books. These men had no honor.

They had been given a despicable mission.

In a bloody assault, they intended to slaughter as many people as they could. It was another use of the devil's favorite weapon – discouragement to the extreme. But there was a catch to it. First, they must get the people to look at them. Before they could murder someone, they had to get the person to look into their eyes. This enables the Night Marcher to claim the victim's soul first. No matter, the Night Marchers have many strategies or tricks to get the poor fools to look at them.

Demoralize them by massacring them in significant numbers.

Death is deeply felt by Hawaiians. In ancient times, they sought relief from their consuming grief through self-mutilation.

Then, these devil soldiers planned to ingest the dead flesh. It was believed that the conversion of flesh into food removed the mana from their enemies that they, in turn, could reap. Cannibalism served to increase their mana. In the earlier days of old, cannibalism was practiced in some South Pacific societies as the ultimate insult to a defeated enemy.

Demoralize them by reducing them to eatable animals.

The flesh would be cut from the corpse and then placed in an imu to cook. An imu is an earth oven, constructed by lining pits with stones. The foods are wrapped in wetted ti or banana leaves, and then they are covered with wet leaves and a layer of earth. The oven reached high temperatures for cooking. The flesh was cooked until it was well done.

Just as they had celebrated on Kauai after the slaughter of the chief's people, these men would sing this mele after the people were dead and vanished from the earth.

Make ke au kaha o piko o ka honua;'oia pukaua

Hua na lau laaa nalo nalo I ka po liolio.

Dead was the current flowing from the center of the earth, they were war leaders,

They rose up as many as leaves and vanished vanished in the running night.

(Charlot, C. and Charlot, John. 1983. Chanting the universe: Hawaiian religious culture. Emphasis International Limited: Honolulu, Hawaii, p. 95).

The demonic men were perverse in their intention to both murder and then eat their dead enemies. They were anticipating with great excitement the evil deeds that they had planned.

It was early afternoon before they stopped briefly to rest. After all, now that they were the devil's property, they possessed supernatural powers, including great strength.

They would attack under the veil of darkness. For Hawai'ians, night is not the mere absence of the day. Darkness has a physical presence of its own. These evil warriors hoped that, after tonight, no new day would arrive.

Many souls would be entering into the unending night of death.

Weak souls, newly separated from their protective mortal bodies, are even more vulnerable to the stronger, voracious spirits that prowl the night. As the soul makes its journey, it is full of *weliweli* or an abiding dread regarding their past transgressions. Their Day of Judgment was at hand.

There was another visceral fear that the Hawaiians held about the soul's journey in the darkness.

Iliilhia fear.

They dreaded the review of their wrong deeds from the scroll by an angel. As they traveled through time and space, they began to vividly remember their transgressions, both large and small. With each remembrance, they experienced the pain that they had caused others. Real empathy pain. Apparently, far worse than the pains of labor.

Hawaiians had projected the image of a soul traveling through the different, dark dimensions as that of a bird, featherless and without protection.

O mihi I ke anuanu, huluhulu 'ole

O mihi I ka welawela I ke 'a'ahu 'ole

Repentant in the great cold, featherless Repentant in the great heat,

In my coverlessness.

(Charlot, p. 93, Chanting)

It wasn't long before the men noticed that the mountain terrain was absent with the familiar sounds of nature. With the exception of black flies, all creatures in close proximity to this small army fled with great fear.

They feared extinction.

Rebellion in Heaven and on Earth

Behold the gods
of Hawaii, the birthplace of lands,
of Hawaii, the birthplace of Gods,
of Hawaii, the birthplace of people!
Gods inside, gods outside,
Gods above, gods below,
Gods oceanward, gods landward,
Gods incarnate, gods not incarnate,
Gods punishing sins, gods pardoning sins,
Gods devouring men, gods slaying warriors,
Gods saving men, Gods of darkness, gods of light,
Gods of the ten skies.
Can all the gods be counted?
The gods cannot all be counted!

(Luomala, Katherine. 1986. Voices on the wind: Polynesian Myths and chants (revised edition). Bishop Museum. Honolulu, Hawaii, p. 63).

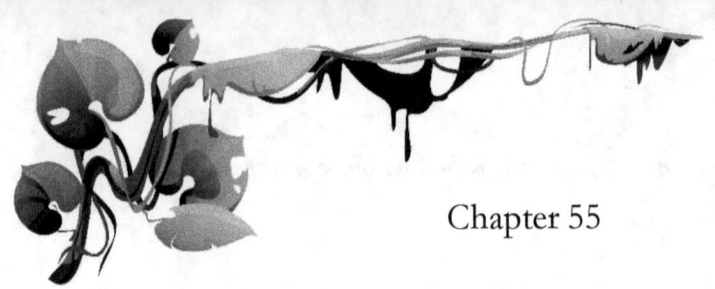

Chapter 55

E lono I kou pomaik'i. Eia!

(Listen to your blessedness. It is here!)

Nothing untoward had occurred after little Hannah had ingested the food that Naomi had brought for the little angel. In fact, she was feeling better than ever.

It appeared that the food had been blessed and delivered from the angel, Naomi. One angel to another. Hannah had gained great strength- great mana- from the blessed food. It would serve her well in the near hours that lay ahead on this epic journey.

Needless to say, Uncle Bert was okay too.

But try telling him that. For the last hour, he had been pissin' and moanin' like he was a dying man, or rather, a dying lizard. Didn't he remember he was already dead?

"I think I'm feeling some better," Uncle Bert said.

"For goodness sake, you were never sick to begin with!" laughed Kate.

Hannah chimed in, "Uncle Bert, you got some imagination! You thought we'd been poisoned, didn't you?" She laughed.

"Look Mom, he's turned a darker shade of green," Hannah said with glee. After all, she was just a kid.

"Haven't you ever seen a lizard blush?" Uncle Bert was clearly embarrassed.

"Okay. I think we've teased him enough, honey," said Kate with a smirk.

"I didn't think Uncle Bert could even get embarrassed, let alone blush!" declared Hannah. "Well as much as I enjoy entertaining you ladies, we should get going." Bert reminded them.

Before their departure, Hannah had a visitor. Kekele, although still in a wheelchair, was on her road to recovery. The hypothermic intervention for the water parasite in her brain had been eradicated.

Thanks to an angel.

Their provisions were packed and ready to go, except they had made a change to their plan. Little Hannah felt so good that they had decided to ride on horses. Both Kate and Hannah knew how to ride. They would make better progress on horseback. The long afternoon stretched ahead. They were hours behind those that went earlier in the day.

By noon, they were on the trail.

Two horses, a mother and child, and a lizard aumakua were off to see the wizard. A wizard who practiced white sorcery.

Both mother and child wore large, wide-brimmed hats. Their fair skin and strawberry hair made them vulnerable to sunburn and heat rash. Their attire included long-sleeved cotton tops and cotton pants and solid footwear. Uncle Bert rode on Hannah's saddle, right near where her hands were holding the reins.

"Whoa!!!" cried Uncle Bert. "I'm gonna fall off with all this bouncing!"

"Be careful, Uncle Bert," replied Hannah.

"I can't with all this horse beneath me! Put me somewhere safe," demanded the frightened lizard.

Little Hannah finally got it. Uncle Bert was not safe and he needed a more contained, stable place to continue to ride up the ever-increasingly mountain trail.

"I know," said Hannah with confidence. "I'll put you in my shirt pocket."

"Great. Now, instead of being terrified of falling off and getting squashed by a horse hoof, I can suffer with claustrophobia in your hot pocket."

Little Hannah chuckled.

"Uncle Bert, don't worry. It's cotton so you'll feel some air through it. Trust me, you'll be okay." She smiled at her ornery Uncle. She understood that he was afraid.

Again, did he forget he was already dead?

"Okay, okay. And, yes I know I'm on a visitor's permit here but, I'm not ready to go back. I want to make sure that you and your Mom are okay. That's all."

Hannah scooped up the lizard and gently placed him in her shirt pocket over her heart.

"It's sort of like a nest in here so, if you don't mind, I believe I'll take a nap." "Just don't snore too loud. I find it very irritating." Hannah giggled.

Kate was laughing too. She had overheard the entire exchange.

"Honey, how are you doing? You feel okay?" inquired Kate.

"I'm fine Mom. Although, my butt is kind of sore."

"That's because you don't have any body fat," suggested Kate.

Her girl was too thin. She intended to fatten her up.

"Truthfully, I am kinda hungry."

"Okay. We will take a break soon and eat and attend to the horses. Till then, let Uncle sleep." Kate added, "Besides, my butt's killing me too!"

Uncle Bert wasn't asleep yet. He chuckled as he overheard the mother and daughter's interaction.

Besides, Bert not only knew that he was deceased; he also knew that he was an aumakua with powerful green mana.

He sighed. They would be okay.

A half-hour later, they were at the first brook site on the trail.

They lead the horses to the refreshing, fresh water brook, allowing them to cool off under a shady tree. Greedily, the thirsty horses drank deeply.

"Hey, can I get out of here!" Bert was obviously awake.

"Hang on to your hat, buster!" said Hannah.

"I'm gonna get sick with all this bouncing around!" complained the lizard with a sour disposition. He popped his head out of the top of the pocket. "Hello!"

Kate laughed and said, "Uncle Bert, you get grumpy when you're hungry. There will be some yummy bugs under that shady tree. That's where we will take a break." She pointed to a nearby tree and then handed Hannah an old, gray blanket.

"Mom, yummy bugs? Really? That's gross."

"Not if you're a lizard," stated Bert. "Lady Bugs are especially good."

"No eating Lady Bugs, Uncle Bert." Little Hannah was firm about that. She liked Lady Bugs. "I'll get our backpack and we'll see what goodies they prepared for us," said Kate. She went over to her horse that was carrying their supplies. The horse enjoyed having it off his back.

Her daughter was sitting against the tree, stretching her legs (and butt). Uncle Bert was cruising nearby looking for bugs, hoping for a buffet. With the exception of Lady Bugs, he would feast!

Kate joined Hannah and laid out some of the food items. When the food was set before her, Hannah's stomach grumbled. There were roast beef sandwiches with a side of pickles, purple sweet potato chips, and a water melon. Hannah wasted no time to dig in given her state of hunger.

The skies remained dark and heavy. Thunder rumbled throughout the mountain cliffs and valleys. Sea birds flew overhead.

"You certainly are hungry!" said Kate, as she watched her daughter consume the treasured food items at record speed.

Kate was enjoying Mele's delights too. That was until the black flies started to bother them.

At first, there were just a few, annoying flies hovering around the food.

"Dang flies!" said Kate with disgust.

Then, about ten more arrived, announcing themselves with their loud, irritating buzz noise.

"These flies are persistent pests! Nasty, dirty flies," grumbled Kate.

"Mom, I think they are not just flies," said little Hannah. Her demeanor was sober. "What do you mean, honey?"

Hannah pointed over Kate's shoulder, her eyes wide.

Kate turned around and looked at the sky. Against the dark skies, a large swarm of ink-black flies was fast approaching, headed right for them. It was a frightening sight.

Swarms of mating flies create black clouds. Besides being vectors for diseases, the female adults, known as gnats, have a nasty bite. Many suffer big, red welts at the site of the bite and they are very itchy. Others suffer a severe allergic reaction. Adult females enter the eyes, ears, nose, and mouth of animals and humans. In the immature stages of development, the flies are aquatic and exclusively inhabit flowing streams.

But, these flies were more than nasty irritants. They were, in fact, the malevolent mu spirits.

"Oh my God! They're gonna kill us! Like the scary monkeys in the Wizard of Oz!" shouted Uncle Bert. "Please Hannah, put me in your pocket again!"

Hannah did so. After picking up the lizard, she stood up as did Kate. Both stared at the incoming swarm of flies, as the volume of the buzz noise increased.

Hannah's heart rate increased, her breathing became shallower.

Hannah didn't know what to do. She really didn't. "Mom, what should we do?"

"Cover your head with the blanket," responded Kate. "Quickly!"

"Don't let them kill me! Please! Don't let them eat me!" cried Uncle Bert. Clearly, he was having a panic attack.

Hannah covered herself under the blanket. She felt Uncle Bert trembling in her shirt pocket.

Kate stood her ground, facing the incoming swarm. The buzzing sound grew, hurting her ears. She covered her ears with her hands. As the got ever closer, Kate closed her eyes and began to pray.

The noise was overwhelming. They must be getting close.

Flies began to land on Kate at a rapid rate, trying to enter her mouth and go up her nose. She swooshed them away with her hands.

Were they trying to suffocate her?

Now they were invading her ears, causing her to cover her ears again. They saw their advantage and resumed their efforts to get access to the inside of her mouth and nose. There was nothing that Kate could do!

She fell to the ground to place her face against the ground. More flies swarmed to cover her body. She was in fetal position. She was sure she was going to die in this horrible way. What would happen to Hannah?

My God! They were crawling all over her, getting inside her bra and pant legs. She wanted to scream, however, she kept her mouth tightly shut.

Kate felt the sun emerge and warm her back. The sound of sea birds filled the air. Suddenly, the flies began to disperse and fly away. Once most of them were gone, Kate sat up and dared to open her eyes.

Naomi stood before her, aglow in the bright sunlight that encompassed her.

"Kate, I heard your prayers asking for help," said Naomi.

"Naomi?" said Hannah poking her head out from under the blanket. "Yes child. Come out."

Little Hannah threw the blanket off and stood up.

"We're saved!" exclaimed Uncle Bert, poking his head out.

Hannah rushed over to her mother. Kate hugged her tightly until Uncle Bert strongly objected and then she tried fixing her daughter's messy hair. "Naomi, thank you for saving us!" cried Uncle Bert.

"Yes, Naomi. God Bless!" echoed Kate.

Naomi laughed. "My dear, you were saved all along. You just didn't know it." It was a

Dorothy-Good Witch of the North moment.

"Hannah?" asked Kate.

"But, of course," said a smiling Naomi.

"Me?" asked the little girl with disheveled hair and a dirty face.

"Child, did you forget that you have been blessed by the Holy Spirit?" Naomi squatted down to make direct eye contact with the little girl. "Use your power, my darling girl. Just listen to the Holy Spirit for your guidance and then you will always know what to do." It was sound advice from one angel to another.

"That's right! Honey-girl, did you forget that you are an angel?" asked Bert. Hannah giggled. "I guess I did."

"I must warn you. If you forget again, I may not be able to help you." Naomi was dead serious.

"I won't forget again. I promise." Hannah looked like an adult in this moment.

The bright sunshine began to disappear and the overhead skies darkened, with no marine birds in sight.

"Heed my warning." And much like the Good Witch of the North, Naomi began to ascend to the heavens above, until she was lost in the darkening clouds.

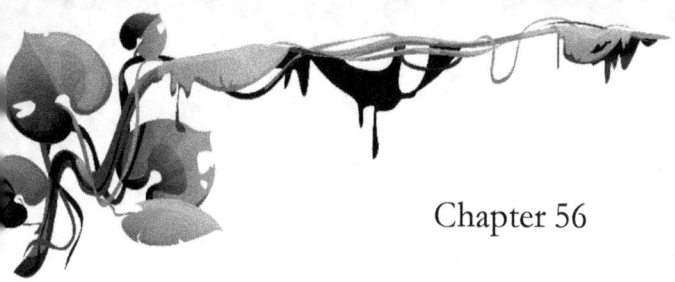

Chapter 56

'O Supernatural times

(These are Supernatural times)

The preparations had been made earlier.

Now, all they could do was wait for Pastor and Puna to arrive.

The day was weaning and the rain had begun falling in earnest as the day cooled. Kimo was with the children, offering words of wisdom and comfort as they waited for the dark night to unfold. A full moon was expected on this fateful night. Of course, that was entirely up to the moon goddess.

The approaching storm was producing stronger winds, some gusting up to 35 mph and the thunder and lightning increased.

"There will be supernatural events," he told them. It was summertime and there was something about the summer that attracts the ghostly and the supernatural. Maybe it's because of the atmosphere or the fact that the moon is closer to the earth.

"What kind of events Dad?" asked Luke. "Like last time?" His voice quivered as his fear leaked through his pores. He remembered the horrors of the days of the great tribulation. He had been used by Satan to attack Hina. Her muteness was a reminder of that horrible period of time. He still struggled with a profound sense of guilt.

"I'm not sure son."

Sobs emitted from Hina. She had not forgotten the horrors of that day either. Kimo scooped the girl up in his arms and soothed her wi th his gentle words.

"Is that my girl crying?" asked Kekela as he entered the dining area where the gang had gathered around the table. The smell of sage lingered on his clothes, announcing his arrival. Ray was with Kupuna Hannah while Kekela took a break.

Hina looked up and saw her beloved uncle and, in a flash, she had run to him, thrown her arms around his waist and tightly clung onto him.

"Hey….. we're gonna be okay, darlin'," said Kekela. "We got righteousness on our side."

"Amen to that," echoed Kimo.

"And how's my man?" asked Kekela as he looked at the unusually quiet boy. David's eyes were wide and he looked scared to death. After all, he lost both his parents during the tribulation days.

David's eyes filled with tears and he tried his best not to cry. Only sissies cry. He looked away to try to collect himself.

"Let's all sit down. I don't know about you but I'm hungry," urged Kekela. Hina heard that and went directly to the area where the food was stored. She prepared him a plate of food. And it was a large, heaping plate of local foods because, despite being very thin, Kekela could chow down heartily.

"That looks good. Hina, can you please make a plate for your dear old dad too?" asked Kimo.

He knew the girl liked the attention. She enjoyed the praise for good deeds.

"Uncle, are we going to see Kanaloa tonight?" asked David who had regained his composure.

"I'm afraid so. He is the enemy we are fighting."

"What about the tsunami and that green mist that's close by now?" asked Luke. Max sat beside him, licking his front paws. He was giving side glances at Kekela's plate of food.

"All weather events can be overcome," responded the wise, blind man who knows about such things.

"But how?" asked the young inquisitive boy.

"By gathering up all the good mana," replied the man who had premonitions. "And by remembering the words and meles of our ancestors."

"But, what are the songs ….." Before David could ask another question, Kekela told the boy that was enough questions.

"How's Kupuna?" inquired Kimo.

"The same." Kekela said no more. Instead he ate. He knew that Kimo was alluding to the fact that when any person lay in an unconscious state, it was supposed by the ancient Hawai'ians that death had taken possession of the body and opened the door for the spirit to depart. Of course, Kupuna Hannah was an extraordinary woman who possessed a deep and abiding faith.

The night would be long and he would need energy. He had seen some of what lay ahead tonight. A vision of death and destruction.

Both Luke and David requested a plate of local foods. Hina was the designated server in the group.

Hina began humming. It was "a place for the universe chant" that she had learned in her hula class:

Upward there upward The birds of the sky

Downward there downward The flowers of the earth

Landward there landward The forest of trees

Seaward there seaward

The fishes of the ocean

Sing the burden of the song: How beautiful the universe!

(Charlot, C. & Charlot, J., Chanting the universe: Hawaiian religious culture. Honolulu: Emphasis International, p. 73).

The gathered group clapped as they so rarely heard Hina make any noise. Max barked his approval.

The little girl smiled.

However, Kekela looked like a hound dog on a rainy day. Sadder than sad. Was he experiencing anticipatory grieving?

Would his people keep their place in the universe?

He returned to his vigil beside the silent Kupuna who was in a deep state that Kekela could not reach. He feared for her. He began to pray because he felt his grip on faithfulness slipping away. Hannah needed him to remain vigilant against the antics of Satan. He would affirm his faith and abiding love for God. Ultimately, their future rested in His hands.

Moments later, David ran into the place where Kupuna lay with her sad guardian.

"Uncle," whispered the agitated boy. "Have you seen Max?"

It seemed that Max had disappeared.

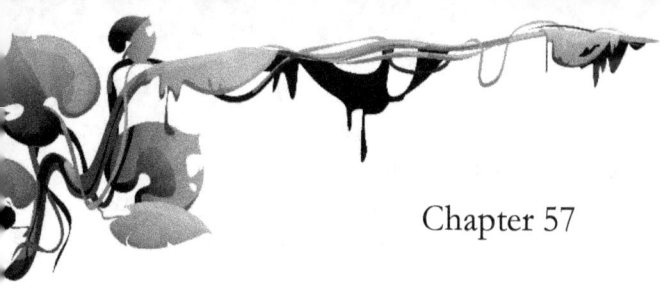

Chapter 57

Ka wai

(The water is the foundation for all natural resources)

Puna, Maui, and Pastor were at the sacred location of the awa water brook. By the time they arrived, they were a weary lot. This included the poor donkey that was slowing down as the trail became steeper.

The blessed awa water would not only refresh them, but, more importantly, it would rejuvenate them as well. It was like an infusion of energy, the power of mana. Rejuvenation was sorely needed to assist them on the final trek up to the sacred caves. The afternoon was waning and the air was beginning to cool. Dark skies were pregnant with moisture and soon rain would offer some relief from the humidity. It was so hot and sticky. There had been a light rain earlier. Surely, it was only a precursor to the storm that loomed ahead. The intermittent thunder was a reminder of the approaching storm. The green mist was advancing ever closer.

As they sat under the shade of the large hala tree, they rested momentarily before removing their boots, socks, pants and shirts. They would both drink and bathe in the awa water. Pastor needed assistance to make it down the grassy slope to the brook. After hours riding on the donkey, his legs were like rubber. Puna held his arm as they made their way into the cooling water.

"Ahhhh….." sighed Pastor. His feet had been on fire. His behind was numb.

"Ahhhhh..is right!" claimed Puna. "Instant relief."

"Son, I couldn't make it without the awa water. I will drink deeply." Pastor sat on the nearby rock and cupped his hands to drink the magic water that some had called the fountain of youth.

He washed his face and arms. It was so refreshing!

Puna came over and poured a canteen of water over Pastor's head. Pastor loved it and shook his head. He felt so renewed.

Like a little boy, Maui jumped and splashed into the brook. Immediately he submerged in a deeper spot. Recent rain had increased the water flow and depth.

"Wow! I've never been in awa water before. I feel so light!" Maui went under again. When he emerged, he was smiling like the Cheshire Cat. Probably, his smile would linger after they were long gone.

"Puna, how much food do we have left? I'm pretty darn hungry!" Maui was revving up. Puna was submerged underwater. When he broke the surface, he said, "Enough."

"How did you hear me, bra?" asked Maui.

"Improved hearing, I guess, from the awa water." Then Puna rose up and headed back to the shady spot under the tree. "I'm hungry too. I'll get our provisions in a minute."

Puna looked up into the branches of the large tree as he felt his father's presence.

Hello son.

He was perched on a high branch, an owl deep in the cool shade.

"Father, you *are* here."

I have come to accompany you for the rest of your journey. Soon your friends will arrive and we shall all go together. That way we will all be safe from Kanaloa and his friends.

"What friends?" asked his son. *Friends of old and friends of new. A special friend.*

"Special?" asked the son.

He has been blessed.

"Is he an angel?"

That is for you to decide.

"Father, will we make it through the night?"

As long as we stay steady in our faith and in our ancestors. Remember, son, you are a warrior. Pu'uwai ha lika.

Heart of steel. Fearless.

"I'm glad you will be with me, father."

Thunder boomed as the sun began to set in the east. The green mist was looming closer. The donkey began braying.

The air was charged with electricity.

Rain began to fall, big raindrops anointing their heads.

The wind began to blow harder, swirling leaves in its wake. It carried a mele that Puna could hear the song of the famous war god, Ku,

The cliffs whence we came

Walking a straight trail,

Climbing a steep one,

Falling with aching knees,

Exhausted, wearied,

Limping, looking askance,

Begging, bold, shameless.

(Voices in the wind, p. 133)

Apparently, the donkey heard it too as he brayed loudly. He began to kick up dirt with his hooves.

"He approaches!" said Puna. As yet, Puna had not told them about his conversation with his aumakua. The others were gathered under the tree now, grumbling about being hungry.

"Who?" asked Maui who picked up on the excitement in Puna's tone of voice.

"He who will help us. A special friend."

The air was filled with a mele as the awa-iku or the beneficent spirits in the form of marine birds blew the unpleasant weather away, and opened the heavens for the sunlight to shine. Once again, they had altered the weather.

'O ke kane huawai, akua kena.

The water gourd male, that is a god.

The noise of people approaching had alerted the donkey first.

Three men emerged from the trail. The clouds parted and a bright ray of sunshine graced the trio.

Mana, Pilikana, and Peter came into view.

It was Peter! How could that be?

"Peter! Is that really you son?" asked Pastor in disbelief. Just the other day, he had given him his last rites. *Had he risen from the dead?*

"How can this be?!" rejoiced Pastor as he approached the beloved boy, uttering praise to the Father.

"He was cured. He was given a miracle," declared Mana. "We witnessed it. It is true," affirmed Pilikana.

"Pastor, it is me." He embraced his father's old friend. Amos had always turned to Pastor in times of trouble.

"It really is you!" Pastor exclaimed as he hugged the young man. He could feel the warmth and vibration of his goodness. Clearly, he possessed great mana.

Puna fell on his knees, aware that he was in the presence of Holiness.

"Your Holiness," said Puna with a bowed head.

"My brother Puna, please get off your knees and hug an old friend," replied Peter who radiated a certain warmth that felt as comfortable as old slipper, familiar slippers.

The two good friends hugged each other tightly as the sun shone down on them. Both heads and hearts had been touched.

"God will deliver us from this persecution as he did for the Jewish people. Peter is our Moses." Pastor made this declaration to everyone as though it were prophecy.

"Let us break bread and be on our way," Peter said, as he removed some food items from his backpack. The others followed suit.

A buffet of local foods was spread out on the blanket. Poi, dried fish, seaweed salad, sweet potato, pineapple and mango, fruit and nut trail mix made by Kate, fresh coconut, and pumpkin mochi.

After praying, they ate quickly. Only the sounds of nature could be heard. Peter, Mana, and Pilikana bathed in the awa water and drank deeply.

Now it really was time to make haste. Thundered cracked the silence.

As the gang of six resumed their journey on the steep trail, more and more marine birds had gathered over head. Leading the flock of birds was a wise Hawaiian barn owl.

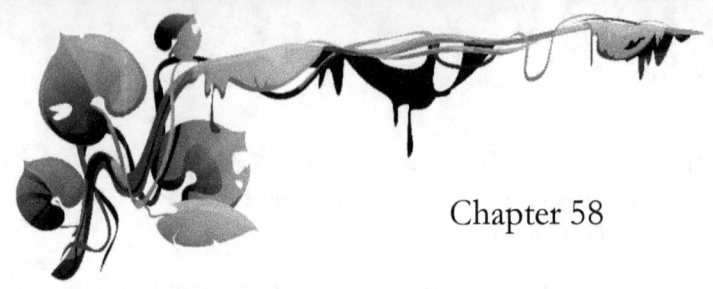

Chapter 58

Nolaika ka! 'o Kalohai.

(Therefore, indeed, you are The Sacrificial Skull.)

The devil's army, under the leadership of Owa, was climbing ever higher towards the sacred caves. They had covered harsh terrain.

The army was well hidden in the mountain forest as the foliage was thick and lush as they plodded along.

Dark storm clouds were overhead. The air was filled with electricity. Lime-green, neon fireflies could be seen off shore.

There was an unusual phenomenon occurring over the ocean waters. Lightning was originating from the energy in the sea, from the bottom-up rather than from the skies to the ocean. As it rose from the ocean, it was merging with the green mist, creating strikes of neon, green lightening against the dark skies. An eerie dark sky displayed the storm in science-fiction fashion.

These Night Marchers had the right backdrop.

Alongside Owa, there was a woman. She was a tall, Hawaiian woman who was very fit and strong.

A woman warrior.

Haumea had joined Satan's army of warrior men whose mission was to kill and eat the lambs.

Her head was covered with ink-black feathers. Like a helmet, they were a thick protective head dress.

They needed to pause to perform a crucial satanic ritual in order to be victorious in their diabolical mission. The evil band of soldiers stopped at a small clearing in the forest. Grunting like animals, they slowly formed a circle. Black flies buzzed around the pungent men.

These men who had forfeited their souls to Kanaloa were now Night Marchers. Night Marchers are the vanguard for Satan. Prior to engaging in battle, they were required to urinate into their hand, rub it all over themselves, and then lie naked and face down. This increased their chance of survival. Not doing so would invite swift death.

Preparing for this aspect of the ritual, they men stripped out of their clothing.

Haumea stood in the middle of the circle. She was holding a ruby-studded crystal goblet that appeared very old. It had a carved skull on the front. She too stood naked. Urine dripped from her hands.

After their urine bath, they were now in a state of readiness to perform the most important part of the ceremony. Satan's bidding was at hand.

Haumea ordered Owa to produce the designated knife for this phase. As he held up the sharp instrument, it glinted brightly even in the diminished sunlight. She also gave him the goblet.

Except for the incessant buzzing of the black flies, there were no other sounds of nature.

In the quiet, Owa lifted his voice and began to chant a mele that spoke of a disappearing people:

Make ke au kaha o piko o ka honua; 'oia pukaua

Hua na lau la nalo i ka po liolio.

Dead was the current flowing from the center of the earth; they were war leaders,

They rose up as many as leaves and vanished Vanished in the running night.

(Chanting, p.95).

The men were so excited about killing their once-upon-a-time neighbors that they began to dance a war dance. Their mounting excitement was evident in their manhood erections. They were lusting for the upcoming killing orgy where they could relish the fear, torture, pain and death of their fellow community members. The folks they grew up with since childhood. Their murderous desires were focused on the local people with whom they had shared birthdays and anniversaries over the course of many years.

These were the intended victims of the nocturnal slaughter and the cannibalistic feast of victory to be held after their friends' blood had been spilled. Not until the ground beneath them ran red with a river of the life-sustaining fluid would they stop. Not until every man, woman, and child had been butchered.

They settled down and became quiet and still. Facing Owa, they dutifully awaited the final phase of the ceremony. It was the final ritual. Owa walked over to a soldier and presented him with the knife.

The soldier took the sharp knife. He then placed it against his left wrist. Swiftly, he slashed the inner aspect over the veins. Blood beaded up immediately.

The blood soon began to flow more until there was a steady trickle. Owa took the goblet and captured the precious fluid. Each soldier followed in the same manner until the goblet was full of their tainted blood.

Owa was the final one to perform the ritual and offer is blood. Deftly, he cut his inner left wrist and allowed the blood drops to top off the crimson nectar.

Owa brought the cup of sacrificial blood to Haumea and offered it to her. She took the goblet and greedily drank each precious drop of blood.

Abruptly, she began to transform into some other dark creature. Her face grew long and thin. Beady black eyes emerged. Her body became smaller, shrinking into the size of a loaf of bread. Her arms had been turned into wings as she became a glossy black raven bird. There was still blood on her emerging beak.

Ravens and crows have long been known to be associated with black magic, evil forces and unseen, unhappy spirits. Larger than a crow, the raven has a heavy bill, shaggy throat hatches, long-fingered wing tips, and a long wedge-shaped tail. An ominous looking creature for sure. Recall Edgar Allan Poe's, "Black Bird of Ill Omen".

After a loud caw, Haumea in her bird-form took flight upwards catching a breeze. She planned to reach the caves ahead of the army of men. She would be a spy until they arrived.

Watching and waiting was her task.

The Night Marchers, dressed in their warrior loin cloths, resumed their journey up the mountain.

Onward Satan's warriors.

After they had departed from the clearing, the only evidence of them being there was a black feather lying on the ground.

The wind picked up and the dark sky opened up with a heavy downpour.

A faint drumbeat could be heard in the wind.

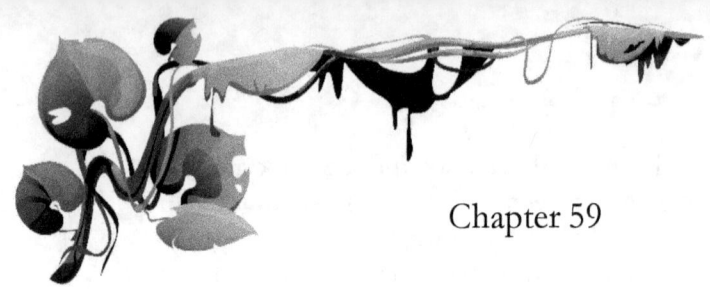

Chapter 59

'olelo 'a'ole e male 'ia

(There will be no wedding)

Lili's temperature was 102.8 F.

She shivered.

She pressed her damp palms against her throbbing temples. Her head felt like it might explode like a live grenade soon.

Too weak to make it to the bathroom, she had just vomited into the garbage can next to her bed. Lili checked the vomitus for blood. Thank God, there was no blood. Yet.

Under the cover of several blankets, she lay in her bed in her small apartment in-residence at the hospital. She realized that soon she would need to be in a hospital room. Dehydration was setting in because Lili couldn't hold anything down in her stomach. With the fluid loss from a high fever and diarrhea, Lili would require intravenous fluids. She had been struck down by the illness that was a guaranteed killer.

I'm sorry Puna.

Lili understood her fate. She knew exactly what lay ahead and it was not a pretty picture. She recalled the painful sores and the bleeding orifices. The bloody vomit and diarrhea. Finally, profound oxygen deprivation at the cellular level would take her. She would bleed out and die from shock and systemic organ failure.

I'm so sorry, my love. There will be no wedding.

Lili couldn't take it anymore. The dam burst as she wept. There would be no children. Nor would there be grandchildren. No more birthdays or anniversaries. No more days at the beach. No more walks on the beach at sunset.

Sobs racked her body.

Through her tears, she cried out," Father, I don't want to die yet. I beg for your mercy and grace." Her voice was tinny with hopelessness.

Thunder clapped outside as the sun began to set. Lightening flashed in her room.

The truth was that Lili had no intention of going into the hospital unit again. She intended to die in this very bed. She'd been in the hospital too much for too long. She couldn't bear the smells of sickness and death, or the sounds of hopelessness and fear, or the unbearable grief of the lost loved one's family and friends.

Frankly, she was done with all that.

Done.

Lili was both physically and emotionally exhausted and, sadly, she had fallen into a state of despair. A deep sorrow filled her chest making it ache.

Had she lost her faithfulness and, in that void, had Satan found her vulnerability?

The devil's wedge perhaps.

She wished that Pastor was here. She had some things that she wished to confess and atone for before the final judgment was made. Maybe that would offer some spiritual relief.

Eventually, Lili cried herself to sleep. It wasn't long before she drifted into a *pokii* dream. A dream from the spirit world with certain messages.

In the dream, it was a beautiful, sunny day. Under blue skies, Lili was walking on the white sand beach that stretched for miles as the ocean waters gently shifted in and out. Her footsteps could be seen in the sand. The ocean glittered in the sunlight on this glorious day. Lili saw Puna up ahead, waiting for her. Her handsome love. And, she did so love him.

His hair was chocolate brown and it shined under the sun's rays. He smiled warmly at her and her heart melted. She could feel his love for her because it radiated from him. He was a very good man. Most importantly, Puna was a man with an unshakable fidelity to the Lord and the word of God.

She trusted him with her life.

But, no matter how far or fast she walked, she couldn't catch up to him. He remained out of reach. She started to feel afraid.

Why couldn't she reach him? Why didn't he come closer? *Look behind you.*

Who said that? Lili knew that she had indeed fallen down the rabbit hole. It was a familiar voice.

Lili turned to look behind her. All she could see was her fading footsteps in the sand.

That's right, child. The footsteps represent your walk with the Lord. When they are washed away by the ocean's tide, they remain forever present.

Lili turned around to look at Puna. He was gone. She was alone.

He remains close and he is waiting for you.

Lili recognized the voice: *it was Naomi!*

A golden cloud floated in the blue sky and Naomi, dressed in a white tapa cloth robe, rested upon it. She smiled kindly at Lili. Like a shot of joy, the smile generated an overwhelming sense of comfort within Lili and she understood that all would turn out well. She realized that she needed to fight rather than give in to her despair. After all, she wasn't bleeding yet. With an intravenous blood-clotting medication like Heparin, she could maybe overcome this illness. A local Hawaiian woman had survived the illness last week.

She would fight the devil's illness with every fiber of her being!

Yes child. It is Satan you are fighting.

Lili looked up at Naomi and smiled brightly, feeling great affection for Naomi's help. The cloud began to lift up towards the heavens. Lili waved as the angel disappeared into the clouds.

She turned to the spot where Puna had stood. He was still gone although she knew that he remained in her heart. She believed that she really would see her true love again.

The sun was beginning to set and she began walking back down beach. She didn't want to get caught in the dark. She couldn't quite recall how far she needed to go to…..

"Lili! Lili!" a voice cried as someone shook her. "Wake up!"

Another familiar voice. A male voice. Dr. Fukina?

She opened her eyes and weakly said, "Dr. Fukina, please stop shaking me."

"Lili, I'm taking you to a private room in the I.C.U. I'll be treating you." He was firm. He was the man in charge.

There was a knock on the door.

"Come in" responded Dr. Fukina. Two nursing staff entered the room with a hospital gurney, including Malia, the charge nurse.

"Let's do it" commanded Dr. Fukina. He was determined to save his colleague. "Ready Lili?"

"Yes. I'm ready." She too was firm.

Twelve minutes later, she was in a hospital bed in the I.C.U. Soon, she was hooked up to monitors and two intravenous lines were going. Ringer's Lactate to keep her blood pressure up and Heparin. Lab work was drawn. An anti-pyretic drug was administered per rectum as Lili was experiencing severe nausea, despite being given an anti-nausea medication.

She resolved to fight by restoring her faithfulness. Perhaps doubt had crept in in the face of so much suffering and death.

But no more! She began to pray.

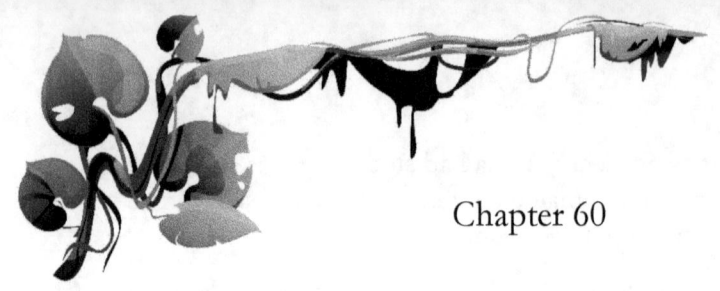

Chapter 60

'olelo he pa'ina 'ekoluu

(A party of three)

Zippity-do-da, Zippity-day.
Uncle Bert was enjoying the cool shade at the sacred site.

After drinking the awa water, he was feeling pretty darn good. Of course, he'd taken a dip in the blessed water too. He was a living sponge of awa water. In fine fashion, he was doing a two-step or rather, a four-step.

"Uncle Bert, are you dancing again?" laughed Hannah.

My darlin', I'm in a dancing mood!

'Save your strength and don't forget to eat some of those disgusting bugs," urged Hannah. "Thank goodness, Mom and I have something besides bugs to eat."

"Are you two talking about bugs again? Really?" chuckled Kate, enjoying their playful exchange. "Well, you're bugging me!"

Hannah laughed at that and Kate and Uncle Bert laughed at Hannah.

"Mom, I'm so hungry!" exclaimed the little, growing girl. There was the other thing too.

Surely being an angel burned up more calories.

"Alright. I'll go get our provisions." Kate walked over to the shady tree where the horses were tied up to a tree, grazing on the tall grass. They had drunk deeply from the brook which would also fuel them for the remainder of their journey.

With blanket in hand, Kate set up their spot to sit and eat under another large and shady mango tree. The air smelled clean and crisp, restoring their lung energy. Despite the thunder and dark clouds, this sacred place was enjoying golden rays from the sun.

Hannah wasted no time to open the food containers. Soon, she was quietly eating dried trail mix that her mom had made especially for her. It consisted of bananas and mangos with shredded coconut and macadamia nuts. In addition, she ate two mountain apples, some Lucky Charms, and taro chips. Coconut sugared mochi, a favorite local candy, was her desert.

"Well, young lady. Are you full yet?" asked Kate who was enjoying some dried fish with some fresh mango from the tree. Instead of cereal and candy, Kate ate several, high-protein energy bars. Mountain apples were seasonal so she also ate two of the sweet-tart fruit.

"Barely!" declared Hannah. Must be burnin' those angel calories!

Kate laughed again and it sure felt good.

"Mommy.... when will we see Daddy and Luke and Hina?" asked the little girl.

"Very soon, honey" said a smiling Kate who was eager to see her husband and other children too.

And I can't wait to meet everyone!

"Uncle Bert, it will be my pleasure to introduce you to the gang!" Kate said with great affection. She wondered when he would return to the ethereal world. Hannah would surely miss him. So would she for that matter.

I guess we should be on our way. Places to go, people to meet.

"Uncle Bert is right. Let's hit the trail. I'm refreshed and ready." Kate collected their provisions and the old, gray blanket and returned them to the backpack. It would seem that the horses were ready to be on the move again. The late afternoon was hot and muggy. The air was heavy, like before a great storm.

The party of three on horseback, a woman, a young girl and a talking lizard, proceeded on the trail to the sacred caves, climbing higher and higher on the steep trail. Thoughts of seeing loved ones danced in their heads. As they continued upward, they could see the green bolts of lightning spik ing the sky. Clearly, this was a supernatural summertime event. But what ghost- god had provoked it?

After two hours on the trail, it seemed like it was getting hotter rather than cooling down as the day drew to a close. Up ahead, there was a huge banyan tree that offered some cool shade and so they decided to take a break and cool down. They had made good time and would soon arrive at the caves.

None of them knew that Hawaiians believed that banyan trees attracted lost spirits, giving them a permanent home.

The unknowing trio sat quietly beneath the tree on the old, gray blanket eating some refreshing guavas, the nectar both tart and sweet. It felt good to rest. It had already been a long, hard day.

Suddenly, the weather changed.

It became hotter than hell and the wind began rippling through the large tree, strong enough to bend the tree.

"Mom, what's happening?!" cried Hannah.

"I don't know but as soon as the wind calms down some, we'll get out of here!" exclaimed

Kate.

"It's so hot I can barely breathe," whispered the little girl. It was so uncomfortable. "Breathe through your nose, honey."

Uncle Bert had fainted from the heat inside the pocket of Hannah's shirt. He had hopped in there when the wind had kicked up.

A funnel of green mist, like a small cyclone, was nearby. Kate tried to reach Hannah to protect her from it but the powerful wind had actually blown her away from the safety of Kate's arms. The ground was trembling as though the Green Giant was strolling nearby.

Suddenly, the funnel of green mist transformed into a cloud that began floating towards Hannah who was now pinned down by an arm of the strong wind. As it approached her, it became a green column that glowed.

It became a pillar of mist that slowly passed through her. Kate watched on in horror.

Hannah was conscious but unable to hear anything or feel the wind. It then became boiling hot. Hannah felt as though she was caught alone in a vortex, feeling both stunned and powerless. She thought that it felt like infinity. Then, she remembered that she was an angel and her heart filled with purity. With a sense of great power, she stood up and ordained that it stop in the name of Him.

And so it did.

The mist disappeared. Thankfully, the air cooled and the wind dissipated. Then, Hannah crumpled to the ground.

She could hear her mother calling out to her.

No longer held at bay by the wind, Kate ran over to her daughter. As she knelt beside her,

Hannah whispered, "I'm okay Mom."

"Can you sit up?" asked Kate. In her hand, she held a flask of awa water.

The little girl moaned as she sat up to drink the water that her mother was offering her. It was so refreshing and, quickly, it revived her. Whatever had passed through her had apparently left no lasting effects.

Drinking from the flask, water trickled down the front of her shirt.

Hey! Are you tryin' to drown me? A sputtering Uncle Bert climbed out of the pocket of

Hannah's shirt.

I had a good, long nap and I'm ready to go! I sure can't wait to meet everyone!

Kate and Hannah looked at each other, shook their heads, and burst out laughing. He'd been snoozing during the whole episode. What a guy!

"Let's get going because it's gonna get dark soon," urged Kate. She gathered their possessions and headed over to the tree where the horses had been tied up.

She stopped abruptly. The horses were gone.

As thunder boomed and green lightning flashed, the dark skies opened up and it began to rain steadily.

Chapter 61

Ainai ka houpo o Kane.
(Land at the breast of Kane)

On this stormy dusk of an evening, Kupuna Hannah remained in a deep sleep state. So far, it had been a completely dreamless state. But not tonight. The arrival of a *pokii* dream changed that as the sun was setting and darkness was at-hand.

Hannah saw herself gathering her people together. They were on the lawn in the park in front of the county building. It was a beautiful day in paradise. The sun shone brightly and the blue sky was cloudless. The turquoise ocean waters were calm, flat as sheets of glass. Yet, it didn't feel alright. Not at all. There was something off and you could feel it in the wind that sounded like it crying. It was the sound of this mele:

Kane comes with the water of life.

Life through the multitudes of the gods! Sacred! Sacred!

Life! Life!

Life through the chief! Life through the gods!

(Luomala, K. (1986) Voices on the wind: Polynesian myths and chants (revised edition). Bishop Museum Press: Honolulu, Hawaii, p. 67).

She shouted to the crowd, "My people! Make ready for a long journey!"

The crowd cried out, "No Kupuna! We do not wish to leave our home!"

"I know. I too regret that we must leave the home of our ancestors, but, sadly, we must. We cannot stay here or we will not survive. Evil has claimed our island."

The gathered local folks grumbled loudly. Some were men were crying and mothers openly wept. It was such a hard thing to take in. Leave their homes, and most of their possessions and their buried ancestors? Leave the only home that most of them had ever known?

An old, bent-over Hawaiian man, cried out, "Kupuna, *pehua e pau ai Keia'eha nui? How will end this great hurt?*"

"We are going to journey to a new land." The crowd hushed. "We will begin again."

Their chief, Kimo, rode onto the lawn riding a small, mutant horse with a large head with pink-braided hair. Purple ribbon adorned the two pink braids. As though it had just come from the Land of Oz, the small horse was purple as well!

He stepped down from the small, purple horse.

"It is true, my friends. Kupuna is right. We must leave this place so that our children may live and go on without us, if need be." Kimo looked very solemn. He too had children to save. Only, one of them was either missing or dead.

"Make ready the canoes, food, mats and *kapa (bark cloth/ cloak)* for the journey," he commanded. "Be mindful! There is no room for your personal possessions."

"He turned and looked at Hannah. "Where is Puna?" he asked.

"I haven't seen him." Her voice quivered with panic. "I can't find him or Lili."

"I'm sorry Hannah, we cannot wait any longer for those that are missing," he said, struggling with his own broken heart.

"Then I shall stay."

"I will not argue with you, my dear friend." Kimo hugged her tightly as tears streamed down his face and he felt her shudder. They both knew it was a death sentence.

There would be others who would not leave, especially the elders. There were others that were too sick to leave.

There were those that were too heart-broken to leave.

Hannah could not leave her son or his future wife.

Feeling panicked, Hannah's heart began to pound in her chest. She felt like she was suffocating! She had to find them! Were they dead?

Anxiety mounting, she cried out, "Help me!"

Her desperate cry for help was heeded. Kai-the-owl-as protector, her beloved husband and aumakua, swooped down in front of her. His large, yellow eyes looked lovingly at his soul mate.

I will be with you, my wife.

She felt less panicked. Kai was here and everything would be okay.

Relief swept over her.

She heard him whisper, *O heavenly One, I know a place. Ainai ka houpo o Kane. I will help lead the way for my people to the new land of Kane.*

She cupped her hands over her face as waves of mercy swept over her. After several moments, she looked up and wiped her eyes.

Kai was no longer there………

Abruptly, the dream ended and Kupuna Hannah returned to a dreamless sleep state once again.

Her blind caretaker never saw her twitching fingers, the increased fall and rise of her chest or the look of fear on her grimaced face.

She had remained silent throughout the disturbing dream. Kupuna Hannah was drawn into an even deeper state of darkness.

Soon, her spirit would become transient in order to survive po or darkness.

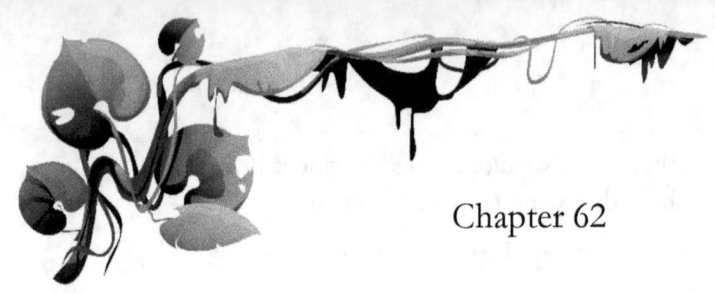

Chapter 62

'olelo mana'o maluhia

(Peaceful feelings)

Lili was burning up with fever.

It was now 103.9 F. She looked like death warmed over.

Her face was wet with perspiration. She looked so pale. The monitors that show her breathing ease, her vital signs, and her oxygen saturation were hooked up but the data that they revealed was not good. She was bleeding internally and anemia had weakened her immune system. Clearly, her condition was deteriorating. Her lab results were clear evidence of her worsening state.

Lili was losing the fight of her life.

Yet, Lili held on to the vision and hope that she had experienced her dream. She was able to recall those peaceful feelings.

She shivered despite the use of several blankets that had been piled on. Her head was throbbing and her eyes were bloodshot and light-sensitive, therefore her room was darkened. Every muscle in her body ached. Every bone felt cold and brittle.

She heard the door opening. The nurses checked on her frequently.

"Lili, its Dr. Fukina. Can you hear me?" asked the doctor. "I want to discuss a treatment that I'd like to try." She looked so pale.

Slowly, Lili opened her eyes.

"Can you please turn off the lights?" she requested.

Dr. Fukina turned off the lights.

"Okay. That's better. Tell me about it." She closed her eyes again. She was very fatigued. "Do you remember Malia?" he asked.

Lili shook her head no.

"She's the local woman who survived this disease," he reminded her. "You two are a match in terms of blood type. I want to give you a blood transfusion using her blood. She has consented already."

"And you're sure her blood type is B+?"

"Absolutely. I'd like to get started right away Lili," said the good doctor to this good woman and colleague.

"Then let's get started. Bring me the consent forms to sign."

"I have them right here." He took out the papers and a ballpoint black pen. He raised the top of her bed to an upright position.

Lili opened her eyes and moaned. He handed her a clipboard with the papers. He had placed a big X beside the signature line.

With difficulty, she signed her name.

And then she threw up. There was blood in her vomitus.

Dr. Fukina rang the call bell. He asked that a nurse come to clean Kate up and change the bed. He ordered another to implement the protocol for administering a blood transfusion.

Time was running out for Lili.

This had to work because they had run out of options.

Chapter 63

He po Kane keia, he ma 'au nein a 'e 'epa o ka po.

(This is the night of Kane, for supernatural beings are wandering about in the dark.)

Pastor Kua was showing signs of great fatigue despite having drunk the awa water earlier.

Puna was concerned. The trail was getting progressively steeper and the high altitude was depleting, especially for an older person. After all, Pastor was well past seventy years old.

"Pastor, we will stop ahead and rest briefly," declared Peter.

They stopped and found a shady tree to sit under and stretch out. Taking a deep breath, they sat or lied down quietly. Pastor was lying down on a bamboo matt, possibly suffering from heat stroke. Because he was so weak, he refused to drink any more water. His flushed face was wet with perspiration. His hands were tremulous. Peter placed a cool cloth over his head. He began to pray over Pastor.

Pastor mumbled an Amen and fell asleep. Peter made the sign of the cross over the dozing man of God.

"Is he gonna be okay?" asked Puna. Pastor was like his father on earth.

"He'll be fine," replied Peter in a confident voice. He nodded and smiled at Puna in a gesture of reassurance.

"Are you sure?" asked Maui. He knew that the Pastor was essential in their strategy to defeat the enemy.

Peter nodded again.

Both Pilikana and Mana let out a deep sigh of relief.

Over the ocean, the skies glowed green. The ominous green mist was frighteningly close!

"How long will he need to sleep? Soon, it will be dark," said Mana." Isn't there a full moon tonight?"

"We have flashlights." Maui knew that it was not just a lack of light that his friend feared, it was the emerging darkness.

"There will be no moon tonight," stated Pilikana.

It was the night of Kane.

According to the Hawaiian calendar, the night of Kane is the one when the moon is completely absent from the sky.

Along with the inky-black night, it would bring a storm of wind and rain.

"We shall let him rest for only half an hour. Then, we will be on our way again. Others will be coming soon to help us on the rest of our journey." Peter smiled.

In the wind, the sound of wind chimes filled the night. Riding on the wave of wind, were swarms of fireflies. They landed around the group, illuminating the area.

"You see," said Peter who was grinning now. His hazel eyes danced with merriment.

"Is Peter Pan coming too?" asked a laughing Maui. Everyone laughed except Puna who remained distressed. He felt uneasy about Pastor.

"Well, if she looks as good as Mary Martin that'd be alright!" grinned Mana. Always thinkin' about women, that guy!

Puna wished that his aumakua, his father, was with him now.

However, the owl-as-protector Kai was needed elsewhere. Kate, Hannah, and the lizard aumakua would need guidance to complete their arduous journey and darkness was fast approaching.

Keeping in close proximity to Pastor, Puna sat down and thought about Lili. He sensed that something was wrong. He felt afraid although he wasn't sure why. In addition, he was worried about his mother Hannah. He too feared for her. Kupuna was his rock. The ceremony tonight must work. His father had told him about the rituals to remove the evil entity inside his beloved mother. Knowing that Pastor was essential to that endeavor, Puna was watching his old friend closely.

Pastor slept deeply.

The darkness came with a moonless night.

Thunder and bright green lightning owned the night sky. The sight of the green mist moving onto the land struck fear in the hearts of the mortal men, women, and children. Like an electric guitar, the wind began to howl. Electricity cackled in the air. An unpleasant odor was present. It was reminiscent of burning tires at the dump.

After thirty minutes, Peter crouched down beside Pastor and kissed his forehead. Expecting Pastor to open his eyes and rise, the others were getting the horses ready. Pastor did not open eyes.

Pastor did not stir.

The night of Kane was unfolding.

The battle was underway. The truth would be revealed this night.

"What's wrong?" asked a concerned Puna, holding back tears. "Why can't you wake him up?"

"I'm not sure," replied Peter. "I think that Satan is interfering." He seemed unsure and perhaps a little rattled.

"I mean it Peter. Please wake him up." Puna was clearly stressed.

"I think we should all pray," offered Maui, his voice cracking.

"I think that that is an excellent suggestion," said Mana, chiming in.

Pilikana stood tall and somber. He started to doubt.

A black raven cawed nearby. The bird was watching and waiting.

"It's the same thing……like my mother," asserted Puna. Fear abounded. Doubt swept in.

Secretly, Puna feared that if Pastor didn't awake and tell him, he had no idea what to do about the gold key hidden in his clothing. As yet, no explanation had been provided except to keep it safe.

In the nearby bushes and behind some rocks, two red eyes glowed.

They came together and prayed, yet Pastor remained in his unconscious state.

Satan longed to separate this godly man from his soul. Kanaloa had targeted both the soul of Pastor and Hannah. Without either one of them, they would be sure to defeat this simple people.

In the dark, icy night that never passes

They pass ceaselessly.

They go far.

(Chanting, p.104)

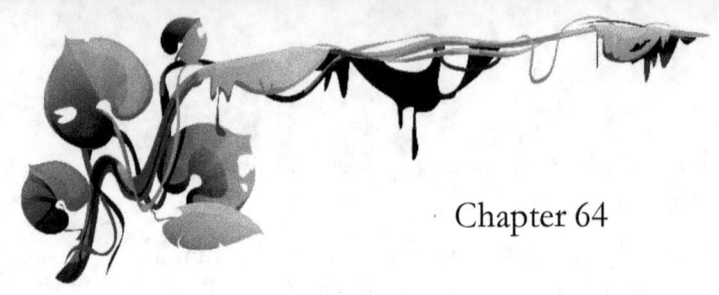

Chapter 64

awa-iku

(Spirits to ward off evil)

Hannah, Kate and Uncle Bert were sitting under the mango tree on this dark, moonless night. With the horses gone, so were the backpacks that held the flashlights. Green lightening flashed against the dark sky, lighting up the night sky like fireworks on the fourth of July. The wind had picked up and the night air was cool. There was a chill in the charged air.

Little Hannah shivered as she laid her head on her mother's shoulder. "What are we going to do Mom?" asked the frightened girl.

Kate hugged her daughter more tightly, "I guess we shall wait for daylight and then continue on our way."

"I don't wanna spend the night out here," the girl complained, with a notable quiver in her voice. "It's so dark." Her hair was dirty and disheveled. Splotches of dirt were on both cheeks.

We'll be okay, Hannah. Uncle Bert chimed in as he poked his head out of Hannah's shirt pocket.

Thunder boomed, startling the little girl. And Uncle Bert.

Yiks! That was too close. But, it's alright. We're okay honey-girl.

"I'm scared Uncle," cried Hannah. "You promise?"

I promise sweetie.

"Uncle Bert is right honey," reassured Kate even though she was worried. Would they arrive too late? Would they be able to survive this night by themselves?

Remember the words of Naomi.

Hannah remembered that she had been blessed by the Holy Spirit and she actually did possess the ability to change things. And so she silently prayed and asked for help and added a thank you. *Mahalo nui loa. Thank you very much.*

Help will be here soon, honey-girl.

Like the speedy expressway, a multitude of lights approached the mountainside where the band of three was located. A humming noise, like the buzz of a small plane, could be heard. It was a mele of hope.

Hundreds of fireflies lit up the black sky, illuminating the area. Like a mystical comet, they streaked across the dark, ominous sky. The tar-black sky of Kane's night.

They were larger than usual, making them seem like little fairies dancing on the wind. It was a Peter Pan moment.

"I'm not sure what you two talked about since I'm not as telepathic as either of you, but you guys sure can deliver," exclaimed Kate as she stared in awe at the approaching light fairies.

Benevolent spirits were going to light the way, making it possible for the trio to soon arrive at the sacred caves. More importantly, they would soon be with the rest of their family.

"Soon, Kimo. Soon," whispered Kate. Her eyes misted up as she thought of her husband.

"Yes, Mommy. Soon I will see Daddy," said Hannah who was tuned-in to her mother. "And Luke and Hina and David and Uncle Kekela and Kumu!" She rushed the words out of her mouth and then took a deep breath.

Me too. I'm gonna meet the whole gang!

The humming noise increased as the glow of the hundreds of lights brightened the surrounding area. Another bird – a Hawaiian barn owl - was leading the multitude of fireflies.

Kai-the-owl-as-protector had arrived with the other spirits. These were the awa-iku spirits who were messengers for Kane to ward off the evil influences of Satan's mu spirits. The owl landed on a nearby log. Tilting his head with a Winnie-the-Pooh expression, he said," *Naomi has sent me and these friends to assist you on the last leg of your journey."*

And we are grateful dear sir. Uncle Bert said with gratitude and a bow.

"We shall light the way and lead the way," replied the wise owl.

Kate clearly heard this conversation and sighed with relief. They were on their way!

Follow the yellow brick road!

The rain was coming down heavy.

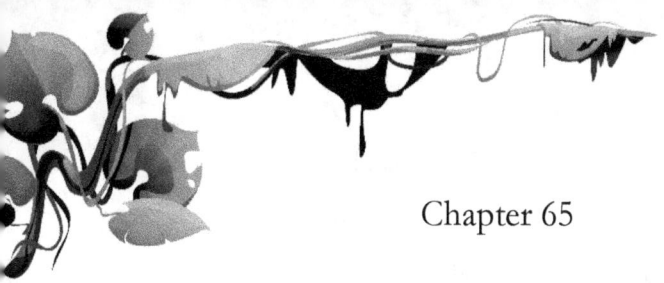

Chapter 65

kamaʻilio telepathic ʻolelo

(telepathic communication)

Despite his apparent state of deep sleep, Pastor was engaged in a telepathic conversation with Kapuna. Making a connection now was imperative if they were going to defeat the evil one who sought to claim the life and souls of these two important agents of light.

The last time that Pastor and Kupuna joined forces, they defeated Kanaloa and his minions. And so they would again.

Or so he hoped. He was having difficulty reaching and connecting to Kupuna. The constant and increasing beat of drums in her head was blocking his attempts. Rather like an internet connection, the connection failed.

How could he break through? A magic password perhaps?

Pastor shouted to her, "Puna! Puna!"

The drumbeats continued, unabated. No response from Hannah. She remained in a deep state of darkness, lost and adrift.

He shouted her beloved son's name again and, then again.

A whisper came back. Mason, is that really you?

"Yes, my dear friend, it is me," reassured Pastor. "I am here to help both of us. We can fight this old enemy, the snake in the grass, the shadow in the night, and the Prince of darkness, who aims to defile us by confining us into the po. But, it won't work. It didn't before because we turned to the light and affirmed our abiding faith."

The sound of the drums was fading quickly.

"Hannah, we must connect to the ao together," declared Pastor.

"I understand, my friend. We shall pray together."

"I ka olelo no ke ola, i ka ola, I ka olelo na ka make." Pastor said, *In the word is life, in the word, death.*

In unison, the two great friends chanted:

Oh, Kane, hear my cry!

Oh, Kane, hear my petition!

Oh, Kane, help me to send Na moo ekahi, the first serpent to the pit,

Oh, Kane, I am Nana ika lani, seer of the heavens,

Oh, Kane, I evoke the ao, the light of my ancestors.

The drumbeats had disappeared.

"Hannah, Puna and the one who will save us are soon to arrive. They shall bring you to the fore." Pastor sent this final message.

As Kekela sat at Kupuna's bedside, he could hear the rain and wind getting stronger outside. It was the night of Kane and Kekela could feel the approaching collision between good and evil. The static in the air crackled like the cellophane on a box of cigarettes. There was an electrical smell in the night winds which served as a reminder that the eerie, green mist was ever- approaching.

He too had heard the sounds of the warriors' drums. A foul, musky smell would announce their arrival.

Suddenly, Hannah began to stir. Her face twitched and her eyes fluttered. Her legs moved under the blanket causing it to fall to the floor. She began to moan.

"'Pastor and Puna will arrive soon," she muttered. And then she was quiet again.

"Welcome back, Kupuna. I look forward to your full awakening, but for now, I rejoice in the fact that you reside in the light again." Kekela transmitted this message without uttering a word.

First, Ray arrived.

"I thought I heard.... or sorta felt Kupuna wake up," exclaimed Ray.

"And, you would be right," validated Kekela. "Although, she…"

He was interrupted when Kimo rushed into the room.

"Is she awake?" Ray rushed his words as well.

More sounds of feet rushing into the cave heading towards Kupuna's bed were heard. Standing before Kekela, were Luke, David, and Hina.

"Kumu, are you awake now?" shouted David.

A smile warmed Kupuna's face. She had heard the boy. In turn, they all smiled at the wise, old woman with great mana. They all loved her and she could feel their mana like beams of sunlight kissing her body and warming her heart.

Besides the drumming, Hannah also heard very loud crickets on this moonless, stormy night.

As the dark night sky blanketed over them like a shroud, they felt the mountain shake and the thunder sounded like a canon being shot out of a gun barrel.

Chapter 66

As the rain pelted down and the wind screamed, Lili lay in her hospital bed, looking so very pale and fragile. Her body, face and hands were covered in red, inflamed and puss-filled sores. Patches of hair had fallen out. She was receiving the blood transfusion. The steady...*beep, beep*...of the heart monitor was a safeguard in the case of incompatibility, toxins or microorganisms. It would take approximately 4 hours to complete the process. Dr. Fukina remained hopeful. After all, all they had left in their toolbox was hope.

So far, Lili had fought the good fight.

But, unfortunately, she was losing the battle.

She lay in her bed in a private room that was darkened because of her sensitivity to light.

Her eyes were so bloodshot from the broken blood vessels. The flashes of green-neon lightning illuminated the room intermittently, giving it an eerie sci-fi glow.

Boom!

A tree branch crashed into the lone window in her room, the pane of glass shattering. The wind rattled the cracked window, thunder clapped loudly, and the sky lite up.

Suddenly, the glass window shattered completely, the irreverent wind blowing into the room made the curtains whip in the strong breeze and caused loose papers to become air born.

White light filled the broken window. And the sweet song of night crickets came in on the strong breeze. Dancing upon the wind were light fairies, each 3 or 4 inches long. The benevolent spirits of Kane to the rescue again. Shining the light of the Lord.

O, Kane.

The light fairies are actually the albino offspring of the Mu clan of the Menehunes that descended from Maui. In folk lore, they are characterized as the leprechauns of Hawaii. Except these were not like Irish leprechauns. They had reddish skin and gold-tinged hair, with blue eyes. These Mu people were known as *urukehu*.

Similarly, like the Irish fairies, the urukehu are a cheerful, merry people. At night when they are working happily, the sound of their mele can be heard. It was the sound of crickets singing all night long. Being nocturnal creatures, they work very hard at night sans pranks and jokes. Once the sun rises, these sun-adverse albinos hide in sacred places.

Swiftly, they flew overhead of Lili's bed, making her shine in their collective light. One by one, each light fairy descended down to her bed and took a position. Soon, they covered all of Lili's body, including her face and head. They became very still, despite the strong wind. Their tiny wings glistened with miniscule drops of dew.

Lili, feel the power of the blood. Remember the blood of Jesus.

It was that same, old familiar voice that both comforted and offered a ray of hope. It was the heavenly angel, Naomi.

"Naomi, is that you?" whispered Lili. She wondered if she was hallucinating, given her feverish condition.

Yes, my dear. I am here with some angels.

"Of course, you are," whispered Lili with a smile. It was not a smile of disbelief. No, no, not at all. It was a smile that affirmed the truth. She could feel the flutter of their tiny wings on her body and face. It created a soothing, angelic feeling.

You will be fine Lili. Soon, you will be reunited with Puna.

Quickly, one by one, the fairies took flight, fluttering their tiny wings franticly. The tiny droplets of dew created a fine mist that drifted down and showered Kate.

The dew was made from awa water.

Lili smiled, sighed deeply, and returned to sleep. She was 2 hours into the transfusion process. Fortunately, she had not experienced any adverse reactions.

Until now.

Her skin started blistering and then peeling as if she had suffered from burns. Large swaths of her skin began to drop off of her face, arms, legs and feet and hands.

She had been tricked!

These were not true fairies. They would not seek to destroy her. Lili's heart rapidly sped up like an automatic gun causing the heart monitor to sound the alarm!

BEEP! BEEP!

Within seconds, Dr. Fukina and the charge nurse came rushing in, expecting to call a code. Lili lay motionless in the bed, looking like a snake that has shed its skin.

"Malia, get me 1 cc. of epi! She's having a reaction to the blood!" demanded Dr. Fukina. He feared she would bottom out and code on them. "What are her vital signs? O2 sat?" He wanted data yesterday.

Malia quickly stated loudly the requested data, "70/45, 114, 26, and 95%."

"Increase her oxygen rate and give her the epi," instructed Dr. Fukina.

Malia quickly implemented the directives that she was given, as Dr. Fukina assessed Lili's condition. He examined her skin, expecting to see spreading, erupting sores as the source of the peeling skin.

This was not so.

In fact, it was very far from the truth. Underneath the peeling skin, there was fresh, new skin. Brand new epidermis! The painful, inflamed, crusted sores were gone. Just like that!

Dr. Fukina was completely puzzled. The transfused blood could not possibly be taking effect this soon. He looked puzzled.

"Vital signs are within normal limits. Oxygen saturation is 99%," said Malia. "Why she's improved so much, well, frankly Dr. Fukina, I don't get it." In a state of bewilderment, there was only one true answer. Malia wanted to shout out loud that a miracle had just occurred. She chose to keep it to herself. Dr. Fukina was a reserved man, not tolerating emotional outbursts.

It was a weird night after all. She actually thought that she had heard the loud chirping of crickets. Who could tell with the rain coming down heavily now on this dark night?

It was now 3 hours since the blood transfusion had begun.

Both Dr. Fukina and Malia knew that something supernatural was afoot. They did not talk about it.

They felt the floor begin to shake beneath their feet. As they felt the tremors, they realized that an earthquake was imminent.

The sirens were going off loudly alerting the town people that a tsunami was fast approaching the island.

And there was nowhere to go for the people trapped within the hospital.

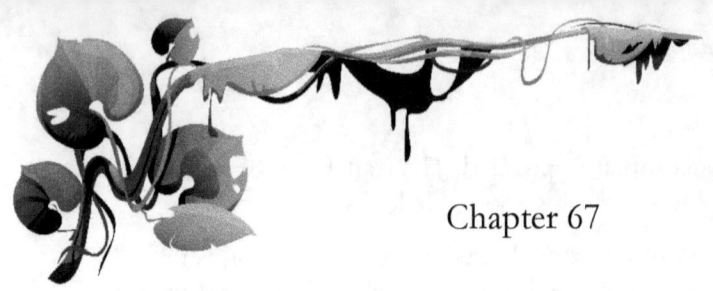

Chapter 67

'olelo e wikiwiki kakou

(Let's make haste)

"He's waking up!" shouted Puna, who had been praying over the pastor, along with Peter and his devoted men. "He's waking up!"

"You're right!" exclaimed Mana. Pastor was stirring.

"Thank you Lord," whispered Peter, as he knelt down beside the pastor and passed his hands over the Pastor's head and body. A white light flashed, like an old-fashioned camera with a flashbulb on it. It provided a dose of healing light that emitted from his hands.

Peter is a man with great mana.

"Hey!!! Why didn't you do that earlier?!" demanded Puna in an angry voice.

"My friend, it is simple. He was not ready until now. He needed to speak to Hannah first."

"My Mom?"

Yes, Puna. Your mother." Peter opened his mouth to explain but he was interrupted by the Pastor awakening.

"He's opening his eyes!" Pilikana shouted. "He's coming to!! Thank God!"

"Stop shouting!" said Pastor as he slowly sat up. "Son, you're makin' a lot of noise."

"Welcome back, my friend," said Peter in his quiet way.

"Pastor, did you speak to my mother?" asked Puna. His pinched face revealed his anxiety. "Yes, son. And she will be fine. Honest." He drank some water that Mana had handed him.

"Help me up please." He extended a hand. Both Pilikana and Puna assisted the pastor to his feet. His hair was matted with leaves from under the tree and his clothes were filthy, as though he had rolled like a pig. His knees wobbled as he found his footing. The two young men held onto him to keep him from falling.

After a minute or so, Pastor shook them off and said, "Okay, I'm ready to get on my ole horse and get to the sacred caves. We need to leave right now. Hannah and the others know that we are coming soon."

"Pastor's right. Time is running out and the weather is about to turn on a dime." As though the weather had auditory powers, a loud *boom* responded in kind.

"Let's make haste," suggested Pastor.

Without further discussion, the men mounted their horses, turned on their heavy-duty flashlights, and moved forward on the steep, uphill trail under the moonless sky. The rain began to fall like a wide-open faucet had just been turned on. It was not a pleasant ride. Quickly, they were as wet as drowned rats. Despite heavy jackets, the men shivered with the biting-cold, gusting winds.

Was a little discouragement creeping into the men's psyches?

Surely not.

Puna was worrying about Lili. He had a bad feeling about her. Somehow he had lost his connection to her. The challenges presented by the inclement weather distracted him somewhat from his fretting.

"Son, stop worrying. Lili's fine too," stated Pastor, reading his thoughts.

"Pastor's right," said Mana. "Lili is your soul mate. You'd know if somethin' was wrong." "I guess," Puna reluctantly agreed.

"Man, I wish that I had a beautiful woman like Lili, bra," said Mana. "I'm sure lonely for a woman!"

"What happened with you and Malia?" asked Pilikana. Mana had a reputation as a ladies' man. It was his Achilles heel.

"She dumped me. I couldn't even get to first base with her and…"

"Enough talk of romance. We must be on our way," declared Peter. "The weather is getting much worse."

Given the sheet of rain pouring down, it didn't take long for a nearby stream to overflow and become a gushing river, headed straight down towards the ocean.

The earth shook.

Thunder rolled through the mountains, green lightning flashed against the ink sky, causing it to glow. Winds were at gale-storm level.

Fortunately, once again, the awa-iku, Kane's beneficent spirits, intervened. These particular spirits had the supernatural powers to change the weather. However, it required great mana to work against these weather conditions. They began to sing a mele.

Kane comes with the water of life…….

The wind ceased. Silence prevailed.

As though encased in a bubble, the rain stopped abruptly over the bedraggled posse of men.

They were provided a clear-weather corridor over the ever-steeper trail. Outside of their bubble lane, the noise of the roaring, downhill, red waters could easily break an eardrum.

Somewhere in the distance, a dog was barking. They must be getting closer to the sacred caves.

A drumming noise in the distance could be heard also. The sound sent a shock up your spine.

Inside the bubble, the air was just right, a comfortable 70 degrees. It appeared that the remaining miles would now be easily negotiated. Perhaps the posse would make it in time. Unspoken, yet understood, a tsunami was on its way, fast-approaching. In silence, they made haste.

The night of Kane was bearing down on them, full speed ahead.

Woman from a Distant Land

Many men were born,

It was the time when the gods were born, Men stood up,

Men lay prostrate (the prostrating tapu prescribed for high chiefs)

They lay prostrate in that far time,

Very shadowy the men who march hither (marchers of the night),

Very red the faces of the gods,

Dark those of the men,

Very white their chins (because living to old age),

A tranquil time when men multiplied,

Living in peace in the time when men came from afar,

It was hence called calmness,

Haumea was born, a woman,

Ki`i was born, a man,

Kane was born, a god,

Kanaloa was born a god, the rank-smelling squid, It was day,

The womb gave birth,

The vast-expanse-of-the-damp-forest, was her next born,

The-first-chiefs-of the-damp-forest, was her next born,

The long-lived man of the two branches of chiefs.

Adapted from Hawaiian mythology-Wikipedia.
En.wikipedia.org/wiki/Hawaiian_narrative.

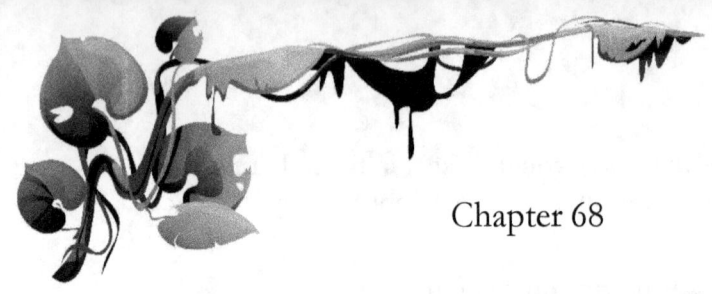

Chapter 68

huaka'i po

(The Night Marchers)

The Night Marchers easily weathered the storm, as they marched upwards carrying their torches which mysteriously never went out despite the heavy rains. In fact, they were partly responsible for the stormy weather. These ghostly apparitions moved with purpose to the beat of the primitive, pounding drums.

Marching the same pathway each moonless night of Kane, they were searching for salvation.

Their purpose was to find a way into the sacred caves to find the leaping point that would give them entrance to the other world, ending their damnation of wandering in the darkness for centuries. Restless and lost in the po, they longed to be with their aumakua.

They were carrying archaic weaponry such as spears and big, sharp knives. Owa was clothed in a decorative helmet and cloak, reminiscent of the days of King Kamehameha. Vivid and bold colors in red and yellow feathers adorned his wispy body. He was the now the leader of the army of mu spirits because Haumea, transformed into an ink-black raven, had gone ahead, undoubtedly wreaking havoc where she could. Spying and improvising ways to interfere with the powerful posse was exactly what Haumea was up to.

She had spied on Pastor, Peter and the others. Since the men of great mana had not yet arrived to the sacred caves, there was still time to disrupt the powerful chain of interconnected individuals required to overcome the mu spirits. She conveyed that message to Kanaloa.

Shape-changer.

Haumea morphed into her old woman persona. Her dark, wrinkled skin and stooped back, allowed her to project a weak image. Hopefully, this would enable her to get closer to the sacred caves and her target. Kupuna Hannah.

She was fully capable of bringing down Haumea with her powerful mana. Joined with Pastor, she was a mighty force to be reckoned with.

Kupuna was in a vulnerable state, but not for long. Time was running out. Hannah was close to surfacing from her state of unconsciousness. She was being pulled by the light, out of the darkness. But until she finally broke through, Hannah could still be dragged back down into the po.

Back to the darkness.

The power of evil knew exactly who Hannah was.

Haumea hoped that she would be mistaken as an old woman from the Hawaiian clan or, better yet, as the old-woman manifestation of the goddess Pele. She hunched over, her back bent, Haumea was dressed in old rags. Her salt and pepper hair was plaited into two long braids. After all, this was exactly the time – a time of crisis for her people - that the fire goddess would show up to render help. Her enormous power made her a *near* impossible entity to defeat. Just like Haumea who had an over-inflated sense of self.

But clearly, not impossible. Kanaloa was a mighty force on his own. He had consumed many dark souls.

And he too was close.

The thing that might give her away was her eyes. The eyes were dark black slits, as dark as her very soul. Frankly, her eyes were haunting if you looked directly into them. Her gaze was cold, void of any emotions except hate. One look from Haumea could send chills up your spine.

Somehow, she would get close to Kupuna Hannah and impose her will to plunge her spirit into a locked, dark box that sat upon a grate above the hot fire pit. Anything less might not contain the Kupuna's powerful mana force. They couldn't risk it.

Haumea had flown and landed near the sacred caves. Already, she could feel the goodness of these Native people. The caves themselves were toxic to Haumea. Upon entering the sacred cave, she would feel different sensations that can be attributed to the mana imprint from previous visitors.

The good imprint from these righteous people.

The torrential rains provided her with cover. She emerged in front of the caves. Which one housed Kupuna?

Remaining in the shadows, Haumea watched and waited.

A tall man carrying a lantern emerged from the closest cave. Another tall man emerged, but he seemed feeble. They stood close to one another under the overhang of vines as the rains beat down like pellets from a gun. Green flashes of lightning interrupted the dark night sky.

Suddenly, there was something else that flashed across the moonless night. A blast of a golden-white explosion crossed the darkness of the Kane night. A pulse of energy ensued.

"Time is running out Kimo," said Kekela, raising his voice. Thunder boomed.

"Is she still deep in her state of po?" shouted Kimo. He wanted to be heard over the noise of the downpour.

"Sadly, she is in a deep dark place," replied Kekela. "If Pastor and his men don't get here soon, it will be too late," he said in a concerned voice.

"They should have been here by now."

"I fear for them." Kekela said loudly. "I also fear for Kupuna."

Overhearing the two men's exchange, Haumea's face displayed a sour smile. She almost cawed in her raven voice. She smelt the faint odor of decomposition in the wind.

It was clear that she had indeed arrived in the nick of time.

So enamored by the information, Haumea failed to see the `elepaio* bird nearby hiding under the shroud of darkness. It would soon sing the last mele of the night. The `elepaio bird is the first native bird to sing in the morning and the last to stop singing at night. The bird's mele is a pleasant and rather loud warble. It is the mele of the moon goddess.

Tonight, let us hope that its final song will be one of celebration.

Chapter 69

maikai me ka hewa

(Good versus Evil)

They weren't going to make it in this storm.

Despite the help of Kai-the-owl-as protector and the luminous albino fairies, the heavy downpour was causing the horses to slip and stumble. In addition, the nearby gushing red river was roaring loudly and clearly spooking the horses.

Yet, a soothing sound was braking through the environmental noises. It wasn't really a noise, per say, but rather; it was more like a *feeling*.

A very good feeling. Like a full tummy of macaroni and cheese.

Kate, Hannah, and Uncle Bert could feel it too.

And then, the rain stopped. The sky overhead brightened. It almost seemed like a full moon had come out! Several stars twinkled in the heavens overhead.

"Look Mom. I see the first star!" exclaimed Hannah as she pointed upwards. A broad smile graced her angelic face. "I'm going to make a wish!"

Kate gazed up at the sky. Sure enough, several stars shone brightly.

I'm makin' a wish too, honey-girl. Uncle Bert stuck his head out of little Hannah's shirt pocket.

"What's going on Bert?" asked Kate. Despite his buffoonery, he understood many things, including supernatural phenomenon. The various elements were at war. Light versus Darkness.

Good versus Evil. Angels versus Demons

He conveyed this through telepathic imagery. He did not speak of the pulse because he knew that each of them was experiencing different sensations from it. It would come to be understood by each of them over the next few hours.

Kate winced. It was as she thought. An epic battle was at hand.

Hannah cried out as she too saw the revealed images. Shivers ran up her spine.

We are encompassed by the light. So we are gonna be okay.

The brightness surrounded them and became their protective shield. Within the safety of their flowing, dynamic bubble, the sound of the pulse, or rather, the feeling intensified. Now it felt like a full tummy of macaroni and cheese *and* a hot fudge sundae.

Kate stopped abruptly.

She felt wetness on her face, as though a mist had seeped into the bubble. She gasped and closed her eyes in an effort to avoid inhaling the mist.

Oh God! Not the toxic mist!

Kate opened her eyes.

The dewy mist wasn't green. Not at all. Droplets of soothing moisture, scented with eucalyptus, bathed her personhood. She released a deep sigh of pleasure. A sense of calm overcame her.

Much like her mother, Hannah was in a trance. She was purring like a kitten. Inside her shirt pocket, Uncle Bert was blissfully snoring.

It was the magic of awa water, the water of Kane. The pulse throbbed like an engorged tick.

It actually sounded like the beat of a heart. It was a very kind and benevolent heart. And it was also a very strong heart.

But whose heart was it?

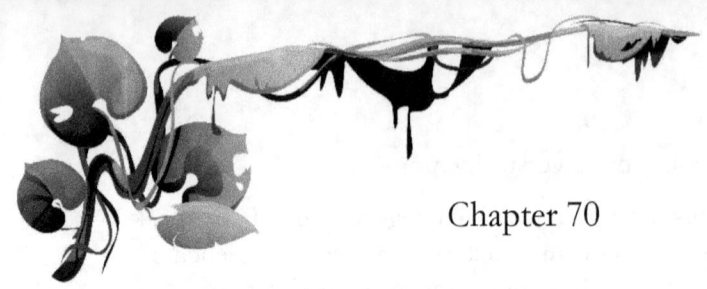

Chapter 70

'olelo ma ke kanaka a me kana 'ilio

(A man and his dog)

Pastor was wide awake and tuned in to every noise and sensation. It felt so invigorating inside their encasement.

"Being inside this bubble, well, it feels like a slice of heaven!" declared Pilikana, grinning widely.

"Perhaps it is," replied Peter.

"What do you mean?" asked Maui. He paid attention to everything that Peter said. "There are divine places here on earth."

"We can sure use some of that!" Mana was feeling fine. Mighty fine. "You mean like the sacred caves?" inquired Pilikana.

Peter just nodded and smiled. He knew that he was the source of this divine energy.

Divine places existed because of the divine nature of an entity that resided in that space. We flock to the holy hands where Christ once walked; seeking a sense of the Holy Spirit. Even after the godly entity left, the powerful mana of righteousness remained. Peter could feel his powers growing. All in due preparation for what lay ahead.

Outside of their protective bubble, the wind howled and the rain pounded down heavily on the ground. Flashes of green lightning streaked across the night sky. The final battle was at hand.

"I hear a dog barking," said Maui. "But I sure don't see a dog." He swiveled and looked in several directions.

"I hear it too." said Pilikana. "It sounds like it's gettin' closer."

Once more, Peter smiled. He knew the sound of the dog's bark. He'd know it anywhere.

Like a galloping horse, Max bounded down the trail towards them with his pink tongue hanging out.

"Max! Look, it's Max!" shouted Puna who was at the head of the troupe.

The horses got excited when Max shot by them and headed straight for his former beloved Master. He barked loudly and jumped up and down. His tail was wagging at a ferocious rate.

"Hey Max! I'm happy to see you too buddy." Peter dismounted from his horse and was quickly knocked down by the overly excited dog. Max pinned him down and began licking his face. "Oh boy! You sure did miss me," laughed Peter as Max slobbered all over him. Peter was covered in dirt and leaves. And love.

There was something more going on between the Master and the dog.

A telepathic communication was underway. Max explained to Peter what had already transpired thus far up at the sacred caves. Max had felt the evil creeping up the mountain and headed directly towards hallowed ground. The putrid smell of the Night Marchers announced their approach prior to their arrival. It smelt like raw sewage or dead animals. Max had caught a whiff of their sickening odor. Moreover, he had *felt* the presence of evil that accompanied the malodorous smell.

Haumea is also close, Max warned.

Peter already knew this because he too had felt an evil entity somewhere nearby, in close proximity.

He did not fear it.

Peter pushed Max off him and stood up.

"Come on boy, we gotta go."

It was time to get going and make haste. Peter needed to assist Hannah very soon before she was plunged into a deeper state of po. They proceeded uphill with Max in the lead.

Outside the bubble, pairs of red-glowing eyes were everywhere…….. waiting for the people to exit their protective shield. The hiss sound of the snakes could not be heard over the noisy weather elements.

In parallel tracts, the group of people (and one dog) and the group of black and yellow - spotted snakes climbed the mountain, with little more than two miles to go to reach the top.

Who knows what awaits them. It wouldn't be good.

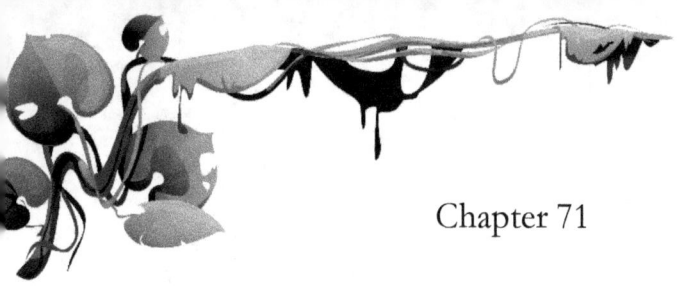

Chapter 71

ka hui hou ana o ka ohana

(Reunification of the family)

"Do you think she heard us? Were we loud enough?" asked Kimo.

"She heard us alright," replied Kekela. "Haumea has very good hearing." They were sitting around the light of the lantern on their eating table. The cave walls danced with shadows.

"She'll be eager to get to Kupuna in her so-called "vulnerable state," asserted Kimo. Their plan was to lure her in and surround her with the white light which is, of course, toxic to her. Right now, Ray was at her bedside. And, the children, of course.

"Let's not make it too easy for her to sense a trap," warned Kekela. He had had a vision of Haumea's old-lady persona and her intention to harm Hannah. Although not fully conscious, she was now muttering words, stirring in her bed, and even smiling as though she found something rather amusing. Clearly, she was awakening.

The truth be known, Kekela had experienced glimpses into Kupuna's mind. He had picked up shreds of a conversation that she was engaged in with Pastor. Thus, he knew that soon Pastor and Puna would be here soon.

Very soon.

He had also had a vision that was a window into the weather events occurring in the ocean waters and the night skies. Through this prism, Kekela saw the raging ocean with surf as high as 300 feet.

Was this the prelude to the tsunami wave?

Green neon lightning persisted as it shot up from the ocean seas. Thunder boomed and shook the earth with the force of an angry giant stomping his feet. The moonless and starless night created a dark backdrop for this night of Kane. And yet, Kekela could swear he saw a comet flash through the dark night. It was a cosmic sign of glory.

Would this night end in a righteous glory?

Or would this be the beginning of the devil's reign for 1000 years?

"The big wave is close," announced Kekela. "That means Kanaloa's soldiers are also close by."

"I thought I smelled somethin' really bad," said Kimo. He had encountered the Night

Marchers army before.

"Let's get ready to greet Pastor and Puna. But first, we must prepare for the ceremony to bring Kupuna back to us." Kekela rose from the table to go bathe and pray. Likewise, Kimo did the same. Before they escaped, the children came into the area.

"Dad, are we really supposed to hide somewhere?" asked Luke. "'Cause I want to fight too!"

"Son, I appreciate your enthusiasm but, no, I can't let you do that." Kimo's tone made it clear that he meant it. "You are in charge of the children, son."

Luke was only sixteen years old. A teenager with raging hormones and ideas of great glory in the battle. At that age, he felt immortal and very brave, placing him at-risk to certainly get harmed or killed. Despite his eagerness to become a warrior, he begrudgingly decided to obey his father.

David was hoping from one foot to another, impatiently waiting to speak.

"Is mommy and little Hannah coming soon?" asked the little boy who was wet and dirty as well as disheveled from looking under bushes here and there for Max. Hina had helped him.

Hina, covered in dirt and spurs, was wrapped around her uncle's legs, clinging to him.

"They will arrive soon." He had seen them on their way and he had already informed Kimo of the vision he had been shown.

David jumped up and down, shouting," Yea! Yea!" Hina let go of Kekela's legs and ran over to hug her father who swept her up in his arms and kissed her forehead. She sorely missed Kate and her baby sister.

"I know. I can't wait to see them both myself," said Kimo with a big, wide smile on his face. He set Hina down as she was getting heavy. Despite her small stature, the prepubescent girl was on a growing spurt.

Luke had turned away so no one could see him wipe away tears from his eyes. Tears of relief flooded him as he heard the news that his mom and little sister would arrive shortly.

No shame there. His father had done the same thing. As a matter of fact, he had wept like a baby.

The reunification of both Kimo's family and Kupuna's family (which includes Pastor although they are not biologically related) would generate more mana for the Hawaiian clan.

"Wait! Quiet!" shouted David. "I think I hear Max barking!"

Everyone paused and listened.

Sure enough, in the distance, Max's familiar bark could be heard.

Everyone paused and smiled.

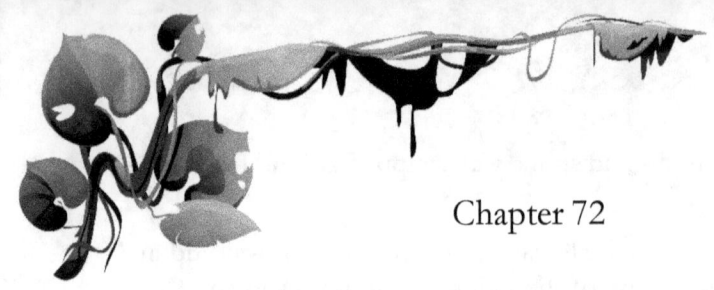

Chapter 72

The urukema people

(Mu descendants from Maui)

Despite the distressing sound of the sirens, Lili was not concerned. She had just been the recipient of a true miracle. Chaos had ensued all around her but she remained calm. Perhaps even content.

She was standing near the broken glass window. The shattered glass on the floor had been cleaned up. Lili felt the strong wind entering her room and battering her face. Her room was on the third floor and it was a room with a view. She gazed up at the night sky and ……. would wonders not cease this night…..

A bright comet streaked across the dark night sky, illuminating the sky and turbulent ocean that was roaring like a lion, tossing and turning, wave heights as tall as twenty-five feet.

Ancient Hawaiian religion looked to the stars to foretell the future. Since the days of the Bethlehem star, many wise men have studied the cosmic clues to gain clarity about what lies ahead.

So Lili asked herself: *What is the meaning of this comet on this particular night?*

Perhaps, it marked the arrival of a heavenly host.

Or could it be a sign of the end of the ages? The Holy Bible prophesizes that there will be many celestial events at the end of time.

No matter. Lili was at peace.

As the brilliant comet passed through the night, white dust particles began to fall from the tail of the comet. Caught on a gust of wind, they were swiftly carried away and they soon headed for the broken window in Lili's room.

Help has arrived, once again, my dear. Behold.

"Naomi."

These are the Mu descendants from Maui. The urukema people. You've surely heard of them.

Naomi's voice was reassuring.

"Yes. I have heard the legends. I have read the stories." Lili was an avid reader of Hawaiian history and folklore.

The benevolent albino fairies knew exactly where to go. After all, they had visited Lili's room before.

Making their cricket noises, they landed on the floor of her room, making a glowing formation. Their fairy wings became still and the spirits fell silent. The sign of the cross was brightly lit up.

Holy, holy, holy.

Now you understand who has arrived. And who sent them.

Lili smiled and nodded.

I have a gift for you. Close your eyes, my dear.

Lili complied with Naomi's instructions.

Her head filled with a glimpse into the world inside the comfortable bubble encasement. She saw Puna and Pastor riding uphill on their horses. She uttered a sound of relief when she saw Puna. Max was in the lead. Then she saw the three other horsemen, followed by Peter!

Peter was alive!

But how could that be? He was dying when she last saw him. Another miracle!

Then the vision disappeared.

In the cold chill of her room, Lili was filled with a warm feeling. She had seen her love.

The still fairies became active again, their wings fluttering as they reformed themselves into a white, living magic carpet. Again, they became still. With their blue eyes wide open, the white carpet appeared as though it was in-laid with blue, sapphire jewels.

It was time for Lili to leave because the hospital would ultimately be annihilated in the hours ahead. She needed to get to higher ground. There would be no survivors for those who had remained in the town. The ocean waters would flood the lowlands. All life forms would be destroyed.

She needed to get to Puna.

It's time to go Lili.

Without any hesitation, Lili stepped onto the living carpet. She felt as light as a feather. She sat down and the downy feathers made her feel like she was floating on a cloud. Without further ado, they took off on a gust of wind, sailing through the night, making that loud cricket noise.

Up, up, and away!

Lili was elated until she sensed a change in the air. In fact, she *smelled* it. A pungent, foul odor. The smell of a dead, decomposing animal.

As she gazed upwards towards the heavens, Lili gasped. A full moon had appeared.

A blood red moon.

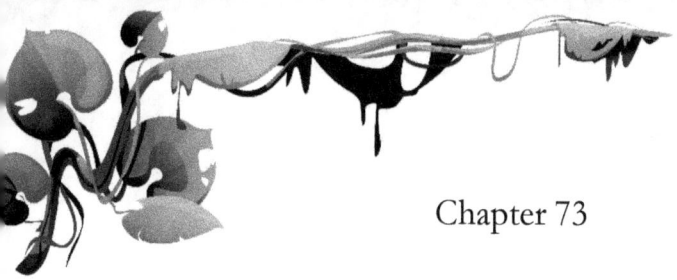

Chapter 73

Ho 'I mai o Makanikeo

(Peace and love are here once more!)

Haumea had readily entered the sacred cave without any interference. No one had noticed her. Or so she thought.

She had entered the dark cavern whose only illumination was the lanterns that created long shadows on the cave walls. The dank smell of the inner cavern pleased her. Quite frankly, it soothed her. Being in this sacred place caused her to feel ill and weaker in her powers. Too much goodness in this place.

She lay on a mat on the hard, cold floor, trying to remain hidden. She was just an old weary woman that was resting in the shadows, well covered in her shawls and scarfs.

And yet, some of the people inside the cave did seem to be noticing her. She could feel them looking at her. This was making Haumea nervous. Maybe she was just being paranoid in her weakened state. After all, they couldn't really detect evil in their presence. They were simple people. Lesser than her and her league of people.

However, there were others who were different. They could readily perceive darkness in their presence. She hoped that they would not pick up on her malodorous smell. There was nothing that she could do about it. It was laden in her very pores.

She heard a dog barking. It was damn close.

Someone else heard the dog barking.

"It's Max! It's Max!" cried David as he ran outside the cave and looked for his beloved friend.

Behind him, there was Hina, skipping with delight.

"Look Hina! I see him running up the trail!" exclaimed the excited boy. Hina smiled widely.

She could now see Max too. He was almost here.

But suddenly, Max stopped dead in his tracks. His bark changed to a ferocious sound. He was really pissed off or scared.

A swarm of black, yellow-spotted snakes crossed the path, directly in front of Max. One of them rose up, and quickly darted his tongue forward, just a fraction from Max's barking face. "Max!!" screamed David who was watching in horror. Hina emitted a loud scream too.

By now, Luke, Kimo, and Kekela had joined the kids and they too, watched in horror as more of the snakes rose up to attack the dog who had failed to retreat. Max was no coward but, in this case, he was gonna get himself killed!

"Max, get away from them!" shouted David who was no stranger to these agents of Satan.

More people had emerged from the sacred caves.

A voice called out," Max, stand down."

Immediately, Max withdrew and crept slowly backwards. Then, he sat down.

Out of the dark night, Peter emerged. His clothes were tattered and torn and he was dirty from head to toe. Still, no one could mistake the divine face of Peter. Son of Amos.

Instantly, they all felt the surge of the pulse. Apparently, the pulse had accompanied them from inside the bubble that no longer existed. For most of the people, they had not as yet *felt* the comfortable, warm and fuzzy sensations that it induced. The air was charged with energy.

"Oh My God! Is that really you Peter?" cried out Kimo. Kekela just smiled discreetly.

Honestly, he hadn't been sure who was going to show up.

Everyone began shouting. Others chanted.

Ho `I mai o Makanikeo. Peace and love are here once more! Sounds of joy and meles of thankfulness filled the air.

Then another loud noise could be heard.

In front of the entrance to the sacred cave where Kupuna lay, a cock crowed at top volume and the crowd grew silent. It was true, their guest had arrived.

All eyes turned and gazed at Peter.

Peter walked up to the slithering mass and waved his hand over the swarm of Kanaloa's vile poisonous creatures. One bite could kill you.

Quickly, the snakes dissipated and slithered away into the dark night. The observers, once again, broke into songs of joy and praise. Salvation had arrived.

Right behind Peter was Pastor, sitting tall but weary on his horse.

"Pastor! Welcome home," shouted Kimo when he saw him. The children had already rushed Max and they were gleeful about his return. Kimo and Kekela approached Peter and Pastor.

"You two are a sight for sore eyes!" declared Kimo, first embracing Peter and then Pastor.

And before anymore words were spoken, Puna and three other horsemen appeared. Introductions and greetings were made all around. Several men took care of the horses that were in need of water and food as well as a cool brushing down. And although there was so much to share, it would have to wait. Right now, they must attend to Kupuna.

Both Peter and Kekela knew time was running out. They were surrounded by evil forces that were creeping ever closer.

The drumbeats were getting louder. The putrid smell was becoming overwhelming. Some were coughing from the toxic odor.

And as the ground underneath rumbled, they gazed upwards to the heavens and discovered the full red moon.

Certainly, a bad omen. They people gasped again as their joy turned quickly to fear.

Weliweli fear.

That profound and absolute feeling of dread for what was yet to come this fateful night.

Chapter 74

Awakening from their blissful state, Kate, Uncle Bert, and little Hannah sat up feeling quite refreshed. They had dismounted and were resting for a while when the awa mist engulfed them. Uncle Bert started singing his favorite tunes from the fifties and sixties.

Love, don't let me be lonely. Tears of a clown. Love me tender. When the red, red robin comes bop, bop, boppin' along.......

"Uncle Bert, please shut up!!" cried Hannah "You're drivin' me crazy!"

They'll be no more....

"Enough! Really, Uncle Bert, settle down. Give it up!" suggested Kate, suppressing a grin.

She was a mess. Dirty, tangled hair, darned in dead leaves and prickly burrs, hung limply forward and obscured an even dirtier, scratched and weathered face. Her red cheeks from both the sun and the wind earlier in their journey were blistered and looked sore to touch. Her torn clothes somewhat exposed her breasts that were harnessed in what was once a white, cotton bra with some pretty lace. Now, it was dirty with dry, red mud and stained with her sweat. Yet, her merry blue eyes still shone from her angelic face. Undoubtedly, Kate was still a beautiful woman.

Geez.... I was just feeling excited about meetin' everyone.

"Well, it's time to get going," said Kate as she helped Hannah up onto her small horse. "Maybe just tamper some of that enthusiasm down until we get there," advised Kate, as she mounted her horse. She was also excited too but, so far, she was keeping it together.

Hannah was also excited, even though the irritable little girl was impatient.

They weren't aware that Hannah had a bad feeling inside her….. weliweli fear had taken hold of her like a dog with a prime rib steak in its grasp.

What was this feeling of dread about? she wondered. She whispered to Naomi. Right away, she got a response.

No need to be afraid, little Hannah. Soon you will be reunited with your family.

Hannah trusted Naomi so she decided to ignore the unpleasant feeling and, instead, she filled her thoughts of her family reunion. Those were certainly happy thoughts.

Their bubble of protection by the albino fairies was a safe place. There was no need to fear anything.

They mounted their horses and moved up the mountain trail, guided by the white, fairy spirits, who were illuminating the way forward. Their distinctive cricket sounds were a familiar mele by now. In fact, the noise had become soothing and therefore, it had a calming effect.

A piercing, loud-pitched caw of a raven bird obliterated the calming moment. The noise sent chills up your spine sending them directly into the cortex of your brain.

Caw! Caw!

A large, ink-black raven landed in front of them. Its beady eyes glowed red.

Geez…. I'm not liking the looks of this dude, said Uncle Bert from the shirt pocket.

Hannah's horse was acting skittish. Clearly, it did not like the black bird either.

Kate called out, "Hannah be careful!"

Caw! Caw!

The bird began to scratch at the dirt on the trail, all the while, getting noisier and noisier. His mele was frightening. It was a very dark and eerie sound.

Evil, nasty bird! Be careful Hannah. Hold onto the reigns tightly!

The horse neighed and began to rise up to escape the aggressive bird, kicking up dirt and red dust.

Yiks! Hold steady, honey-girl.

"Mommy! Help!" Hannah was losing control of her horse. After all, she was only a tiny bit of a thing. "Help me!" Her voice quaked with fear.

Caw! Caw!

"Hold on honey. I'm coming!" screamed Kate as she watched with horror as the scene unfolded in front of her eyes. Hannah had fallen off her horse. The horse was long gone. She fell pretty hard and just barely missed hitting her head on a rock.

"Oh my God Hannah!" screamed Kate. She was already dismounted and running towards her daughter. As she got close to her, the large, evil bird-creature approached unfettered.

Caw! Caw!

The red eyes glowed like the full crimson moon. Deadly intent showed in those devilish eyes.

Without any fear, the bird began to peck madly at the ground. It was advancing on Hannah, unconcerned by Kate's presence.

"Mommy, make it go away!" screamed the terrified girl.

"Shew! Shew! You wretched thing!" yelled Kate. She was leaning over Hannah, protecting her as much as possible. "Dammit! Get away from her!"

Caw! Caw!

The bird took aim and darted its sharp beak at Hannah's face. In alarm, Kate quickly pulled her daughter close to her, covering her face with her hands.

"Ouch!" cried Kate. She had been struck. Her left hand was bleeding. The bird had taken a small chunk out of her forehand. While she had removed her hands, the raven wasted no time. It pecked at Hannah's face, plucking a small piece of her right cheek. Hannah's painful scream was unnerving.

Uncle Bert's head was stickin' out of Hannah's pocket.

Hang on baby-girl.

Uncle Bert jumped out of the shirt pocket and ran down Hannah's arm. Within seconds, he was sitting atop the bird's beak. He released some kind of toxic spray that caused the bird great discomfort. The beak was beginning to melt and give off a foul odor. Injured, the bird retreated.

But before it retreated, the raven had thrown the offending lizard off of his beak and onto the hard ground. Then, the creature used both of its feet, which had sharp talons, to stomp on the lizard.

Uncle Bert lay motionless on the ground. Blood began to pool around his lifeless body.

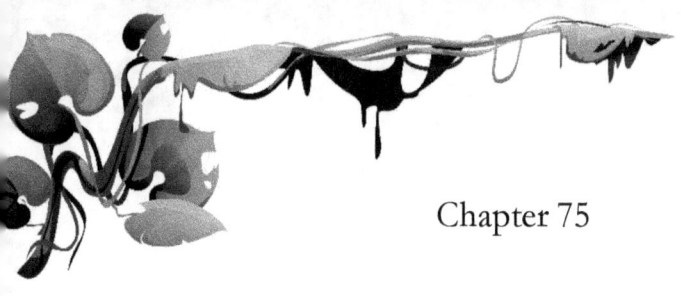

Chapter 75

The ceremony had begun.

In the dim light of the lanterns, the requisite players were all there and accounted for.

Kimo, Kekela, Pastor, Peter, Puna and the three horsemen of great merit and great mana gathered around Kupuna's bed. The lingering smell of sage used to cleanse the area remained.

Beside her bed, the tapa mat awaited for her to rise. Joining hands, they began to chant:

Oh, Kane, hear my cry!

Oh, Kane, hear my petition!

Oh, Kane, help me to send Na moo ekahi, the first serpent to the pit,

Oh, Kane, awaken Hannah ika lani, seer of the heavens,

Oh, Kane, I evoke the ao, the light of my ancestors.

Oh, Kane, hear our prayers, release the light from the darkness.

Shadows danced on the walls and the whispers of the others in the cave could be heard in the background. Many of them were praying, generating more mana, focusing on their beloved Kupuna.

They could feel a surge of energy when they had joined hands and, as they chanted, the pulse increased……………..

Until it abruptly stopped.

"There is one among us who is part of the darkness now, take your leave before you are destroyed by the saber of white light," ordered Peter. "We must break the chain."

Looking baffled, everyone let go of their joined hands. Who among them was tainted? Maybe turned.

With laser vision, Peter stared directly at Mana.

"I didn't know! Honest, I didn't know Peter!" declared Mana. "She was just a beautiful woman…... I mean, I didn't know it was *her*! It was just for some fun."

His Achilles heel.

Mana failed to recognize that the young and beautiful Hawaiian woman that he had recently bedded was the human form of Haumea. He had slept with the devil!

"You must leave this cavern at once," order Peter.

"Where will I go?" asked a panicked Mana. He got no response. Everyone was staring at him now with disappointment shining in their eyes and the shame that he felt was feeling was enormous. He turned to flee but his way was blocked.

There, standing before him was the beautiful, Hawaiian woman with whom he'd shared some moments of great passion. Haumea. The old lady persona was gone. The temptress had returned.

"Aloha Mana. Nice to see you again, my love," coed Haumea and then she laughed heartily.

"What? Has the cat got your tongue?" she asked playfully. Then she stepped in front of him, only inches away from his face. "You can do better than that, baby," she said. She seductively touched her breasts. Quickly, she leaned in and forced a kiss upon his lips. Mana tried to push her away but she held onto him more tightly and kissed him more deeply.

When she let him go, he fell to the ground.

Mana's body began to shake as a seizure overtook him and caused his arms and legs to jerk. Blood oozed from both of his ears. He gasped deeply once and then he laid still, eyes wide open with the look of death.

Mana was dead.

The good mana that the group had intended to generate had been corrupted by the evil presence and evil deed that had just occurred in this, once sacred, cave.

Kupuna was plunged further into the po.

The mana in this place was tinged with smell of raw sewage. Evil left its mark.

"All of you step away from Hannah," ordered Haumea. No one moved.

"Step away unless you want to end up like your friend here." Haumea let out a hideous laugh, *Caw! Caw!*

"None of us are leaving. We are not leaving Kupuna's side. Amen," said Peter. He gazed into her black eyes…… pools of darkness that made him feel ill. He groaned out loud and held his stomach, his face pinched with pain. Blood dripped from his nose. His ears were ringing, and his vision was blurred.

"Not feelin' so good, man of God?" Haumea smiled again.

Despite his discomfort, he began to pray. The others joined hands and began to pray along with Peter.

They felt the pulse.

Another outburst of laughter.

"No one is leaving this place. We can agree on that," said Haumea, dead serious. She was ready to act. How dare they defy her!

Peter stepped forward, silently in prayer. He wore a ceremonial, white tapa robe.

"Madame, you cannot defeat the power of the Lord," stated Peter calmly. "You are so naive Peter." mocked Haumea. "So stupid…"

Peter threw a small bottle of awa water that he had brought with him and he threw it in

Haumea's face. She screamed a sound of agony that pierced the night.

Caaaaaw! Caaaaaw!

Within several minutes, Haumea was transformed into a black raven. She flew up and out of the cave, out into the red moon night. Left behind, was her clothing and shoes. They lay in a puddle on the floor.

It was just a temporary leave. She would be back again soon.

The drumbeats were very loud and the putrid smell was overwhelming. The Night Marchers had arrived.

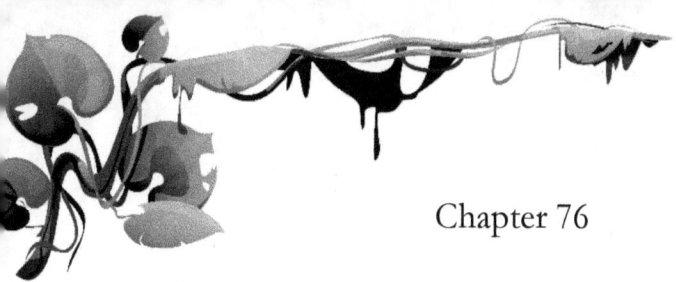

Chapter 76

I k ʻolelo ke ola, I k ʻolelo ka make

(In the word, there is life; in the word, death.)

Little Hannah was inconsolable.

Uncle Bert was dead.

"It is very sad, honey. I miss him too," said Kate, holding back her own tears.

Hannah sobbed loudly, her body shaking with her grief.

Kate had gathered her up in her arms. She was rocking her gently.

"Shhhhh….. it's gonna be okay," said Kate, trying to comfort her sweet, little girl.

Kate and Hannah buried Uncle Bert under a tree, under the shade. They said a prayer together.

After a while, Kate helped Hannah up on to the saddle on her horse. She mounted her horse and, once again, they were on their way, on the last leg of their arduous journey. They both were exhausted, both physically and emotionally.

"Soon we will see Daddy and Luke and Hina." Kate soothed herself with that thought.

Hannah remained silent.

Only the sound of the horses' hooves and the fairy noise could be heard as they slugged up the trail.

A mele began out of nowhere.

Kane comes with the water of life.

Life through the multitudes of the gods!

Ahead on the trail, a fine white mist hung in the air. A woman on horseback emerged   from the fog. Her white horse was a magnificent creature that had an unusual eye color of amber, like whiskey in a crystal glass. The woman was tall. Long, red hair like fire hung down her back. Her beauty was breathtaking causing one to pause. Her skin was like ivory and her high cheekbones and full lips were the evidence of her majestic beauty. But, her eyes….. they were mesmerizing….as blue as the aqua blue of the ocean waters. Dark, long eyelashes dressed her hypnotic eyes and her cheeks were as red as an apple. Hannah presumed her to be Sleeping Beauty at first. Indeed, this woman had a powerful aura about her.

Clearly, she was not of this earthly world.

She nodded at the mother and daughter. Approaching slowly, the woman came up beside Hannah. She was dressed in a colorful, tapestry skirt and a bright red and gold flowing blouse. A headdress of vivid colored feathers sat upon her shimmering hair of fire. Smiling, she reached into her skirt pocket and produced something. A very noisy something.

Finally, I'm out of that deep, dark and hot pocket! I was suffocating, especially when we were flyin'! Not a pleasant place to be, I assure you. Not at all. I was so overheated…it was like a sauna, for goodness sake!

It was Uncle Bert! It was an intact and a very-much-alive Uncle Bert!

Cheer up honey-girl! Uncle Bert needed repairs but I'm back now. They gave me a new body, so to speak. I'm just dandy again, honey-girl! Good as new and new is good.

"Uncle Bert! I missed you so much!" squealed Hannah. Her face shone with delight. Her heart soared, like a sky rocket at night.

The woman handed the beloved lizard to Hannah. She let him crawl on her face and tickle her nose. Then she held him close and kissed his nose. He squirmed in response.

Yuk! I'm happy to see you too baby girl but no more kissing.

"Wow, Uncle Bert. You never cease to amaze me!" said Kate, who was beaming with delight too.

Zippity-do-da, Zippity day....

He was doing his two-step again. He was showing them it was really and truly him. Little Hannah and Kate laughed in amusement as well as in relief.

Another miracle.

The woman smiled and then she turned her white horse around to lead the way forward.

She was quite regal and possessed a great presence.

Who was she?

Her appearance had readily snapped Hannah out of her revere. The woman was a real princess! Hannah could just tell.

"Mom, I think she must be a real, true princess!" "Maybe so Hannah." She was not of this world.

Kate didn't know what to think! So much that had occurred this night that was inexplicable and it was far more than she could sort out right now in this moment. Frankly, supernatural events are inexplicable by their very definition.

This woman of great fortitude spoke only the following words,

I ka olelo no ke ola, I ka olelo na ka make. In the word is life, in the word, death.

They had no choice but to follow this mysterious woman. Intuitively, Kate trusted her.

Since the arrival of the woman, Kate could really feel the upward tick of the pulse. Obviously, Hannah and Uncle Bert were feeling it too. Like old times, they were laughin' it up like two old drinking buddies from college.

As they moved up the trail, the two of them were singing and jabbering the whole way. A feeling of joy was the air that they breathed. Kate laughed at the two and her heart was filled with the spirit of love and a trust that all would be fine in the days ahead. They would face the unknown as a family. Their reunification would reconnect them all to each other. This would create an unbreakable chain. Nothing is stronger than love.

They could hear Max barking so they knew that they were close.

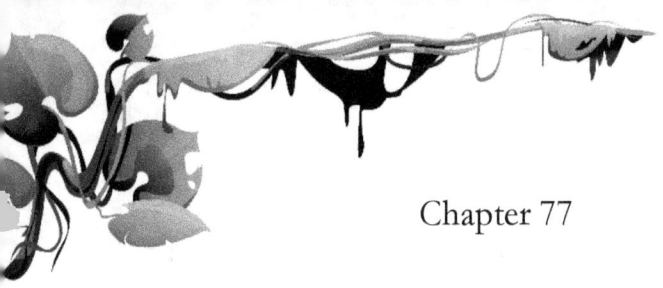

Chapter 77

kani nui ka moa

(The cock crows loudly)

Pastor had collapsed in a heap on the ground. When Kupuna was pulled into the depths of the vast darkness, Pastor, who was strongly connected to Hannah, was also pulled into the under tow. Now, he was entangled in the state of po with Kupuna. It was quite a setback.

Either both would be lost or together they would prevail.

Ray was shaking Hannah as if it might actually help though it was just foolishness.

Kimo spoke first," We must do this in a different place. But not now, later. The Night Ma rchers are just about here and we must prepare to fight them. But remember; do not look into their eyes. Try not to look at them at all. Ray, go gather our people together."

"Dad, what'll happen if we look at them?" inquired Luke.

"They will take your soul and then your life," warned Kimo. Both David and Hina heard their father's warning and remained silent. The younger children were very afraid. As advised, they planned to hide in a secret location.

Ray returned and told Kimo," Your people await you."

From both of the caves, the Hawaiian clan had emerged and assembled outside under the blood red moon. The rain had stopped. The awa-iku beneficent spirits had been sent by Kane to manage the wind and the rains at the sacred caves. In the near distance, the torches of the Night Marchers glowed.

Their fate had been cast.

Kimo wasted no time. They were all expecting Kupuna to emerge and speak to them.

"My friends, it is with great sadness that I must tell you that Kupuna remains in her dark state. But just for now."

The crowd looked to Peter to say something about that. Couldn't he help her? Wasn't he a practitioner of 'ana'ana or white magic?

Peter could hear their unspoken thoughts. "I will help her as soon as we have dealt with the Night Marchers. Do as Kimo forewarns, if they see you looking at them, the Night Marchers will kill you unless an ancestor recognizes you and claims you as their blood. Lay face down on the ground as a sign of respect, but whatever you do, do not look at them."

The crowd quickly dispersed to go find a place to lie down and protect one's self. Family units stayed together. Some covered themselves with blankets or with pillows over their heads.

Some clutched a lucky aumakua or a lucky fishing lure to use as a protective factor. Others held a rosary or a cross.

The torch lights grew closer. The drumbeats were loud.

The horrific smell prevailed. The conch was blown.

The Night Marchers had reached the location of the sacred caves. Suddenly, the drumbeats ceased.

Holding their torches, they did surveillance of the situation. All was quiet. The Hawaiian people were inside the sacred caves. Kupuna was located in one of them. She remained an important target.

A group of Night Marchers entered the first cave.

A second group entered the second cave that housed Kupuna. Their terrible stench entered with them. Shudders could be heard as the locals recognized how close the men were to them. Hidden in corners, under blankets and other items, they tried to keep still. All of them had their eyes closed tightly. Younger children were talking and crying, sensing the absence of the pulse and the strong presence of evil.

Luke, David and Hina were in the back of the cavern, but away from Kupuna's area. The men were protecting her and Pastor. They were in a recess in the wall of the cave. It was a small inlet in the wall, not quite hidden.

They had piled a heap of clothes and blankets on top of them, hoping to keep themselves well buried. They could hear them moving about, whispering to one another. They heard a young girl scream which, in turn, lead other children to scream as well.

"What's going on?" asked a frightened David, his voice trembling.

Luke shushed him. "Stay quiet. And close your eyes!"

Hina held on to Luke, holding his hand tightly. She was shaking.

Despite the clothing and blankets, Hina shivered. She kept her eyes closed and prayed that she would see her mother again, and little Hannah. Tears ran down her pale cheeks.

They could hear the men praying around Kupuna and Pastor Mason.

There was shouting, others screaming, and the smell of copper filled the air. Blood was being spilled.

"Wait! He is my flesh and blood. I claim him as my son!" shouted a distressed mother. Her son did not look like her. The verdict was in......not of the same blood.

Using a machete, the boy that had looked at him was brutally killed. The wailing mother had looked at the men in her outrage. They dispensed with her quickly.

Unfortunately, the pure horror of it all caused some to look at the Night Marchers. Chaos ensued and others died violently. Yet, David, Hina and Luke stayed under their covers, refusing to look anywhere, eyes remaining shut. They were in the throes of illilhia fear.

Hina began to squirm. She began making noises.

"Shhh," warned Luke.

"Ouch!" cried David. Now he was squirming too. "Shhhh!" Still, Hina cried out, through her tears.

"A centipede bit me!" David was really moving around.

And they drew the attention of one of the evil men. He began removing the heap of clothes and blankets, disrupting the pile of clothes. Several large centipedes fell out of the clothing items. They scurried away.

"Whatever you do, don't look at him," reminded Luke in a whispered voice as the man kept removing more items from the pile.

They could hear Max barking outside of the cave.

Then, in the deepest part of the dark night, the cock crowed loudly, announcing an unexpected guest, just as it had been foretold.

Did they get it right this time?

Everyone paused except those who were overcome by anguish at losing a loved one. Minutes passed slowly but no one had arrived as prophesized.

More minutes passed.

The evil man focused on the trio he had just uncovered. He roared loudly at them, kneeling down on the ground. He sniffed them, especially Hina as he was drawn to the smell of urine. She had covered her shut eyes with her hands.

Next, he prodded Luke and sniffed him but he got no response. Luke remained still, quiet and kept his eyes tightly shut. He too had covered his eyes with his hands. Silently, he was saying the Lord's Prayer.

Getting no response from Luke, he moved on to David. He got down beside him and gave two big blows of his breathe that was as foul as a decomposing animal that lay in the hot summer sun. It brought to mind maggots and black, slimy worms and crawly things.

David started to gag. He was gonna throw up, his body shuddered. He retched several times, causing him to sit up as he rocked and held his stomach. Seeing the boy's vulnerability, the large man came around front, knelt down and looked at David. The boy had his eyes shut. The evil man blew several more breaths into the boy's face. David started retching again.

He began to throw up. The warrior man laughed. It was an ugly sound.

"Shut up you faggot!" cried out David, eyes open and wild. "I hate you!"

Right away, Luke cried out, while keeping his eyes closed, "Uncle Ray, come claim David as your own flesh and blood!"

Hina was in fetal position, curled into a small ball, keeping her eyes solidly closed and listening to every word.

"Uncle Ray!" screamed David as he felt wetness down his legs.

Max began barking madly. What was going on outside of the caves? They heard the sound of horses fast approaching.

They *felt* the pulse once again, stronger than ever.

The pulse seemed to agitate the Night Marchers. It was making them feel weak. The man focused on David tried to raise his knife against him but he could not. His arm was too weak.

A tall, striking woman with firey red hair and blue eyes entered the cave. The pulse escalated to a higher level. Following behind her, was Kate, little Hannah and Bert. But no one had noticed yet.

"Who is she?" asked David who had moved over to sit by Luke.

"I don't know. Maybe a queen or something majestic like that," replied Luke. "Aloha Hina," said Kimo from Kupuna's bedside.

The moon goddess Hina looked around the dark cavern with only the light from the lanterns; yet, she was able to bear witness to the death and destruction as a result of the Night Marchers. The smell of copper filled the cavern.

Blood.

Blood spattered on the ground.

Blood on the scattered clothes and blankets on the ground. Blood all over the people who were dead.

For centuries, she had witnessed their debauchery in their relentless search to find the passage to the other side on the night of Kane. This night was no different.

"Hello Hina," said a beautiful, young Hawaiian woman in the deep shadows of the cave.

"Haumea, we meet again," replied Hina in a strong and confident voice. In her right hand, she held a saber of white-golden light, drawn from the moon. Hanging on a rope on her left hip was a calabash or a coconut gourd that, according to legends, contained the moon and all of the stars.

"I am much stronger this time," warned Haumea. "We have collected many souls."

"And I am on the right side. The side of righteousness. Aligned with the Lord." The very utterance of those words stung the Night Marchers. They retreated to the deep recesses in the large cavern.

Haumea laughed in scorn. Or was it fear?

"Your King cannot help you now but mine can. He has great powers," stated Haumea. "He can give you all your heart's desires."

However, Hina was not tempted by false promises or seduced by shiny objects. Not by a long shot. Therefore, the serpent had no power over Hina, goddess of the moon and ocean. An agent of the light.

Haumea quickly morphed into her black raven persona and attacked Hina, aiming for the eyes with her razor-sharped teeth.

Caw! Caw!

Hina grabbed the raven by its one claw and flung it away but not before Haumea bite her deeply with her sharp, knife-like beak. The bird spits out an eyeball now dripping with blood.

Hina had been badly wounded with impaired vision so she did not see the next strike coming and it came with great speed.

Caw! Caw!

Haumea aimed for the jugular vein in Hina's neck. "Hina!" shouted Kimo. Others cried out.

Slam!

The large bird hit hard against some kind of invisible shield. Upon the direct hit, the shield became a wave of white, fluid motion.

The albino fairies flew in a V formation, headed towards the stunned and fallen bird. As they descended, their mele could be heard. The cricket noises grew louder.

Caw! Caw!

Haumea had recovered. The bird immediately took flight, clapping its large, black wingspan and sweeping away the little fairies like a large broom. Rather like a witch's broom.

One by one the fairies fell to the ground.

The evil bird flew towards the mouth of the cave in an effort to escape the powerful fairies but it was of no use. Here too Haumea encountered an invisible shield. Once again, she was stunned but she recovered more quickly this time. And in that very brief period of time, Haumea morphed into reddish-brown colored particles that trans positioned themselves into a sturdy cockroach that scurried into the dark recesses of the cave.

The fairies covered Hina's face and her injuries were repaired as good as knew. Just like

Uncle Bert!

Another sound emerged in the background. It was the sound of chanting.

O Kane,

Hear our pule, There is casting off!

I am casting thee off!

Do not come to possess this spirit again.

For she is Kupuna, powerful in mana,

Let her not be a seat for thee again.

Do not try to know her again.

For she is Kupuna, a keeper of knowledge,

Go and seek some other medium for thyself in another home.

Let it not be she, not at all.

For she is Kupuna, blessed by the Holy Spirit,

I cast thee off for I am weary of thee!

I cast thee off, for I am not afraid of thee!

I cast the off, for I am expelling thee!

Behold our people, Thou are taking them. Holy, holy is our Lord.

The Night Marchers remained powerless on the ground but soon the energy field surrounding them would change in an involuntary drive to return to a state of homeostasis.

Time was running out. Their putrid odor had subsided for a while but it was fast returning.

The people felt things changing too and began to hide under blankets, cots, and clothing.

They were in the grips of Iiliilani fear. They cried and they cowered.

Hina called out, "Oh ye of little faith! Do not hide in the dark when the white light fills your space. Stand proud and remember that we are a righteous people."

Pulse….Pulse….PULSE…

On a breeze, the awa-iku or the beneficent spirits sent from Kane, road into the cave, and suddenly, the air became as fresh as an ocean breeze on a sunny day. The distinct smell and taste of sea salt was in the air.

They appeared more like ghosts than fairies. Wispy white spirits. The pulse was intensifying.

The Night Marchers were rendered helpless by the powerful white mana that had filled the cave. They detested light, repelled like vampires.

And like vampires, they transformed themselves into raven birds and fled from the sacred caves.

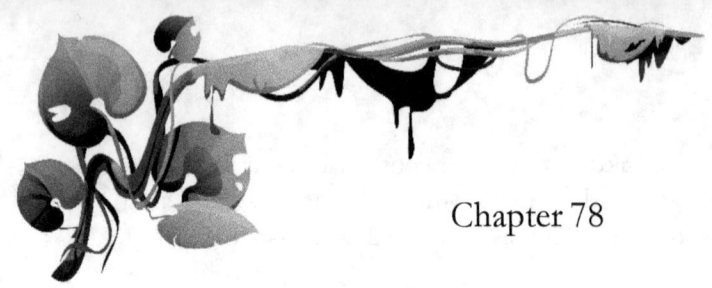

Chapter 78

Lani mau loa

(Eternal heavens)

The neon green mist had come ashore and hovered over the lowlands. The ground continued to rumble. The receding beach being pulled away by the approaching tsunami suggested that the giant wave would exceed 300 feet.….at least.

At the hospital, under the direction of Dr. Fukina, all the staff was at the bedside of their patients. After all, no one should have to die alone. The hospital was dark as the generators had been shut down except for those needed to maintain the monitors, pumps, oxygen and suction function.

Heaven knows why but I guess it's hard to pull the plug on someone. Or did a little hope sneak in there?

After observing Lili's miracle cure, Dr. Fukina possessed the knowledge that those things which are unseen are the evidence for those things which are seen. He waited for the invisible world to intervene in this earthly plane. In these moments, Dr. Fukina became to know the Almighty God of the heavens and the earth. In these moments, he saw a glimpse of life everlasting.

Outside the windows in the hospital, the neon mist glowed creating an eerie picture right out of a sci-fi movie. Dr. Fukina was ready to meet his maker. He was not afraid. He understood that a watery grave awaited him as the gigant wave approached. He had not been able to tell his community that the sickness that had afflicted them was radiation poisoning.

The island would remain inhabitable for centuries to come. Where it had come from, he had no idea. Perhaps an atomic bomb explosion. Pure speculation on his part.

He wondered how many other Polynesian islands were affected? Were we at war with Russia? What a frightening proposition!

Is this the end of time for humanity as prophesized in the Good book? He now knew with certainty that there is an eternal heaven.

A sickly Dr. Fukina waited quietly in his office, prepared and ready for the massive wave that was about to engulf the island, including the local hospital and staff. He heard the winds picking up, shaking the window so it rattled loudly. Was the howling wind from the approaching storm or was it evidence that the night marchers were on the move?

Once again, he gazed out the window. Perhaps he could see the torches of fire that the night marchers always carried as they approached in the dark. Just then, he had a coughing fit that caused him to throw up bloody mucus. Breathing deeply he heard the death rattle in his lungs. He wouldn't last much longer.

Suddenly, a bright light shone through the green mist. A shooting star perhaps?

A vision of the beautiful moon goddess Hina appeared in his head. The oldest goddess in ancient Hawaiian legends, Hina represents a strong female energy with great healing powers. She is the goddess of both the moon and the ocean. Her beauty is breathtaking.

Suddenly, his office door opened and three of his beloved nursing staff waltz inside. Malia, Kakalina and Mele had joined him. Each nurse had on a uniform that was no longer white, now it was covered in red blood. They were showing the symptoms of radiation poisoning. Kakalina's beautiful, thick blue-black mane had big chucks of missing hair. They had bleeding gums and missing teeth that made their bloody smiles grotesque. They had lost so much weight that they looked like stick figures. Most of all, they were bone weary.

The malodorous smell of death hung in the air.

Profound anemia from internal bleeding rendered them as weak as newborn kittens. All three laid down on the carpeted floor to rest. Dr. Fukina and his three friends were falling into a deep sleep. This man and his faithful nurses had lived lives of great service. They're eternal reward awaited these godly people. As they finally lapsed into a coma, each was escorted by their amakua to the bright light in the heavenly skies. On their upward climb, all four of them heard the mele of Kane.

They would be long gone when the gigantic tsunami wave swallowed up the hospital.

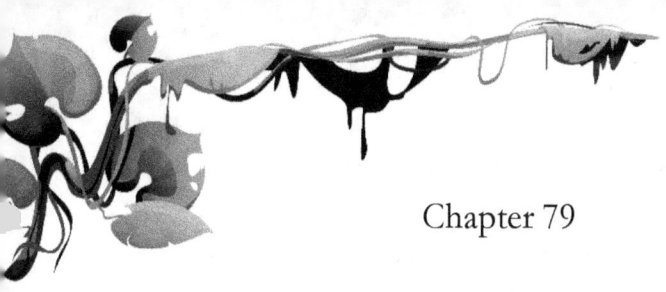

Chapter 79

Kuleana

(Area of responsibility)

Mrs. Tanaka, wife of the E.R. Doctor Tanaka, knew with certainty that her husband would never leave his patients' side. He would remain with them until the end. She was very proud of for him. He was fulfilling an oath that he had taken. However, she could not think about that right now.

Much like her husband, Mrs. Tanaka was a dedicated teacher. She understood that it was her responsibility to lead these students to safety. And the elder, Tanti, too. They would have to climb up the mountain to the Calvary cross. But, how was that supposed to happen with a 72 year old man and six teenagers?

As Mrs. Tanaka pondered this impossible situation, she looked up at the blue sky and she began to pray. She noticed a flock of large, white birds approaching the island. In a V formation, they were right overhead. They were carrying something in their strong beaks. As the birds drew closer, she could see their azure blue eyes. The eyes of the Big Birds of Kane. Somewhere close by, an owl hooted like a cheerleader.

"Now I know I'm old, but I'm a thinking that our ride has arrived," smirked Tanti.

The teenagers were looking up at this wondrous site. The majestic birds were swooping down right in front of them!

"Are you sure that we ain't hallucinating??" asked a chubby adolescent boy named Willy. "These are supernatural times," replied Tanti.

Eight large Birds of Kane stood before them.

Next, an owl swooped down beside the birds. It was the owl-as-protector, Amos. "Tanti is right. Your ride up the mountain to the sacred caves awaits you," said Amos.

Each Bird carried a large gourd with a rope attached. Each person had their own gourd. They would have to stay crouched inside as the Bird carried them, on the wind, up the steep red Mana cliffs of the mountain side.

"I don't think I want to do this...." a shaky, girl's voice said.

"You are completely safe in the gourd of Kane. There is nothing to fear," claimed Amos. A test of faith.

Tanti went first. He was laughing as the Big Bird flew away with him. Next, the four girls and two boys, flew upwards in their sturdy gourds. Lastly, their beloved teacher followed suit.

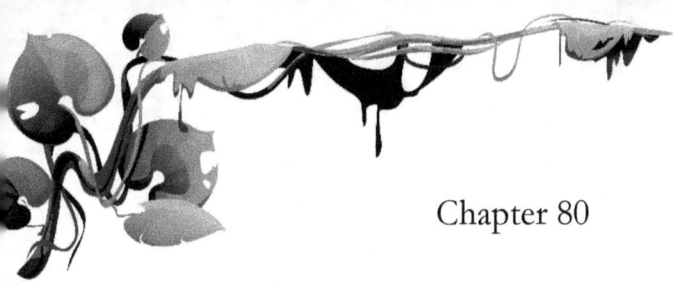

Chapter 80

Hina-i-te-marama

(Hina of the moon)

It was little Hina who first noticed them. She could see her Mom and little Hannah in the dark shadows of the cave.

She let out a joyful noise and yelled, "Mommy! Mommy! Hannah!" All eyes turned in awe. Mute Hina had finally spoken!

Kimo ran up to the wife and daughter that he had missed so much. Hugs and tears were flowing at the family's reunion. Hina was crying the most. For so long, her pent up feelings were finally being released. She had endured much sorrow for such a young girl.

The godess Hina's work was not yet done. A gigantic wave was approaching rendering them with no escape route. Flooding in the lowlands was increasing with every passing minute. Once again, Hina asked her people to gather around her and, once again, the ohana (family or group) responded. Pastor stood tall beside Kapuna Hannah. His beloved people stood together and waited to hear her speak. Such a motley crew, including the dog! Yet, none had been affected by the cancer causing radiation. Hannah's daily noni drink had prevented them from suffering from any inflictions from the poisonous radiation.

"Pastor you have been a spiritual warrior throughout this attack from Kanaloa" asserted Hina, as she smiled at him with great pride. "One more thing must be done."

All eyes turned on Pastor. He remained stoic.

Hina spoke again. "Kapuna Hannah you must lead us in a pule. We must pray with a grateful heart that we have been saved." Little Hannah was by her side. Big Kapuna, little kapuna.

In the years ahead, much knowledge of Kupuna healing would be transmitted to the next generation. Little Hannah would have a large footprint in the Hawaiaian peoples' future. There was so much to learn about the medicinal remedies found in the mountains and tropical forests. Puna was already well versed in these matters concerning the *aina* or land and the unique plants found in the tropical islands. However, nothing could cleanse these lands because radiation will never leave the soil. It causes permanent contamination.

They all gathered in a circle and held hands. Nobody intended to break the chain. They raised their sweet voices up to the heavens with love and praise for Kane. The one true God.

Kimo shouted, "Amen!" Kekela followed suit. Kate crossed herself. Others wept at their salvation.

Puna and Lili stood together, as she rested her head on his large, comforting shoulders. Their love for each had grown through these trials.

True love abides.

A pule to thank the gods for their protection through such perilous times was given with thanksgiving in their hearts. Max danced around the group as he was feeling the good vibes. In a corner, a green lizard was dancing too! Max let out a happy bark of excitment. The lizard was singing, *Zippity do da, Zippie de day!*

Little Hannah smiled. Uncle Bert was such a kick! Hina turned to Pastor.

Out of a deep pocket, Hina pulled out a small, koa box. It required a key to open it.

Hina said to Pastor, "I believe you hold the golden key that fits in the keyhole on the wooden box."

"Indeed I do Hina." Thank goodness Peter had given him the key. He pulled it from his pocket. It gleamed in the benevolent light. The smell of awa puhi or white ginger filled the air.

Pastor inserted the golden key into the koa box. He turned the key and *Viola*, the lid popped open. Sitting inside the box was a crystal amulet, shining like a diamond in the sky. The white light that the amulet generated filled the cave. No more po.

Light over darkness.

A rush of wind blew into the cave. Riding on the breeze were the albino fireflies, adding more white light into the cave.

Shrouded in the white, healing power of the amulet, people started feeling a full sense of renewal. Weariness melted away. Regeneration replaced it. They began to sing the mele of Kane.

The singing stopped when the goddess began to speak. "Kimo, I am calling on you next," said the goddess.

KImo waited for further instructions.

"It is you, and only you, that can see the words written inside," directed Hina. "Go on, pick up the amulet."

Kimo picked up the amulet. It had a pulse. Kimo's face shone like a full moon in the illumination from the amulet. He examined it more closely and *behold:* a map had appeared!

"This is the map you will use to navigate to your new destination, northwest from this land," explained the goddess. "There is still one more thing."

Kimo looked at Hina. Her blue eyes sparkled. Her smile was warm and loving.

"Kekela, please come up here with us," she requested. He moved to the spot where they stood.

"Kimo, there is something in your pocket that we need."

Kimo reached into his pocket and pulled out a white feather. "You mean this?"

"Yes."

"Pass the feather over the bright amulet." Kimo does as instructed.

"Now pass the feather over both of Kekala's eyes." And so he did.

Kekela felt a warm sensation. He also felt the darkness in his eyes start to dissipate and, remarkably, his vision was starting to come back. He shouted out, "I can see! I can see!"

The cave dwelling group knew that they had just witnessed a miracle. Their gleeful noises filled the cave with good mana.

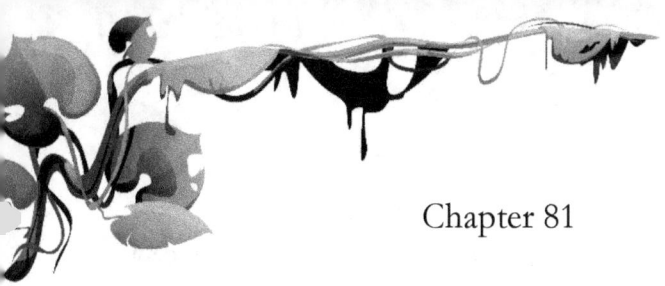

Chapter 81

Ahu kupanaha ia Hawai'I 'imi loa

(Wonder heaped on wonder in regard to Hawai'i searching for)

They could hear and see thunder and lightning. It seemed pretty close.

Hina said the god Lono was nearby.

Most of the folks inside the cave were gathering up the few belongings that they were permitted to bring with them. Besides, they were going to be sailing in a large Polynesian canoe that was already waiting for them. Only what was absolutely essential. There wasn't a lot of space.

But how could they possibly get from the mountain top to the canoe?

Outside the mouth of the caves, there was a great rucus. The screeching of birds was reaching high decimal levels. Everyone, inside the safety of the caves, ran to the mouth of their sanctuary to see what the heck was going on.

Surrounded by Hawai'ian barn owls, a Hawai'ian man of regal stature, stood before them. His aura was golden as was the flower of the gourd fruit that he wore around his neck. After all, the flower was considered sacred. The god Lono was also the god of agriculture. The cave dwellers looked upon this apparition with amazement.

The god Lono had arrived.

The strong winds had ceased.

Gone was the thunder and lightning. A calm ocean remained.

The night was still.

"I am here to ensure that the wind and waves cause you no troubles as you set out for new lands." His commanding voice was like the ocean depths.

"Kimo will lead you good people to a new land," said Lono. "He will take you to a beautiful Hawai'ian island in the northwest. He has the map. I will be nearby during your journey just in case you encounter inclement weather. Your amakua will also remain close." Right on cue, several owls hooted. Uncle Bert briefly stuck his head out of little Hannah's pocket.

Pastor stepped forward, standing with the god who, united with the goddess Hina, had helped to save them from a death sentence. *Hikapoloa!* The united will of the gods prevailed. "We were blessed by our holy trinity. Without faith, none of us could have been saved. It is faith that is the bridge between the earthly realm and the divine heavens above. A connection to the everlasting, living God. With Him, nothing is impossible."

Murmurs of prayers of gratitude warmed the crowd. A group of albino fairies flew into the cave generating warmth and bright light. They would be guiding the way with their illumination.

"O Lono, please tell us how we are going to get down the mountain to the canoe?" asked a nervous Kapuna Hannah. "And some of us cannot swim. The poison remains in the lands."

"Kapuna Hannah, we are going to fly off this mountain on the wings of angels."

Mrs. Tanaka, Tanti, and her group of teenagers smiled. "I will send you off with a chant," declared Lono.

"O my land standing force, hid thy face! Be lost, lost to view on the voyage.

Let me be lost to you in launching from my land.

Let my land standing out be lost!

Hide thy face as I bid farewell,

And bid me conceal, hide my sorrow.

As I say aloha, say aloha to the woods of my land till by and by."

(Adapted from Voices on the Wind, p.168)

Now, they were ready to depart from the island that they had once called home.

"The large, white Birds of Kane will take you safely to the canoe," explained Lono. "They are already outside waiting for their passengers."

"I'm scared. What if I fall off?" asked Luke. Alemea was standing beside him. Eyes wide in wonder, Little Hannah echoed that fear. Even Max barked his concern.

"Hold tightly to their neck feathers and you will be fine."

"It's safe. I rode one here," said Mrs. Tanaka. Tanti and the teenagers nodded their heads in agreement.

And so, each person began to board their flight.

Because the god Lono had cleared out the bad weather and had somehow stopped the giant tsunomi wave, the night sky was twinkling with stars. The full moon was no longer blood red. Instead, it shone brightly in the night's tapestry, lighting the way to the new land. Magestically, the new dawn that was emerging added bright pink and orange colors to the tapestry of life that lay ahead for these rightous people.

Ka la hiki ola. The dawning of a new day.

References

Ancient Hawaii civilization: a series of lectures delivered at the Kamehameha Schools, by E.S Craighill Handy and others, Rev. ed. Rutland, Vt., C.E. Tuttle Co., 1965

Ancient Hawaii. Words and Images by Herb Kawainui Kane. (1997). The Kawainui Press: Captain Cook, Hawaii.

Anderson, Johannes, Carl. 1873-1962. *Myths and Legends of the Polynesians.* Rutland, Vt., C.E. Tuttle Company, 1969.

Berney, Charlotte. *Fundamentals of Hawaiian Mysticism.* Library of Congress Cataloging-in- Publication Data. 2000.

Charlot, C. & Charlot,J., *Chanting the universe: Hawaiian religious culture.* Honolulu: Emphasis International. 1983.

Grey, George. *Polynesian Mythology.* Edited by W. W. Bird. Christchurch, New Zealand: Whitcombe and Tombs Ltd, 1965.

Hawaiian mythology-Wikipedia. En.wikipedia.org/wiki/Hawaiian_narrative.

Hawaiian Mythilogy: V. Kane and Kanaloa. http://www.sacredtexts.com?pac/hm/hm07.htm

Hawaiian Mythology: Part Three. The Chiefs: XIII.Mu.and www.sacred-texts.com

Hawaiian Godesses by Serge Kahili King. www.huna.org/html/hawaiian_godddesses.html.

http://barnowlsberkely.org/hawaiian-owl

http://www.solarnavigator.net/history/captainjamescook

http://www.mythichawaii.com/cook-haw

http://www.cycleharmony.com/stories/everyday-goddesses/hina-the-hawaiian-moon-goddess.

http://www.kaahelehawaii.com/pages/culture_ipu.htm

Kalakaua, His Hawaiian Majesty. *The Legends and Myths of Hawaii.* Rutland, Vermont: Charles E. Tuttle Company, Inc., 1972.

Kamakua, Samuel Manaiakalani. 1991. *Ka Po'e Kahiko: The People of Old.* Bishop Museum Press: Honolulu, Hawaii.

Kane, Herb Kawainui. 1997. *Ancient Hawaii.* The Kawainui Press. Captain Cook, Hawaii.Museum Press: Honolulu, Hawaii.

Kikawa, Daniel I. *Perpetuated in Righteousness: The Journey of the Hawaiian People from Eden to the Present Time.* Library of Congress, Kaneohe, Hawaii: Aloha Ke Akua Publishing, 1994.

King, Serge. 1983. *Kahuna healing: holistic health and healing practices of the Polynesia.* Theosophical Publishing House. Wheaton, Ill., U.S.A.

Knudson, Eric. *Teller of Tales: Stories from Kauai.* 1946. Mutual Publishing Paperback Series. Tales of the Pacific. Honolulu, Hawaii.

Kupihea, Moke. *The Seven Dawns of the Amakua: The Ancestral Spirit Hawaii.* The Library of Congress. Rochester, Vermont: Inner Traditions, 2001.

Luomala, K. (1986). Voices on the wind: Polynesian myths and chants (revised edition). Bishop Musuem Press: Honolulu, Hawaii.

Poisonous Plants of Paradise: First Aid and Medical Treatment of Injuries From Hawaii's Plants. Susan Scott and CRaig Thomas, M.D. University of Hawaii Press, Honolulu. 2000

Puku'i, Mary Kawena. 1994. *The Water of Kane and Other Legends of the Hawaiian Islands,* revised edition. Kamahameha Schools Press, Honolulu, Hawaii.

www.ingramcontent.com/pod-product-compliance
Lightning Source LLC
LaVergne TN
LVHW021755060526
838201LV00058B/3103

http://www.cycleharmony.com/stories/everyday-goddesses/hina-the-hawaiian-moon-goddess.

http://www.kaahelehawaii.com/pages/culture_ipu.htm

Kalakaua, His Hawaiian Majesty. *The Legends and Myths of Hawaii.* Rutland, Vermont: Charles E. Tuttle Company, Inc., 1972.

Kamakua, Samuel Manaiakalani. 1991. *Ka Po'e Kahiko: The People of Old.* Bishop Museum Press: Honolulu, Hawaii.

Kane, Herb Kawainui. 1997. *Ancient Hawaii.* The Kawainui Press. Captain Cook, Hawaii.Museum Press: Honolulu, Hawaii.

Kikawa, Daniel I. *Perpetuated in Righteousness: The Journey of the Hawaiian People from Eden to the Present Time.* Library of Congress, Kaneohe, Hawaii: Aloha Ke Akua Publishing, 1994.

King, Serge. 1983. *Kahuna healing: holistic health and healing practices of the Polynesia.* Theosophical Publishing House. Wheaton, Ill., U.S.A.

Knudson, Eric. *Teller of Tales: Stories from Kauai.* 1946. Mutual Publishing Paperback Series. Tales of the Pacific. Honolulu, Hawaii.

Kupihea, Moke. *The Seven Dawns of the Amakua: The Ancestral Spirit Hawaii.* The Library of Congress. Rochester, Vermont: Inner Traditions, 2001.

Luomala, K. (1986). Voices on the wind: Polynesian myths and chants (revised edition). Bishop Musuem Press: Honolulu, Hawaii.

Poisonous Plants of Paradise: First Aid and Medical Treatment of Injuries From Hawaii's Plants. Susan Scott and CRaig Thomas, M.D. University of Hawaii Press, Honolulu. 2000

Puku'i, Mary Kawena. 1994. *The Water of Kane and Other Legends of the Hawaiian Islands,* revised edition. Kamahameha Schools Press, Honolulu, Hawaii.

www.ingramcontent.com/pod-product-compliance
Lightning Source LLC
LaVergne TN
LVHW021755060526
838201LV00058B/3103